Captain Jerry Ya... ...e-
rior to the Yak gr... ...00
meters he fired sh... ...ns
and watched the Yak run right into the tracers. The
Russian craft shuddered and smoke poured from
behind the propeller, the plane seemed to shrug and
nosed toward the ground.

The fighter immediately behind it came through
its predecessor's smoke like an avenging angel, cannon firing and no deviation in course as it headed
straight for Jerry.

Jerry rolled to the left and dove at full speed before
pulling the Eureka up at a steep angle to come up
behind the Yak. At least that was the plan. He snapped
Satori—every P-61 he flew induced *satori*—around
and the Yak wasn't there.

Immediately he rolled to the right and tracers
streamed past the cockpit. He felt two rounds hit the
fuselage as he fought for altitude. Glancing over his
shoulder he saw the sun flash off the Yak's wings as
it pulled up to follow him.

He became aware of the radio chatter.

"Dave, you got one on your tail!"

"Good shooting, Currie, but watch out for the belly
gun on the one behind it."

"Colonel Shipley, you got one coming straight
down at you!"

Jerry looked back at the Yak. It had reached its
performance ceiling and rolled back in a dive to lower
altitude. Jerry roared down on the now vulnerable Yak
with his wing guns blazing.

BAEN BOOKS
by
STONEY COMPTON

Russian Amerika

Alaska Republik

ALASKA REPUBLIK

STONEY COMPTON

Alaska Republik

This is a work of fiction. All the characters and events portrayed in this book are fictional, and any resemblance to real people or incidents is purely coincidental.

A Baen Books Original

Baen Publishing Enterprises
P.O. Box 1403
Riverdale, NY 10471
www.baen.com

ISBN: 978-1-4391-3417-7

Cover art by Kurt Miller

First printing, March 2011

Distributed by Simon & Schuster
1230 Avenue of the Americas
New York, NY 10020

Pages by Joy Freeman (www.pagesbyjoy.com)
Printed in the United States of America

To the memory of
Maisie Rose Verley Reynolds Grandgenette
1899–1972
One of the first strong women I ever loved

Acknowledgement

I owe a heartfelt thank you for the efforts of my superb critique group: Walt Boyes (who also nailed the title), Paula Goodlett (who not only critiqued but also edited), Jeff and Inna Larsen, Leonard Hollar, Karen Bergstralh, Sarah Maisie Compton Campbell, and of course, Colette Marie who also doubles as my muse.

Thanks to Toni Weisskopf and her crew at Baen Books for publishing my work.

I must also say that Kurt Miller's dynamic covers have probably sold more of my books than all the nice reviews. Thanks, man!

★ Prolog ★

68 miles south of Delta, Russian Amerika

First Lieutenant Gerald Yamato found himself in the twin-thirty crossfire from three tanks. He felt Satori shudder with each hit, and there were a lot of hits. For a blissful moment he thought he could stay in the fight.

Then his controls went mushy and the solid stream of smoke from his engine compartment burst into bright flame washing back over his cockpit. Another minute in this situation would kill him. He immediately ejected the canopy and rolled the bird over; after jerking his seat restraints free, he threw himself into the smoky wake of his doomed P-61 that screamed out of control down into the awesome canyon a thousand feet below the battle.

Lieutenant Yamato wrenched his chute around so he could see as much of the battle as possible. While he watched, one of the Eureka fighters suddenly flamed, trailed smoke and exploded.

"Looked like Christenson's ship," he said to himself, feeling his heart lurch. Mike was the squadron mascot, a classic brilliant, self-doomed fuck-off.

A tree drifted past and he realized he had better pay mind to his own predicament, for him the fight with the Russians was over. An explosion from below pulled his attention to the bottom of the valley. His fighter had impacted at the edge of a river.

Someone had claimed it was the Delta River.

The wind pushed him farther down the huge canyon. The artist in him took a quick moment to appreciate the majestic beauty of the valley. The miles-long ridge on the far side rippled in shades of reds, pinks, greens, and even light purples, like a Technicolor layer cake cut and toppled on its side.

Abruptly the pragmatic flier took over and he worked his chute in order to come down near the river, rather than hang up in the middle of the forest bordering both sides of the obviously swift-moving water. Even before the ground rushed up and grabbed him, he wondered what equipment he had and would it be enough?

His landing was textbook: take the shock with his feet together and collapse in a rolling tumble. Unlike the field back in the Napa Valley, this one was covered with boulders and rocks the size of his head.

He landed on a small boulder and his feet slid off to the right. He threw his arm out and instantly jerked it to his side again—he couldn't risk breaking it. His shoulder took the majority of the impact and immediately went numb. Jerry threw out his hands and stopped himself.

The parachute settled on the rocky floodplain, began to fill from the constant breeze moving alongside the water. He pushed himself up and jerked the shroud lines, collapsing the silk. His shoulder hurt like hell but he swiftly pulled the lines into a pile at his feet.

Just as his hands touched the silk canopy, he heard a massive explosion from above. He looked up the incredible slope. At first he saw nothing but smoke pouring down from the road on the canyon rim. Then he saw awful movement.

At least nine Russian tanks avalanched down the steep wall, rotating in deadly decent, thunderously smashing flat the rocks and trees before crashing into each other or bouncing farther out into the canyon. Huge boulders and entire swaths of trees boiled in a descending dust-shrouded dance of death.

Behind the maelstrom tumbled a boulder larger than any tank, gouging out sixty-meter-wide swaths of mountainside before spinning out into the air again, following the doomed Russian war machines into the abyss.

A multitude of conflicting thoughts ran through his head as he waited for his companions to finish their preparations for the impending trek. First Lieutenant Jerry Yamato realized he had run out of options. As an officer of the Republic of California Air Force his first duty was to complete his mission.

Well, getting shot down in combat certainly ended my mission.

He would never forget the vivid memory of enemy fire hitting *Satori* and the sudden lack of control as the P-61 Eureka transformed from sleek fighter plane into burning debris falling out of the sky. Rolling the bird over so he could open the canopy, jerk his seat harness free, and drop out of the cockpit through the flames roaring back from the engine had taken less time to do than it would to describe the actions.

The ache in his shoulder attested to his poor landing.

Of course there had to be boulders all over the ground!

His other choice had been to land in the fast-flowing river that threaded through the boulder field. Parachuting into moving water became a recipe for disaster. He accepted the aching shoulder as a reminder of choosing the lesser of two evils.

His second duty was to return to his command as soon as possible. Well, that was finally about to commence. However he hadn't counted on being attacked by a survivor of the Russian armored column that his squadron had all but destroyed.

How a man could fall into a valley along with tanks and armored personnel carriers and still live loomed nearly beyond belief. Sergeant Cermanivich had not only survived the fall, he had also tried to kill Jerry with a rifle. Jerry's aim with his service .45 kept the sergeant alive.

Jerry had aimed at the man's head and hit the rifle in his hands instead. The blow had knocked the Russian sergeant off the rock on which he sat and in his condition took him out of the fight.

Or took the fight out of him, Jerry mused.

Then things really got complicated. Jerry had an unconscious prisoner who didn't look as if he could live another hour and he stood in the middle of an unknown, vast wilderness that happened to be enemy territory. The 117th Fighter Squadron had flown many miles over Russian Amerika and the only sign of human habitation or toil had been the road over the mountain pass where they attacked the Russian armor.

To be honest, he had considered putting the damaged

Russian out of his misery. For all Jerry knew, this son of a bitch might have shot him down! Killing a man in combat could be considered duty; putting a bullet through the brain of an unconscious man from three feet away seemed like murder.

So he woke the soldier and met Sergeant Rudi Cermanivich, who had been the gunner on the lead tank—which meant he *was* the son of a bitch who shot Jerry down!—and when he tried to stand he passed out again. With a simple litter, Jerry dragged the mercifully unconscious sergeant back to where he had left his parachute and other gear. After a very long, exhausting time he thought he should be in the right area, but his gear had vanished.

Suddenly a beautiful woman appeared who had enough words of English to ask if he spoke Russian. And then he saw stars when a rock hit the back of his head. Once he regained consciousness, tied securely with his own parachute lines, he met Pelagian, a six-foot-tall, muscular man who had the blood of numerous races flowing through his veins.

Piercing blue eyes and skin the shade of coffee with cream made for a very arresting figure. His wife, Bodecia, stood all of five feet and with her chiseled beauty, looked mostly of Alaska Native ancestry. The beautiful woman who had rendered him witless in more ways than one was Magda, their daughter.

After Jerry and Rudi both explained their presence, Pelagian had freed them and offered them assistance. A great weight lifted off Jerry's shoulders at that moment. He and the sergeant just might live through this after all.

When he explained he had been shot down while fighting in aid of a Dená revolution against the Czar the effect on his rescuers had been electric. It seemed they were all on the same side, except Rudi, of course. Pelagian and his family had been in the bush for months and knew nothing of the battles fought between Russia and the Dená Separatist Movement and their allies.

Jerry wondered if these people could really get him and Sergeant Rudi Cermanivich out of the wilderness alive. He glanced at Magda who happened to look at him at the same time. Interest shone in her eyes and that buoyed him immensely.

Well, I joined the Air Force for adventure. Mother always told me to be careful of what I wished for.

★ 1 ★

Pelagian felt relief that he didn't have to kill the Californian. However, he maintained a close, unobtrusive watch on Lieutenant Jerry Yamato. So far the young pilot from the Republic of California impressed him. He could have killed the Russian tanker sergeant and it would have been the fortunes of war. The sergeant would not have hesitated, in fact had twice tried his best to kill the pilot and not succeeded. If he had there would have been two bodies to bury out here in Rainbow Valley.

Instead, they were all busy rigging a litter to haul Sergeant Rudi Cermanivich to Delta where he could get decent care without being jostled all over the length and breadth of Russian Amerika. Sixty-odd miles were nothing for a healthy person, a few days walk. But carrying a litter through what had suddenly become enemy territory might evolve into a much larger challenge.

Lieutenant Yamato had told them about the Dená revolution against the Czar, about the Battle of Chena, and the death of Slayer-of-Men, Pelagian's good friend and cousin to Bodecia. His wife had not shown much

7

emotion, but he knew what to look for on the face of the woman he loved. She had taken the news of the death hard, rock hard, and he pitied any Russian soldier who fell into her gunsights.

Along with their daughter, Magda, they had watched the sleek warplanes attack an unseen Russian armored column far above them on Baranov Pass near Rainbow Ridge. At the beginning there had been fifteen aircraft diving and firing. Only seven flew away to the north after the shooting stopped.

They had witnessed the destruction of three of the planes, including Lieutenant Yamato's; the fourth had been destroyed out of their line of sight. Having been a military pilot in another time and another place, Pelagian knew how close the lieutenant must have been to the men who died back there. He would carefully choose the time to discuss the battle with Lieutenant Yamato.

Magda moved around Jerry like a cat, curious but very wary. Pelagian didn't dwell on that aspect of the situation since it didn't involve him. He knew his daughter could handle herself, physically and emotionally.

Bodecia finished testing the knots on the litter and gave him a long look and a sharp nod.

"Let's go to Delta," he said, and slipped into the harness bearing the weight of the front of the litter.

Jerry Yamato stumbled again. How far had they walked? How long had they been walking? The litter bearing the wounded Russian tanker sergeant had to weigh two hundred pounds at the very least.

Pelagian wore the parachute harness bearing the front weight of the litter as if it were a light cloak.

The rope sling in the back cut into Jerry's shoulders and he gripped the end of the litter, constantly lifting it with raw, blistering hands to ease the burden on his aching shoulders. He could barely move but he gamely continued.

Following the man wasn't difficult; Pelagian inspired confidence.

The dogs, bearing a goodly share of the load tied to a pole between them, which supported the right and left sides of the litter, seemed as fresh as when they started the journey.

Bodecia, Pelagian's small, sharply handsome, shamanistic wife, and Magda, their stunningly beautiful daughter, both carried heavy packs with the air of being on an amble in the park. Jerry refused to whine about his condition. He stumbled again.

Pelagian said, "This is a good place." And everybody stopped moving. The women dropped their packs and immediately unslung the dogs from the litter.

The dogs wandered around and thoroughly marked the area. Pelagian nodded to Jerry and they lowered the litter to the ground. For the first time Jerry noticed the clear creek running parallel to their route, and the high grassy meadow surrounded by mountains in which they found themselves. Back and legs aching, he lowered himself to the ground and lay down.

"Lieutenant, wake up. You must eat." Magda's voice ended Jerry's dream and his eyes popped open. She knelt next to him, holding out a wooden bowl full of steaming, savory smelling food.

He scrambled to a sitting position and took the bowl. "How long was I asleep?" From the warmth in his face he knew he was blushing.

"A few hours. Not to worry, you were exhausted. After we eat everyone will sleep."

Pelagian and Bodecia already sat cross-legged on the ground, eating.

Nodding dumbly, he shoveled what proved to be stew into his mouth. Large chunks of meat enhanced by carrots, potatoes, and unknown herbs made for a completely satisfying meal. The worn spoon boasted the twin-headed eagle of Imperial Russia on its handle.

"Nice silverware," he said, glancing at Bodecia and grinning. "The Czar give it to you for a wedding present?"

"No, I traded beadwork for it," Bodecia said.

Jerry wondered if the woman ever smiled. He noticed Rudi still slept, but the bloody, fouled uniform had vanished and clean blankets covered him. Jerry hadn't thought about what Rudi's personal condition might be.

I'm trained in wilderness survival, yet I feel so stupid here, he thought.

"Is there a wife waiting for you in Castroville?" Magda asked.

"No. I had a girlfriend, but she 'found somebody else' just before the war started. In a way I'm glad I'm not tied down right now. You never know what's going to happen in a combat situation."

"Then the relationship was not serious to begin with?"

"I wanted it to be for a long time, but no, I don't think it ever was."

Magda frowned. "So why did you not seek a serious relationship?"

Jerry set his empty bowl beside him, contentedly

patted his belly, and stared into her lustrous eyes. "I'm still working on it."

She smiled and blinked. "I'm sure you are." From behind her she produced two blankets.

"Here is your bedding. I'll see you in a few hours." She stood and walked away.

He watched her body move under the soft moose-hide and wondered if there was a sweetheart waiting for her back in Delta, or wherever they called home. Straightening one blanket on the ground he wrapped the other around him and fell asleep as soon as he lay down.

His plane flew straight toward the flashing muzzles on the row of tanks but his guns wouldn't fire, nor could he make the aircraft turn away from what was sure to be instant death in mere moments. Bullets hit his plane; chunks of metal ripped away, the canopy fragmented in silent explosion. He pounded on the stick to make the bird turn but it wouldn't. Something hit his foot and he jerked out of the nightmare, still shuddering.

"Wake up, Lieutenant," Pelagian said from some-where in the clouds. "We're leaving soon."

Jerry let the dream ebb as he lay in his wadded blankets. The ubiquitous daylight felt cool to his sweating face. The aroma of cooking food brought him completely awake.

After rolling his blankets together he set them near Rudi's litter. The sergeant smiled at him.

"Fighting dream battle, yes?"

"Yes. How did you know?"

"Have been in army long time, it happens to most."

"How long until the dreams stop?"

"I'll tell you when mine do."

Jerry thought about that for a moment, and then shook his head. "So, how do you feel, Sergeant Cermanivich? You look better than the last time I saw you."

"For first time since Colonel Lazarev's tank was blown off ridge, I don't hurt. People rarely appreciate lack of pain. But from now forward, I do."

Bodecia walked over and handed them both bowls of food. "If you wish to heal, Sergeant, you will stay in that litter for two more days. Then you may walk on your own, if you are capable."

Jerry looked down at his bowl, potatoes and six small eggs fried sunny-side up.

"I feel good to walk now."

"If you walk today, you will be dead by the end of tomorrow. You have many injuries, which need at least that long to begin healing. Two more days in the litter and you may live to see grandchildren."

"Where did you get fresh eggs?" Jerry asked.

Bodecia nearly smiled. "Birds lay them everywhere, you just need to know where to find them."

"I'm glad you knew. Thank you."

Bodecia actually smiled and nodded her head before turning back to her family sitting around the campfire.

"Please help me sit up," Cermanivich said.

Jerry grabbed the man's wrist and hauled him to a sitting position. It took much less effort than he thought it would. Rudi gasped, sat still for a long moment, then began eating and looking around at the same time.

"We are not in last remembered location. River is different, and ridge is gone. Who carried me here?"

Between bites Jerry told him about the dogs and the litter lash-up.

"You helped carry me?"

"I told you, our war is over until we can return to our own people. Don't you agree?"

Cermanivich looked up from his food. "I agreed in concept, I never believe you mean it."

"Oh hell, Rudi, I don't mean it. I'm going to shoot you the first chance I get."

"Do not believe that, either," Rudi said with a laugh. "You are very different from other armies I have fought. I do not think you are good soldier, but you are good man, for which I remain grateful."

"Thanks, I think," Jerry said, running back over it in his mind, trying to decide if he should feel insulted.

Pelagian loomed over them before sitting next to the litter. "We will sleep in Delta the day after tomorrow, if you both can handle the pace. I realize that neither of you are Yukon Cassidy."

Rudi lay back and grinned. "Is no problem for me."

"Lieutenant?" The blue eyes gleamed at Jerry.

"I've had a night's sleep and a full meal, you bet I can handle it."

"Good. Today you wear the harness in front."

"But I don't know where I'm going."

"Just follow Magda," Pelagian gave him a wolfish grin. "You can do that, can't you?"

"Definitely," Jerry said, holding the man's gaze. "Who's Yukon Cassidy?"

"A warrior of legend, and he holds his own. I am honored to have him as a friend."

"Will I meet him?"

"If you are fortunate."

A half hour later they stretched out down the trail headed north. Jerry found his stride and, in addition to watching Magda in front of him, appreciated the landscape around them. They climbed a ridge and dropped down into a wide valley.

In the distance Jerry noticed a mountain he had seen from his plane. At this elevation it loomed even more majestically. He called ahead to Magda, "What do you call that?"

She glanced back to see where he pointed, followed the direction with her eyes and came to a complete stop.

"That is Denali. A holy place for our people and the heart of the Dená Nation."

"Oh. It sorta reminds me of Mt. Shasta back in the Republic."

She turned to him, eyes shining. "You also have a holy mountain?"

"Not everybody regards it that way, but yes."

Bodecia walked back down the trail to them, her eyebrows arched. "May we continue now?"

Pelagian chuckled and said in a low voice, "I wouldn't waste any more time if I were you."

Jerry grinned back over his shoulder. "I thought you were in charge here."

"A woman is not property, and husbands who think otherwise are living in a dream world. My friend Bob told me that and he was right."

"He sounds like wise man," Rudi commented. "Is permissible to sing?"

"No!" Jerry and Pelagian said simultaneously.

"You two worry me."

The lower elevations of the valley brought more water, standing and active. They forded two cold, fast-moving creeks. Jerry noticed early that they followed a trail; a mere suggestion in some places and well defined in others. Now the trail bore unmistakable wheel tracks as well as those of human and animal.

"How much farther to Delta?" Jerry asked Magda.

She dropped back and in a low voice said, "Just beyond the mountain you see in the distance there." She pointed. They were going through a vast stretch of willows, more bushes than trees; the tallest stood no more than two meters.

"Why are you whispering?"

"Because we are very near a redoubt, and we do not wish to explain your presence to the Russians."

"Listen to her," Rudi said in a low voice. "They would kill us all."

"Even you?" Jerry whispered.

"I am among enemies and still breathe, therefore traitor to the Czar. The Imperial Russian Army is bereft of nuance or sentiment."

"Do you want to go in alone?"

"How to explain presence in this condition? I am too many versts from my command, perhaps deserter? No, I stay with you."

A birdcall drifted back and Pelagian snapped, "Quiet! Get off the trail."

Magda spoke to the dogs and they followed her into the brush. She led them down into a small depression and spoke again. All four dogs quietly lay down, tongues lolling. Pelagian slipped out of his sling and pulled a hatchet from the pack Magda had carried.

"You all wait here quietly," he said. He disappeared toward the trail.

Jerry unbuckled the harness and gratefully let it slide to the ground. Not since flight school when he was a cadet had he expended this much effort on a continuous basis. He eased to the ground next to Rudi's litter and fell into a light doze.

Something pressed firmly over his mouth and his eyes popped open to see Magda holding her other hand up, index finger over her mouth. He nodded his head and she took her hand off him. She handed him his automatic.

He dropped the clip enough to see it was still full. As he quietly pressed the clip back into the pistol butt, he looked around, finally catching Magda's eye again. He elaborately shrugged.

She knelt down beside him and pointed toward the wall of brush between them and the trail. Suddenly he heard the voices. Unknown voices, speaking Russian.

Jerry slowly pulled the barrel back on the automatic until he could see the round in the chamber. He glanced around.

Rudi lay belly down on his litter, holding a huge revolver in both hands and aiming toward the voices. Both Pelagian and Bodecia were nowhere to be seen. Jerry's heartbeat increased and his mouth felt dry.

The summer sun beat down from a cloudless sky and mosquitoes circled round them. Sweat stung his eyes but he didn't move. The voices were no more than fifteen meters away; he could hear boots scuffing the small rocks and dirt on the trail despite the breeze high in the willows. The constant wind wasn't strong enough to get down to where he crouched.

Time hadn't slowed this much for him since he had to watch an ice cube melt when he was a child. Back then he had been restricted to a chair until the ice turned to a puddle. Now he had no idea what was required of him other than staying alive.

The voices receded slightly and Jerry's heartbeat slowed. He smiled over at Magda just as she unsuccessfully tried to muffle her sneeze.

One of the unseen voices said something short and sharp. Silence grew and Jerry's heartbeat increased. The barrel of his .45 trembled and he wished he could stop sweating.

"Yaaaahhhhh!"

Three Russian soldiers burst through the brush, nearly overrunning them. Two held rifles at high port, the third led with his machine pistol pointed forward.

Jerry, Magda, and Rudi all shot the man with the machine pistol, who fell flat in front of them, instantly dead. The other two soldiers jerked their weapons down toward the three. Multiple shots rang out and both men lost all coordination and collapsed, dead before they hit the ground.

Silence reigned as dust motes drifted and settled.

A hoarse shout in Russian from beyond the brush: "Shout out, comrades!"

More silence.

Abruptly a heavy weapon opened up, spraying the area with large caliber rounds. Three rounds hit the dead Russian directly in front of Jerry, causing the corpse to jerk as if it felt the damage.

Somewhere out in the brush Pelagian said, "Damn, they hit me!"

"Father!" Magda yelled and started to her feet.

Jerry grabbed her arm and jerked her back down. She turned on him with bared teeth. "What do you—"

Thick fire stitched through the brush over their heads, blowing the small trees in half with single rounds. The sharp scent of sap and cut wood joined the light haze of cordite in the air.

"We have to put an end to that one," Rudi said with a growl. "You go left, I'll go right."

Before Jerry could say anything, Rudi grabbed the machine pistol out of the dead corporal's hands and wriggled into the brush, grunting with effort. Jerry grabbed one of the fallen rifles and quickly made sure it was loaded.

"Stay here and shoot anyone who comes crawling through the brush. We'll be on our feet."

Magda stared at him with wide eyes. *"Da."*

Jerry crawled through the dust and weeds, slowed when he came to an opening in the brush before him. This was another reason he hadn't joined the infantry: he hated being dirty.

He stopped in front of the opening, listening intently. Panting, he heard pain being unsuccessfully suppressed.

"It's Yamato," he whispered and pushed through the opening.

At the side of a wounded Pelagian, Bodecia held a machine pistol, pointing at Jerry. As soon as she saw his face she aimed at the brush in front of them.

"He's hit in the side," she said a low, emotionless tone.

"I need the automatic weapon."

They silently traded weapons.

"Thanks, I'll be right back." Jerry crawled as quietly as he could away from the couple before turning toward where he knew the enemy lurked. The heavy willows moved in the breeze and were easy for him to negotiate but he knew the top portion of the branches signaled his advance. He backed up and moved down into a small swale before stopping to rest.

The hammer of the heavy weapon followed the bullets chopping down willows wholesale, right where he had turned back. He shrieked, "Ahhh!" and hoped for the best.

The fire ceased and he immediately squirmed down the leveled path, appreciating how much the downed willows suppressed the dust. If the Russian gunner believed his cry, Rudi might believe it too, and do something foolish.

But what if the Russian didn't believe his cry, what if he was waiting for a stupid first lieutenant to stumble through the trees so he could cut him in half?

His heart hammered and Jerry found it difficult to swallow. Heat suffused the entire universe and he tried not to think about water. Suddenly he ran out of the downed willows and stopped. With his mouth hanging open, he desperately listened for any sound beyond the bluish-green leaves screening him from the threat beyond.

The rattle of a machine gun belt carried through the dusty air. Jerry decided the gunner was reloading. He sat back on his haunches and rose to his feet, hunched over and terrified. He decided it was now or never.

He charged through the willows and into the open.

★ 2 ★

90 miles east of St. Anthony Redoubt

For at least the thousandth time, Lieutenant Colonel Samedi Janeki wished the Imperial Russian Army would line tank hatches with rubber or something softer than steel. His kidneys were taking a beating as the Imperial 5th Armored rumbled toward Chena Redoubt from Tetlin Redoubt.

The Russian Amerika Company could certainly profit by making the Russia-Canada Highway more travel friendly. The smallest stone in the semi-packed surface looked larger than his fist. But then his column of 30 tanks, 15 trucks and assorted other vehicles were tearing along at 15 kph, which made it impossible for his driver to avoid the larger rocks.

As his Zukhov jarred over yet another small boulder, his radioman broke in on his comm channel.

"Colonel, communication from St. Nicholas Redoubt!"

"Patch it in, Kerenski." A click transferred him to a different frequency. "This is Lieutenant Colonel Janeki of the 5th Armored."

"Janeki," the voice came through scratchy, "this is Skalovich."

"Georgi, my friend, how are you?" They had been friends for over twenty years and Georgi, a full colonel, now sat behind an impressive desk in St. Nicholas Redoubt as deputy commander of Northern Land Forces in Russian Amerika. Georgi would get a star before Janeki did.

"My health is good, thank you, Samedi. But I must make you aware of bad news."

"I'm being replaced?"

Colonel Skalovich forced a laugh. "No, nothing like that. In fact at the moment you are irreplaceable. Lazarev and the Flash Division have been destroyed crossing the Alaska Range."

"Destroyed, by whom?"

"The Republic of California Air Force." Janeki could hear the disgust in his friend's voice. "They've also cut the road. Now everything must go through Tetlin first."

"Don't worry, Georgi, the 5th Armored can handle the mission."

"I am not finished with bad news, Samedi. Tetlin Redoubt is under armored attack from the east."

"California again?"

"No, the First People's Nation. They have taken the British Army out of the war and are hitting Tetlin with at least three dozen tanks. You took all our armor with you, didn't you?"

"As ordered," Janeki said, angry that his voice had tightened along with his jaw.

"I know those were your orders, I issued them. This FPN thing caught us flat-footed. We do have artillery and infantry there, and they are offering a stiff resistance."

Janeki instantly felt mollified. "Do you want me to stop my advance and return to Tetlin, Colonel?"

"No. You should be linking up with your old mentor Myslosovich within twenty-four hours. He has lost his ass at Chena and will be full of doom and gloom. Turn him around and hit Chena again, we need to be as deep into Dená territory as possible when the cease-fire order comes down."

"Cease-fire order? Why would they do that, we're just getting started in this wasteland. Only a small fraction of the army has been committed to stop this piddling revolt."

"It's not common knowledge yet. Imperial Command is trying to pull its fat out of the fire, but most of the Pacific Fleet went to the bottom day before yesterday, courtesy of the Republic of California Navy."

"Oh, Jesus," Janeki breathed into the microphone.

"It gets worse, Samedi. No sooner than the diplomats asked for peace terms, the Japanese Navy started shelling Naval Base Kodiak."

"The Japanese?" Janeki shouted. "Where the hell did they come from?"

"It seems the Kolosh are pulling the same crap on us the Dená did. Only they asked the Japanese for military aid rather than the USA or the ROC."

"Who *isn't* up here messing in our internal affairs?"

"As near as we can figure, the CSA, Republic of Texas, and Deseret."

"Well that's a damned relief, no religious zealots to worry about!"

"I don't think the Mormons have an army as such."

"Mormons? I was speaking of the Confederacy, wild-eyed Protestants to the last man."

Colonel Skalovich's laugh was genuine this time. "I'm glad you still have your sense of humor, my friend, because you're going to need it."

"Any idea when this cease-fire order will come down from on high?"

"No. We know the Baltic Fleet has steamed east to help, but we don't know if they will be in time to make a difference. In my opinion, high command has put Alaska further down the list of important things to think about. I think they're worried about Mother Russia's east coast with the Japanese threat."

"So we are fighting a lost cause, Georgi?"

"Perhaps, Samedi, perhaps."

"Not if I can help it, old friend!"

★ 3 ★

Tanana Hospital, Dená Republik

"What is the status of our army, General Eluska?" General Grisha Grigorievich, commanding general of the fledgling Dená Republik Army asked impatiently from his hospital bed.

Paul Eluska flashed a shy grin and then settled back into his new role.

"Sorry about your leg, Grisha. I sent them California paratroopers under Colonel Buhrman and Major Smolst with a platoon of our guys after the retreating Russians. Between 'em they got about two hundred men. Then Colonel Jackson showed up with his California Rangers, another two hundred men, and I told him to go find Colonel Buhrman's group and help out."

"Are the Russians still fighting or just getting the hell out of Huslia?"

"They ain't nowhere near Huslia, Grisha," Paul said with a frown. "They're headed for Delta."

"I'm just trying to be funny or something, can't do much else with this leg all trussed up. What's in Delta?"

"That's where St. Anthony Redoubt is, with a small

Russian garrison that's never seen combat yet, all fresh and ready to go."

"Any idea how many?"

"Last I heard from Doyon Williams, right at a hundred."

"What kind of armor?

"I think they got three tanks, a couple small cannons and a helicopter. They just guard the RustyCan Highway, Grisha, and provide a place to stay for traveling Russian big shots."

Colonel Wing Grigorievich cleared her throat and put her hand on her husband's arm. "General Eluska, have we any information on Russian movements south of Delta?"

"All we know is what Grisha's flight spotted on the way to Chena. The FPN Army is headed north, and there was a column of tanks and other vehicles ahead of them. I think it's safe to say they're Russian."

"That was two days ago. I thought the Russians had asked for terms," Grisha snapped, frowning at his broken leg.

"St. Petersburg did ask for terms." Wing cleared her throat again and continued, "But their army has yet to wave any white flags or show signs of stopping. They're probably trying to gain as much territory as they can."

A knock sounded on the closed door.

"General Grigorievich?" Sergeant Major Nelson Tobias' voice came through the door at a respectful level in cadence with the rap of his knuckles.

"Please come in, Sergeant Major," Grisha said.

Tobias pushed open the hospital door and stepped inside, barely, before straightening to attention. "We have priority messages from the USA and the ROC commands."

"What do they say?" Colonel Wing Grigorievich asked. She put her hand on her husband's bed and the general covered it with his.

"The ROC has sent her fleet north into the Gulf of Alaska which includes air support."

"And the USA?" Grisha asked.

"Claims one of their submarines sank a Russian destroyer in Clarence Strait, in the Russian portion of the Inside Passage."

The fifth person in the room broke his silence, "It seems our people are going to get the aid they requested."

Grisha smiled at his cousin, Captain Pietr Chernikoff, of the Tlingit Nation Army.

"Whatever happens, Pietr, our old world is gone forever."

"Do you really think it can get worse than it was, Grisha?"

"I don't know. Ask me a year from now."

"There's one more thing, General," Sergeant Major Tobias said, his mouth working as if he smelled something unpleasant.

"Yes?"

"The Imperial Japanese Fleet shelled and effectively destroyed the Imperial Russian naval base at Kodiak at 0200. Imperial Russia has declared war on the Imperial Japanese Empire."

"My God!" Grisha blurted.

"That's insane!" Wing said.

"That was not supposed to happen!" Pietr's tone carried anger.

"What do you mean by that?" Grisha snapped.

"We asked them to posture, nothing more." Pietr's face had gone as pale as possible. "They would demonstrate and then leave. We were sure we could get the Russians to back down."

"You made a treaty with the *Japanese*?" Grisha felt stunned and terrified at the same time.

"At the time we felt we had no other choice..." Pietr's voice trailed away.

"Now that's what's insane!" Wing said. "Did you leave any soft spots in your treaty's perimeter? Some place they could break through with impunity if it served their purpose?"

Pietr's face flushed and he opened his mouth to respond, eyes dark and brow constricted. But he held his tongue long enough to digest her words. His mouth snapped shut and the frown lost contour and dissipated.

"Perhaps," he said and his face reddened further. "I would need to revisit what I urged to be signed."

"Can you rescind the treaty?" Grisha asked.

"Unlikely, cousin."

"So we potentially have a new war to consider."

"Grisha!" Wing blurted. "We have no navy, we barely have an army. The Japanese have both in numbers we can't defeat."

"She's got a couple of good points there, Grisha," Paul Eluska said.

"But we have allies, no?" Grisha searched all their faces but found no answer.

"Japan has a *huge* navy," Wing said in a gentle voice.

"I must get in contact with my brother Paul," Pietr said. "As soon as possible."

"I'll introduce you to our communications people," Wing said. "Follow me."

★ 4 ★

40 miles northwest of Delta

Major Joe Coffey of Easy Company, 3rd Parachute Infantry Regiment, Republic of California Army, hustled through the woods and dropped next to his commanding officer. "They aren't doing much rear guardwise, Del, uh, Colonel Buhrman."

"You're out of shape, Joe," the colonel said with a wide grin only partially covered by his walrus mustache. "How far ahead are they?"

"No more'n half a click, shit, I couldn't run farther than that,"

"Do they know we're back here?"

"Don't think so. They seem more worried about what's in front of them. They don't act like an army in full retreat."

"Good. But if they figure out we're back here, it could get hairy and damn fast. Nothing like a cornered rat for a real fight."

"Kinda reminds me of that Spanish fight over in the Arizona no-man's-land. Remember that?"

"How the hell could I forget it?" Colonel Buhrman said with a snort. "Only time I've ever been suckered, and by the sheep-humping Spanish at that!"

"But we kicked their asses," Major Coffey said through his grin.

"And we lost four good men because we weren't paying attention."

Coffey's smile evaporated. "Yeah, that's right. Better keep our act together on this one, huh?"

"Couldn't have put it better myself. Where do they have their tanks?"

"Way forward. You'd think they were attacking instead of retreating."

"I've come to the conclusion that General Myslosovich likes to kid himself. He never retreats, only attacks. That suggests he's vain and can be bullshitted. Good thing to know about your enemy."

"Sometimes you scare me, Colonel Buhrman."

"I must be losing my edge, used to be you were in constant terror of me." He grinned again.

Joe laughed. He and Del had gone through the Presidio together. The officers the Republic of California Military Academy provided could more than match anything offered by West Point, VMI, TMI, or Sandhurst.

It had taken Joe Coffey nine long years to make major; marginal peacetime was hell for a soldier. But Del had made colonel in the same amount of time. Joe felt no envy; Del was the smartest man he had ever met. Give him another five years and he'd have stars on his shoulders, no doubt about it.

"Constant terror? Naw. Worried that we might not live through your latest adventure, maybe. You always pull us through and I'll take that to the bank."

"As if you ever had anything left over to put in a bank!" Colonel Buhrman was still grinning.

★ 5 ★

63 miles south of Delta

Rudi could make out the hulking armored personnel carrier through the light screen of willows. He aimed toward the machine and waited for movement. Moments before he had heard the death cry of the Oriental-Californian pilot.

Despite his self-avowal not to dwell on it until later, Jerry's face flashed through his mind. He was beginning to like that boy, even if he was a goddamned first lieutenant. Now this pustule-infested, borscht-eating, lice-picking, mouth-breathing, self-abusing son of a bitch in front of him had ended Jerry's life.

Rudi tried to maintain his sergeant's distance. Something clinked and he focused. Another clink.

The whoreson is reloading his heavy machine gun. He painfully pulled himself to his feet and stepped as quickly as he could through the willows.

The corporal behind the twin 9mm machine guns jerked his head up in surprise and quickly brought the muzzle around to bear on Rudi. A burst of automatic fire blossomed a row of blood roses across the corporal's chest and toppled him lifelessly over the edge of the gun tub onto the mud-scarred trail.

Jerry Yamato let his weapon drop to his side and grinned at Rudi. "I knew you were going to try something crazy. But your timing was perfect."

Rudi felt something other than pain inside him. He grinned and pointed to the armored personnel carrier. "Is good to insure there are no others."

Jerry walked around the machine, poked his weapon inside the troop compartment and let loose a string of shots. Silence fell over the area.

"So how far is it to the closest redoubt?"

"I would know this how?" Rudi asked, gesturing with his unburdened hand. "I am as new to Russian Amerika as the lieutenant, and like you, I no longer have my maps."

"Good point." His face went bleak. "Jesus, I nearly forgot, Pelagian has been hit."

As quickly as possible, Rudi followed Yamato into the brush. The amount of pain he constantly suppressed had lessened over the past day, for which he was grateful. To tell full truth, he felt fortunate to be alive.

The forever fall down the mountain did things to him that other men would not have survived. Being obstinate helped, he felt sure. But Bodecia had worked magic on him and saved his life. She had also put clean clothing on him and replaced his boots.

He owed these people. It had been a very long time since he felt that way about anyone. It occurred to him that he felt more loyalty to them than to anyone or anything else.

Pelagian lay on the ground, using part of the parachute for a pillow. Bodecia knelt beside him, her back to the others, working on the wound. Pelagian appeared gray and wrung out.

Rudi wondered where all those worry lines on the man's face had suddenly come from.

"Magda, come on in," Jerry called. He surveyed the couple on the ground. "How is he?"

"I've stopped the bleeding. Now I must remove the bullet."

"It didn't go through him? That's amazing."

"We think it hit a branch first. We were both out of the line of fire and we believe the bullet was a ricochet. It could have been worse, but this is bad enough."

Magda crept up as if her sudden presence would frighten.

"Father is wounded?"

"Yes, but I am going to take out the bullet; all of you can help me."

"How will you remove the bullet?" Rudi asked.

"I have ways. Sergeant, you move over here," she pointed, "and, Lieutenant, you go right there."

Immediately both men knelt on either side of the fallen giant.

"Hold him; this will probably hurt."

"What can I do?" Magda asked in a girlish voice.

"Get hold of yourself and then give me every bit of your strength you can."

"Beloved," Pelagian said in a papery tone. "For you I would endure anything."

"Good," Bodecia said with starch in her voice. "Now don't move."

Rudi followed Jerry's lead and rested his hand on the wounded man's arm. Bodecia cupped her hands over the blood-oozing wound and closed her eyes. The muscles in her neck and jaw stood out, slightly quivering.

Magda stood directly behind her mother, as close as she could without touching. She tensed her body and she lifted her face to the sun.

"Uhhnnn." Pelagian went rigid, sweat popped out on his face and chest. His eyes rolled far back and Rudi thought the man would faint.

"It's coming," Bodecia said in a gasp.

Rudi thought he saw white light between her palms, but realized that was impossible.

Pelagian arched his back, straining against their hands, as Bodecia held her still-cupped hands over him. A gout of blood erupted from the man's side with a small *poitt* sound and Bodecia grinned as Pelagian fell back in a swoon.

"I got it," she said.

"Got what?" Jerry asked.

Rudi knew, but he wanted proof just the same.

Bodecia opened her hand and a bloody lump of disfigured lead rested on her palm.

"This was the easy part. Now I must make him heal."

"That fast?" Jerry asked.

Bodecia and Rudi laughed in unison.

"No," Bodecia said. "It will take time."

"After seeing that," Jerry said. "I believe you could do almost anything."

"I can't hurry time, which is a good thing, because that's all we have."

Magda slumped to her knees and rested her head on her mother's back.

"What can we do?" Rudi asked. He felt a deep, nearly religious awe and affection for this healer.

"See if you can get that machine started. We need to get to Delta as soon as possible."

"As you wish, Bodecia." Rudi looked up at the lieutenant. "Do you know engines?"

"I know they run on gas and oil. Don't look at me like that, I'm a pilot; I have a ground crew to keep my plane operational."

"Come with me anyway."

As in most Imperial Russian Army vehicles, a key was not needed. Ignition began with the push of a button. But on this vehicle, pushing the button produced a flat click.

"Damn." Rudi opened the engine compartment and began tugging on wires and prodding at components. "Look inside for tools."

"Yes, Sergeant."

Rudi grinned. "No disrespect intended, Lieutenant."

Yamato dropped a toolbox on the fender next to Rudi. "Is the battery damaged?"

"Excellent question." He followed the wiring back to a compartment under the floorboards. The battery leaked acid from three bullet holes. "No, is not damaged. Is destroyed."

"Oh shit, really?" Yamato stuck his head in the compartment and retreated immediately. "I thought I didn't hit anything."

"Would seem you are better shot than appreciated."

"How are we going to get them out of here, Rudi?"

He gave the younger man a bleak look. "How do I get *me* out of here?"

Yamato went silent. Rudi didn't like that. He suspected the man produced crazy ideas when he didn't talk.

"Let's go give them the bad news," Yamato said.

"*Da.*"

Bodecia looked up when they returned to the small clearing.

"Battery was destroyed in the fighting," Rudi said. She looked blank.

"The battery supplies the electrical power to start the vehicle and stores additional power from the generator once the vehicle is running," Yamato said.

Rudi looked at him. "Thought you knew nothing about it."

"My dad is a mechanical engineer; something must have rubbed off."

For an instant Rudi remembered his father, drunk and beating Rudi's mother, right before Rudi knocked him flat with a pick handle. That was the day he had joined the army. He had only fifteen years at the time.

"Rudi, you okay?"

"Yes, of course." He looked at Bodecia again. "The lieutenant describes situation succinctly. Under present circumstances, vehicle is inoperable."

"I understand. When you said 'battery' I thought of guns for some reason. Sergeant, get back in your litter. Magda, get my pack."

The young woman hurried off and was back in an instant. "Here, Mother."

"Thank you. Now go fetch yours and make sure your water bottles are filled." Magda hurried off again.

Bodecia stared up at Yamato. "You and Magda must go get help."

"What? Why us? I mean, I thought you fixed him."

"He will not die. But it will take twice as long for him to heal out here as it would in the village. And sooner or later someone will come looking for that machine and its crew."

"Good point," the lieutenant said.

In his comfortable litter, Rudi tried not to smile. Bodecia could run a recruit training center better than any three sergeants he knew.

"But why Magda and me?"

"Pelagian is wounded, I must care for him, and the sergeant cannot travel as far and fast as you need to go."

"Why can't I just go and leave Magda here?"

"You would be lost within three hours without a guide, wouldn't you?"

Yamato stared up at the sky and scuffed one foot. Finally he whispered, "Yeah, probably."

Magda returned with a pack on her back and looked down at her mother. "Who is going with me?"

"Take Consort and Arrow and—" Bodecia pointed at Jerry and Magda grinned. Rudi's laugh broke free.

"What's so damn funny?" Yamato demanded.

"You lose at cards, yes?" Rudi asked.

"Yeah, mostly. What's your point?"

"You possess honest face, Lieutenant. What happens in your mind ends up there. Please to be careful, we need both of you."

"I'll do what I can."

Magda bent and kissed her father's cheek, then touched her mother's hair. "The Czar Alexander Highway is not far. Five days at most and we'll be back."

"Find Frank, be careful, and hurry."

"Come on, Lieutenant." Magda whistled for the dogs and left the clearing without looking back.

★ 6 ★

Russia-Canada Highway, east of Tetlin Redoubt

General Spotted Bird surveyed the burning perimeter of Tetlin Redoubt through his field glasses. No movement. No resistance for over two hours. "Okay," he said with a growl into his microphone, "send in the braves."

Infantry rose in both directions on the wide front, established earlier through cannon and other heavy weapons fire, and moved forward with caution and practiced alertness. The occasional crack of a rifle would bring the troopers down onto their bellies, but they didn't hesitate in their advance. No rounds came their way; the enemy offered a total lack of resistance.

"Whattya think, Fires-Twice?" General Spotted Bird asked, squinting over at his adjutant.

The tall Sioux glanced at his commanding officer and nodded toward Tetlin. "I'd send in the Dog Soldiers if it were up to me."

"Why?"

"They handle the unexpected somewhat better than our less experienced troops, and they won't walk into a trap."

"Agreed. Make it happen."

Colonel Fires-Twice motioned to the radioman. "Contact Major Guthridge and tell him to execute Plan Prairie Fire at once."

"Yes, sir." The sergeant flipped switches on the large radio attached to the wide tank hull and spoke rapid Navaho into the microphone.

Colonel Fires-Twice cleared his throat and glanced at the general again.

"You got something to say, say it," the general said, peering through his field glasses.

"We've run out of civilian liaison units. There were more towns in British Canada than we thought."

"Don't worry about it, Franklin." General Spotted Bird lowered the field glasses and bent his mouth as close to a smile as he could. "We're in Russian Amerika now, and every place we take will be given to our northern brothers-in-arms."

"Why are we doing that? We've already taken most of British Canada. If we're not out for conquest, why the hell are we still risking FPN lives?"

General Spotted Bird peered through his binoculars again. "For the big picture, Franklin, for the future."

"I'll take your word for it, General."

"Sirs," Sergeant Yazzi, their radio talker broke in.

"Sergeant?" General Spotted Bird gave him his full attention.

"Captain Guthrie says there is a man named Cassidy who just drove in and demands to see you. Says he was sent for."

General Spotted Bird grinned for the first time that day.

"Indeed he was sent for. I sent for him. Have Mr. Cassidy brought forward at once."

Sergeant Yazzi spoke into the microphone for a moment and then lapsed into silence.

Colonel Fires-Twice gave the general a look. "Is that Yukon Cassidy you sent for?"

The general glassed the field again. "Yeah. Know him?"

"We were friends when we were boys. I haven't seen him since he got pissed and joined the Royal Canadian Rangers back in '73."

General Spotted Bird dropped his binoculars to his chest and gave the colonel a level stare. "You never told me you knew him."

"You never asked, sir."

"Why was a white kid living in the FPN?"

"His dad was one of those back-to-the-land rustics in the late '50s. His mother is Hunkpapa Sioux, so he's half Indian."

"How long did the father last?"

"He's the chief administrator for the big hospital in Sioux Falls, still married to his wife after all these years."

"That's amazing. Most of those guys went home after three months. What was Cassidy like as a kid?"

Colonel Fires-Twice grinned and shook his head. "He got me into more damned trouble than any five other people put together. Always had a scheme that would make us some money, get us horses, or much later, find wild women."

"And you haven't seen him for over fifteen years?"

"The few times he came back to Pa Sapa to visit I was out patrolling one of our borders. You know his record pretty well, General. How is that?"

"He's worked for me off and on for the last ten years. Best facilitator I've ever seen."

"I can easily believe that. He was always good in tight situations. One time he and I—"

A battered utility with a lodge top screeched to a stop beside the Brulé tank and both men watched a solidly built man of medium height climb out and look up at them.

"General Spotted Bird, you sent for me?" His gaze wandered over to the other man in the wide tank hatch. "Frank, is that really you?"

"With your permission, General?" Fires-Twice said with a wide grin.

"By all means, Colonel, go greet your friend."

Colonel Franklin Fires-Twice vaulted out of the hatch, landed on the hull and then jumped to the ground. He and Cassidy grabbed each other in a fierce bear hug and danced in a circle, pounding each other on the back. When they pulled apart General Spotted Bird saw tears on the faces of both men.

"I've thought about you every damn day," Franklin said. "Always wondering what you were up to, where you were, who you were—"

"You're looking good, Frank." He wiped his eyes with a grimy sleeve. "And a full colonel, too! I always knew you'd get somewhere if I just got the hell out of the way. I've kept up on you, too. Two Valor Shields in one career is a record, isn't it?"

"So they tell me. It is *so* good to see you, my brother!"

"We can't let this many years separate us again, agreed?"

"Agreed!"

"Now I have to report to the general." Cassidy turned and looked up at Spotted Bird. "Any word on our outlaw?"

"The Freekorps went through here over a week ago. They jumped the border in the middle of the night without killing anyone. The Russians had other fish to fry and put the incident on the back burner. Where they went from here is anyone's guess."

"Was Riordan with them?"

"Oh yes. Our witness was very sure of that point. Riordan's scout car nearly ran down the guy's kids. Riordan had the driver stop and he screamed at the kids for being in his way."

"That asshole never changes, does he?"

"There's a firefight ahead of us—we're taking out Tetlin Redoubt—but we can get you around the fighting and headed northwest if you wish."

"I would be most grateful, General Spotted Bird."

"You're after Riordan?" Franklin Fires-Twice asked.

"I'll bring him back to the First People's Nation to answer for his crime, my friend."

"Isn't he surrounded by mercenaries?"

"So I've heard."

"But how—"

"I'll see you when I get back, Frank. Please stay safe."

"You too, Wayne."

Cassidy crawled back into the battered utility and started the engine. Then, with a wave, he swayed off down the road stretching north into the heart of Russian Amerika.

★ 7 ★

57 miles south of Delta

"*Majeur!* We have sighting of Russian military." Captain René Flérs exclaimed through the window of the command car, jerking Timothy Riordan out of a deep sleep.

After waiting ten beats for his heart to slow, Riordan squinted his eyes and stared at his executive officer. "Are they actually *attacking* us, René?"

"*Non!* Perish the very thought. They know nothing of our presence."

"Then you should have carefully touched my shoulder and spoke in softer tones," he said softly. Then he screamed, "I nearly *crapped* myself when you startled me! Ten days of busting ass on the road takes it out of a man!"

"My apologies, Majeur Riordan," Flérs said as he cringed. "I was merely attempting to notify you in the most expeditious manner at my command."

Riordan sat up and glanced around. "Don't worry about it, this time. So what's the situation?"

"Corporal N'go and Private Kyle report they have made visual contact of a small group of Russian Army vehicles and soldiers. They are at the junction where the road turns north again."

"Small, how small?"

"Two tanks, six armored personnel carriers and three trucks. No more than forty Russians."

"Good work, René!" Riordan jumped to his feet and adjusted his uniform. Squaring his beret he flashed René a quick smile.

"We're going to come out of this better than we are going in."

René smiled.

★ 8 ★

58 miles south of Delta

Jerry fought his mixed emotions. He was in a combat situation among people he didn't know, and had no idea of their viewpoint on anything other than killing Russians.

He felt an increasing attraction to Magda. Sure, he had always appreciated a good-looking woman and would vie with his buddies for their favors. Even the engagement to Andrea had been more lark than not and the sex had been awesome at first.

Somehow this was different. But was that due to the fact that she knew more about the current situation than he did, and he needed to prove dominance or something? This sudden change in the situation didn't give him pause but it certainly put a new twist on things.

She was a very strong-willed person, physically brave, obviously intelligent, and would probably kill him if she thought it necessary.

"This is the kind of girl my mother would like," Jerry muttered, remembering how much his traditional mother had disliked Andrea.

Ahead of him, Magda stopped and peered back

over her shoulder. "Shut up," she hissed. "This *is* Russian territory."

Jerry gave her a crisp salute and forgot Andrea. Watching Magda's body move under the moosehide was much more interesting.

All of his gear had been returned and he kept a weather eye on the compass embedded in the hilt of his survival knife. Even though she weaved around rock fields and brush too dense to penetrate, Magda maintained a bearing of NNW. Without the compass, Jerry knew he would have been lost within a half hour, even if he knew where he was going.

Bodecia had been generous with her three-hour guess. The two dogs fanned out on either side of the trail, never barking nor chasing the small animals spooked by their proximity.

They crossed a crude road indented with the passing of tracked vehicles. *Tanks or armored personnel carriers*, Jerry decided, *or both*. After moving out of sight of the road he reached out and touched her arm.

She wheeled and the muzzle of her machine pistol pointed at his stomach. "What?"

"Aim that somewhere else, if you don't mind. I'm on your side, remember?"

The muzzle dropped to her side. "Why did you stop me?"

"How long has it been since it rained here?"

"You want to talk about the weather?"

"I want to know how old those tracks are back there. They were well defined but dry. They could be a day or a month old, but they haven't been rained on."

She had the courtesy to blush. "I'm sorry. I keep underestimating you, don't I?"

He shrugged. "You don't know me from Adam, as my mother likes to say. All you know is that I can fly a plane."

"Thank you." She awarded him a quick, dazzling smile. "It rained here four days ago. We had a downpour. Is there any way to determine their direction?"

"Not that I can tell. But tracking wasn't my easiest merit badge."

"Let's go back and take a quick look," she said. "Maybe I can see something you didn't."

With a gesture he offered her the lead. She declined. He carefully retraced their path.

The ground had been churned many times in the past. The willows were broken off or worn away for a full ten meters. The vehicle hadn't been alone. Jerry could count three different sets and thought there might have been four.

After pointing this out to Magda, he hesitated and then said, "So what else do you see?"

"Nothing. But perhaps there are things we should look for and ponder their significance."

"You have an extensive vocabulary for a girl who was raised in the middle of Russian Amerika."

"We call it Alaska. Both of my parents are well read and like to discuss what they read. One can learn much just listening, let alone reading. We should look for things they dropped or dragged."

"Equipment?"

"I was thinking more in the order of oil drops."

"Oil drops. How can that tell us their direction?"

"If they were moving at speed, the drops will point in the direction they were going."

"Okay, let's look for oil drops."

"Won't take long," she murmured, walking past him while searching the ground along the road. "They don't take care of their equipment."

"That could get them in a lot of trouble out here in the middle of—"

"There!" she said, somewhat more excited than he thought she would be.

They weren't oil drops. Someone riding in the vehicle had emptied dark liquid, quite a lot of it. The largest splash mark lay southernmost, the constantly diminishing smaller marks pointed north.

"Damn," Jerry muttered. "They're going the same direction we are."

"Yes, they are."

He looked up at her. "Thank you for teaching me that."

"You're welcome. Let's go, we're almost to the Czar Nicholas Highway."

He followed Magda and her dogs into the brush. For an hour he silently followed, trying to keep his mind on the situation and destination rather than where her presence led him.

"Let's stop for a while," Magda said. She sat on a large rock, which now seemed rare. "Would you like some squaw candy?"

"The kind your father gave me?"

While opening her pack she gave him a smirk. "And what other kind would there be?"

He barked an embarrassed laugh, feeling more vulnerable than he would ever admit. "I meant the smoked fish. Don't be silly."

Her face went solemn and she handed him a strand of salmon. "Why would you call me silly? That's something one says to a child."

"My God, Magda, you are most definitely not a child!"

Her face softened and he felt his body relax. This didn't seem to be the place to explain how attractive he found her. But it did seem like the right time.

"I think you're amazing, beautiful, and dangerous, in that order. I would happily accept any sort of sweet you offered me."

She grinned. "That was pretty good. Let's go now."

He followed her as she moved lithely down the trail, watching the land ahead of her and her feet never stumbling or stepping in the wrong place. Yamato decided her toes had eyes. With a start he realized his complete trust in her.

"Where did you attend university?" she asked in a normal voice.

"University of California at Bakersfield. Majored in history."

"California history?"

"North American history, I think it's fascinating."

"From what I've heard and read, it seems very jumbled up, all those nations at each other's throats, alliances against alliances yet often on the same side in a larger war."

"Where did you attend university?" he said with a laugh.

"Two years at Metropolitan Collége in St. Nicholas and I took my bachelor's from Simon Frasier in British Canada with double majors in philosophy and biology."

"Why are you living like this if you don't have to?" he blurted.

"Because I want to, maybe?" She gave him a long, level look over her shoulder before continuing on down the trail. "I've been teaching Dená children at Delta. There is no higher calling than teacher."

"How old are you?"

She chuckled softly without looking back. "One never asks a lady her age. Didn't they teach you that in school?"

"No." He laughed. "But my mother tried."

"And how old are you?"

"Twenty-eight last August. I've been in the RCAF for almost four years."

"How much longer are you obligated to serve?"

"Two more years and a few weeks, if I decide to get out."

"Why would you stay in the military? Do you like being told what to do?"

"I like the feeling that I'm contributing to my country and getting to fly planes at the same time." He felt nettled but tried not to show it. "I think we all owe our country something."

"So why not teach?"

He laughed again. "Not even the military tells you what to do as completely as do public school administrators. Or hadn't you noticed?"

"Good riposte. I give you points. I left my position in January."

"Why?"

"Bloody administrators, that's why. Let's just say we didn't agree on curriculum."

Jerry remained silent for a few hundred yards. The more he learned of her, the more attraction he felt. He decided she had to be at least twenty-four.

"So, is there a boyfriend or fiancé waiting for you back in Delta?"

"Not really."

He nearly asked what that meant before deciding he didn't want to know. Not yet, anyway. The next four questions that popped into his head were instantly rejected.

Throughout their trek he watched everything they passed, trying to remember landmarks in the event he had to retrace the route alone.

Well, if I can just find the trail.

Magda suddenly stopped and hunkered down into a crouch. The dogs vanished into the trees. Jerry instantly moved off the trail and into the brush before stopping.

"What?" he said in a hiss.

She held her hand up for silence and then moved. And disappeared. Try as he might, he could not see where she went. He heard a voice.

"But we have an armored column advancing from St. Nicholas, Major. How can you insist we need your Freekorps, especially at such an exorbitant price?"

Educated Russian, Jerry decided. Freekorps?

"We're all veterans of armed conflict, Captain. We know what we're doing and how to do it as expediently as possible. You tell us what objective you want taken and we have it for you in three days or give you fifteen percent off."

Jerry couldn't place the accent—Europe, maybe. He had heard the term "Freekorps" before, in OCS; the major was a mercenary.

"What would be the price of taking Chena Redoubt?"

Major Mercenary's laugh lacked humor. "We are a company, not a brigade. But we could do it in a month for five thousand British pounds."

The Russian captain laughed with great amusement. "Hell, for that much I would conquer it!"

"No discretionary funds, I take it?"

"Nothing like that. Besides, the Californians have deployed troops and antiaircraft batteries throughout the area. Is suddenly whole new war."

"Yes, I know. And you're losing."

"We have suffered setbacks, yes. But not losing, no."

"As you wish. It really doesn't matter to me."

Jerry edged forward; he wanted to see these men.

"I find your attitude offensive, Major Riordan."

"I don't mean to be personally offensive; tactically offensive, yes. I like to think I am a realist."

Through the screening branches of three willows, Jerry saw them. The Russian's field garb gave off small puffs of dust as he walked. Major Riordan wore mottled camouflage and an incongruous red beret.

"As you wish. If you don't mind, I must return to my command. There is great battle raging near Chena and my armored scout company has been ordered to the front."

"Very heroic, I'm sure you and your men will acquit yourselves honorably." Riordan lagged behind the captain and put a whistle to his lips. Abruptly he pulled his pistol from its holster, and blew twice on the whistle before shooting the captain three times in the back of the head.

Jerry nearly cried out. He knew war was brutal, but this was—

A fusillade of weapons fire blazed from a near distance.

Riordan grinned down at the captain's body. "Now it becomes clear, does it not? You either let me in the game or risk losing everything. Now I've got your money *and* your armour." He marched off down the dry wash toward the sound of motors revving and men cheering.

Jerry could clearly see the dead captain's ruined head. His stomach lurched and he lowered his head close to the moss and years' worth of ancient leaves before he let himself vomit. Taking a pull from his canteen, he rinsed his mouth as best he could.

I've got to find Magda.

Acutely alert, he edged out onto the trail.

★ 9 ★

Dená Provisional Capitol, Tanana, Dená Republik

"We have a quorum," President Nathan Roubitaux said with a firm gavel rap. "The War Council will now come to order."

Representative Blue Bostonman quickly stood and stared at the president.

"Representative Bostonman, do you have something to say for the good of the order?"

"I move that the Dená people need to form a civilian government immediately. There are treaties and permissions being thrown around that will affect them for years." She dropped back into her seat.

"Do we have a second for Representative Bostonman?" Nathan asked.

Every hand shot up. Nathan pursed his lips and stared around the room long enough to rein in his anger.

"Very well." His voice rapidly chilled like a northern front. "The floor is open."

Five of the seven delegates stood.

"We'll do it in reverse alphabetical order," Nathan said with a frosty smile. "Mr. Ustinov?"

"The people have fought a very costly war, still not finished from what I have heard. We claim to be the Dená Republik, but are not republik in fact, perhaps a military state?"

"Maybe a military dictatorship?" Eleanor Wright said with a growl.

Nathan rapped his gavel twice. "One at a time, please. Everyone will get his or her chance to speak. Did you have more to say, Representative Ustinov?"

"If we do not create a representative government, the people will turn on us. *I* will turn on us!"

"So noted, Mr. Ustinov." Nathan pointed to another delegate. "Representative Wright?"

"You don't know your alphabet, Nathan," she said with a quick smile. "When we leave this meeting today, we have to tell our constituents when there will be a constitutional convention and how they will pick people to serve on it. Without a constitution we have nothing; we'll be a big tribe, not a nation."

Nathan held up his hand, "Eleanor, we're still fighting a war. Every village has people in the field. How can we select delegates to a constitutional convention if everyone doesn't have a chance to vote?"

"C'mon, Nathan, that's the least of our problems." Her dark eyes flashed in irritation. "We can distribute ballots to every man and woman in the Army and they can vote for the people they want. Everybody gets one vote and every district gets one delegate, sounds simple to me."

Anna Samuel from Fort Yukon stood up. "I think it's my turn to speak, Nathan. Eleanor is right. We can't keep telling everyone that nothing can be done until the war is over.

"The Russians have asked for a cease-fire and the British have folded their tent and run off in the night. This war is finished for all intents and purposes. You—we—cannot drag our feet any longer." She looked around the room, making eye contact with every other delegate before sitting down.

More hands shot into the air and Nathan held both hands above his head. "Okay, I surrender. If you want a constitutional convention, you'll get one. We need at least three people to work together to set up the delegate election."

Every hand in the room shot up again.

"We need to do this logically," Nathan said. "Claude, you're as downriver as a person can get and you know the diplomatic ropes: you're selected. Gennady, you're about as upriver as a person can get and still be in Dená country: you're number two."

The room grew even quieter as they waited for the third committee member to be chosen. Nobody questioned Nathan's right to make the selection; after all, he was the president.

"Anna, you're midriver, and you know folks from all over the Dená Republik, so I think you'd make an excellent, third committee person."

Anna stood. "Thank you, Nathan. Claude, Gennady and I have a lot of work to do, so as soon as we decide when this election will be held, we're going to leave this body and convene our committee."

"How much time do you need?"

Claude stood. "I think we can have it all organized to hold an election three months from today. Assuming, of course, that we have logistic help from the military."

"So ordered," Nathan said with an insincere smile. "Now we must decide whether or not to officially consider the unification request from the provisional Tlingit Nation."

Blue stood. "Since we all have a lot to do, why don't we just consider the question and skip the first part?"

"You're out of order!" Nathan said, rapping his gavel.

"But she's right," Anna said with a grin. "There's too much fancy stuff to wade through if we do everything your way, Nathan."

"Do we offer the Tlingits a unification treaty or not?" Nathan said with some heat.

"This is why we need a real government," Gennady Ustinov said. "We need to put the best minds we have to working on this idea."

"General Grigorievich, do you have a question?" Nathan asked.

Grisha lowered his hand and rested it on the arm of his wheelchair. "More of an observation, Mr. President. The Tlingits, my people, are just as tired of Russian domination as you are. You know them, have traded and intermarried with them for centuries before the Russians ever *discovered* Alaska. The concept of an Alaskan Republik is as forward-looking and sensible as anything I've heard yet. My recommendation would be to send a delegation to them to confer and come up with a workable plan for unification."

"Thank you, General," Nathan said, looking around at the others. "Any other thoughts on this?"

Andrew Isaac stood. "I think we should send the general. He knows his people and he knows us. Wing should go with him as his wife and as a fellow delegate. If we can't trust those two, we can't trust anybody."

As soon as Andrew sat down, Joanne Kaiser called out, "I move we vote on it."

"Second the motion," Gennady said.

Moments later Grisha and Wing were declared ambassadors to the Tlingit Nation.

"Now if we can just get you there safely," Nathan said.

★ 10 ★

Akku, Russian Amerika

"The Tlingit Nation Army is in a very tight place. I'm not sure we can get out with everything we want," Captain Paul Chernikoff said, pacing back and forth in the small room. Rain tapped on the windows and wind sighed through the towering spruce and hemlock outside the building.

"Define your terms, please," General Sobolof responded in a quiet tone.

"The Japanese have attacked Russian Amerika, but not the Russian mainland, unprovoked and without warning at the very moment the Russian Pacific Fleet was destroyed by the California Navy. We made a grave error when we signed the military aid pact with Japan—we left the option of taking action up to them. We asked for a paper tiger and got one with steel claws instead."

"Did you not support the pact, Captain?" General Sobolof asked.

"Yes, sir, in the strongest terms possible. I think the Japanese naval attaché perhaps duped me, and I should have anticipated that possibility. I didn't."

"No need to fall on your sword, Captain. We all agreed to the pact."

"It's just that I remember being very outspoken and possibly rude, General Sobolof."

The general grinned. "I was once your age, Captain, and had just as big a mouth. What's past is past; we cannot change that."

"No, sir, we cannot. My brother has secured the cooperation of the Dená people as well as that of the ROC and the USA. The US fleet is sortieing out of the Kingdom of Hawai'i, preparing to engage the Japanese fleet if all other options fail."

"What other options are there?"

"Frankly, General, none."

"What are the Californians doing?"

"One of their submarines sank a Russian warship in Alaskan waters; other than that they are watching and waiting. In the meantime we are completely cut off from the Pacific by the Imperial Japanese Navy."

"Are the USA and the ROC declaring war on the Empire of Japan?"

"That depends on whether or not the Japanese pull back."

"So what happens if the USA and the ROC save our asses from the Japs? Are they an instant enemy also?" General Sobolof poured himself a glass of water and then drank it. He slammed the glass down on the table between them.

"Are we reduced to choosing who our new master will be?"

"The Dená Nation is sending a delegation to us, to explore the possibility of an Alaskan Republik." Captain Paul Chernikoff said it as if it were an afterthought.

"Who suggested this republik?"

"My brother did, General. It just came to him, the possibility, that is, and he ran with it."

"I think you and your brother have just redeemed yourselves, Captain."

"Do you mind if I sit?" His relief was evident.

"Of course not."

Chernikoff dropped onto the chair and sighed. "The most positive thing about this delegation is they're sending our cousin, General Grigorievich, as head of the delegation."

"Grisha?"

"You seem surprised, General Sobolof. Why?"

"Wasn't he cashiered from the Russian Army?"

"Yes. He also led the Southern Dená and when the truce was called, the Dená made him commanding general of their army."

"How can that be? He's not even an Athabascan."

"Personally, I think they thought he would fail, and he didn't. Our northern brothers are doing something I think we should copy, immediately."

"What?" General Sobolof asked in a guarded tone.

"Reward ability with increased responsibility. Grisha went from a rescued slave to a general in less than a year."

"And we don't?"

"With all due respect, General Sobolof, we never see the individual, we only see the kwan."

The older man blinked and looked toward the rain-soaked window. "Perhaps there is something to what you say. I will bring it up to the others. Let me do the talking; you do not have the rank to push a thing like this."

"Believe me, General Sobolof, I am very aware of that."

★ 11 ★

65 miles south of Delta

"Sergeant," Bodecia said, "would you please bring me the other pack, the one Pelagian was carrying?"

"Please, name is Rudi to person who saves my life. Of course I will." He hurried off before she could respond. He had never been good at social skills, which served him well in his career.

In the Russian Army one agreed with one's superiors and instilled respect and obedience in one's subordinates. As an enlisted man he could rise no further than command sergeant major. Lieutenant Yamato's squadron had obliterated Rudi's command.

Colonel Lazarev came to mind. He hadn't liked the man, but he had respected him. Rudi hadn't found any trace of the colonel's body. But he had been standing in the turret when the tank fell into the canyon.

Rudi found the pack near the place where Pelagian had been hit. He hefted it, winced at the flash of pain in his chest and side, and hurried back to Bodecia. The day seemed too warm to bear.

As soon as he dropped it next to her, Bodecia

tore into it and pulled out the mottled green silk of Yamato's parachute. She shook it out and started tying it to saplings.

"Help me, Rudi. We must build a shelter to keep him out of the sun and rain."

Rudi glanced at the cloudless sky. "Is not raining."

"It will. And the sun is strong this time of year."

In twenty minutes they fashioned a tent, which could shelter up to five people if they were friendly. They gently moved Pelagian into the shade and piled their gear close. Rudi carefully pulled in large rocks to make the position defensible if the need arose.

The pain flashed in his chest again and he grunted.

Bodecia peered at him with her obsidian-black eyes. "How are you feeling, Sergeant? The truth now, I'll know if you dissemble."

"Is Rudi, please. I ache most of the time, sleeping has become difficult, this gives me much weariness."

"You should have said something. I could have—"

"Please, is of no account. I am alive because you save my life. I do not complain, you asked me."

"I could have given you something to help you sleep. You should let me finish my words."

"I already know what you will say. If I take medicine to sleep, I lose survival edge, I don't let little wrong noises wake me, and we all die. I am well able to endure small discomfort, please not to worry."

"I, or the dogs, would know if someone came close. I could wake you. You need to heal as fast as you can."

"How would you know if dogs also sleep, or wander? You don't sleep at all? You are only healthy person here, must stay that way."

"Rudi, look deep into my eyes, yes, right now."

He stared, more out of politeness than curiosity. She wasn't a hard woman to look at.

"Good, you're getting close, now concentrate on what you see in there."

He started a smile but it died halfway. Something moved in the back of her eyes, something there and not a reflection.

"Do you see shapes or people? Do you see yourself, or what you wished to be? Look deep, push your senses, and open your heart and mind."

At first they were shapes. Slowly they coalesced into a startling image of Natalia as he last saw her. Her laughter abruptly crossed an unfathomable abyss to brush his ears.

He sat transfixed as completely as an opium eater. He could taste Natalia's tears, feel her hands in his, and smell the lavender defense with which she blocked the world. He smiled at her for a long time.

"Ser— Rudi, you need to wake up now." Bodecia's voice insistently pushed into his contemplation, eroding his smile. He jerked at her touch and woke.

He pushed himself upright and shook his head. "I have been asleep?"

"Quiet. There's something out there, along the river. The dogs and I heard it."

"Were voices?"

"No, it might be an animal." She continued to whisper. "If it is, it's a big one."

Rudi licked his lips and tried to peer through the brush. "What animals live here?" he asked in a low voice.

"Well, no lions or tigers." Bodecia gave him a grim smile. "But we do have caribou and moose, brown bear and black bear, lynx, wolves, fox, and even muskrats."

"Real bears?" His voice rose slightly.

"Shh. *Da*, not like the kind Jerry wears on his chest."

He thought of the lieutenant's flight wings: a roaring bear head with wings on either side of the skull.

"California grizzly is national symbol," he showed a deprecating grin. "Have been extinct sixty years, perhaps more."

"The Alaska variety sure isn't. If it's a bear out there, all we have to do is make a lot of noise and it will probably leave."

"Probably? Why would it not?"

"It might be hungry."

"Oh, shit."

"Unless a bear is very old or injured, it would not be hungry this time of year. They live on fish, rodents, berries, and grubs. All are plentiful in late spring."

"Then why is it here?"

"These creeks are full of grayling and trout. Didn't you notice?"

"No." He knew she was toying with his fears, but knowing that it probably wasn't a hungry bear calmed him. "What about the dogs, will they go with me?"

"If there is trouble, I will send them to help."

"I will see what is there."

"Rudi, all sport aside, please be careful. Do not ever come between any animal and its young. If you do, it is the last the thing you will do."

He stared into her eyes where all humor had evaporated. This wasn't a joke.

"*Da*." He picked up the rifle and ensured the firing chamber held a round. Thirty years of lessons and memories spread through him. A hunter of men, he carefully edged into the brush.

★ 12 ★

30 miles west-northwest of Delta

Colonel Del Buhrman waved his hand downward and the sixty men within view around him sank out of sight into the brush and trees. He pulled himself down behind a rock wreathed with bushes and peered ahead. A Russian soldier, his rifle carelessly resting across his shoulder, briefly ambled toward them.

Buhrman rested his elbows on the rock and eased the rifle barrel through the bushes, centered his sights on the man's chest and waited. His index finger caressed the trigger.

The soldier stopped, peered back down the trail, and shrugged. He turned around and disappeared.

Colonel Buhrman pushed on the safety and moved the weapon to his side. Major Coffey slid up next to him.

"What's the good word?"

"They have no idea we're back here. Pass the word that the guys have done an excellent job of being invisible and Colonel Buhrman is pleased."

"If I knew where they were, I'd tell Benny's guys that too."

"Joe," Buhrman's glance held a smile, "they might not even be out here. Wherever they're at, we're all on the same side."

"Sometimes it's hard to tell. You know that Benny will be where the action is, and that's out here. Maybe I should have joined the Rangers. At least I'd get my name in the paper on a regular basis."

"Notoriety is a double-edged sword, Major Coffey. If they don't know who you are, they can't blame you for not living up to their expectations."

"How do you do it? No matter what I say, you point out how good I got it—and I always believe you!"

Colonel Buhrman laughed. "That's one of the things I like about you, Joe, you're gullible."

They laughed quietly together.

"Tell Major Smolst I'd like to see him," Colonel Buhrman said.

"Right away." Major Coffey vanished silently into the brush.

Colonel Buhrman leaned against a tree a few feet from the large rock and slid down to a sitting position. He appreciated the respite but his eyes constantly moved over the terrain ahead of him.

Major Smolst suddenly squatted next to him. "You wanted to see me, Colonel?"

"You're good, Heinrich. I didn't hear you coming."

"I didn't want you to, sir."

"You're ex-Troika Guard, aren't you?"

"Yes, sir. Over twenty years."

"Well, I'm glad you're on our side and not theirs." Buhrman nodded toward the rock in front of him. "How many Dená are with you?"

"A hundred and ninety-five, not counting me."

"Any of your guys know this country?"

"Two are from Delta, and have hunted this area all their lives."

"Perfect. I'd like to speak with them at their earliest convenience."

Smolst nodded. "I'll go get them now. You going to be in this spot?"

"Yep."

★ 13 ★

58 miles south of Delta

Shouts of dominance and victory carried through the copse of willows and black spruce. A shot rang out and the cheering intensified. Jerry felt near panic. Where was Magda? Had they found her?

He stepped out onto the path, almost standing over the Russian captain's body. A quick glance about found nothing and he steeled his resolve to go into their midst after her. He checked the machine pistol, making sure the safety was off.

"Lieutenant!" The whisper came from behind him and he whirled about to see Magda and the dogs deep in the willows.

"My God, you're safe!"

"Shut up!" she hissed. "They are just down the road. If they catch us, they will kill us: you and my dogs immediately, me after they have had their fun."

Jerry joined her in the brush. "What do you want to do?"

"What do you want to do?"

"You're my guide, Magda. I agreed to follow your lead."

"You saw what he did to the captain. These are rogues, without honor or discipline."

"I think they have discipline," Jerry said, maintaining his whisper. "But I don't think they have any honor. Which to be honest, I considered just an abstract concept until about five minutes ago."

"So what do we do?"

"I wish I knew what they were going to do. If they are headed for Delta, we have to take a different route—are there any?"

"Of course there are, but we're talking about an extra day's worth of walking. They will take the highway; we'll have to follow the game trails."

"Then let's not waste any more time. I'll follow you."

"We need to move fast in order to warn the DSM."

"The what?"

"The Dená Separatist Movement. That's who you're fighting for."

"I thought this war was all new to you?"

"The war is," she smiled, "but we've been part of everything else all along. Come now, we need to hurry."

Frigid water swirled around Jerry's hips as they forded yet another fast-moving tributary to the Delta River. The only good thing about being in the middle of a cold creek, he decided, was the lack of mosquitoes. The invasive insects droned in clouds all around the horizon.

Magda gave him something to rub on his exposed skin but the devils still found entry into his shirt and hovered around his face. As they approached the shore, he could see them hazing above the water.

"Do you have any more of that stuff?"

She pulled a vial from her pouch and handed it to him. "Use it sparingly; it's all we have left."

He rubbed it behind both ears and on the back of his neck before closing the vial tightly. Hours ago he had pulled off his flight suit and now wore his khaki fatigues.

He pulled the flight suit out of his bag, held it under water and, as they neared shore, wrapped it around his head and shoulders. Cold water cascaded over his face as he hurried up onto the shore.

"Move fast, maybe we can lose most of them," he all but shouted.

"Make a little more noise and the Russians will bite you permanently!"

Jerry slowed and looked back at her. "I'm being eaten alive by flying needles and you're worried about Russians? They won't be out in this; they're all sitting around smudge pots drinking vodka."

"If you believe that, I'll just let you stay here and die."

Jerry bit his tongue to stop his heated answer. This was not the way to save Pelagian, Bodecia and Rudi. Nor was this the way to serve the Republic of California and the Dená Separatist Movement.

"I'll try to make less noise if you will," he said in his most jocular tone.

"Oh, now I'm the one making noise!"

He stopped moving and stared at her, watching her eyes widen and her lovely bosom heave with the emotion she felt, and appreciated the color blossoming in her face.

"What's wrong with you?" he asked in a low voice.

She blinked and looked away. "Sorry, just edgy I guess. I didn't mean to upset you. Let's go."

She followed the game trail and he followed her. For a moment he considered kissing her, and the sudden realization that, more than anything else, he wanted to do just that jarred him. He dwelt on what that would mean.

At any other point in his life he would have taken the chance of getting his face slapped. There was always another girl around the corner in California. But this girl, no, he corrected himself, this *woman* was different. Not to mention there weren't many corners out here.

Alaska was so different from California he didn't bother with comparisons. They came from different cultures, but both had completed college. Her calling seemed to be education, he wasn't sure of his.

Casual pairings didn't seem to be the norm here, but then his contact with locals and local mores could only be described as limited. Did he find her attractive enough to marry her? He mulled that: *maybe*.

"You hungry?" she said over her shoulder without looking at him.

"A little."

She twisted and tossed him the ubiquitous strand of squaw candy. He wondered if it were possible to get tired of it. As he chewed, he thought about being married to Magda.

He bit the side of his mouth and yelped.

She whirled and was in front of him in an instant. "What's wrong? Are you choking? Are you okay?"

Jerry held his cheek and explored the spot with his tongue, staring intently at her. "Yeah, I'm okay. Just bit the side of my mouth."

"Oh." She seemed disappointed, started to turn away.

"Magda, you are unlike any woman I've ever met and I am overwhelmingly attracted to you. I don't know if the intensity I feel is part of the situation we're in," he waved his hand toward the distant forest, "or exactly what I would feel if we met in San Francisco. I just know that it's there."

She stared at him with her lovely deep blue eyes and listened intently as he spoke.

"You're an honest man, Lieutenant Jerry Yamato, and I appreciate that and what you just said. I can't even think about you and me in that way until we get help at Delta. Once my father and mother are safe, I'll consider you again, I promise."

"Deal. Lead on."

"Listen," she said and her eyes lost focus. "That's an engine."

Jerry cocked his head to the side and instantly heard the metallic grinding of a tank. He turned and peered toward the sound. Both dogs stared intently in the same direction. Jerry wondered if they could actually see something.

"They're off to our left, so they're not following our tracks. Is that where the highway is?"

"Yes," her brow furrowed, "they'll always be ahead of us."

"How far away is Delta?"

"Fifty, maybe fifty-five kilometers. A couple of long days of hiking no matter how you look at it."

He glanced at his watch. Six hours had passed since they started. Quickly he did a self survey and decided he felt pretty good.

"Can we pick up the pace and make it by morning after tomorrow?"

She smiled. "I've been holding back for you." Magda turned and charged down the trail.

Jerry worked to match her pace. Did she take every question as a challenge? As they moved, he kept one ear on the engine noises.

If the machines got any nearer, he had to have a plan. Mosquitoes buzzed past but Magda's pace gave them the added bonus of moving faster than the insects could fly. Jerry swatted one off his face.

Of course you could still run into them.

★ 14 ★

63 miles south of Delta

Moving silently through undergrowth choked with decades of dead leaves and branches taxed Rudi's skills and current physical abilities. Every few steps he stopped to listen intently and rest.

Nothing moved save for the constant whisper of wind across the willows and black spruce. The susurration filled the silence at the edge of his awareness and he missed the sound of teeth on foliage. He spied something dark ahead, but seeming stationary, he dismissed it.

He quietly spread the willows with his rifle and left hand and stared up into the face of a moose. A covey of thoughts flashed through his mind: moose were incredibly large; it was as surprised to see him as he was to behold it; his left hand was impossibly far from the rifle in his right hand; he didn't know where to shoot this thing if he even got the chance, and he was totally terrified.

The animal's eyes grew wider by half and it abruptly pulled back and centered its weight over the back legs. Rudi knew it was going to use its front legs for combat and he threw himself to the side and scrambled madly through the thicket, ignoring the lightning flashes of pain throughout his body. Behind him the moose smashed down through the haze of sweat he knew he must have left in his wake.

It crashed into the willows behind him. He turned ninety degrees to his left without slowing. The moose gained on him, snorting and slamming huge, splayed feet down on the thick gravel.

Dogs barked in excitement somewhere behind him.

Rudi turned to his left and ran through the slashing willows, desperately trying to avoid anything that could truly trip him up. Three strides later his right foot caught in the middle of a three-trunk sapling and he hit the ground hard. Unhealed wounds ripped anew and the cascading pain lofted him into the edge of shock and unconsciousness.

Cool, wet strokes brought him awake and he jerked as memory returned.

"Lie still, Rudi," Bodecia said gently. "You've opened some of your wounds."

"Where is moose?" He tried to see all around him.

"Gone. It was probably more scared of you than you were of it. Griz and Kodiak ran it off."

"Not possible to be more frightened, would have died from fright."

She laughed. "I'm glad you didn't lose your sense of humor."

He tried to smile but couldn't find it. "I run from a beast, a man I would fight, but from beast I run."

"If you hadn't run it would have killed you. That was the only thing you could have done."

"You are kind. I ran like coward. I have failed person who saved my life."

"You are being far too melodramatic. That was a cow moose, she had a calf with her, and she thought you were a threat to her baby. If you hadn't run you would have been kicked to death in moments. I am not presenting puffery, merely facts."

"*Da.*"

"How do you feel?"

"As if I may die."

"Here, drink this." She held a cup to his lips and he drank deeply. The astringency of the liquid nearly caused him to vomit, but he held it back.

"What is this?" he asked with a gasp.

"Relief."

Darkness swam up around him, rolled over him, and pulled him down into it. He surrendered without a fight.

★ 15 ★

60 miles south of Delta

Bodecia sat between her two mumbling patients and two drowsing dogs, listening to the birds and wondering how Magda and Lieutenant Yamato were faring. Her daughter was one of the smartest people she knew, but Bodecia had witnessed the spark between the two young people.

"Attraction equals distraction," she said quietly to the rocks in front of her. She checked the constantly simmering stew and the low fire in a shallow pit beneath it. Her fire made little smoke and the constant breeze pulled it away from them.

She had enough to deal with here; she didn't want to worry about Magda too. Very vividly she remembered meeting Pelagian the first time and how completely her desire for him blotted out everything else. She smiled at her sleeping husband of twenty-eight years.

Rudi mumbled something and jerked in his sleep. The man possessed devils and she suspected he had not come to terms with all of them. His total loyalty moved her.

Rocks hit other rocks somewhere on the far side of the screening willows and she quickly grabbed the rifle. Gravel crunched under a foot within ten meters of her.

Blood pounded in her ears and her hands shook slightly as she aimed the rifle at the noise.

Off to her left a voice said in Russian, "Did you find anything?"

Griz growled deep in her throat and Bodecia quickly squeezed her muzzle. The dog quieted and along with her brother, Kodiak, stared intently toward the sounds, body tensing to spring.

The steps faltered and stopped. "No, Sergeant. Nothing but damned willows and rocks."

"Come on back," the first voice commanded. "We need to rig this tow."

"Yes, Sergeant." The man walked away toward the disabled armored car.

"Whoever killed them are long gone by now. Probably another DSM ambush."

Bodecia felt her heart slow closer to normal. Rudi thrashed again and began mumbling. She clamped her hand over his mouth.

If it's not the dogs, it's the men!

He subsided and she held the rifle firmly in both hands, waiting to see what would transpire next. Where had they come from? She had heard no engines.

Perhaps the constant breeze had worked against her. She jerked with the realization that if the wind shifted slightly, the Russian soldiers would smell the smoke from her fire. She caved in the sides of the pit on the wispy flames and they ceased to exist with no telltale plume.

She stood as tall as she could and peered around, seeing nothing other than the vast willow forest and the rushing creek.

Where were they?

☆　　☆　　☆

"Take up the tension," a man's voice bellowed in Russian. "Don't snap the cable."

Bodecia, moving as quietly as possible, continued piling dead brush on top of the parachute. After chopping off all but two thirds of a meter from the support poles, she now tried to disguise their low-profile shelter. The parachute nearly blended with the surrounding area and she stopped, listening intently.

"Make sure it's in neutral," the second voice said.

They didn't like each other, she decided. Good, they both will fixate on their irritation, perhaps relaxing their vigilance.

"That's the middle position, right, Sergeant?"

"Private Gordonin, if you give me any more shit I'll break your arm."

Bodecia smiled at the animosity in both voices. Her enemies were enemies.

"When I wave, you brake for both of us, understand?"

"Yes, Sergeant."

This time she heard the engine crank up. How had she missed that before?

"We only need to go a few hundred meters, so keep it in a straight line."

"Yes, Sergeant."

A few hundred meters? Fear coursed down her spine. She found the strongest willow within sight and carefully climbed the slender trunk.

The Russians moved away from her toward a mass of parked vehicles about three hundred meters away, somewhere between thirty and fifty machines, she thought. Most of the machines had guns of various sizes mounted on them. Another two hundred meters beyond the vehicles squatted clusters of tents with soldiers milling about.

The whole Russian encampment was no more distant than the lengths of two soccer fields.

Bodecia eased back to the ground, thinking hard. If they had strayed but a few meters off the path and taken the line of least resistance, they would have walked into the middle of that. But the Russian motor pool lay between the camp and her.

How did they not hear the exchange of gunfire earlier when Pelagian was hit? Between the wind and willows, she decided, much went undetected. Or the gunfire had been ignored as commonplace.

She checked both her patients. Then, taking only her berry bag, hurried off toward the Russian encampment. She moved quickly but quietly, both dogs silently flanking her.

In minutes she saw the dirty brown of military vehicles through a screen of willows. She edged into the open and looked around. Nothing moved.

Bodecia sidled up to a small truck and saw the ignition button waiting to be pushed. But would they hear her? She felt sure nobody would see her, as the truck was much smaller than the tanks and great tracked vehicles between her and the tents.

The wind blew away from the camp, so they probably wouldn't hear her—unless there was a patrol close by. Throwing caution to the constant wind, she climbed into the back of the truck and surveyed the area.

Nothing moved. She jumped down and swung behind the steering wheel. The engine caught immediately and she pulled out of the rank and turned sharply. In moments she was crashing through the willows.

Maybe we'll give the kids a lift.

★ 16 ★

48 miles south of Delta, Russian Amerika

"Magda, I need to take a break."

Welcoming his words, she immediately stopped and sat down next to a tree, leaned on the trunk and let her eyes close. "Okay."

Both dogs sank to the ground, tongues lolling and eyes watchful.

"Stay where you're at; I'll be right back."

Her eyes flew open. "Where are you going?"

"To add to the water table, okay?"

"Good idea, take your time." She moved into the trees and relieved herself. She went back to the tree she had been leaning on; it seemed comfortable.

A Steller's jay squawked irritably from high in a spruce tree, where the incessant wind kept its perch in constant motion. High, puffy clouds dotted the brilliant blue sky. The day sparkled for Magda and she wondered about herself.

Her feet and back hurt. Even though she and her parents had been trekking for weeks, they hadn't pushed the pace nor kept moving if someone were tired. Her stamina needed work.

Arrow crept over to her and pushed his nose under her hand. She absently scratched the dog's ears and pondered their situation.

Jerry moved silently toward her.

What am I going to do about him?

She liked him a great deal, but beyond that she wasn't sure. There had been other men, boys really, whom she had affected that way. Jerry was the first mature man, to her way of thinking anyway, who was obviously attracted to her, other than Viktor Mitkov. She pushed the thought of him away.

On one hand, it was terribly flattering. On the other, it felt frightening. What would he expect of her this quickly? Sex? Marriage?

Jerry was the first Californian she had ever met. But she had heard stories about their excessive lifestyles and licentious ways. She had heard the same sort of stories about the French.

"How are you holding up?" he asked. She saw nothing but concern in his face and felt touched.

"I'm fine. This is the farthest I've walked at one time in my life. Anyway that's what my feet are saying."

He laughed. "What a relief to hear you say that. My feet are killing me but I was afraid you'd think I was wimply if I mentioned it."

"What's wimply?"

"You know—weakling, unmanly, that sort of thing."

"You don't have to worry about that. I think you are a very strong, good man."

To her astonishment, he blushed and looked away.

"Thanks, I appreciate that. Just let me know when you're ready to continue."

Feeling a little worried, she pushed herself to

her feet. The dogs rose effortlessly and moved out to flank her. Although confused, she wanted nothing more than to kiss Jerry.

"Okay, follow me."

"Happily," he said.

She heard engine sounds in the distance and her lethargy dissipated instantly. The ache in her feet seemed to disappear and she moved swiftly down the trail. Behind her she heard the comforting tread of Jerry's feet.

★ 17 ★

Village of Angoon, Russian Amerika

"I would like this meeting to be extremely productive, very succinct, as brief as possible," General Sobolof said. "For all of us to meet in one place, especially in these times, is just short of lunacy."

The nine men in the room followed him with their eyes; nothing else moved.

"Captain Chernikoff, would you please bring everyone up to date?"

Paul Chernikoff stood and glanced around at the hard eyes now intent on his face. He nodded.

"Many of us, myself and my brother included, argued for a pact with the Japanese which we finally signed. Our shortsightedness has come home to roost much more quickly than any of us would have guessed. The Japanese are well into a conquest of our part of Russian Amerika.

"If they win, we will not only have a new master to contend with, but a much more alien one than the well-known Russians we are struggling to escape. The Japanese are multitudes of degrees more militant than the Russians, and they will enter every aspect of our lives if they succeed in this campaign."

Colonel Fredrik Paul jumped to his feet and waited.

"Colonel Paul?"

"Do you have any suggestions on what we, as the Tlingit Nation Army, should do to prevent this from happening?"

"We are far too small to act on our own," Chernikoff said with a shrug.

"Don't the Dená have allies from the southern countries?" Colonel Gregori George asked.

"Yes. They have an alliance with both the United States and the Republic of California. Both of which, by the way, in the persons of their military liaisons, promised us military aid if we so wished it."

Lieutenant Colonel Samuel Dundas shot to his feet, didn't wait to be identified. "Then why the hell aren't they on their way with what we need?"

"Because, Colonel, my brother didn't have the rank to agree to it."

"Paul, he was our envoy; he had our full confidence to act as he saw fit," Dundas said.

"That's true, Sam, he did. But he thought if we were going to change masters, you all should have a chance to vote on which one."

"Change masters—what do you mean?" Colonel George asked.

"We have to face reality, Colonel. Whichever country grants us military aid is going to want something for it. We don't have gold like the Dená or oil like the Eskimos. All we have is salmon, cod, and halibut. How many guns can you get for a halibut?"

"Depends on how damn big it is!" Colonel George said with a snort. Everybody in the room laughed with him, including Paul. When the laughter died down, General Sobolof cleared his throat.

"Pietr was right on this one. They'll want bases, treaties, more of our life than we want to surrender so quickly after winning it from the Czar."

"So we sit on our ass and do nothing?" Lieutenant Colonel Dundas raised his eyebrows as he spoke and then glanced around at the others.

"No, Sam!" General Sobolof shouted. "We run out there and get our asses shot off, let 'em kill the whole TNA in one swoop. That what you want?"

"No, General, of course it isn't. But there's a war on and it affects us in every possible way. And we're just sittin' here watching it all go by like a buncha school kids."

"If we are to exist at all, Sam," Paul said in a low voice, "we have to stay quiet right now. There are people out there helping us, but all we can do is absolutely nothing."

General Sobolof nodded.

Sam stared at each person in turn, and then said, "Sounds like crap to me!"

"Fine," General Sobolof said and clapped his hands, "we're unanimous then. How many agree we should formally ask the USA and the ROC for military aid immediately?"

Only Sam's hand did not rise.

"There is also the question of unification with the Dená and the creation of an Alaska Republik," Paul said. "Our northern brothers have agreed to send a delegation to explore the possibility. But that will all be so much star gazing if the Japanese conquer the Russians here in the panhandle."

"Say what?" Lieutenant Colonel Dundas said.

Paul glanced at the stern visage of General Sobolof

and felt his face go ashen. He had agreed to speak to the others!

General Sobolof raised his hand to still the sudden buzz in the room.

"Don't worry, Captain Chernikoff, all is well. Gentlemen, the captain brought up a subject he thought had been presented to you before this. Due to my harried schedule, I haven't had the time to cover the topic with any of you. I'm sorry."

"Maybe we could cover it now?" Lieutenant Colonel Dundas said in a sarcastic tone.

"Colonel Dundas, I know you're new to this military thing," General Sobolof said with steel in his voice, "but you're also getting close to pissing off a kwan leader. You're stacking the deck against yourself, Sam."

His previous scowl vanished and Sam Dundas suddenly looked worried. "I apologize if I suggested offense, General Sobolof."

"Not to worry. Captain Chernikoff's brother is on a trip to visit his cousin, General Grigoriy Pietrivich Grigorievich, Commander of the Dená Army."

"Grisha is in command—" Colonel Gregori George stopped himself with an effort. "My apologies, General, but you couldn't have surprised me more if you had said he was the man in the moon."

"It *is* surprising," General Sobolof said with a sage nod. "Especially considering the fact that a year ago he was a prisoner in one of the Czar's penal camps. With this hiatus in fighting, the Dená are sending him and his new wife, a colonel in the same army, to us as emissaries."

"But we are a rebel army, General," Colonel George said, "not a government."

"The Dená started in the same manner," Paul said. "Then they had each village elect a representative to send to an assembly where they thrashed out a basic government."

"Why don't we just have all the kwan chiefs decide on a government?" Colonel George said. "That would save a lot of trouble and time."

Paul Chernikoff and Sam Dundas were the only two men in the room who were not kwan leaders. But Sam was the son of a kwan chief and knew that one day he would lead his people. Chernikoff cleared his throat.

"If it had been the Tlingit Army, my cousin Grisha would perhaps be a major. The Dená have traditional chiefs, but they also have legislators, a war council, and a president. Some of those people are traditional chiefs, but the majority are not."

"What are you implying, Captain?" Colonel Paul asked in a frigid tone.

"Our people have a rigid caste system. Tradition has always outweighed ability and that has not changed in hundreds of years."

"Our system works for us, Captain Chernikoff," Colonel George said. "Let the Dená do as they wish."

"The Dená are creating a republik. Republik means equal representation for all. Every person above a certain age has a vote."

"Even women?" Colonel George asked in evident surprise.

"Yes, even women. Over half of the delegates in the Dená assembly are women. And they have done an excellent job of directing, and fighting in, the war against the Russians."

Silence settled on the small room. One by one, all eyes found General Sobolof. Chernikoff kept his silence and waited; he had done his part.

"Like it or not, we are in the midst of change," General Sobolof said. "We wish to govern ourselves, to throw off the Czar and his cossacks once and forever. It surprises none of us that we cannot do this thing alone; we need help from outside."

"General, if I may interrupt a moment?" Colonel Paul said. "Would it be worth destroying our culture in the process of freeing our people? The kwan is the backbone of our people—"

"But not the muscle!" Chernikoff blurted. "The people are the muscle, and the chiefs and leading families have always been the brains. It is time the whole of our people had a say in their lives."

"That is a very radical statement," Colonel Paul snapped. "This is not the time for radical deviation from the way our people live."

"Throwing off the Czar and the Russian government isn't radical? They have been our masters for over two hundred years—is *that* not tradition by now?"

"Captain Chernikoff," General Sobolof said, "I think we all get the point of your commentary. Please allow us the courtesy of debate."

"Of course, General."

"You may leave the room now."

★ 18 ★

Tanana, Dená Republik

"No," Wing said as sternly as she could. "We aren't taking any large weapons."

"But this is the rifle General Grigorievich used in the Second Battle of Chena, Colonel!" Sergeant Major Tobias' eyebrows went as high as his tone of voice.

Grisha laughed. "Don't worry, Sergeant Major, I'm sure I won't need it in Akku."

"Very good, General." Tobias left the room.

"He's like a mother hen!" Wing said in a low voice as she sat down beside him. "Sometimes I feel I'm a rival to him for your affection."

Grisha put his arm around her shoulders, pulled her over and kissed her.

"If that's the case, he lost."

"Well, I wasn't worried about him winning!"

"Neither was I."

She peered at him. "Grisha, you've changed somehow. You don't seem as uncomfortable as you once were with what you're doing."

"I finally realized that I was no longer a charter boat skipper in chains, but rather I was a person of authority in charge of the lives of many good people. The thing that has saved me in the past, and now, is my ability to change: to assess the situation correctly and embrace it completely. I have accepted the fact that I am now a general and must think far beyond myself if I am to do the job I have been given."

"I think I'm who I always was." She looked at him with new eyes.

Two knocks sounded on the door and Sergeant Major Tobias stepped through.

"Guess who?" Wing muttered.

"Colonel Jackson wishes an audience with you, General. What should I tell him?"

"Show him in, Sergeant Major Tobias."

"Very good, sir." He shot Wing a glance and then exited.

"I think the sergeant major and I shall have a little chat," Wing said, "about his chances of promotion."

"There's no higher enlisted rank than sergeant major," Grisha said.

"True. But he might be a corporal, soon."

"Grisha!" Benny Jackson strode into the room and then stopped short. "Sorry. General Grigorievich, how good to see you again."

Grisha smiled and reached up from his wheelchair. "Benny, it will always be Grisha to you."

"Thank you, sir!" He shook Grisha's hand and looked over at Wing. "And the most exciting woman I know, such luck I have. How are you, Wing?"

She embraced him. "It's good to see you, Benny," she said into his ear, "what do you want?"

He pulled back with a laugh. "Damn, I hate it when a woman is smarter than I am."

"Another woman, you mean." She smiled again.

"Wing!" Grisha said with a frown.

"No," Benny said in a more somber tone, "she does have a point."

"I know you're a busy man, Benny," Grisha said. "What can I do for you?"

"In a way, it's something I can do for you. Do you, personally, have a problem with the Republic of California rendering aid to the Tlingit Nation?"

"Christ, no!" Grisha tried to sit up straighter, but the full leg cast kept him pinned to his chairback. "I couldn't be happier! They will be under the Japanese yoke within weeks if they don't get help, and we can't help them."

"I don't trust your current government, but I trust both of you. We've all shared privation, defeat, and victory together. There is no stronger bond among humankind."

"No argument," Wing said, her eyes shining. "Finish what you started to say."

"We're going to declare war on Japan if they don't withdraw from Alaskan and Californian waters. I understand you two are the new Dená ambassadors to the Tlingit Nation. Congratulations. Be ready to move south on a moment's notice, okay?"

"Why?"

"We're supplying your transport and it's to our advantage to have you down there right now. They trust you. Something about a kwan?"

"Yeah, that means a lot to them," Grisha said. "Will you be going with us?"

"No. They pulled me out of the field to ask you about the potential alliance with the Tlingits. My government thinks we have a bond they can manipulate, so they obviously don't know you very well."

Wing grinned but her tone bore an edge. "And you're not trying to manipulate us?"

"No, Colonel Grigorievich, I'm not. I might try that with your government, but not with the two of you."

"Thanks, Benny," Grisha said. "We appreciate that. Now get back to your command."

★ 19 ★

Tim McDaniel's odinochka

Although feeling the room was far too small for all the people jammed into it, Cassidy pulled the door shut behind him and stood quietly, assessing the scene.

Timothy McDaniel's *odinochka*, situated three miles outside Chistochina on the edge of the Saint Elias Mountain Range, occupied a prosperous location. The twenty-meter-by-twenty-meter building was sectioned off from the entrance by two long counters. One served as a bar, now thick with loud inebriates.

The second counter served for dry goods and other merchandise and was populated by two patient Indian women who waited for the proprietor's attention. A pall of tobacco smoke wreathed the heads of those who stood. Cassidy didn't like the stink. Never had.

Stale beer, unwashed bodies, and the sharp bite of cheap whiskey also mingled to overwhelm his nose.

"Yukon Cassidy? We haven't seen you around here for at least a year!" Cristina Petitesse seemed ageless. He remembered she had looked this wrinkled and jaded ten years ago.

He had never seen her inhale her trademark Russian

cigarette. It was as if her lungs filled through her nicotine-stained fingers. She blew out a cloud of acrid smoke.

"What can I do for you?"

"Petrol for my utility, a mug of beer, and some answers." He noticed the drop in conversation around him as more of the denizens quieted to hear the stranger's words.

"Petrol is six coppers a liter, and four coppers for the beer," she said, waiting for payment.

He slapped money on the bar. "And how much for the answers?"

"That all depends on the questions." She turned and pulled a tap handle over a smudged mug. She set it on the bar as if making an offering, but the four coppers disappeared before his hand touched glass.

"Looking for a man called Riordan, Major Tim Riordan."

He drank off half the beer without examining the mug.

Cristina frowned at the name, but Cassidy recognized her *I'm thinking about it* look and waited. Her eyes returned to his.

"Never heard of him. Is he in this area?"

"He's somewhere in Russian Amerika, that's all I know."

"Well, for once you know more about the situation than I do. No charge. I'll have Boris top off your utility."

She turned away and the ambient conversation resumed its previous volume. Someone nudged his left elbow. He looked down at a small, heavily bearded man. No, small didn't come close. This person stood barely more than a meter and a quarter.

"Who are you?"

"Someone you need to know!" The surprisingly deep voice held no question, only assertion. "You've got one chance in four to get out of this room alive."

"Wha—"

"And one chance in six to get back through the gate before you bleed to death, no matter how fast you drive."

Cassidy glanced around. Nobody paid them the slightest heed. He tried not to grin as he lowered his gaze to the man. "Nobody seems to give a damn whether I'm here or not."

"Just for drill, shut up and listen. Two of Riordan's men are in this room. They'll want to know why you're looking for their boss. If it's not to give him, and them, a job, it means you're one of the growing throng who wish to see that bastard Irishman dead. So, which is it?"

Cassidy surreptitiously glanced around again.

Still no detectable interest.

He looked back to his informant, no longer feeling like smiling.

"So which ones are they?"

"The first one will remain unknown for the moment. I'm the second one."

Cassidy grinned. "You're looking for another job, aren't you?"

The beard moved and Cassidy saw a flash of teeth.

"You're pretty quick for a guy your size. Your chances of living just changed dramatically, *if* you make the right decision."

"Which would be to hire you?"

"Yes. You need a guide and someone who knows the Freekorps and can fight at your back."

"Nobody gets behind me that I don't trust implicitly. So far you don't fit that description. Hell, I don't even know your name."

"Listen hard," he spoke quickly, "we don't have the time to go over it a second time. I am Roland Delcambré, a man of wit and education who has fallen on desperate circumstances. I hired myself out as a mercenary soldier to..."

Cassidy snorted what began as a laugh.

Delcambré's hard, dark eyes burned up at him. "You have a big man's attitude. Don't confuse size with ability. You haven't seen me shoot."

"Forgive me, you look more the poet than the warrior. Please continue."

"Perhaps I also misjudged you," Delcambré again flashed his grin. "You're pretty good at sucking up for a man your size."

Cassidy bristled and his good humor vanished. "Okay, you little—"

The snick of a sling blade flashing to rigidity, and the slightest touch of a fine, sharp point under his scrotum, decreased the latter's size by half.

"The thing you big guys don't seem to realize is that someone my size is very much closer to your *weak* spots."

"Make your point, verbally, if possible, and let's be done with it."

The blade vanished.

"I am a mercenary, and a good one. I can shoot the eye out of a camp robber at 150 yards."

The screeching, constantly active Steller's jay bobbed in Cassidy's mind for a moment. "And?"

"I'm one of Riordan's intelligence agents. The big guy with me is my bodyguard."

"Which big guy?" It took all of Cassidy's willpower not to look around the room with new eyes.

"The *promyshlennik* by the door. The one who looks like he's deep in his cups? He hasn't had a drink."

Cassidy turned his head and scratched his neck sporting a disbelieving look on his face. He spotted the bodyguard, noted the hard stare from beneath the lowered eyelids over a falsely jovial mouth.

"Alright. I believe you. Are you as good at your job as he is at his?"

"Much better. He's stupid and happy where he is. I am looking for other employment."

"Why? Seriously?"

"Listen, I've been serious from the first. *You* were the one with size prejudices that got in the way of rational thinking. This is your last chance to hear me out; would you like to use it?"

"I don't apologize twice. What's your proposition?"

"For half of what you earn and find, I will lead you to Riordan, if you wish, or help you avoid him: your choice."

"I really don't make all that much."

"I'll keep that in mind. So here's the situation. Potempkin over there is waiting for me to either scratch my chin, or pull my ear."

"*Potempkin*—what kind of a name is that?"

"He was named after the ship his grandfather was on; they shot a bunch of traitors or something; you'd have to ask him about it right before he cuts your throat."

"And what would you do first to get my throat sliced, scratch or pull?"

"Scratch," Delcambré said, flashing his smile again. "Scratch means 'kill' and pull means 'no worries.'"

"You're scared of him, aren't you?"

"Okay, I'm now completely convinced you are my mental equal and I would be happy to share your circumstance, no matter how miserable, if you would just say the word."

"Can you cook?"

"Yes, but I don't clean and I am utterly subservient and devoted to women when it comes to sex. Just wanted to make that clear."

"It seems we agree on a great deal."

Cristina materialized out of the crowd. "You owe me sixty coppers or the equivalent for the petrol."

Cassidy counted out six silver coins into her steady hand.

"Thanks, and good luck with your questions." She stared hard at Delcambré before disappearing into the crowd.

Cassidy grinned. "Okay, pull your ear and let's get out of here. I'll hit him high and you hit him low."

"Gawd, you're smart enough to be a general!"

"Charge!"

They both stood. Roland pulled his ear theatrically and they walked straight toward the *promyshlennik*. Potempkin jerked to his feet, eyes flashing up and down between them.

"Is he the one Riordan is looking for?" He stared at Roland, who finally nodded.

"Yeah. Come on." He nodded toward the door and charged ahead. Cassidy stayed right behind Roland but also kept an eye on the battleship at his back.

Once out in the fragrant, soft, impressionistic glow that passed for evening in the high subarctic spring, Roland abruptly stopped and turned to Potempkin.

Cassidy could smell a hint of wood smoke in the clear, cool air.

"You have two choices. Go back to Riordan without me, or stay here."

Potempkin frowned at him.

"Oh, there is another choice: die."

Understanding thrummed through Potempkin like the strike of a cathedral bell.

Grabbing the hilt of his sheath knife, he sneered, "And who would be killing me? You or this clumsy oaf with you?"

Knives flashed in the soft light and the last thing Potempkin heard through fading pain was: "Both!"

★ 20 ★

55 miles south of Delta

Bodecia couldn't rouse Rudi. Pelagian had stumbled to his feet at her bidding and crawled into the leaf-mattress bed she had made in the back of the truck. She had spent a frantic twenty minutes stripping the leaves off willows to cushion the men.

Rudi endured her increasingly heavier slaps on his face without even blinking. She stopped; her hand hurt anyway. Abruptly she rose and went to the water skin, brought it back and dumped half a gallon on his head.

"Ahhh, what, why did you do that?" Rudi's eyes had yet to open.

"Wake up, now, Rudi. I need for you to move."

His eyes squinted open. "So bright here. Where, oh, is you."

He pushed himself up, groaning with the effort. Once upright he rested, breathing hard.

"*Da*, what do you require?"

"I want you to get in the back of that truck. I'll help you."

"Thank you," he said through a wheeze as she helped him stand.

She led him to the truck and he crawled into the back and lay down next to Pelagian.

"Will not ask where you obtained vehicle, but grateful you did."

She covered them with the parachute and packed more leaves in between them and the sides of the truck bed. Their gear also offered some cushioning. She glanced around the area, decided she hadn't missed anything, and climbed into the cab with the dogs.

The engine caught on the first turn and she pulled away from their refuge in low gear. The trail proved easy to follow, but the uneven ground caused the truck to bounce and sway. She slowed even further so the truck felt more like a small boat on a medium sea.

Bodecia had hated being on the ship that took her to college in Vancouver, British Canada. The ocean seemed so alien, so unnatural, that she couldn't sleep the entire four-day voyage out of fear they would sink. After she settled in the omnibus, which would take her to the campus, she fell so fast asleep that an emergency medical crew was called and they took her to a hospital.

She grinned at the memory. Ever after, the other students called her "Rip." At least the truck sailed solid ground and the rolls felt gentle rather than tempestuous.

"This is a lot faster than walking," she said to herself.

The landscape bobbed up and down in all three of the rearview mirrors. She began glancing from mirror to mirror, comparing the different views of the same thing. She held on the right mirror, and then shifted her vision to the left mirror, just in time to see it explode. Two hammer-blow reports shook her at the same time.

Stifling her involuntary flinch, she stared at the inside mirror and beheld a Russian armored car directly behind them. The gunner at the top of the small turret aimed his heavy machine gun down into the back of the truck, at Pelagian and Rudi.

She slammed on the brakes and spoke sharply to the dogs, "Home! Now!" They leaped through the open window and vanished into the ubiquitous willows and birch.

She envied them.

"Who are you?" the Russian lieutenant demanded, his hand resting on his holstered pistol. "And who are these men?" A sergeant and a corporal stood on either side of him, training their automatic weapons through the truck window at her.

"I am Bodecia," she said in fluent Russian, "a healer of the Dená people. The large man in the back is my husband, the other is a man we found in the forest."

"What's wrong with them?"

"The man was injured in a great fall, or so he said. He has internal injuries, which I treated. My husband was shot by unknown assailants."

"His wounds wouldn't have anything to do with the dead crew of one of our armored cars, would they?"

The sergeant and corporal exchanged knowing looks.

Bodecia thought fast. "I don't think so, not unless they were wearing different uniforms."

"The Freekorps, Lieutenant?" the sergeant blurted.

"Shut up, you idiot." The lieutenant returned his steely gaze to Bodecia. "What kind of uniforms did they wear?"

"I wasn't paying close attention." She reached out with all her senses and repeated the words that came into her mind. "But they had splashes of different drab colors all over them, like that silk in the back of the truck."

"That isn't merely silk, it's a parachute. Where did you get that?"

"Near a crashed plane far up on the Gakona River. The pilot had jumped out but the parachute didn't slow him down enough. We buried him there."

"Do you know why it crashed?"

"We heard many guns firing. I think it was shot down."

"Exactly where on the Gakona River was this?"

"Near Rainbow Mountain."

"Then the radio report was true—"

"Sergeant Platnikov, if you say one more word I'll have you *shot!*" The lieutenant stared at Bodecia again. "And you decided you could take Imperial Russian property with impunity. Why?" He kicked the door of the truck.

"You had many; we had none. My patients couldn't walk and I wished to get them to more medical help than I can provide. I didn't realize there was an encampment there, too."

"Because you didn't bother to look, or you're lying. We don't leave fleets of vehicles in the wilderness unattended. Everybody knows that. The penalty for stealing the Czar's property is instant death."

She felt weak with sudden fear. Her hand still clutched the machine pistol at her side, but there were three surrounding the truck and one manning the heavy machine gun in the armored car. She couldn't get all four of them before they shot her.

"Lieutenant!" the sergeant said in an urgent tone.

The lieutenant twisted to face his subordinate while pulling his pistol out. "I told you—"

"Aircraft, sir."

"Oh."

"Three aircraft to the north!" bellowed the gunner on the armored car.

"Get your glasses on them," the lieutenant screamed. "Are they Yaks?"

"No, sir. They're not Russian."

"Can you see any identifying insignia?" Fear radiated from him.

All three men next to the truck fixated on the aircraft. Bodecia decided this was the only chance she had to get her patients out alive. She eased into second gear and popped the clutch; the truck lurched off like an Arctic hare.

She swung to the left for a hundred meters and then swung back to the right. Heavy machine gun fire blasted the willows where she would have been had she not swerved; then it started following her. Three aircraft roared over her at very low altitude and she slammed on her brakes to stare in the rearview mirror.

The gunner now fired at the planes, as did all three of the men on the ground. Flying gravel, dust and rocks, thrown up by the bullets from the wing guns on the planes, obscured her view. Above the cloud of dust and debris, she saw the three planes lift and veer toward the concentration of Russian vehicles.

When the dust settled, she clearly saw the three Russian soldiers splayed in attitudes of death in front of the burning armored car. She wondered if the planes were going to come back and strafe the truck.

She needed some way to identify them as allies or

noncombatants. Her gaze fastened on the emergency medical kit and the solution bloomed in her mind. She ripped items from the kit, crawled across the hood to the roof of the truck and was finished in moments.

Grinning, she swung back into the cab, cranked the engine over and drove as fast as she could for Delta.

Moments later the three aircraft buzzed low over her and the middle plane waggled his wings. Then they disappeared over the horizon.

Bodecia laughed out loud.

★ 21 ★

40 miles south of Delta

Magda held her hand up and Jerry halted, quickly surveying their horizon, seeking threat.

"We need to turn here," she said.

He sighed in relief and followed her gaze.

"How do you know? This is the third trail we've crossed."

"Because from here I can see Denali framed between those two trees. I can't show you proof in one of those travel books, but you can believe my decision."

"Well, you're going to follow that path, therefore I will also follow it."

Magda chuckled. "You're not following the path. You're following me."

"Which will take me to the same place anyway. Yes?"

"Yes. So keep up." Magda turned away.

"Wait," he said in a very authoritative tone.

She swung back. "What?"

"What's on this trail? Is there anything I should be aware of in order not to get killed?"

She gave him a rueful smile. "I'm sorry, you're right. Yes, there is a Russian *odinochka*, which must be avoided even though I think there will be nobody there."

"Why do you think that?"

"There will be a woman, probably Dená, like me. But her man will be gone to the Russians. Word travels fast in the bush, especially this close to the Russians. There are always people going somewhere else, and they talk.

"Once her man hears of the Dená attacks he will immediately hurry to the nearest redoubt to profess his loyalty and total ignorance of what is happening in Russian Amerika. These men are a waste of good women."

"Are they also Indians?"

"Some. Most are part Russian, a few are French Canadians."

"Does Russia get along with French Canada?"

"I thought you were the one with the worldly education of North America."

Jerry suspected a sneer, but ignored it. "Historically they have been at odds since Napoleon marched into Russia. Even though he went no farther than the Berezina River before having second thoughts and withdrawing: he upset the czar.

"Despite the fact he won eastern Canada from the English, then an ally of Russia, diplomatically the two countries agree on more than they disagree. You mentioned French Canada and I wondered if there was something going on here not covered in my studies."

Magda smiled. "Most of the Frenchmen here are refugees from French Canada. They are radicals but have their uses to the Russians. If they do not cooperate with the government, they will be deported back to Montreal."

"Where they would be shot." Jerry nodded.

"Or lose their heads to the guillotine."

"How long do you think they would be away?"

"No idea."

"So we should avoid the..."

"*Odinochka.*"

"...at all costs."

"Isn't that what I said in the beginning?"

He thought hard while he followed her and the silent dogs. "Yeah, but I needed to know why, that okay with you?"

"Sure, just don't stop when you talk; we waste time that way."

He puffed along for a few minutes. "There anything else ahead that I need to know?"

"Yeah. Don't make a lot of noise; we're in Russian country."

"Okay," he said in a low voice she probably didn't hear. "Thanks."

They walked along a wide valley for a few miles. A low drone caught his attention.

"Listen!" Jerry hissed. They both froze and sank back under the trailside trees. A rapidly growing growl now hung at the edges of their ears. Both dogs peered into the sky.

"Those are P-61s!" Jerry shouted, dancing out into the open.

Three aircraft roared down the valley toward them, no more than 200 meters above ground.

"They came looking for me, they came looking for me!" He jumped up and down waving his arms.

Watching him, Magda suddenly teared up. He thought his comrades had forgotten him. With her mother and father she had witnessed much of the air attack on the ridge and knew how fierce the fighting had been.

She wondered if Jerry knew how many of his fellow pilots had died that day. In the time since they had been together, she had completely forgotten to mention the subject. So many things had happened...

The planes roared over them and the middle craft waggled its wings as they lifted to higher altitude.

"They saw me!" Jerry was nearly hoarse. He turned and grinned at her. "They saw me, Magda."

"I'm glad they know you're here. I just hope they can send a land party to help us."

He went still for a long moment and then looked around. "Yeah, they'd play hell landing here, wouldn't they?"

"Come on, I'll bet they're waiting for you in Delta." She moved down the trail.

"Here comes another one," he said in a tone full of hope.

A single plane flew low over them and a small parachute capered down in the turbulent wake.

Without a word Jerry raced to where the small chute would land and caught it in his hands. Ripping off the square yard of silk, he threw it aside and tugged at the lead-weighted cylinder. In moments he unscrewed the white metal device and the cap fell into his hand.

Jerry pulled a small roll of paper out and tossed the tube away. Magda picked it up and stuffed it into her pack next to the small parachute and the white metal cap. They might be everyday junk to Lieutenant Gerald "Bigshot" Yamato, but they were treasures to her.

She had only figured out five uses for each item before Jerry said, "They want to know if I am who I am, and if we have three allies behind us in a truck."

"Truck?" they said together.

Magda jumped in immediately. "If anyone can find a tool they need within a hundred miles, my mother can. She once found a 9mm wrench my father needed to repair his plane; she found it six miles away at an old mine site."

"Your father is a pilot?"

"My father is everything," she said fiercely, nearly tearing up again. She stopped and thought for a moment.

Damn, I'm getting my period!

"We have to signal by pointing to our left for 'yes,' and to the right for 'no.'"

"Okay," she said. "I'll point where you point."

As they pointed with all four hands, the aircraft roared over them again and waggled its wings as it angled up into a sky the color of her mother's old trade beads.

"I sure hope we didn't just save the collective asses of three Russians," Magda said.

"Damn. I didn't think of that."

"Don't worry," she said with a wide grin, "it's Mother. I was just scattering your mind."

★ 22 ★

51 miles east-southeast of Delta

The speedometer registered 10 km and Bodecia knew insanity lurked within a few more miles at this mind-numbing pace. If she increased the speed, it tossed her patients around like dried fish in a wagon. The rapid flight from the Russians had nearly thrown Rudi out of the truck bed.

She had apologized as she made him comfortable once again. Pelagian lay askew, but comatose. A small fear grew inside her but she didn't look at it.

So now she advanced slowly, worried she would lose both of them if she sped up, or Pelagian if she didn't. The aircraft hadn't come back. The huge smoke column prominent in her rearview mirror attested to some success in their mission.

She wondered if they had already known about the large concentration of Russian machines or if they had just come looking for Jerry Yamato. *Either way*, she mused, *they did pretty good*.

And saved my aging butt.

The broken willow limbs, almost exactly a meter and a half off the ground and repeated every fifty

113

meters, told Bodecia she followed her daughter and the lieutenant. Her smile widened. In all her years she had never met anyone like Magda.

Even as a small child, Magda knew her own mind. From the time she was 22 months old, she picked her own clothing and would wear nothing else put on her. At four, when asked if she planned on taking another bath, she replied: "It's my body and I'll do what I want with it."

That's when Bodecia knew she had a challenge. She and Pelagian had decided during a five-minute conversation that they had an equal to guide, not a child to rear. And to be friends with her daughter at this point in their lives was such a joy.

Magda always had a vote and a damned good reason for it. She excelled as a teacher but had no administrative leanings whatsoever. Bodecia had been worried about her emotional distance to everyone around her.

"Not any more," Bodecia all but shouted aloud. "She's smart; she won't do anything foolish until the times are safe for such things, I'm sure."

The trail ended at the Czar Nicholas Highway and she eased the truck up onto the more level surface, shifted gears and increased speed.

Hours later Bodecia fought fatigue, feeling stretched beyond her own bounds. Carefully she stopped the truck and killed the engine, just sat in the seat and listened. She knew the road was cut off behind her, thanks to Lieutenant Yamato's squadron, and since the Russians knew it by this time, nothing would be coming toward her.

Slowly, the birds called, tentatively at first and then back to full-lunged declarations of territorial dominance. She unwittingly drowsed. Sound of movement woke her.

She listened, waiting with accelerating heart to discover if she faced danger. There, a scraping sound behind her. She twisted, and through the rear window saw Pelagian trying to crawl out of the truck bed.

In a flash she was out of the cab and beside him, holding his arm to ease him back into a more comfortable position.

"What are you doing, husband, trying to hurt yourself?"

He lay back with a small gasp and peered up at her.

"I thought I had been taken prisoner. Where did you get this vehicle? Where are we?" He flashed his usual "Captain Alaska" facade for a moment but faded fast.

"I think we're about forty-eight or forty-nine miles out of Delta." She went on and told him about the truck and the Russians and the fighter planes.

"I'm sorry I missed all the excitement," he said with a wheeze.

"Let me look at your wound," she said, using a firm no-nonsense attitude.

Pelagian acquiesced without a murmur, adding to Bodecia's unease. She carefully peeled off the bandage and laid it aside.

It took all of her self-control not to curse.

The wound wept with a foul-smelling discharge. The raw edges of the bullet hole presented an angry, raw appearance. It wasn't healing and she didn't know what else to do.

Rudi suddenly sat up upright, and then groaned.

"Be careful, dammit, you're injured."

"Apologies, I'm sure." He squinted at Pelagian. "How is he?"

"Look for yourself, Sergeant."

"Your wound is infected," he said to Pelagian. "Must be sterilized."

"How?" Bodecia asked.

Rudi gave her a wry grin. "So happens our needs mesh. Human urine is sterile and I have a quantity."

"You're going to piss on me?" Pelagian returned the wry smile. "All I can say is, it better work."

"You're right, Rudi. I'm surprised I had forgotten that," Bodecia said.

"Please to hold him up, and look away," Rudi said.

She braced Pelagian up and looked away toward the north, toward Delta. They had to be no more than three hours from town.

Where are Magda and Jerry?

The sound of water ceased.

"That wasn't so bad," Pelagian said, "hardly any sting at all."

Bodecia wiped the wound with the cleanest cloth she owned. "Now I will pack it with fresh sphagnum moss."

Rudi frowned. "Moss?"

"Sphagnum is also sterile."

"Ah, good to know."

She wrapped him with her last bandage. "Would it be better for both of you to sit in the cab with me?"

"It couldn't be any worse," Pelagian said.

"Agree."

"Well, let's get going then."

Bodecia drove with lip-chewing determination, dodging every large rock she spied in the road surface.

The truck bumped and jerked across the road as the two passengers grunted or moaned with each small collision.

"Why are you driving so erratically?" Pelagian asked, exasperation evident in his voice.

"I'm trying not to hurt you."

"Just get there so we can be finished with this."

"Agreed, speediest route is best," Rudi said breathlessly.

"As you wish, gentlemen." She stepped on the accelerator and nearly hit the tank leveling its 80mm cannon at them. She slammed on the brakes but neither of her passengers complained.

"Is Russian tank," Rudi whispered.

"Turn off the engine, please," Pelagian said quietly.

On each side of the tank, four men with machine guns covered them.

"Sure." She switched off the engine.

The men were not soldiers of the Imperial Russian Army. She studied them carefully. All four held their weapons steady, never relaxing, never taking their eyes off the occupants of the truck.

Their uniforms were not the solid brown of the Russian Army, but more like the parachute Jerry had used: mottled patches of drab colors that blended easily in the shadows—just like the uniforms she had pulled out of the air for the dead Russian lieutenant. For the first time in a very long time, Bodecia felt frightened.

"Well, the letters made with gauze, on the top of the cab, say 'Dená,' but who are you people?" a voice said at her shoulder.

She started and swung her head around to look at

the questioner. Like the others, blotches covered his face and matched his uniform, yet without disguising his relative youth and sharp handsomeness.

"Who are you?" she asked without thinking.

He snapped to attention. "Major Riordan, commander of the International Freekorps, and pleased to meet you."

"Bodecia, wife of Pelagian," she said, trying to keep the heat from her voice.

"Now there is a name I have heard." Major Riordan smiled and nodded at the two men in the cab. "Does it belong to one of these men?"

Before Bodecia could speak, Rudi stiffened to attention.

"I am Pelagian, and I am the ruler of this land on which you trespass."

"You don't fit the description."

"My people protect me. I am described in many ways."

"None of them mentioned your heavy Russian accent, but they did admire your mastery of five Athabascan dialects." In Kuitch'an, Major Riordan asked who was the other man in the truck cab.

"You are wasting our time," Bodecia put all her irritability into her voice. "I have two injured men here who must get medical attention soon. We don't care who you are, just leave us be."

Major Riordan said something to the nearest soldier, who immediately vanished into the willows and birch bordering both sides of the trail. The other soldiers continued to cover them with their weapons.

"Madam Bodecia, we care very much about who you are. Our intelligence discovered that you and your

husband," he pointed at Pelagian, "are well regarded
locally, therefore you have great value."

*How did these strangers know so much about the
area?*

"Great value? You plan to kidnap us for ransom?"

"Crudely put, but essentially true. Please surrender
the ignition key." He held out his hand.

She glanced around at the leveled weapons; none
had wavered. Bodecia looked up at him. "Russian
military vehicles do not have ignition keys; only a
button one pushes."

"That's true, I had forgotten. Please exit the vehicle."

"My husband and our friend..."

"Will be cared for immediately."

The soldier returned followed by five men, two of
whom carried collapsible litters.

"What's the problem, Major?" asked the oldest man
in the group.

"We have two injured men, Doctor Revere. What
are their injuries, Madam Bodecia?"

She spoke to the doctor, "A gunshot wound in
the large man and internal injuries from a long fall
in the other."

The other four men opened the truck door and
transferred Rudi onto one of the litters before reach-
ing for Pelagian.

"Who shot him?" Major Riordan's voice went crisp.

"Russian soldiers."

"They caught you stealing this truck?"

Doctor Revere carefully removed Pelagian's bandage
and peered at the wound.

"No. I stole this truck because they had shot my
husband and I needed to get him home."

"How long ago was he wounded?" the doctor asked.

"This morning? Yesterday morning? It's been at least eight to twelve hours ago. I know it's infected."

"Quite the opposite, I'm happy to say. Seems to be healing nicely."

Bodecia pushed through the soldiers and looked for herself. The angry redness had mellowed to a scab-edged pink. She wondered what Rudi had been drinking the previous twelve hours.

"For the record, Madam Bodecia," Major Riordan said behind her, "you and your two companions are my prisoners."

"So you're not really an army, you're bandits?"

Color appeared high on his cheeks and his voice tightened. "We are the finest mercenary unit in all of North America, and we're sure not worried by anyone south of Texas, either. You are possible enemy combatants and therefore a threat."

"Two wounded men and an old woman?" She laughed in his face. "Take responsibility for your actions, Major. You're really a bully and a thief."

"Why are you trying to make me angry?" The tightness slowly leached out of his tone, and he focused on her.

"Because I don't like you."

His smile bordered on glacial. "I'm beginning to feel the same way about you." Riordan motioned to a trooper who moved up next to Bodecia. "Corporal Burnett will see to your accommodations. If you cooperate there will be no problems, if you don't cooperate, you will be the problem."

"This way, ma'am," Corporal Burnett said.

Bodecia followed him.

★ 23 ★

Tanana Aerodrome, Dená Republik

Grisha didn't look down as he moved on crutches toward the aircraft. For an instant, his mind flashed back to the last plane on which he had left this place—they all looked alike to him. He increased his speed as he pressed forward.

"Grisha, please slow down," Wing said in a low voice, "or I'll trip you and have you carried in a litter."

He immediately slowed. He harbored no doubt his wife and adjutant would do exactly as she said. A warm effusion of affection swelled through him and he knew he was a lucky man.

"Yes, Colonel," he muttered over his shoulder.

"General Grigorievich, welcome to our flight."

Grisha stopped and stared at the attractive young woman standing at the bottom of the ramp.

"Anita! How is your arm?"

"Thanks to you, it is just fine. It is so good to see you under happier circumstances, sir."

"This is my wife, Colonel Wing Grigorievich. Wing, this is Anita; she and I have traveled together before."

Wing smiled and took her hand. "Yes, I heard all about it. So pleased to meet you."

"And you, Colonel! Now if you will both step this way."

"Is this the same plane?" Grisha asked, looking around.

"Indeed it is, General."

Grisha moved up the steps at a slow, but steady, pace. He could sense Wing behind him, ready to catch him if he fell. The leg was nearly healed, but he didn't want to jeopardize it with undo stress before it fully knitted.

"I'm not an invalid!" he barked over his shoulder.

"That's fine, Grisha," Wing said, "because I'm not a nurse."

He laughed despite himself. She was absolutely the best thing that had ever happened to him. Life without her was unimaginable, and at this point, would be unbearable.

. He abruptly stopped on the second-to-last step. Wing immediately grabbed his right elbow. Grisha turned and kissed her astonished mouth. Then he moved into the aircraft.

"That was very unmilitary," she said as harshly as she could.

"And very satisfying." He grinned to himself and took a seat, the same one, he reflected, from which he had attended to Anita.

Wing slid past and dropped into the seat next to him. "Where are they taking us?"

"I give you points," he said. "You've waited over fifty hours to ask that question."

"You mean it wasn't a military secret?"

"Not from you."

She punched him in the arm with painful force. "You moose turd! I've been going crazy wondering what I should pack for us and you've known all along where we were going and could have told me!"

"I'm sorry," he said instantly. "But I needed to know which came first: the adjutant or the wife. I treasure you on both counts, you know that."

"So where the hell are we going, *General*?"

"To a former British Air Corps base in Puget Sound. There we will transfer to a Californian submarine which will deliver us to Angoon, Russian Amerika."

"Aren't the Californians and the US navies fighting the Japanese in those waters?"

"I need to tell my adjutant the answer to that?"

"At this moment, I'm a wife. So how much Japanese activity has there been in the area?"

"They've moved their focus south, a long way south. The RCN fleet is moving against them."

"Good." Wing glanced around. "Do you think the Tlingit Nation will ally themselves with us?"

"Militarily, without a doubt. Politically, I honestly don't know. The Tlingits are an incredibly stratified society. The kwan leaders have been in power for a millennium."

"Sounds promising," Wing said in a flat tone. "So why are we wasting our time?"

"We may not be wasting anything. If we can get the leaders to actually join us as a true republic, they will have to change their rules. And it would be in a manner where they would not lose prestige. So in a way, it would be a double victory for them."

"But they wouldn't run things any more, Grisha."

"At this moment they are facing the fact that the Japanese could easily be their new rulers. I think they're ready for a little help into the twentieth century."

"Are they really that devious?"

"The word you're looking for is *complex*."

"All strapped in?" Anita asked.

Grisha smiled at her. "How about *you* strapping in as well?"

She laughed and sat across the aisle from them.

"Prepare for takeoff."

They all glanced up at the speaker.

The four engines revved and the plane abruptly jerked forward, sped down the runway and soared into the sky.

"What's our flying time, Anita?"

"Depending on head winds, about six and a half hours, General."

"Please, call me Grisha."

"Thank you, Grisha. I am honored. Would you both like something to eat?"

"The last time you asked me that—"

"I ended up wearing your lunch," Anita said and laughed. She sobered quickly. "I thought we were all going to die that day. You not only helped me physically, you helped me hang on mentally."

"Not everyone gets sucker-punched by an aircraft."

Anita laughed again. "That's for damned sure!"

"Can I help you prepare the food?" Wing asked.

"Oh, no, but thank you, Colonel. I don't do much on these VIP flights anyway."

"Please, Anita, I would like you to call me Wing. Vee-eye-pee?"

"Very important persons. Like it or not, that's how the crew regards you, including me."

"We're just soldiers," Grisha said. "You're just as important as we are."

"Whatever you say. Now, what would you like to eat?"

★ 24 ★

Delta, near St. Anthony Redoubt

Jerry's feet hurt. "Can we take a break?" he asked.

Magda glanced back at him. "Ten more minutes, okay? We're really close."

He decided to go as far as the next bend in the trail and if it stretched on through the boreal forest with nothing else in sight, he was going to sit down for at least half an hour. The more he thought about sitting, the more he anticipated finding nothing but more trees.

A dog barked as they entered the bend. Consort and Arrow answered in unison, and then fell silent. Two hundred meters away sat a cabin flanked by a massive woodpile and small outbuildings. Beyond the cabin sat more buildings of varying sizes.

Two dogs raced toward them in total silence. Magda laughed and bent to greet them. "It's Griz and Kodiak. Mom and Dad must be here already!"

Wood smoke drifted in the air as well as the savory odor of frying meat. Birds flew past and their chirping filled his ears with comfort. He felt weight he hadn't before noticed lift off his shoulders.

Magda slowed so he could catch up with her.

"Welcome to Delta, where the Delta River flows into the Tanana River. This is where I was born and have lived most of my life. Now follow me and stay close."

She led them down a small path skirting the edge of the village.

"Why are we going this way?"

"Because I don't want to talk to the Russians who man the garrison here."

"Russians? Here?"

"They think they still own the place, remember?"

Jerry had registered it as a fact, but only mentally; he knew she felt it viscerally, and he must also or suffer greatly.

They moved down a heavily shaded corridor in the closely woven willows, which nearly became a tunnel. Birds darted and flew in panic from the humans. He wondered what their chances would be if they encountered Russian soldiers in here. Slim, he decided, very slim.

When he looked forward again, three men blocked their path. All four dogs wagged their tails. Magda didn't slow her pace and for an instant he wondered if she saw them. One of the men opened his arms wide.

"Little Magda, how good to see you!"

She responded in kind, throwing her arms open and racing forward, "Uncle Frank!"

They hugged and laughed. Jerry and the two men with Uncle Frank eyed each other warily. Magda spoke rapidly in what Jerry supposed was the local dialect of Athabascan.

Uncle Frank became agitated, glanced up at Jerry and then focused again on Magda.

"Your father is wounded?"

Magda nodded.

"When Kodiak and Griz came in, I thought you and your family would be here soon."

"The dogs are here but not my parents?"

"Yes, and your father is wounded, so—"

"The Russians must have captured them!"

"We'll figure it all out, don't worry. And who is this?" he nodded toward Jerry.

Before Magda could answer, Jerry snapped to attention and said, "I am First Lieutenant Gerald Yamato, Republic of California Air Force. My P-61 was shot down in a battle with a Russian armored column."

"I am Franklin Isaac, the doyon for this area. This is my friend and associate, William Williams." William smiled and nodded. "And this is my friend, Yukon Cassidy."

Cassidy, who was the shortest of the three, nodded and smiled.

"We heard about that battle, Lieutenant," Frank said. "Your squadron eliminated a threat we thought would have to be fought right here in Delta. In the name of the Dená people, I thank you."

"Uh, you're welcome." He felt embarrassed but couldn't decide why. "Do you know how many of my people survived the fight?"

"I am not sure, but I think I heard the number seven."

"Seven. We went into that fight with fifteen birds. Can you put me in touch with the airfield at Fort Yukon?"

"No. The Russians still hold the small redoubt here, as well as all the communications."

"How did you hear about the battle?"

We have people inside the redoubt, but they have no authority over the Russians."

"Jerry," Magda said, "tell them about the Freekorps."

Jerry told them what he had heard and seen. "We don't know where they went, but we heard engine noises off to our right. I'm not sure when that stopped."

"It faded about four hours ago," Magda said. "I thought they might be following one of the tributaries back up into the hills. We didn't see them on the highway."

"Do you have any idea how many there are?"

Jerry and Magda shook their heads in unison.

"Those are the people I'm looking for," Cassidy said.

"Any idea how many Russians were in this group?" William asked.

"No idea at all. How many Russians are here?" Jerry asked.

"Fifteen officers and ninety enlisted men. About half the enlisted are trained well enough to actually fight." Frank grinned. "But the garrison has three tanks and a lot of heavy weapons."

"How many people do you have in your DSM cell?" Jerry asked.

"What makes you think we have a cell?" William asked.

"You're Dená. I'd be more amazed if you didn't have an organization here. You already mentioned spies in the Russian garrison."

"We slightly outnumber the Russians, but we can't match their fire power," Frank said. "But we've got to get out there and help your parents, Magda."

"Did the three fighters come by here?" she asked, gesturing at the sky.

"Planes? No."

"I thought my mother had already picked up a vehicle. But, with the dogs here, I'm no longer sure."

Frank nodded down the path. "Tell me about it while we get ourselves organized."

Twenty minutes later they sat and talked over tea.

"I sent out three men who know the country," Frank said, draining his teacup. "Give them a day and they'll know what's going on and why."

"What about my parents and Rudi?" Magda asked.

"William's getting the supplies we need. As soon as you two get some rest, we'll go after them."

"I'm not tired," Magda said.

"Yes, you are," Frank said, his lips twitching toward a smile. "And look at the lieutenant, he's almost asleep."

Jerry forced his eyes open in the cozy kitchen of Frank's home. "I can keep up with you!"

"I'm sure you could, Lieutenant Yamato. But you'd be of more use to us and yourself if you recharged your batteries."

Jerry couldn't argue with him. He wasn't just tired; he was exhausted. He couldn't remember ever being this tired before in his life. Magda had to be nearly out on her feet, too.

"Four hours of sleep and we'll start, okay?" Frank said glancing from one to the other.

Jerry nodded.

Magda sighed. "Okay. But just four hours."

Frank pointed to two doors. "You each have a room if you wish."

Jerry felt his cheeks grow warm. "Thanks, see you in four hours." He entered a small, clean bedroom containing two single beds and a dresser. As he shut the door he heard Magda say, "It's not like that, Uncle Frank."

"Whatever you say," Frank said with a chuckle.

Jerry's eyes popped open and he wondered what it was that woke him. For a long moment he couldn't fathom his location. Then it all flooded back.

He sat up in the comfortable bed and looked across the room. Magda slept on the other bed, curled in a fetal position with the sheet pulled tight around her shoulders.

So much for trust, he thought. But then he realized that her defensiveness might not have anything to do with him. There was a lot happening in her life just now that might induce something less than open, welcoming arms on her part.

He turned, pulling his body free of the light sheet and blanket, and slipped into his boots. As he secured the lashings, he glanced around the cabin. He could live in a place like this, he decided.

Varnished peeled logs fit tightly atop each other, creating a snug bedroom boasting one window. The yellow cedar window frame brought warmth from outside and spread it liberally throughout the room. The plank flooring felt cool and sturdy under his feet, and nowhere a sliver to be found.

Jerry had spent months living in the Sierra Nevada Mountains every summer for five teen-aged years. As a counselor he had one of the better cabins in the camp. The difference between this house and those cabins was the difference between *Satori*, his P-61 Eureka fighter, and an AT-9 Sacramento trainer.

They both fit the description, but in such different ways.

He looked back at Magda again and found her staring at him.

"Hi," he said. "How do you feel?"

She looked at him, her head still partially buried in the pillow, and smiled. "I'm fine, how are you?"

"Quite rested, thanks."

Her eyebrows arched. "What time is it? How long have we been here? Why did they let us sleep so long?"

Jerry peered at his watch.

"It's eighteen hundred?" He looked up at her. "Six in the evening. We've been here about six hours, if I remember right. What was the last thing?"

She popped out of her bed as if spring-loaded. In a few seconds she had slipped into her hide boots and rushed out the door.

"Good thing I had a head start," Jerry muttered, following her.

Magda didn't hesitate, but hurried down a flagstone path to a larger house. She slammed the door open with the heel of her hand and disappeared inside.

"Doesn't anyone knock in this country?" Jerry said loudly, following on her heels. If someone took offense at her lack of manners, he might have to rescue her.

"Frank, where *are* you?" she shouted.

The house felt empty. Jerry wondered if she had gone to the wrong cabin. He started to suggest his question, but—

"Damn him! They've gone without us. That low-down, condescending, hubristic son of a bitch went without us!"

Relief surged through Jerry and he silently thanked

Frank and William and whoever else went with them. He focused on Magda, realizing he had to get her calmed down or end up following her through these woods carrying anything between an automatic weapon and a spear.

Magda was certifiable, as his grandfather used to say. She didn't hesitate to consider consequences, just acted. Or did she?

In controlled circumstances, she was quite deliberate, such as their first meeting. He frowned, upset that he had jumped to conclusions.

He had worked so long and hard on that one.

"So what should we do?" he asked.

"Nothing, damn it! I hate being treated like a-a..."

"Well-loved young woman?"

She started to answer, and then suddenly her eyes bored in to his. "By whom?"

"Your parents and your uncle, dimwit!"

"He knew I wanted to go along," she said, close to a pout.

"He also knew you were exhausted, ready to drop, and completely overwhelmed by circumstances."

She frowned at him but it faded into a moue. "You're right, dammit, Lieutenant Yamato."

"But."

"But it's my fight, too!"

"He knows that, and he respects it. That's why he had to trick you to get you to sleep long enough to do some good."

The moue solidified into a frown. "You'll get nowhere with me by being right all the time!" She stomped into the next room.

After four silent responses he elected to say nothing.

He followed her into a kitchen and realized how hungry he had become.

"Can you handle a moose steak?" Magda asked.

"Better than it can handle me," he quipped with a smile.

"Good. That's about all we got." She stoked a wood range and tossed sticks into the firebox, opened the flue a quarter turn. "Rare, medium, or well done?"

"Medium. I'm a medium kind of guy."

"No, you're not. I wouldn't like you if you were medium." She burrowed into the refrigerator and pulled out a plate holding two large pieces of meat. "I don't believe the Republic of California picks medium guys to fly their fighter planes."

She dropped each steak into its own pan and began pawing through the spice shelf. "No, First Lieutenant Yamato, I think you're more of an extreme guy"—she looked at him over her shoulder, nearly hiding her smile—"who isn't afraid of risk and is always looking for an adventure. Right?"

The steaks sizzled in the pans and the aroma of cooking meat touched his nose. His stomach growled. She filled his thoughts.

"Never thought about it that way, but to a point you're right. You have to want to fly more than anything else in the world to make it through flight school, not to mention put up with more military bullshit than you ever imagined."

"But you did it," she said, still smiling and turning toward him. "Because you're an extreme kind of guy."

She crossed the small space between them and kissed him; he wanted it to last forever. She finally pulled away and he saw something new in her eyes.

"You get through this safely, Jerry. We have a lot to do together." She turned back to the stove and flipped the meat.

Jerry decided he was in love. He wasn't sure exactly what that would mean to him in the future, but more than anything, he wanted to grow old with Magda and love her as much as possible every single day.

"I'll be careful," he said. "I promise."

★ 25 ★

St. Anthony Redoubt, Russian Amerika

"Colonel Romanov, we have lost all communications with Taiga 10 command."

Colonel Stephan Romanov sighed and tore his gaze from the natural beauty outside his office window.

"When did they last report in, Sergeant Severin?"

"Yesterday at noon. Captain Kobelev said they were eager to advance whenever the order came."

"Nothing since noon yesterday?" Romanov chewed his lip and wondered at this turn of events. Until a year ago this had been pleasant, if boring, duty.

"It's either faulty equipment or the damned Dená," Sergeant Severin said.

"I hope you're right about the first part." Despite his aristocratic name, Romanov's grandmother was a Yakut from Siberia and he held deep sympathies for the Dená. He tried to keep his attitudes to himself, but others had noticed.

A visiting colonel once asked for an Indian woman for the night.

Stephan had frowned. "I'm not a whoremonger, Colonel. You'll have to solicit for yourself."

"You do not know women who—"

"No. You'll have to ask one of the privates."

Thankfully, the colonel let the matter drop. Romanov would not allow his men to molest the local women nor mistreat any of the civilian population. He preached brotherhood to his troops and had a corporal lashed within inches of his life for drunkenly beating an old Athabascan man.

Now this stupid war has made a hash of everything, he thought. Not that he blamed the Dená. In fact he felt they were right: St. Petersburg had abused the Alaskan peoples for over 200 years and it was time for a change.

Colonel Romanov glanced up guiltily at his sergeant to see if the man had interpreted his silence correctly. The sergeant was staring out the window.

"Are the pilots sober today?"

Sergeant Severin snapped his head away from the window. "I don't know, sir. Shall I send an orderly?"

"Yes, do that. Have the orderly tell them that I require a reconnaissance mission. Now."

The sergeant grinned and pressed a button on his desk. A private walked in and snapped to attention.

"Turgev, go to the officer's quarters and tell the pilot-officers they are to report for a mission immediately."

"Even if they are drunk, Sergeant?"

"Even if they are drunk, Private Turgev."

The colonel and the sergeant grinned at each other as soon as the door shut behind Private Turgev.

"What if they wreck the helicopter?"

"We'll be rid of both of them. That's worth a helicopter, don't you think?"

"As long as I don't have to pay for it," the sergeant said with a laugh.

"If they're not drunk, they will be suffering hang-overs large enough to split rocks." Colonel Romanov chuckled.

"Perhaps Taiga 10 received orders from the front and we were not informed, Colonel?"

"I thought of that already, but dismissed it for two reasons. First, I am in nominal command of the force since I am the district commander and would have been notified as a courtesy and for protocol if nothing else. You know how much the army loves protocol.

"Second, we are between their last position and the front, unless there is a new front to their rear. But Alaska Command would have notified us of that also, no?"

"I certainly hope so," the sergeant said.

The door to the office banged open and two blonde men stumbled in, cursing and complaining.

"Colonel, we are in no condition to fly today, we can barely walk!" Captain Ivan Fedorov said without so much as a salute.

"My brother is right," Captain Georgi Fedorov chimed in. "Besides, this is our stand-down week and—"

"Silence!" Colonel Romanov bellowed, not allowing himself to smirk when both men flinched in pain. "This is not the St. Petersburg Officers' Retreat. We are in a war."

"We know that," Georgi mumbled, "but we—"

"Taiga 10 has not reported in since yesterday at noon. This is not only unusual, but also alarming. The only way we can contact them is by motorcycle messenger or helicopter."

The pilots looked at each other. Ivan scratched his unshaven jaw.

"I have already dispatched a motorcycle messenger, but I want an aerial reconnaissance as well. Now."

Ivan straightened into a semblance of military bearing and gave Colonel Romanov a weak salute. A moment later Georgi copied his brother.

"As you wish, my Colonel," Ivan said in a ponderous tone. "We leave as soon as the helicopter is warmed up."

"Yes," Georgi said with a firm nod.

"The maintenance crew has already started the machine," Romanov said. "By the time you reach the flight line, it will be ready to fly."

Both pilots turned as one and shuffled out of the office, leaving the door open behind them. Georgi's voice drifted back to them, "I told you we should bring the vodka with us."

"Holy Mary, Mother of God," Sergeant Severin said in a low voice. "How did they get through officers' training, let alone flight school?"

"Their father is a nobleman and supporter of the Czar. Those two uniforms on his worthless sons are a gift from a grateful ruler," Colonel Romanov said. "Therefore, they become our problem."

"How do they fly that thing?"

"I don't know and I don't care. All I want from them is a report about Taiga 10 or word of their deaths."

★ 26 ★

39 miles south of Delta

"What are you all doing this far from home?" Major Riordan inspected Bodecia through narrowed eyes.

"Going for a walk, if it's any of your business."

"Forty kilometers, one way, on a walk?"

"We enjoy trekking. Now leave me alone."

"You have a choice, madam. You can answer my questions now or after we string your husband up by his thumbs and carve on his belly for a while."

"In a fair fight my husband would kill you in moments. But you know nothing of that; you're just a damned grouse-hearted bully. I will tell you nothing or lies—your choice."

"You place him in peril."

"He placed himself in peril, I just went along for the exercise."

"If I had three subordinates like you, I would rule the world."

Hatred burned from Bodecia's eyes. "You are as full of shit as a Christmas goose."

"Lock her up, Corporal," Riordan snapped. "Now!"

He watched the corporal of the guard usher the

small woman out of his tent. Riordan felt angry enough to spit nails. Never in his life had he met such an intractable, insolent bitch.

She reminded him of his late mother.

Perhaps I should just shoot her now and get it over with.

What were they doing out here? Spying on the Russians? There was nothing else; they couldn't have known about the Freekorps.

Lieutenant Grudzinski pushed open the tent flap. "Major, there is a helicopter out there."

"Headed this way?"

"Difficult to tell, sir. It seems to be quite erratic."

"Show me," Riordan said, grateful for the distraction.

They moved briskly into the center of the camouflaged vehicles and tents. Lieutenant Grudzinski pointed north, "There, sir."

Riordan trained his field glasses on the machine, keeping it in view with difficulty as it dipped and yawed.

"It's Russian, but the pilot must be drunk, or very clever. Never have I seen such an unmilitary flight pattern."

"I'd vote for drunk," Grudzinski said with a nod.

"Shoot it down, Leonard." Riordan returned to his tent.

★ 27 ★

39 miles south of Delta

Captain Ivan Fedorov pulled the stick back and the helicopter leveled out. It always took him a few minutes to get the feel of the craft after being away from it for more than two days.

"Like a woman!" he exclaimed.

"Who is?" Georgi said, continuing to stare out the side window.

"This sodding helicopter, you dolt. What did you think I was talking about?"

"I never know. What is that down there?"

"Where?"

"Over on the left there. See all those hummock thingies?"

"They're probably hummocks, you idiot."

"But some have barrels, big ones."

"By the balls of St. Peter, you're right. I'll get a little closer."

"If they are what I think they are and we get any closer, they will shoot hell out of us."

"You're right again, Georgi. So what should we do?"

"Well, if they're Russian, they either won't shoot at us, or miss us if they do."

141

"True, Georgi. But what if they aren't Russian?"

"Then we are already in very deep shit. We've been here too long."

The helicopter abruptly leaned to one side and then leveled again. Georgi glared at his brother. "Wha—"

A high-velocity shell shrieked past them.

Georgi's glare popped into surprise. "Get us out of here!"

Ivan already had the helicopter in a tight turn when two more shells burned past.

"Look at them, dammit, while I fly this stupid machine. How many hummocks are there? Do you see any troops, or insignia?"

"Shut up so I can think!" Georgi bellowed.

Ivan turned hard and flew directly at the encampment. Several large shells whistled past, aimed where the helicopter might have been had they not changed course. Ground fire, some of it larger than hand-held weapons, winked up from the camouflaged equipment.

Suddenly the canopy perspex starred in three places and small bits of the heavy plastic danced across the floor. Rounds buzzed past their heads and the helicopter jerked with the hammer blows.

"That's what I wanted to know!" Ivan twisted the flight path into a "U" and pushed the throttle to maximum. "Took them by surprise, didn't we?"

"Mostly," Georgi said slowly, staring down at his feet. "We took a few hits."

Ivan snapped his head around. "Are you injured?"

"Perhaps a little. A bullet went through my thigh."

"St. Michael preserve us! Put a tourniquet on the damned thing, Georgi."

Georgi fumbled around, peering around in the

cockpit as if looking for his other dress glove. "What should I use, d'ya think?"

"Shit, you're going into shock, damn you. Georgi, listen to me. Take off your belt and tighten it around your leg above the wound. Do it!"

Georgi pulled his belt off in one move and wrapped it around his leg and tightened it as hard as he could. "The thing is, my brother, every so often I require some direction. The amazing part is that you always seem to know when that moment arrives."

Ivan banked and roared in a straight line for their aerodrome at St. Anthony Redoubt. "Are you still losing blood?"

"No, the flow has ceased. But I seem to have leaked a great deal."

"It's all that alcohol in our blood. We've thinned ourselves to a dangerous level."

"My God, you're right. We could bleed to death twice as fast as anyone else with the same wound."

"Probably four times as fast," Ivan said, glancing sympathetically at his brother.

"Get me home."

"What did you see back there?"

"Four, maybe five tanks, six or seven trucks. Over a hundred soldiers in a position to shoot at us when you went insane back there."

"You know as well as I do, if you don't scare the game it won't flush."

"Or fight," Georgi said agreeably.

"Exactly. And as reconnaissance pilots, we need to know how many will fight."

"I think I remembered that part, Ivan. But I don't remember discussing the part where we charge the enemy in a helicopter with only one gun which you didn't see fit to use."

"To tell the truth, I forgot we had it. It probably isn't even loaded." He thumbed the cover up and pressed the trigger mounted on the stick.

Rapid roars boomed in front of them and the helicopter slowed near stalling speed. Ahead of them the tops of several large trees blew into flinders.

"Stop shooting, give this thing some petrol!" Georgi screamed. "The goddamned cannon is loaded. Now get me home!"

★ 28 ★

38 miles south of Delta

Rudi peered through the mosquito-net-covered slats of the hospital wall. The Freekorps numbered about two hundred effectives. It reminded him of the Russian Troika Guard: multiple shades of skin, a variety of languages, and they all spoke English when on duty. Except in the Troika Guard, the language had been Russian.

But what are they doing here? Had the Czar hired mercenaries to bolster his odds against the Dená and their allies?

Somehow Rudi didn't believe that. This outfit reminded him of the vultures in Afghanistan, except the Freekorps smelled both death and profit.

As near as he could tell, all of the effectives were cross-trained. He wouldn't wager against any of them in a target-shooting contest. They would not be an easy foe to conquer.

His cot jiggled which meant someone had just walked up the steps of the hospital. Rudi sank back on his pillow and closed his eyes. He hoped they would not change the huge bandage they had wrapped around his torso; he had almost worked the stiffness out.

"Your hands and arms are torn and bruised, your whole body has been battered, and you have internal injuries which should have killed you," the doctor had told him after a thorough examination. "Yet you seem to be healing at a much faster pace than if you were in a modern, well-equipped hospital. How do you account for that?"

Rudi had grinned at him. "Perhaps because I lead an exemplary life?"

The doctor laughed all the way to the door, where he called a nurse in to help him bandage Rudi. The nurse was a hulking man with surprisingly gentle hands. It still hurt when they tightened the bandage around him.

The floorboards creaked as someone approached. Rudi wondered if they were visiting him or Pelagian, or just checking on both.

"Sergeant, are you awake?" Bodecia asked.

"Awake." His eyes flew open and surprise filled him to see her alone. "Have you evaded the guards?" he whispered.

She nodded. "It's easy if you know how. Has Pelagian wakened yet?"

"No. They gave him an injection and he went into a deep sleep."

"Good, he'll heal quicker that way. How much have you observed?"

"I would put their number near two hundred, give or take twenty. They have six tanks and four armored personnel carriers, some with Russian Army markings, and a fleet of trucks." He stopped, thinking hard. "Oh yes, and one motorcycle."

"Very good, Rudi. Our numbers match. Now I am

worried that since they have allowed us to see so much, what do they plan to do with us?"

"Ransom is the only thing I have heard. I· do not believe they have a political stake in this war, only an interest in money."

"But surely they realize our side has no money. We are all at the end of our possibilities. That's one of the things that has precipitated this·war."

"My armored company was ordered here. If the Czar tells me to fight, I obey. If he tells me to stand down and relax, I obey. This"—he gestured at the hospital walls—"is all new to me."

"Yes," she said. "As Pelagian says, 'I am orating to the ordained.' I am worried about what they will do to you and Pelagian."

"If you can escape," Rudi whispered in an urgent tone, "you must do so!"

She smiled and shook her head. "No, I am too much bound up in that man's life to leave. I would rather die with him than live without him."

Rudi looked at the sleeping Pelagian, then back to her.

"You have no idea how much I envy him at this moment."

★ 29 ★

38 miles south of Delta

Bo Thomas slowly crawled backward from the ridge of the knoll before turning. Frank Isaac and William Williams leaned forward at his approach. Back at the ridge Yukon Cassidy remained on his stomach, peering through binoculars.

"They got a bunch of people down there, maybe hundred fifty, two hundred. They got tanks and them things that have big machine guns and haul troops."

"Armored personnel carriers?" Frank asked.

"Yeah, those. And a bunch of trucks."

"Shit," William said in a reverent tone. "We're in over our heads." He eased forward to a vantage point and raised his binoculars.

"Why are they here?" Frank said.

Bo shrugged and Frank patted him on the shoulder. "Good work, Bo. Now get back to the others and tell them to stay very quiet."

"Can I tell them what I saw down there?"

"Absolutely."

"Okay. See ya." Bo evaporated into the brush.

Frank slowly took position between Cassidy and William. "Whattya see?" he whispered.

Williams spoke first, "Same thing Bo saw. But what I don't see is Pelagian or Bodecia."

"Are there any large structures where they might be held prisoner?"

"Well, there's close to two dozen vehicles where they could be held, and there are two large tents."

Frank squinted his eyes. "I can't see for shit any more. Are either of them marked as a hospital?"

"Yeah, the biggest one." He pulled the binoculars away and looked at Frank. "You getting old or what?"

"Unless you're dead, you're getting older all the time, right?"

"Good point."

Cassidy spoke up, "Hey, I see Bodecia."

"Where? What's she doing?"

"She's walking up to the hospital tent. The guard doesn't seem to see her. She went in."

"I'll bet my trap-line against yours that's where they've got Pelagian," Frank said.

"No bet," William said. "Okay?"

"Yeah, no bet." Frank scooted back into the dense tree line. "This is more than we can handle. It's more than the Russian garrison can handle."

"Hell, it's more than all of us put together can handle," Cassidy said, joining them.

"Not necessarily," Frank replied.

"Colonel Romanov, Doyon Isaac is here to see you," Sergeant Severin said.

"I hope this isn't more trouble. Please show him in."

The colonel stood as the doyon entered.

"Thank you for seeing me on such short notice, Colonel Romanov."

Romanov shook the offered hand. "I am never too busy to see you, Doyon Isaac. Please make yourself comfortable."

"We have a mutual problem, so I will get straight to the point."

Romanov nodded.

"There is a small army of mercenaries up on Boris Creek, small by army standards, that is. They number around one hundred fifty to—

"Two hundred effectives," Romanov said. "Your intelligence is very good, Doyon Isaac. But how is this your problem?"

"We are very aware of the fighting north of here between the Dená and the Russian military. The fact that it has lasted over many months gives us all hope we had been afraid to admit before now. We've heard nothing for almost a week, but prior to that things had quieted and—"

"The Republic of California has entered the war on the side of the Dená separatists by dropping 900 paratroopers on Chena three days ago. They will be defeated by the armored column moving north from St. Nicholas."

"Your high command hasn't told you about the battle of Rainbow Ridge?"

"What are you talking about?"

"A squadron of ROC P-61 Eureka fighters destroyed most of the armored column, and blew large gaps in the road to the pass. The surviving vehicles are stranded until the road can be repaired in both directions."

"Propaganda, perhaps?" Romanov countered, feeling a void in the pit of his stomach.

"I had no idea you were unaware of the battle. Over half of the attacking squadron was destroyed."

"I knew about the battle, and the destruction of the armored column; what I didn't know was that I had a spy among my communications people. We have other reserves in the area." Romanov didn't like this verbal chess match, especially since they had lost contact with their only reserve—Taiga 10.

"Good, because the Freekorps is a very real threat to this village and your garrison. If you believe the Russian Army can effectively deal with the threat, I am much relieved."

"What other choice is there?"

"We could join forces. I don't have a lot of people under arms, but perhaps enough to make a difference."

"A Dená Separatist cell would aid the Russian Army?"

"Part of the Dená Republik would help foreign troops stationed here by the Czar to defend the village of Delta and in so doing also defend St. Anthony Redoubt."

"Republiks have a sordid history in North Amerika. They're always breaking off from each other and starting new ones. Look how ineffective they render each other south of here."

"In fact," Doyon Isaac said, "they're all fighting between themselves right now. Yet the USA and the ROC have both sent troops north to help us. The Dená Republik is already fact, Colonel Romanov."

"Why are you interested in helping the Russian Army combat a band of mercenaries?"

"Two reasons. You have always been fair and as respectful as possible to my people. As far as the mercenaries are concerned, we are in this together: they will kill indiscriminately, not just Russians."

"My grandmother was of the Yakut People. They and the Athabascans share many traditions. I treat your people the same as I would treat my own family."

"I had no idea," Doyon Isaac said, visibly moved.

"I sent out our helicopter this morning to check on Tai...on our reserve force. The helicopter encountered an unknown force and heavy fire. One of our pilots was severely wounded."

"Do you want our help?"

"Your people know this country better than my men ever will. If you could provide ground reconnaissance, I would be most appreciative."

"Consider it done."

"Thank you, Doyon Isaac."

They shook hands and the Athabascan left the office.

"Sergeant Severin, sound officers' call!"

★ 30 ★

Delta, Russian Amerika

The scrape of an opening door pulled Jerry Yamato's attention away from the remains of his meal. Magda jumped to her feet as William Williams entered the room.

"Well, you're both up," he said cheerfully, heading for the teapot on the stove.

"You were supposed to wake me after four hours," Magda snapped.

"Yeah, well we were out messing around in the bush about that time. Besides, Frank said his favorite niece needed her sleep."

"Where is Uncle Frank?"

"Over talking to Colonel Romanov."

"Who's that?" Jerry blurted. Fear vibrated through him and he wondered if these Indians weren't as antagonistic toward the Russians as he had been led to believe.

"The Russian commander of St. Anthony Redoubt," Magda said. "What's he doing over there, William?"

"Making a deal that might save all our lives. Don't worry, Lieutenant, he's not selling you out, nor are you a bargaining chip. The Freekorps have more men than the Russians and us combined."

"You're joining the Russians?" Jerry suddenly realized

that up here rules might change with the wind. The look on Magda's face reflected his own turmoil, making him feel better.

"Think of it as them joining us," William said. "Colonel Romanov is not your ordinary Russian officer; he has a heart."

"I wish I could ask Rudi about this."

"As soon as you're ready to go, we're going to go rescue your parents," William said to Magda.

"Rescue? From what?"

"The Freekorps have them. We saw your mother going into their hospital tent, so we assume your father is in there too."

"Are they what I think they are?" Jerry asked. "The Freekorps, I mean?"

"Mercenaries from what Yukon Cassidy says, and well-armed ones at that. They must have hired out to someone other than the Russians or are just out for conquest. Cassidy is after their leader for crap they pulled down in the Nation."

Magda bounded out of her chair and grabbed her machine pistol. "I'm ready. Let's go."

Jerry drank up his tea and followed her out the door. Thirteen men stood near the cabin, all carrying weapons. Magda hesitated and then laughed.

"What is this, a class reunion?"

Birds chirped drowsily in the dark trees and the light breeze invigorated Jerry. He could smell wood smoke and leather. Twelve of them smiled, the thirteenth glowered at him. "Heard you could use some help, Magda," one of the others said.

"That's true, Alexi, and I appreciate every one of you being here."

"Nothin' else to do around here, y'know?" another said.

"Thanks, Eric. Guys, this is First Lieutenant Jerry Yamato of the Republic of California Air Force. His fighter was shot down in a fight with a Russian armored column that was on its way here. Jerry lost five of his friends in that fight."

"Welcome to Delta, Lieutenant."

"Glad you're here, man."

"Thanks for helpin' us out."

Every man except the thirteenth made him welcome and he felt emotion rising within him. They all went silent and everyone looked at him. Jerry hated public speaking.

"It's a privilege to be here, thank you."

"Here's Frank," Williams said. "Everyone listen up."

Frank's face looked grim and Jerry noticed the smiles of moments ago had all evaporated.

"Okay, what we have out there is a small army of mercenaries which outnumbers us about twelve to one. We are going to rescue Pelagian, Bodecia, and a Russian named Rudi."

"A Russian. Why do we give a shit about a Russian?" Alexi asked.

"Ask Jerry, here, sometime. Rudi's on our side; leave it at that. So we have to create a diversion without getting any of our people hurt while getting Magda's folks out safely."

"With just seventeen of us?" Eric asked.

"No, the Russian garrison here is going to give us some help, too." Frank picked up a stick and began drawing a diagram in the dirt. "Okay, here's the setup."

☆   ☆   ☆

38 miles south of Delta

Clutching his machine pistol in a sweaty right hand, Jerry Yamato carefully crawled through the brush surrounding the Freekorps' motor pool. Like each of the five men with him, he carried two explosive charges that were not supposed to detonate without a radio signal on a specified wavelength. He fervently hoped the Freekorps didn't have any radios on that wavelength.

He stopped and the men behind him melted into the brush. Jerry put his face down between his arms and waited while a silent perimeter guard of two men no more than fifteen meters away inched past in the long dusk of the subarctic evening. After a few minutes Jerry carefully peeked up, half expecting to see them standing over him and grinning while pointing their weapons at his head.

They were gone. He lifted up onto his elbows and began crawling again. He sensed his squad moving behind him.

Never before had other men depended on his leadership. That was one of the things he liked best about being a fighter pilot: if he screwed up he was the only casualty. Now five other lives depended on his ability and leadership acumen, so he was being cautious. He also didn't like being dirty.

And he didn't like Viktor Mitkov, "the thirteenth man" as Jerry thought of him. Not only had Viktor not welcomed Jerry, at his first opportunity he had shouldered Jerry away from the others and spoken quickly.

"Magda and me are gonna get married, so don't get any ideas, Hero Fly Boy."

Even though the man was much larger than him, Jerry wasn't cowed. He had met bullies before, and they all had believed their sheer size would open doors for them.

"That's odd," Jerry said in a musing tone. "When I asked her about it a couple of days ago, she said there was no one special waiting for her back in Delta. Are you sure she knows about this engagement?"

As he goaded the bigger man, Jerry had carefully pivoted on his feet. Realizing Viktor lacked more than a modicum of intelligence he expected a physical attack. As if responding to a script, Viktor lunged at Jerry, arms wide to crush the wise-ass pilot.

But Jerry ducked under the man's arms, placed his right leg in front of Viktor's right shin, and as the man stumbled over the obstacle, Jerry kidney-punched him as hard as he could. Viktor landed on his face, gasping in agony. Receiving a kidney punch makes it difficult for one to breathe.

Jerry knelt down next to the man and spoke into his ear.

"You approach me again with malice and I'll kill you. That's not a threat; it's a promise. And if you treat Magda with respect and regard her as a thinking person, she might actually end up liking you; but you do not—in any way, shape, or form—own her. Do you understand me?"

Then he leaned on the injured kidney and Viktor cried out.

"Yeah, I understand!"

"That's good. Because we're going to need your help."

Then they had commenced this mission.

Jerry pushed through more brush and nearly collided with an armored personnel carrier. He thought his heart pounded loud enough to be heard fifty meters away. Following the drill they had agreed on, he touched the machine and waved his arm once.

This one would be the first target. His squad crept past him and infiltrated through the parked vehicles. Jerry crawled under the APC and carefully pushed the sticky explosive against the steel hull under the engine compartment.

After his long crawl through the brush and sphagnum moss, the underside of the machine reeked of cold steel, heavy engine oil, and petrol. All of his senses seemed hyperextended and even the earth and crushed foliage beneath his hands felt alien. He strained to see through the deep shadows.

Did they have alarms that could be tripped?

Something above him made a *clink* and he froze. When his heart slowed and the pulse thudding in his ears decreased, he could hear voices murmuring above him. He realized there were mechanics working on the engine.

Never before in his career had he been this close to people he knew would die because of his actions. For a moment he wavered, seeking a way around this fatal intimacy. But he knew if the tables were turned, they would not hesitate to kill him.

They are mercenaries, after all!

He slithered across to the other side of the machine and placed the second explosive on the fuel tank armor. After inserting a detonator in each deadly lump, he crawled back toward the fresh-smelling woods. A new confidence surged through him when he easily spied the wind-broken birch they had agreed on as a rendezvous point.

Clarence Charly already waited as Jerry crawled up.

"Man, that was pretty fast work," Jerry whispered. "Good job, Clarence."

"There wasn't any reason to hang around, y'know?" His quick grin revealed poor dental hygiene.

Max Demientieff crawled up and rolled over on his back. "No more of this creepin' around shit for me," he said in a low voice. "Just give me a rifle and tell me who to shoot. Okay?"

"That's next." Jerry grinned at them as the rest of their squad came into view.

Viktor, the last man in, gave him a level look and nodded. Jerry nodded back. He pulled the small radio unit out of his pocket and pressed the button to give the go-ahead signal.

★ 31 ★

38 miles south of Delta

Major Timothy Riordan glanced at his watch and then at the sky. "This 'midnight sun' crap is irritating."

"*Oui*," Captain René Flérs said. "If you wish to do something under the cover of darkness, you must move quickly before the sky she lights up again."

"And it doesn't get dark until it's bloody late at night!" Riordan shook his head. "Have the scouts reported back yet?"

"*Non*, and most confusing it is. I expressly told them to return before the midnight. Perhaps they have become disoriented and lost?"

"I'd be more willing to bet this has something to do with that Russian helicopter yesterday afternoon. That thing took more hits than a whore on payday, yet it stayed in the air."

"But she did not return, *oui*?"

"That doesn't mean a damn thing. We didn't scare them off, René. They're going to come at us in a different way. That's why we've got to move out tonight."

"The men are resting, but in full combat dress. The prisoners are under guard in the hospital. The machines are fueled and ready to leap into action."

Riordan laughed. "All I have to do is push the button, is that it?"

"*Certainment; mon Majeur.*"

The major's eyes never rested on one spot more than a few seconds. Only under fire was he able to stay still. Tonight his executive officer struggled to keep up with Riordan's pace as they walked the perimeter of their camp.

"What's Pelagian's condition?"

"Doctor Revere says his wound improves *trés* quickly. He should be ambulatory by week's end. The Russian also rapidly heals, but nothing like the large man."

"Did you double the guard on the woman as I ordered?"

"*Oui.* She is unsettling, that one. My *grand-mère* would say she has the evil eye."

"Keep that crap up and you'll have me believing she can summon the black mariah or call down a banshee. She's just an old woman who fights with her mouth. But she is damn good at it."

"Where is roving patrol?" Captain Flérs asked, looking around in the twilight haze of midnight in summertime Alaska. "We should have encountered—"

An abrupt wave of concussion and heat swept across them as one of their three fuel trucks and two armored personnel carriers exploded in a thunder of detonations, lighting up the camp and surrounding forest by throwing burning fuel in all directions. Liquid fire cascaded down on four of the six tanks and both of the remaining APCs.

"*Merde!*" Flérs shrieked. "We are under attack."

Riordan already had a whistle clenched in his teeth. He blew three sharp blasts, paused and repeated himself. Spitting the whistle out he screamed, "As if that fooking explosion wouldn't wake the very saints themselves! Go direct the damage control crew; I'll direct the counterattack."

The men raced away from each other. Riordan saw figures flitting about at the edge of the camp. He pulled his pistol out and fired the clip empty.

All was for effect. Despite his keen marksmanship, he knew hitting anything over fifty meters away would take an act of a very forgiving or forgetful Catholic God. His men boiled out of their four-man tents, armed and alert.

The fire silhouetted them perfectly if you were watching from the forest, Riordan realized. His thought became a cosmic cue as gunfire erupted from the trees. Ten of his men went down in the first few seconds.

The first group of mercenaries took cover and returned fire, shooting at the muzzle flashes in the shadowed woods. Another armored personnel carrier exploded in the middle of the motor pool, spraying the area with pieces of metal as lethal as bullets or shrapnel.

The camp seethed with pandemonium: men screaming in anger or pain, weapons firing nonstop, and the roar of an out-of-control fire created the backdrop of a scene from hell. Riordan looked around, assessed the situation, and knew he had to make quick decisions or they were lost to a still unseen enemy.

He ran over to his men while bullets snapped and buzzed past his head. Something bit his right ear and he grabbed it to discover the lobe shot away. The old, blind, killing anger surged through him and he fought it. If he went berserk now they would all die.

"Concentrate your fire, sweep the woods. Where's the mortar crew? Bring up those fifties on tripods!"

He glanced back at the raging fire. It looked out of control. Every time his men attacked the flames, they were cut down.

How the hell did they surround us? He picked up a rifle lying next to a dead Freekorpsman.

"Sergeant Ombekki," Riordan grabbed the quick African. "Take charge here. I'm going to get some of our heavy weapons into this."

"Yes, Major!" His filed teeth gleamed in the firelight. "I will hold them."

Riordan raced toward the motor pool. Two of the tanks pulled away from the fire and he resolved to promote the men inside: the hulls had to be hot as ovens. Two burning trucks abruptly whomped into pillars of flame as their gas tanks burst.

A figure dashed from the forest and threw something at the lead tank. Riordan snapped the rifle to his shoulder and shot the man dead. Fire gushed over the side of the tank.

"Gasoline bombs, damn them!" He fired into the forest where the man had appeared. He emptied the clip then threw the rifle down and sprinted for the remaining armored personnel carrier.

Behind him one of their heavy machine guns opened up, firing long bursts. Riordan scrambled up into the gun tub on the APC and grabbed the twin fifties. With a shriek he pulled his hands free—the metal was hot enough to blister flesh.

He ripped his shirt off and tore it in half, quickly wrapping the cloth around his hands. The heat from the burning vehicles less than thirty meters away was nearly overwhelming. Now he was *really* pissed off.

He fired sustained bursts into the forest. If he

saw movement, he blew the area to pieces. Enemy fire slackened as both tanks fired machine guns and cannon into the forest even as fire licked over the leading hull. Riordan became aware that enemy fire hadn't just slackened; it had stopped.

"Cease fire!" he bellowed. "Cease fire!"

The order echoed around the perimeter and the crackling flames seemed magnified in the sudden stillness. The heat defeated Riordan and he jumped down off the APC, shaking his hands free of the smoldering shirt rags.

"Officers on me!" he bellowed. "Sergeants, assemble your men. Everybody attend to the wounded." Firelight reflected redly off his sweaty arms and chest.

The grim triage began immediately. Every member of the International Freekorps knew that if their wounds were too grave for them to travel, they were dead. They didn't own an ambulance.

Captain Flérs hurried up to him and rattled something in French.

"English, René, English!"

"*Oui*. Yes, Major. We have lost a great deal of machines and men."

A gun went off near them as a mortally wounded trooper's misery ended.

"How many men?"

"Sixty, perhaps, seventy?"

"How the hell did they get past our patrols and perimeter guards?"

René shrugged. "Who is the enemy—Russians, Dená, somebody else?" He shrugged again.

"Well, I know we got at least one; let's go look at him."

Riordan hurried over to where the man had tumbled in death. A large amount of blood covered the ground, but the body had disappeared.

"Perhaps they are wraiths," René muttered.

"Bull crap, they're just men," Riordan snapped, peering around the woods with half-maddened eyes. "Get me a korpsman for my hands."

★ 32 ★

Delta, Russian Amerika

Moans of pain, the unusual sound of a man openly crying, and constant movement swirled around the operating table in the middle of the ancient cabin.

"Put your hand right there and push down," Bodecia ordered.

The sweaty, blood-soaked, young Russian corpsman pushed down on the mangled thigh of the wounded soldier. The steady spurt of blood reduced to a dribble and Bodecia poured fresh, hot water over the wound and cleaned it as best she could. She packed the wound with sphagnum and wrapped it tightly with a bandage ripped from a sheet.

"Tape that down," she said, moving to the next, and last, casualty.

Whistles out in the forest just before midnight told Bodecia what to expect. With practiced ease she had slipped from her cell and made her way to the mercenary hospital tent. The guard thought all threat would come from the forest.

When she moved up behind him with the rock held

in both hands, he didn't even look around when she bumped the tent.

"That you, Felix?"

She fervently hoped the blow didn't kill him, but she knew it would keep him out of the coming battle. A small battery lantern glowed inside the large tent and she immediately moved to Pelagian's side.

"Wake up, my husband, we are leaving this place." She pinched his nostrils together and in a moment his eyes popped open.

"Wha—"

Her hand pressed over his mouth and she repeated her words.

"I'm so hungry," he whispered.

She produced a strand of squaw candy and while he chewed, she moved over to Rudi.

"Sergeant, wake up."

"I woke when you entered the tent," he said in a soft voice. "Is it all going to start now?"

"Yes," she said and smiled. "Did you hear the birds calling?"

"Other than owls and loons, birds don't call at night. I thought it might be a message for you."

"A message for us. Come on, get up, we need to get out of this camp."

"What about the guards?"

"They're not going to see us. Please help me with Pelagian."

Rudi moved slowly but didn't seem to be in pain. Pelagian was close to his old self.

"I'm fine, Bodecia, you don't have to hold me up."

"Good. Now humor me and hang onto my arm."

The trio moved to the door of the hospital. Bodecia

motioned for both men to stop. She pulled a small battery light out of her pocket and flashed it three times towards the dark forest.

A single light flashed once and then something in the mercenary motor pool exploded.

"That's our cue, gentlemen. Head for the trees where you saw that light."

In less than a minute they traversed the gulf from prisoner to citizen without so much as a shout being raised against them. But pandemonium reigned on the far side of the camp. Weapons of every caliber seemed to be firing as fast as possible.

"So good to see you folks!" Doyon Frank Isaac yelled as they met under the foliage. "Does anyone need help, support, wheelchair?"

"Just get us to the rear, please," Bodecia said. "I know it's going to get wicked lively over here very soon."

"I have just the guide for you," Frank said with a wide grin.

Magda appeared out of the gloom and hugged her mother and father at the same time.

"Oh, I was so worried about you!" both women said in unison.

"Where's the lieutenant?" Pelagian asked.

"Over with the people creating the diversion. You'll see him later."

Heightened gunfire tore the air along with more explosions.

"Let's go," Magda said. "We have a support camp and field hospital set up for the wounded."

☆   ☆   ☆

Bodecia laid her hand on the last casualty, a young Russian private whose head was all but hidden by his field dressing. She couldn't find a pulse.

"Private, are you still with me?"

No answer. She pulled off the bandage and realized he had probably died soon after being hit. They lost more troops than anticipated, but they had pulled the Freekorps' teeth.

Over the past four hours Bodecia had taped, sewn and patched up three-dozen fighters. Four of them were women and over two thirds of the wounded were Russian. She felt confused by Frank's alliance with Romanov. They were Dená; weren't the Russians the real enemy?

She stepped out into the cool dawn, leaned against the wall of the building and sank to a sitting position. Given more than a minute of silence, she would have fallen asleep.

"Jesus, man, I sure wasn't ready for them guys to shoot hell out of the forest."

"Yeah, Arkady and Vitus were right next to me and the bullets just tore 'em apart."

Sixteen dead didn't sound like a lot, she thought. *Except when you knew every one of them. And we're not even fighting Russians.*

"Mother, are you okay?"

She looked up at her beautiful daughter.

"I'm fine, Magda, just very tired."

"I thought that might be the case. Come on, I'll walk you home."

She let Magda help her to her feet and through the brightening day they walked down a familiar street.

Her mother and grandmother had walked through this very same dust, yet this morning it all looked different.

"How is Lieutenant Yamato?"

"He's fine. He's sleeping. William said he fought like a demon last night."

"You like that young man, don't you?"

"He *is* a man, not a boy, Mother. Yes, I hold him in very high regard."

"I already know what he thinks of you."

"How do you know that?"

"I watched his eyes when he looked at you." Bodecia smiled at her daughter. "All I'm going to say is this: you don't really know him yet. But in the greater sum of things that might not matter."

"So far I like everything about him. But I told him I couldn't think about him and me until you and father were rescued."

"He agreed to that?"

"Instantly. He's not stupid or full of himself like, like other people I've known."

Bodecia's smile didn't get beyond her eyes as she mentally supplied names for both categories.

"I know he's not like us; he has Asian and Californian ancestry..."

"Magda, race is not a consideration here. Your father is part Irish, African, and Danish. I am Athabascan and New England Yankee."

"As I said, he's not like us."

"Does this fact bother him?"

"I don't think so, Mother."

"Then drop the subject. It's not worth your time or consideration."

"You don't have any problem with his ethnicity?"

"Was there some portion of 'drop the subject' that you didn't understand?"

"No, ma'am."

Bodecia stopped and considered. Magda hadn't used "ma'am" since she was nine years old. She held out her hand and stopped her daughter.

"Magda, look at me. I'm on your side. I know you well enough that if you decide to do something, you have thought it out in all its complexity.

"I trust you and I love you. You do what you think is right. But I reserve the right to geld any man who hurts you in any way. Agreed?"

Magda's beautiful grin broke across her face and she hugged Bodecia tightly.

"Agreed, Mother. Agreed."

★ 33 ★

St. Anthony Redoubt, Russian Amerika

"Doyon Isaac, I have received messages that our forces at Chena, at the Battle of Chena, that is, that the Russian Army is falling back in some confusion." Colonel Romanov sat at his desk and stared at the man seated across from him. "This puts me in a unique situation, which I'm sure you can appreciate."

"Are they counting on you for reinforcement or rescue?"

"No. They know we are a small garrison. They have inquired about Taiga 10, but I already made a full report regarding the International Freekorps and our temporary alliance."

"And their response was . . ."

"Forceful, anticipated, and completely out of touch with the reality of the situation." He smiled briefly. "They mentioned the possibility of a court-martial."

"Have you answered them?"

"No. First I wanted to talk to you about options."

"Options. You have a small command, yes. But you are on the only road between British Canada and Russia. A defeated Russian army is coming from the northwest and, if my intelligence is correct, there's an armored column between here and Tetlin headed northwest, and all are going to arrive here eventually. You will soon be knee-deep in reinforcements and all spoiling for a fight. What option do you have other than to wait for all of them to arrive?"

"We fought together well last night," Romanov said. "The mutual support bordered on extraordinary, and we accomplished our mission. Your intelligence is correct, a column is headed northwest from Tetlin Redoubt."

"But?" Doyon Isaac said.

"I have been ordered to apprehend all members of the Dená Separatist Movement in my district and hold them for interrogation."

"Have you identified any?" Doyon Isaac smiled.

Romanov smiled back. "I have some suspicions, but no proof. But to be honest, I have no interest in following those orders."

"Court-martial aside, don't they shoot people for not following orders?"

"Only if they can prove it."

"It sounds to me as if you are limiting your own options, Colonel."

"Perhaps. I have been following the battle reports closely and it seems obvious that Russia is losing this war. Perhaps St. Petersburg isn't willing to risk more troops in Alaska for whatever twisted political rationale, and is prepared to cut her losses.

"Obtaining military assistance from North Amerikan countries was a brilliant stroke. I believe that in a very short time the Dená Republik will be recognized by the entire world. The Imperial Russian Army will soon be leaving Alaska."

"Well, this part of it," Doyon Isaac said. "I'm not sure what will happen in St. Nicholas or farther south in Tlingit country."

"I believe it is inevitable that the Czar will relinquish all claims in North Amerika. The sentiments which provoked this war are also being heard in the Russian Far East; people are tired of being subjugated."

"So, your options boil down to what?"

"I wish to stay here. There is nothing in Russia for me, hasn't been for over a decade."

Doyon Isaac finally looked surprised. "I see. If the Imperial Command hears about this, they won't bother with a court-martial, they will summarily execute you."

"Only if they are in control of the situation when they arrive. I have talked to my officers and noncoms. Those who did not accept my way of thinking have already headed southeast toward the Tetlin column."

"Your way of thinking being...?"

"I, and the remainder of my command, wish to join the Dená Republik. If you'll have us."

Doyon Isaac, grinning from ear to ear, sprang from his chair and grabbed the colonel's hand.

"Welcome! You are all so very welcome!"

★ 34 ★

St. Anthony Redoubt

"This is Dená Southern Command, Delta One, we read you, over."

Jerry stared at the microphone, wondering why he suddenly feared communicating with his command. He suppressed the thought and pressed the send button.

"This is First Lieutenant Jerry Yamato, Republic of California Air Force. Are there any representatives from my unit there?"

"ROCAF? I thought you guys all flew away a long time ago, but then I don't get out much."

"I was shot down in action over Rainbow Mountain."

"Oh, you're that guy! Wait one second, please."

Jerry looked around the Russian radio room. A beefy sergeant with two-inch gold, double-headed, crowned eagles equally separating the six gold chevrons on his arm watched him closely. "What 'guy' is that?" he asked in a voice laced with frost.

Jerry tried to smile. "They probably mean the one who was shot down and lived to tell about it."

"This makes you famous, *da*?"

"Damned if I know. I've been out—"

"Yamato, is that really you?" Even through the static Jerry recognized the voice.

"Fowler?"

"Yep, that's you all right. Where you at?"

"Delta, St. Anthony Redoubt. Is the whole squadron there in Chena?"

"I'm not in Chena and I can't say where we are; the Russians are probably listening. St. Anthony Redoubt! Are you a prisoner?"

"Negative, but for the same reasons I can't get into specifics. Is the skipper there, too?"

Fowler's voice instantly lost its exuberance. "Jerry, the skipper bought the farm in that attack. So did Christenson, DeForest, and Barton. Major Shipley is the skipper now. He recommended Major Hurley for the Medal of Honor."

Jerry's eyes suddenly brimmed with tears. Major Hurley had represented everything good about the officer corps. He never told you where to go, he led you.

"Who was it that flew over me the other day, dropped the message?"

"Major Shipley, Currie, and Kirby. They said you were with a good-looking woman. How'd you pull that off?"

"You know my animal magnetism. I'll tell you about it when I get back. There's a field here; can you guys arrange a pickup?"

A different voice suddenly boomed from the speaker. "Lieutenant Yamato, this is Major Shipley. I'm glad you're still with us."

"So am I. Good to hear your voice, Major."

"They're telling me we have to cut this short, so

here's the deal. For the time being I need you right where you're at, to act as liaison and, if it comes to that, forward spotter.

"You people have a large Russian force running north up the RustyCan to bite you in the butt. We'll give you all the air support we can, but that's about it."

"Yes, sir. I understand."

"You're a good man, Jerry, and I know you'll uphold the honor of the air corps."

"Yes, sir." Jerry stiffened his spine and nearly saluted the speaker. The carrier wave dropped into total static.

"Welcome to the infantry, Lieutenant," the sergeant major said with an evil grin. "The colonel wishes to see you now."

Jerry noticed the headquarters building consisted of a variety of gray stone. The dark gray stone floor bore hundreds of scuff marks with stolid endurance. Medium gray walls, broken with elusive splashes of color in military posters, remained otherwise unforgiving and impermeable.

The colonel's door, at least, was dark brown oak. Jerry knocked on it twice, and then waited.

"Enter," said a loud voice rigid with authority, never doubting instant compliance on the part of the listener.

Jerry opened the door and stepped into a comfortable office decorated with lace curtains; an oriental rug covered most of the stone floor, and the colonel rose to his feet behind a beautiful cherrywood desk.

"First Lieutenant Gerald Yamato reporting as ordered, sir." He gave him the best salute he owned.

The colonel stiffened to attention and returned the salute. He smiled and gestured to a chair in front of Jerry.

"Please sit, Lieutenant Yamato, enjoy being off your feet while you can. I am Colonel Stephan Romanov, late of the Imperial Russian Army. Even though a number of my men and I have joined the Dená Republik Army, I have been left in nominal command of our little band of volunteers."

"Yes, sir," Jerry said, waiting for the real reason he was here.

Romanov smiled. "I understand that you are new to the area, flew in from California?"

"Flew most of the way, walked the rest."

Romanov laughed far more than the situation warranted. After a few moments of deep breaths, he said, "Thank you, Lieutenant, I needed to laugh at something."

Jerry had remained deadpan throughout. "You're welcome, sir."

"We're faced with overwhelming odds. I'm sure you've been told we have the remnants of an angry, defeated army coming at us from the north and a fresh, fully complemented army of retribution coming at us from the south. Unless we fade into the bush, where the remains of a band of pissed-off mercenaries still lurk, we have nowhere to go."

"What is your plan, sir?"

"Who said I had a plan?"

"You and Doyon Isaac did great quite recently. I know, I was there."

"Yes, so I heard. In fact you showed great courage leading the infiltrators and sappers. If I was still in the Russian army I would decorate you for your actions."

"Thank you, sir." Jerry felt a wave of astonishment sweep over him; the colonel actually meant it!

"No, I thank you. I need your help again: what should we do here and now?"

"I'm a first lieutenant from another nation's military; I don't even know the country. Why are you asking me?"

"For some of the same reasons you just mentioned as well as the fact that you are a warrior. Perhaps I was at one time, but for the past eleven years I have been an administrator."

"Have you spoken to Doyon Isaac about this?"

"Yes, he recommended you as an advisor."

"Oh." Jerry thought for a moment. He had sorted things out, but he needed to put them in the right order. "We need reconnaissance, on the ground and in the air. Do you still have aircraft?"

"We have a Sikorsky helicopter, which is almost repaired, and an old Grigorovich fighter."

"A Grigorovich. How old is it?"

"I think it was built in the late '40s."

"Does it fly?"

"Beautifully. But our last fighter pilot left three years ago and our drunk—our helicopter pilots won't touch it."

"Does it still have armament?"

"A 20mm cannon on each wing and 7.62mm machine gun in each wing root. Our mechanics have kept it in perfect condition, as a pastime more than a duty. They run the engine up each month just to keep it functional. Have you flown such a plane?"

"We trained in old fighters for months before they would let us touch a P-61 Eureka. Would you allow me to take her up and see what's going on in the neighborhood?"

"Provisionally. First we must make contact with your people so they don't shoot you down. Then you must convince the chief mechanic that you won't hurt his pride and joy."

"Lead me to him, sir."

★ 35 ★

Delta, Russian Amerika

"I'm fine, I tell you! Please stop this incessant questioning," Pelagian said.

"It's only been a few days, my husband," Bodecia said as contritely as she could. "I wanted to be sure your wound had knitted."

"Frank is making deals with Russians, there are armies advancing on us from both directions, and I have been completely out of the action for a week!"

"You know Colonel Romanov is an honorable man. Why are you doubting his sincerity?"

"Because he's a Russian! They have no more control over their emotions than a Frenchman does, they just look at the situation in darker terms."

"Pelagian, the man is part Yakut. He's only part Russian."

"They're more like Eskimos than they are like us."

"Stop talking like that this instant!" she snapped. "It's beneath you. Where is your head?"

"I'm angry, damn it! I have worked for years to create a sovereign nation for the Dená. And when it finally starts to happen, I get winged by a damn ricochet and am on my back for a whole week."

She shrugged. "Ricochets happen if you're around guns. It's not your fault, nor mine. It's kismet, why not accept it?"

Pelagian opened his mouth, frowned, and then closed it. She watched him think and felt more in love with him than ever.

"You're right, I haven't accepted this for what it is." He gazed into her eyes. "I'm sorry if I've been a bit of a shit. You've done an incredible job of getting Rudi and me through this. You are the most extraordinary woman I've ever known and I'm so happy you married me."

She hugged him tightly. "That's one of the reasons I love you—you know when to retreat."

They both laughed.

"I am so transparent to you," he said.

"But I like what I see."

The door opened and Naomi Jim filled it. "Hey, looks like my patient is much better."

Bodecia released her husband and moved across the room to her friend. "That's because you're such a good nurse, Auntie Naomi."

"Well, Auntie Bodecia, that's because he had a healer with him. He's a very lucky man."

"You're both right," Pelagian said. "Now I have to get out of here. Where's Frank?"

"Doyon Isaac is over at the redoubt," Naomi said with a sniff and gave him a slight curtsy. "And you're welcome."

"Thank you, old friend," he said, suddenly hugging her to him. "You know I love you."

He vanished through the door.

"He just wanted to get around me," Naomi said with a chuckle.

★ 36 ★

Port Lemhi, Republic of California

"No, Wing," Grisha said with a sigh, "you can't move your rook like that."

"Damn! I thought you said this was a war game. How can soldiers only move in certain ways? It doesn't make sense."

General Grisha Grigorievich laughed at his wife's expression until she impaled him with her "you're walking on thin ice" look.

He coughed. "Look, it's just a silly game, don't worry about it."

"I'm not worried, I'm pissed! This game is too formalized to be a true depiction of war. Why did you think I'd like it?"

"You said you wanted to learn chess..."

A brisk knock rattled the door.

"Come in!" they shouted in unison, him grinning and her glaring.

Sergeant Major Nelson Tobias stepped through the door, assessed the situation, and snapped to attention. "General, Colonel, our next transport is here and they are ready for us to board."

"Finally!" Wing said. "We've been here for a whole damned day!"

"Thank you, Sergeant Major. We'll be along in a few minutes."

"General, Colonel," Tobias said as he nodded. The door closed behind him.

"You've been hell on wheels this trip," Grisha said. "You've scared Tobias into acting like a subordinate instead of my mother, and you've got me wondering if I can talk to you without endangering my life."

When she looked at him her eyes widened and her fierce demeanor melted into one of compassion. "Grisha, I wouldn't do anything to hurt you, you know that."

"Not on purpose," he said with a chuckle. "Now let's go see what they have us doing next." He grabbed his crutches.

They exited the building and entered a staff car, a long, dark affair with leather seats and a glass window between them and the driver. Grisha remembered the hidden microphone in the console of his boat and didn't believe for a second that anything they said while in the car would not be recorded.

He abruptly realized he had not thought about *Pravda* for weeks, perhaps months. For the first time, he truly understood that the years skippering his boat were the last when he was truly his own master. Now he had responsibilities and interrelationships that demanded most of his time and might possibly take his life.

He was fine with that. If he could turn things back the way they were, he wouldn't do it. Something shifted in his head and he completely accepted the turn his life had taken; not only accepted it, but welcomed it.

"Grisha, did you hear what I said?" Wing asked.

"I'm sorry, but no, I didn't."

"Are you feeling worse?"

"Actually I feel better than I have in a very long time. Have I told you lately that I love you?"

She laughed and his heart warmed.

"About half an hour ago, if that."

"Oh, good. You remembered."

The car stopped and a muscular, blonde RCN officer with a wide grin opened the door for them.

"General, Colonel, I am Lieutenant Commander Darold Hills. My friends call me 'Bud.' I will be your RCN liaison for the rest of your journey. Would you come with me, please?"

Grisha smelled the sea and the lush forest, transporting him emotionally to the Alexandr Archipelago. The horizon revealed a landmass in the distance. The port teemed with military life.

Huge cranes loaded transports while troops marched aboard. Bosun pipes shrilled from a variety of quarterdecks and, as they watched, a ship slipped its lines and slowly made its way toward the open water.

"Commander," Grisha waved at the activity, "what is going on?"

Bud presented his wide, easy smile. "We're at war, General. The Japs declared war on us in the middle of the f—, uh, the middle of the night, and we're going to make them wish they had waited for morning and thought about it first."

"We have been in transit. When was war declared?"

"About 0300. I'm not sure of the exact time, but they did wake me up for officers' call."

"Did they declare war on anyone else?"

"Not that I know of, sir. But then there are a lot of things they don't tell me."

A large man stood by a gangplank, waiting as if he had nothing else to do for the rest of the day. Lieutenant Commander Bud Hills saluted the man as they approached. Grisha noted the fellow had three half-inch rings on his cuffs.

"This is Commander Josh Vandenberg, also known as PacSubFlot One."

Commander Vandenberg laughed at the expression on Grisha's face. "Welcome to Pacific Submarine Flotilla One, General and Colonel Grigorievich. The RCS *Mako* is the most modern boat in our fleet and I'm proud to be her skipper."

Grisha returned the salute and then shook hands with the submariner. "So you're our next ride, Commander?"

"Yes, General, and honored to have the opportunity to be of service to two heroes of the Second Battle of Chena."

"They tend to toss that 'hero' term around a bit too easily to suit me," Wing said. "Commander, we appreciate your assistance to our cause. I thought all naval vessels were called ships, you called yours a 'boat.'"

Commander Vandenberg's grin was infectious. "Colonel, submarines were called pigboats when they first entered the fleet, since they were made out of pig iron, and the boat part has stuck." He cracked his knuckles loudly. "We submariners persuaded the surface fellows to drop the 'pig' part."

Grisha and Wing laughed.

Behind them, Grisha heard Sergeant Major Tobias chatting with Lieutenant Commander Hills.

"Please," Commander Vandenberg said with a wide sweep of his arm, "come aboard our shark boat."

The gangway angled down to the narrow deck of the RCS *Mako* where two men waited.

Grisha handed his crutches to Wing and grabbed the steel handrails of the gangway, swung his body back and up so both legs hooked over the railings and he easily slid down to where the railing bent and anchored itself in the bottom planks.

Both men on the submarine laughed in surprise when the general landed and stood tall in front of them.

Grisha turned and saluted the Bear flag hanging limply on the stern, then turned to the lieutenant wearing the Officer of the Deck armband.

"Request permission to come aboard, sir."

The lieutenant returned the salute with a practiced snap and said, "Permission granted. Welcome aboard, General Grigorievich; it is an honor to meet you, sir."

Grisha glanced down at the name tag on the officer's uniform. "Thank you, Lieutenant Walls. What does the 'D' stand for?"

"Douglas, General. But I answer to 'Doug' just as fast."

Wing stepped off the gangplank and poked Grisha in the ribs, muttering so only he could hear: "You ever pull another stunt like that and I *will* break your leg again!"

"And this is my lovely wife and adjutant, Colonel Wing Demoski Grigorievich. Keep her safe and I hold you all in my heart forever."

Lieutenant Walls saluted Wing, then turned to the enlisted man at his side. "Allow me to introduce Chief of the Boat Keith Busch, our leading enlisted man."

Grisha shook hands with the chief. "Gentlemen, I was in the Russian Army for a number of years and had little to do with the Russian Navy, so I'm at sea here in more ways than one."

"If there's anything we can do to make this easy for you, General, you just let us know," Chief Busch said.

"Well, for starters, I can understand that crossed anchors indicate a bosun. But what does the device between all those stripes on your arm mean?"

"That is a diagrammatic representation of a sound wave, General. I am a master chief sonarman bumped up to serve as the senior enlisted man on the RCS *Mako*."

"I'm sure the California Navy picks only the best."

"General, I'm certainly not going to argue with you."

Commander Vandenberg stepped toward the open hatch in the center of the deck. "General, Colonel, if you'll please follow me, I'll show you to your quarters."

As they went down the steel ladder, Grisha commented, "I know that submarines don't have guest accommodations, Captain. So who is giving up their stateroom for this trip?"

"They told me you were very perceptive, General. You and your wife will be sharing my cabin, and I apologize that it's not larger than a standard telephone booth. But I am also impressed that once on board you addressed me as captain. Not many non-sailors are that well versed with naval protocol."

"I owned my own boat for ten years, and it was important to me that passengers knew I was the captain. Thank you for the compliment."

The compartment was small, but the bunk was adequate for both of them as long as they liked one another. Wing stared at the curtain that served as the only door.

"The entire crew treats that like it was made of three-inch oak, Colonel," Captain Vandenberg said. "Including me."

"I truly appreciate that," she said. "Thank you for your hospitality, Captain. Now I need to sleep." She slid the curtain closed.

★ 37 ★

St. Anthony Redoubt

"Lieutenant Yamato, this is *Vzvodnyi Unterofitser* Yuri Suslov."

Yamato looked at Colonel Romanov. "I apologize, my Russian is barely existent."

"No apologies needed, except mine. This is Sergeant Yuri Suslov, chief aviation mechanic for St. Anthony Redoubt. The Grigorovich is his pride and joy."

Sergeant Suslov, having popped to attention when Romanov entered the immaculate hangar, saluted Jerry.

Jerry returned the salute. "Sergeant, may I please see your aircraft?"

"The aircraft belongs to the Czar, it has been my honor to keep it mechanically fit. Of course you may see her, *Poruchik*."

"Our guest has no Russian, Yuri, please keep it all in English."

"Excuse me, Lieutenant, I meant no—"

"Don't worry about it." Jerry waved. "Where's your bird?"

The sergeant gave him a gap-toothed grin and led the way. The hangar was huge, even for Californian sensibilities. A large tarp hanging from the rafters made an effective wall across the end of the building. After edging around one end of the rank, heavy material, Jerry beheld a jewel.

The deep blue cowling blended into a polished aluminum fuselage. The three-blade propeller promised power. The windscreen spotlessly protected the cockpit, waiting for a pilot. Prominently displayed on the fuselage was the imperial twin-headed eagle, looking freshly painted in black, red, and gold.

"My God, Sergeant," Jerry's voice had gone husky. "She's beautiful."

"Thank you, sir. My men and I have put many hours into this machine."

"May I take her up?"

"You are the flying officer shot down a few days ago, yes?"

"Yes, that's true. I fly P-61 Eurekas."

"Please to bring her back in the same shape?"

"I have to do a recon mission. I will do my best, I promise you."

"I can ask no more than that." Sergeant Suslov shouted at his men and they pushed open the great door in the front of the hangar. Others pushed the aircraft out into the sunshine resulting in reflections painful to the eyes.

Romanov thrust a map into Jerry's hands. "This has the areas we spoke of earlier all marked for your reference. Be careful, just look around, and do not get aggressive."

"Are the guns loaded?"

"Of course they are, Lieutenant," Sergeant Suslov said. "If they weren't, she wouldn't be a war plane."

He waved Jerry toward the ladder hung over the edge of the cockpit.

"I am acutely aware that I am not wearing a parachute." He mounted the ladder and dropped into the seat. On the other side of the cockpit a corporal helped him into his straps, tightening them firmly.

Jerry surveyed the abbreviated instrument panel, and glanced around.

The corporal gave him a sad smile. "I'm sorry about the lack of parachute, Lieutenant, there isn't enough space; you'll just have to bring her back."

"I must admit, that's a very strong incentive. What's her top speed?"

Sergeant Suslov, standing on the ladder Jerry had used, handed him a leather helmet and a pair of goggles, and double-checked all the straps. "Approximately 410 kilometers per hour, sir."

"What's that in miles?"

The sergeant looked thoughtful, then said, "About 255, I think."

"What's her ceiling?"

"About 7,500 meters and she has a range of 600 kilometers before refueling."

"So that's around 25,000 feet and 370 miles, *nyet*?"

"I was led to believe you had no Russian," Suslov said with a laugh as he slid to the ground and removed the ladder.

Jerry flipped the ignition and nodded to Sergeant Suslov who waved at the men in front of the huge engine. They immediately began walking the prop to turn the engine over. Jerry switched on the magneto and the engine coughed, sending the prop into a brief spin before stopping.

He increased the throttle and the men resumed turning the prop, displaying more skittishness than previously.

The engine popped and the prop spun lazily as the men leapt away. Jerry grinned and opened the throttle, running the engine up until the aircraft rocked in its chocks. He pulled the leather helmet tightly onto his head and eased the goggles up to his forehead. After he tightened the chinstrap, he held his fisted hands butt to butt with thumbs sticking out in opposite directions, made eye contact with the sergeant and jerked his hands apart.

Suslov repeated the gesture to his men and they simultaneously pulled the chocks away from the wheels. The plane danced forward slightly as Jerry ran the engine up to maximum revolutions.

The roar of the engine filled him and he breathed deeply, intoxicated by the power at his fingertips. After moving the rudder back and forth and his flaps up and down, he released the brakes.

The Grigorovich abruptly sped down the packed-gravel taxi strip and onto the macadam runway. Jerry slowed to turn into the wind before fully opening the throttle and releasing the brakes. The fighter hurled itself down the runway in a satisfying blaze of speed.

He grinned and pulled back on the stick. The Grigorovich roared into the air and Jerry laughed.

Damn, I'm home again!

★ 38 ★

20 miles east-northeast
of St. Anthony Redoubt

General Taras Myslosovich felt empty. His armored column retreated east at a steady 7 km per hour. Less than a third of his original force rolled down the road with him.

Wounded soldiers lay on every flat surface of the tanks and APCs, some being held by unwounded but exhausted friends. The rear guards had to trot in order to keep pace and therefore had no idea what was behind them. Most didn't care.

"It's unthinkable," he repeated. "How can the Czar allow foreign military adventurers to interfere with internal Russian matters like this?"

Lieutenant Colonel Bodanovich, his adjutant, fighting shock, hovered near complete collapse. His ruined right arm had stained the bottom of his field dressing a dark red. Myslosovich felt it his duty to keep the colonel distracted and alert.

"I think the Czar sent us to dissuade them, General," Bodanovich said with an air of abstract discovery, ". . . and we failed."

"How dare you speak to me like that?"

Bodanovich worked to focus on the old man, finally giving up. "Because you need to hear the truth or completely lose what army you have left, and the men don't deserve that. And it no longer matters what I say because I know I am dying."

"Don't be absurd. You are wounded in the arm; that's not fatal."

"The bleeding has yet to stop, I need medical attention, and all of our combat surgeons are lying dead back there by that little stream. I'm not stupid, merely terminally flawed."

"You make no sense whatsoever!"

The command car slowed and stopped.

Myslosovich slapped his baton on the back of the driver's seat. "I did not order you to stop."

"The scout car has stopped, General," the driver said over his shoulder. "The lieutenant is walking back toward us."

Myslosovich peered through the windscreen and visually verified the sergeant's words. "Why has he stopped?"

The lieutenant jogged up to the general's side window, stopped and saluted.

The general rolled his window down. "What is it, man?"

"The road had been blocked, General. Our men are clearing the obstruction as fast as they can."

"Tell them that Lieutenant Colonel Bodanovich is dying and we need to find medical aid immediately!"

"Yes, General Myslosovich!" The lieutenant saluted and ran forward.

Myslosovich turned to his adjutant. "There! They will have us down the road in mere moments. Sergei?"

The lieutenant colonel was slumped in the seat, staring at the floor but seeing nothing.

"Oh, Christ!" Taras felt tears well up. The overwhelming feeling of grief nearly unhinged him. He angrily rubbed at his eyes.

A rap on the window brought him up short: the lieutenant again.

"There's an aircraft, General. Perhaps you should have a look?"

Glad for the diversion, the general climbed out of his command car and accepted the proffered binoculars, peered through them.

"My God, that's an old Grigorovich IP-1, and in splendid condition, too. I haven't seen one of those for thirty years."

He shoved the glasses back to the lieutenant. "Take a hard look at that. It's something you can tell your grandchildren about—you'll sure as hell never see another one!"

He burst into tears.

★ 39 ★

2,000 meters above St. Anthony Redoubt

The Grigorovich roared into a wide descending turn and First Lieutenant Jerry Yamato couldn't suppress his grin. *Satori*, his destroyed P-61, could have outrun this old bird; even flown rings around it. All the same, this plane had heart and soul, and Jerry had fallen in love with her.

He forced his mind back to the mission. The retreating column was mere miles from Delta but inching along.

He twisted the supple craft eastward and flew over Delta again, glancing down to see if he could spot Magda. No such luck.

Approximately three miles down the road he spied the remaining Freekorps. Jerry easily recognized the scorched hulls on the tanks and APCs as his handiwork.

The retreating Russians and the Freekorps were about to meet. Remembering his first encounter with the Freekorps, he figured the Dená didn't have to worry about the retreating Russians; they probably wouldn't survive the introduction. Then he flew in a wide circle around Delta, admiring the braided Tanana

River and the smaller Delta River feeding into it. Earlier he had flown north and saw what had to be the Salcha River also joining the Tanana.

Magda told him that the Tanana finally flowed into the Yukon some 200 miles northwest of here near the small village of Nuchalawoya, which in the local dialect meant "place where two rivers meet." Tanana was just a few miles downriver from there.

Jerry spied the road again and flew east-southeast. After ten minutes he saw dust on the horizon and flew wide of the disturbance. He dropped down to 300 feet and aimed straight for the center of the dust cloud. At full speed he crossed the Russia-Canada Highway and saw it was packed with military equipment from tanks to troop carriers.

He waggled his wings and soldiers waved. If they had all fired at him, he would have been riddled. Pulling back on the stick, he rapidly gained altitude and looked down the road as far as he could see.

His blood went cold when he saw the second column, no more than five kilometers behind the first one. It was as large as the leading element if not bigger.

Delta doesn't have a chance!

He turned and flew a straight line back to St. Anthony. With all of these visitors, people had to be warned.

★ 40 ★

Delta, Russian Amerika

"Is the hospital all packed?" Bodecia's voice sounded tight as a fiddle string, Magda thought.

"Yes, Mother. And all the medical personnel have already moved everything up to the Refuge. Do you have everything from the house that you can't live without?"

Bodecia stopped and looked at her with an expression of surprise. "Of course not! How can I save the afternoon light coming through my kitchen window, or the doorjamb where we measured your growth for fourteen years?

"I have a lifetime of memories in that house, and most of them are good. How can I save them"—she tapped the side of her head—"except up here?"

Magda wondered if her mother knew she was crying. Her own tears startled her and they hugged each other and wept. While she stood there holding her mother, she wondered when the older woman had become so small and thin. Magda suddenly felt fiercely protective and angry at the circumstances causing so much upheaval and turmoil.

"We'll get through this, Mother. We both have years of memories ahead of us. What's happening right now will be a strong one."

"Don't forget your sewing machine," Bodecia said with a sniff. "A girl who's looking to get married needs a sewing machine."

"I'm not 'looking to get married,' Mother."

"Oh, save it for later; just make sure you don't forget it."

"I won't." She watched her mother hurry off to direct someone to do something, and she smiled. Her sewing machine was one of the first items she had put in the cart for the trip up the mountain.

She saw Jerry on the far side of the square, just leaving the Russian compound. He peered around at the people rushing about. When he finally looked in her direction, she waved, and was rewarded with his smile and instant motion toward her.

When he reached her, he took her in his arms and kissed her. It seemed the most natural thing in the world to her, and she kissed him back. He held her tightly to him for a long moment.

"Okay," he said, dropping his hands to his side and staring at her with his puzzled-boy expression. "What's the Refuge?"

"I'll tell you while we're driving our truck there. We're completely loaded and ready to go."

They moved swiftly through the village to the house where she had spent her entire life. The Russian truck Bodecia had liberated sat waiting.

"You said loaded; that thing is overloaded! If we hit a good sized bump, we'll break an axle."

"You'll have to drive slow, Lieutenant Yamato,"

she said sweetly, "and try to remember you're not in California any longer."

"Haven't had trouble keeping that one straight," he said.

Jerry pulled the driver's door open and found Rudi sitting in the seat, a pistol in his hand.

"What do you—oh, is you, Lieutenant. Are we to leave now?"

"How are you feeling, Rudi?" Jerry asked.

"Not good as unused, but nearly there, I am told."

"Are you riding up to the Refuge with us?" Magda asked.

"Yes, if I may."

"Great. Scoot over to the window; three of us will fit in here."

Jerry eased the truck forward. The chassis groaned with the load but the engine didn't falter. He pulled in behind a Russian Army lorry and maintained a thirty-foot distance.

"So where is it we're going?" he asked.

"The Dená Separatist Movement has been around for about twenty years, but didn't really have any muscle until about five years ago." She noticed both men listened carefully. "That's when my mother, father, and I, joined."

"You are revolutionary, Magda?" Rudi asked with a trace of amazement in his voice.

"Yeah, I am, okay?"

"Of course, but you are young, and to be five-year veteran already gives me astonishment."

"Yeah," Jerry said. "I'll drink to that."

"I'm a sergeant of scouts, for what it's worth. Anyway, we knew the day would come, that this day would come, and we'd have to leave the village or be destroyed. So we built the Refuge."

"How long did it take before you finished?" Jerry asked, easing the truck through a series of potholes.

"Who said we finished? There is still much to be done before it's comfortable, but it's serviceable right now."

"Is like a redoubt?" Rudi asked.

"The village council knew about this large cave and kept it a secret from outsiders, like the Russian Army or any *promyshlenniks* who might be passing through."

"Any what?" Jerry blurted.

"Ah, *promyshlenniks*," Rudi said. "They are hunters and woodsmen, very brave and adventure-seeking. Russian children read tales about them."

"Which are all lies," Magda said, putting daggers into her words. "They're a bunch of filthy, drunken rapists who think they own Alaska and everything in it. They lie, steal, cheat, and would sell their mothers to the Spanish if it meant they wouldn't have to do honest labor for a week. They're lazy cowards who will kill you for your shoes and you must never trust one of them."

"Whew," Jerry said.

"I was approaching that part," Rudi said in a hurt tone. "But she is affirmative. Worse than Russian Army I think."

Magda patted his knee. "Much worse, and not as good in a fight."

Rudi preened and looked around. "We climb into mountains?"

Magda stared through the windscreen, trying to see the land as if it were the first time. Spruce and birch covered the hillside at this elevation, although the largest spruce were no more than four meters in height and were probably 200 years old.

Within another hundred meters of elevation, the trees thinned to solitary stalwarts claw-rooted into the rocky soil and bent away from the prevailing wind. Brush and lichen grew thick between the increasing number of rocks and boulders. The constant breeze grew stronger.

"We worked hard on this redoubt. There's probably something like this near all the Dená villages."

"You will win this war." Rudi spoke with the conviction of a man who has just comprehended universal truth.

"Why do you say that?" she asked.

"Russian high command believes you are all wastrel rabble, to use as basic labor but for nothing complicated. They have no idea what they fight."

"Thank you, Sergeant Cermanivich. That is the finest compliment I have ever received."

Rudi shrugged. "You are welcome. Is true."

The truck slowed as it climbed up the increasing slope. Jerry pushed the accelerator against the firewall and held it there.

"This crate won't last much longer," Jerry said.

"It doesn't have to—look." She pointed ahead to where the lorry had suddenly found level ground and turned between two large boulders. Their truck gained power when it leveled out and Jerry had to hit the brakes to keep from rear-ending the lorry. Magda watched Jerry's mouth drop open when the lorry drove into the mountain.

"Holy Shasta, that's one hell of a cave!" Jerry said.

"It'll hold the whole village comfortably."

"What about the Russians?" Rudi asked.

"They'll fit, too, but it will be a bit of a squeeze."

"This is all well and good, but how could you defend it?" Jerry asked.

Magda smiled and looked at Rudi. "Did you see them?"

"The gun emplacements? *Da.* I made count of four."

"You missed two. I didn't expect Mr. Flyboy here"— she bumped her head on Jerry's shoulder—"to spot them. But you've had a lifetime in armored divisions. I'm glad you missed two of them; that means we did it right."

Jerry looked dour.

"Hey, did I hurt your feelings?"

"There's no place to land a plane."

"You mean the Grigorovich?"

"Yeah. They'll destroy it or steal it."

A man with a hand torch waved them to a parking spot near the cave wall. Jerry parked the truck and switched off the engine. The area thundered as other vehicles followed them into the cavern. Sound bounced off the rock walls to collide with itself.

"Jeez, I don't know how much of this I can take." Jerry put his hands over his ears.

"You flew an open cockpit aircraft this morning. I've been up in those things—they're deafening."

He grinned at her. "Well, next time wear a helmet. The one I used was great."

"Pardon for my asking," Rudi said, "but what now?"

"Now we set the trap," she said with as much authority as she could muster.

★ 41 ★

Delta, Russian Amerika

"Something about this bothers me," Jerry said.

"What would that be?" Doyon Isaac asked.

"I'm flying under false colors; what if they shoot me down?"

"You probably wouldn't survive the crash, but I don't think that's your point, is it?"

"They could hang me as a spy."

"Lieutenant," Colonel Romanov said, rising from the couch in the corner. "You are still wearing your uniform. If you are ordered up in a craft with the wrong insignia, that's merely the fortunes of war—we use what we can get. You couldn't be mistaken for a spy."

"I sure hope you're right, Colonel." He faced Doyon Isaac again. "I'm ready to go."

"Remember," Colonel Romanov said, "don't engage them, just piss on their boots."

"Yes, sir." Jerry zipped up his flight suit and, carrying his helmet under his arm, walked out to the command car waiting for him. They drove out onto the airfield where Sergeant Suslov and his mechanics waited next to the Grigorovich.

205

As soon as he had climbed out of the truck at Refuge, a Russian lieutenant had given him orders to return to the redoubt: he had a mission to fly. It had taken him twenty minutes to walk back down the mountain, waving at people and vehicles streaming up from Delta. He still only counted three gun emplacements.

Jerry thanked the driver and got out of the command car. When he turned to the sergeant and the ground crew, they all stiffened to attention and saluted. Jerry returned the salute.

"Is she ready?"

"Yes, Lieutenant Yamato," Suslov said. "Where did they tell you to land after the mission?"

"Chena, if I can. Fort Yukon, if I can't."

"They will think you are the enemy. They might shoot you down."

"I'll lower my landing gear when they approach; that's the sign of surrender."

The crew frowned together as they considered his words.

"Then I'll be back with modern warplanes to help defeat the enemy."

"Not all are enemy, Lieutenant Yamato," one of the corporals said. "My brother is a conscripted gunner with the Fifth Armored en route from Tetlin. I would hate to bury him."

"Tell him how good you have it. He might join us."

"I hope he is offered the opportunity."

Jerry climbed up into the cockpit and went through his brief preflight. In moments they had the engine turning at full revolutions. Two minutes later he soared into the sky.

After climbing to a thousand meters, he surveyed the ribbon of road. In the distance to the northwest, he saw the dust cloud of the retreating army headed toward Delta. To the south he saw the lead column no more than ten kilometers from St. Anthony Redoubt.

He angled over and caught the approaching armored column from Tetlin in his sights; in moments, he tore down through the sky at the leading elements. Somewhere in his head he knew this was a sucker punch, but when you're outnumbered, you try to even up the fight.

The Russian scout car stopped to see what he was going to do. He zoomed over the car and bored toward the main column at full speed. At 500 meters, he began firing.

★ 42 ★

RustyCan near Delta

"We are being attacked by an antique?" Lieutenant Colonel Samedi Janeki shrieked at his driver. "Order them to shoot that damned thing down!"

"Yes, Colonel." As the driver radioed back to the main column, heavy fire erupted behind the car.

"Good. They didn't wait."

The Grigorovich finished its strafing run and roared back up into the sky. It didn't seem to be hit, nor did it return.

"I want an officers' meeting in ten minutes. Have an appropriate space created."

The driver snapped orders into his microphone, passing coronaries on down the chain of command. He pulled the car over to the side of the road and parked.

"Would the colonel prefer tea or vodka at the meeting?"

"Provide both, let them choose. Leave me be now; you make the decisions for ten minutes."

The driver grinned and slid the thick glass window shut, sealing off the passenger compartment from the

driver. Two trucks screeched to a stop beside them
and men boiled out with equipment and began chopping down trees and clearing ground.

Lieutenant Colonel Janeki flipped through the sheaf
of papers from his dispatch case.

"There," he muttered. His finger ran smoothly down
the page and stopped near the bottom. "St. Anthony
Redoubt is garrisoned by fifteen officers and ninety
lower ranks. Minimal artillery, three tanks, and support vehicles."

He raised his face to the glass and peered through
it. "But they have an aircraft." His soft voice aided
his train of thought. "So what else might they have
which St. Nicholas Redoubt doesn't know about?"

His mind didn't register the tent being erected
by twelve silent, sweating men. Personnel swarmed
around the car like crazed hornets, but none touched
its polished metal sides.

Lieutenant Colonel Janeki glanced at his watch,
straightened his tie, and rapped on the window with
his swagger stick.

The driver immediately got out, came around the
car, and opened the door closest to the now complete
tent. Three enlisted men stood at attention behind
the two tables laden with meat, cheese, vodka bottles,
cups, and a samovar already emitting the aroma of
steaming tea. Seven officers stood in a precise rank
on the other side of the tent.

The lieutenant colonel walked to the table and
picked up a slice of ham but, before putting it into
his mouth, said, "Gentlemen, please join me."

The officers crowded around the table filling plates,
grabbing and filling cups. By the time they were ready

to eat, the lieutenant colonel had strolled to the far end of the tent and rapped his swagger stick on a large-scale map of the area.

"This is the situation. The garrison at St. Anthony has mutinied and gone over to the Dená rabble. According to the roster forwarded from St. Nicholas Redoubt, we are talking about a hundred men. They have three tanks and assorted support vehicles."

"Then the aircraft was not from the redoubt, Colonel?" Major Brodski asked.

"It had to be, who else would attack us?"

"Did the Third Armored have any aircraft, Colonel?" Major Chenkov asked.

"No."

"So if they have an aircraft, no matter how antiquated, what else might they have that the high command does not know about?" Major Brodski's tone edged into the rhetorical.

"You've asked the same question I had earlier, Leonid," Colonel Janeki said, slapping the crop against his thigh. "I think we should prepare to assault a heavily armed and well-entrenched foe. The Indians are probably under Russian command."

He stopped and thought for a moment. "Pyotr, request St. Nicholas to send me the personnel file on the commander of St. Anthony, soonest."

"Yes, Colonel," a stocky major yelped. He saluted and left the tent at a run.

"Leonid, leave one tank at the rear, move the others up to the front rank. Nothing makes the enemy piss his pants faster than seeing a wall of Russian armor advancing toward them, guns blazing."

"Yes, Colonel." The major turned to a lieutenant

and spoke quickly. The lieutenant left the tent at a run, stuffing a last bite of sausage into his mouth.

"Did that damned plane do any damage?"

"Twelve men dead, another eighteen wounded. One lorry totaled and bits and pieces shot off the tanks and APCs here and there." Major Brodski took another sip of vodka.

"So all they did was slap our face." The lieutenant colonel's facial muscles tightened and he stared at his officers through slitted eyes. "Before this is over, I want that pilot in front of me."

★ 43 ★

3 miles south of Delta

Major Timothy Riordan felt tense enough to shatter. His scouts had warned of a large Russian redoubt ahead of them, so they had taken the first northbound secondary road they found. After much twisting and turning, reconnoitering of other side roads and many dead ends, they had at last found the Russia-Canada Highway.

Knowing they still were not beyond discovery by a Russian patrol, Riordan didn't allow himself any elation over the successful evasion. Now one of the scouts was tearing back to the column on his motorcycle.

"Stop the column!" Riordan snapped. He stepped out of the command car as the scout slid to a stop beside him.

"Major, there's a Russian column coming toward us. There's something odd about them—they don't have any scouts out. I damn near ran into them."

"From the north? How big of a column?"

"Bigger'n we are, Major."

"Damn. Well, I guess we have to try diplomacy." Riordan turned to his command sergeant major. "Rig me a white flag, John. We're going to make some new friends."

Captain René Flérs, still sitting in the command car, said, "Do you think we shall ever arrive at Klahotsa, Majeur?"

"René, if you can't say something positive, just shut the hell up."

A white flag was tied to the radio aerial on the command car. Riordan swung into the seat next to the driver. "Let's go meet some nice Russians. Oldre," he said to the scout, "get up there and stop in the middle of the road when you see them. Wave a white flag. We're right behind you."

"Somebody have a spare white flag?" Oldre asked in a petulant tone.

"Here, Tom, just wave this." Sergeant Major Douglas handed him a dirty pillowcase. "It's close enough."

Oldre motored away.

"Okay," Riordan said to the driver. "Keep up with him. Sergeant Major, keep the column here; put out pickets."

The car accelerated after the motorcycle. Oldre stopped in the middle of the road less than half a mile from the Freekorps column. He parked the motorcycle in the middle of the crude road and waved the cloth over his head.

The command car pulled up behind the motorcycle.

"Do not show a weapon unless we're fired on," Riordan ordered.

"Yes, sir," the driver said, frowning at the advancing Russian scout car.

Riordan slipped out and, holding both hands over his head, walked up the road toward the Russians. The scout car slowed and stopped fifty meters away. Two soldiers with rifles jumped out and aimed at Riordan.

"Hold your fire," he yelled. "I am not your enemy."

A lieutenant followed the soldiers. He kept his pistol holstered, but his right hand firmly rested on the butt. He hesitated for a moment, and then walked toward Riordan.

"You wear a uniform I do not recognize. Who are you?"

"I am Major Riordan, commanding officer of the International Freekorps." He lowered his arms.

"Mercenaries," the lieutenant said flatly.

"That's one description," Riordan said.

"Have you just come from St. Anthony Redoubt, Major Riordan?"

"No. We decided the times are too contentious to risk startling a garrison that could do us major harm. We went around it."

"Where, exactly, are you going?"

"The village of Klahotsa, up on the Yukon."

The lieutenant's pistol slid partway out of its holster. "You're joining the Dená and you think we're going to allow that?"

Riordan quickly held both hands out in front of his chest.

"No. In fact we're on our way to fight the Dená. Could I please speak to your commanding officer? I would like to explain our situation only once."

Without taking his eyes off Riordan, the lieutenant lifted his left hand and cocked his index finger. One of the two soldiers ran to his side.

"Yes, Lieutenant?"

"My compliments to the general. Tell him we have

encountered a group of mercenaries, strength unknown, whose leader wishes to speak to him."

"Yes, Lieutenant!" The soldier turned and ran back to the scout car. As soon as he crawled in, the car turned in the middle of the road and raced toward an approaching dust cloud. The second soldier stood with his weapon ready, but no longer pointing at them.

"I heard there was a big battle up north," Riordan said. "How'd it go?"

"*How* did you hear of any such battle?"

"We had radios," he jabbed a thumb toward the aerial on the command car. "We eavesdropped."

"You what?"

"We listened in."

"Then you know what happened at Chena, don't you?"

"Not completely."

"Ask the general."

Riordan wished he had the lieutenant in his outfit. The man was a real hard-ass.

"Where are you from, your home town, I mean?"

"That's none of your business."

"Good enough." Riordan realized the lieutenant would be hostile no matter what he did, so he just waited. The minutes seemed to stretch into hours but a quick glance at his Swiss watch showed it had only been ten minutes since the scout car left.

Private Oldre eyed the lieutenant with an unmilitary scowl.

So much for diplomacy, Riordan thought.

A high-powered, luxury sedan approached at a high rate of speed.

This would be the general.

The limousine stopped within a foot behind the soldier and the driver jumped out and opened the back door. The general took his time, his lack of speed due more to his corpulent body than anything else. He squared his shoulders and then dropped back into a slouch as he moved forward, idly slapping his thigh with a riding crop.

"What's this all about, then?"

Riordan snapped to attention and gave the general a perfect parade ground salute, rigidly holding it until the general returned with his own half-hearted wave. "Good afternoon, General. I am Major Riordan of the International Freekorps."

"Hmm, yes. I am General Myslosovich of the Imperial Russian Army. Exactly what are you doing here, Major?"

"Attempting to get to my new place of employment: Klahotsa on the Yukon."

"That entire area is held by the Dená Separatist Movement, a terrorist group in rebellion against the Czar of Russia. Any aid to them is a crime against Russia."

"My employer, Mr. Bachmann, is loyal to the Czar and wishes to hold his part of the Yukon free of the Dená rebels. We have been hired to assist him."

"Bachmann? Never heard of him," Myslosovich said with a shake of his head. "Until we can verify this person's existence, let alone his political position, I'm afraid we'll have to sequester you and your men."

"What if we don't agree to that, General Mysloso-vich?" Riordan said in a hard voice.

"You have no choice! We could annihilate you in moments—"

"Begging the General's pardon," Riordan interrupted, "your people seem to be incredibly disorganized. My scouts tell me that your column is in disarray, which coincides with our interpretation of your radio messages of a few days ago. In short, General, you are in retreat and in no shape for a fight."

The lieutenant bristled, pulled his pistol from his holster but kept it pointed at the ground. "Say the word, General Myslosovich, and I'll shoot this man myself."

The general held his hand up. "He has a point, Lieutenant Andreanoff, much as I hate admitting the fact."

"Perhaps we can assist our employer by assisting you, General?" He turned his head to the side and told Oldre, "Tell the column to advance."

Myslosovich turned to his driver. "Bring the column forward, now."

While Oldre spoke into a radio, the driver turned the heavy automobile and drove away.

"I mean no threat," Riordan said. "I just want you to see what we have to offer."

General Myslosovich gave him a thin smile. "I'm sure. And by the same token I would like *you* to see how much in *disarray* my column might be."

Behind him, Riordan could hear his people and machines moving up. Ahead, he could see the Russian column advancing with all the implacability of a glacier.

A higher engine whine cut through the massed cacophony of the two armies.

"Here comes that plane again, Major Riordan," one of his men yelled. "Looks like it means business this time."

"Track it," the General commanded. The two commanders stood next to Myslosovich's command car. Riordan nodded to General Myslosovich. "I suggest you have your crews prepare for attack, General."

"From a venerable old bird like that? Besides, she has Imperial Air Corps markings."

"Are you in contact with the Tetlin column?"

"No. We are traveling without communication at this point. ROC fighters destroyed our radio truck, and all of our field units have depleted their batteries. Even our tanks cannot communicate; many lost their antennae in the battle and the one that didn't lose its antenna has a broken radio. It is all very vexing!"

"So you have no idea if that plane is friend or foe."

Myslosovich grinned. "We'll know soon, won't we?"

The shriek of bullets abruptly ripped past their ears, tearing up ground, the command car, and some hapless soldiers, all before the sound of the plane's guns reached them.

"Damn!" Myslosovich screamed, diving behind trees bordering the road.

The column fired back and, from his position next to the general, Riordan saw pieces of the plane shred into the air. But it roared overhead without a single cylinder missing a beat and curved away to the north. The aircraft buzzed into the distance and the sound faded.

Riordan turned to the fat old man hiding behind the trees.

"Well, you certainly called that one. What're your thoughts on the next tank or APC we encounter? Friend or foe?"

Myslosovich pulled himself to his feet and presented

a baleful look. "How dare you speak to me like that. I could have you shot!"

Riordan glanced around. "No, I think not. What I do think, however, is that you need me a lot more than I need you."

"To what end?"

"You're running around here like you own the country, no scouts farther out than ten minutes, no attempt at discipline, stragglers from here to hell and gone. Have you mustered your people since the battle? Do you have any idea how many men you have left?"

"That's staff work! Do you think I am some sub-private with nothing better to do?"

"No, I think you're a politician in uniform. You have no concept of how much trouble you are facing and yet you're sure of victory. You're retreating, General, retreating!"

"And there's a superior Russian force headed this way at speed," the general said. "And the officer in charge is my favorite subordinate, I made him what he is today."

"Well, I'm here and he's not. Do you want my help or not?"

"Only if you apologize instantly."

"I'm sorry if I hurt your pride, but it was imperative that you see the reality of this situation. They're going to hit us again and we must be ready."

Myslosovich slapped his thigh with his riding crop and stared at the major through puffy eyes. "What do you suggest?"

Riordan spun away, turning his back to the old man, primarily so his wide smile wouldn't be seen. He waved and shouted, "I need the long-range radio, now!"

He turned back to the general. "Why don't you make contact with your people at St. Anthony Redoubt. We'll take it from there."

General Myslosovich sucked in his gut momentarily and puffed out his chest. "Superb idea. I am grateful for the opportunity, Major Riordan."

A corporal hurried up to them. "Here's the radio, Major."

"Thank you, Corporal Mader."

Riordan held the field radio out to General Myslosovich. "General?"

Myslosovich glanced around and the lieutenant moved up and accepted the radio.

"Thank you, Major," the lieutenant said, then twisted dials and switched on the unit. "St. Anthony Redoubt, this is Third Armored, General Myslosovich commanding, over."

Static. They waited, all staring at the radio. Myslosovich opened his mouth and the radio crackled into life.

"Third Armored, this is Sergeant Desonivich. Except for me, and a few others, the garrison has joined the Dená. They are in the process of abandoning the redoubt as I speak. If you act quickly, you might stop them."

"Who is the commander there?" the lieutenant snapped.

"At this point, *I* am."

"Where is the rest of the command?"

"All I know is they all left—our personnel, the Indians, everybody."

"You don't *know* where they went?"

"Lieutenant, I was told I'd be shot if I followed them. So I stayed in the radio shack with four troopers."

"Only *five* of you remained loyal?"

"No, sir. A few men, seven I think, left this morning and headed south toward Tetlin."

The lieutenant stared at the general, shock and dismay radiating from his eyes. "Why did the five of you not go with the ones who joined the Indians?" The lieutenant's voice held massive sarcasm.

"We hate it here, sir. We are all from the Black Sea area and this place gets too cold to believe."

Myslosovich cleared his throat.

The lieutenant immediately regained his professional mien. "General?"

"Tell him to lead a reconnaissance party at once, or *I'll* have him shot!"

The lieutenant grinned ghoulishly and snapped into the microphone, "Did you hear what the general said?"

"Yes, sir. We're leaving as soon as you're finished talking."

"Then go!"

"Try to reach Fifth Armored," the general said.

"Fifth Armored, this is Third Armored, please come in." The lieutenant stared down at the radio. "This damned thing just died on me!" He snapped off the radio.

"I'd appreciate it if you'd be a little easier on my equipment, *Lieutenant*," Riordan said in his best command voice. "Our batteries were low and that was the last functioning set we had."

Riordan knew his tank radios still worked but he was damned if he was going to bring more Russians into this if he could help it. The odds were building in his favor.

"My apologies, sir, and thank you for the use of your radio."

Riordan smiled. "You're quite welcome. General, what do you want to do?"

"Find them." Myslosovich's voice was glacial. "And hang every mutineer and filthy savage from the nearest tree!"

"Very good, sir. If you'll allow me . . ." he turned and blew his whistle. "Scout One, on me!"

He composed himself and turned back to Myslosovich. "I'm sending my most seasoned men out to probe ahead of us. As soon as they see the enemy they will return at once. Their scout car moves a hell of a lot faster than an armored column."

"Sounds reasonable," the general muttered, suddenly deflated. "I'm going to see to my staff." He walked toward the command car and stopped short. The vehicle sat on three flat tires and the body and engine were peppered with bullet holes. His driver lay sprawled in the front seat with most of his head destroyed.

Riordan watched the old man's shoulders slump and knew he had just inherited an army.

★ 44 ★

Refuge

Sitting on the highest point above the Refuge, Pelagian and Magda both lowered their binoculars.

"He did it," Pelagian said.

"Yes. Did you see any smoke coming from the plane?"

"No, but I could hardly see the plane; the action was at least five kilometers away."

Magda sighed, staring into the distance where the plane had disappeared. "I really like him, Papa. I like him a lot."

"So your mother tells me. Did he speak of his family?"

"He mentioned that his father was a mechanical engineer. I don't remember him saying anything about his mother."

"He has certainly done everything he could so far."

"Yes, yes he has."

"But if he ever hurts you, I'll cut his heart out."

Magda smiled at her father. "You'll have to wait your turn."

They laughed in unison and rose to their feet as one.

"I'm to direct the defense of St. Anthony. Would you like to join me?"

"Since I plan to be there anyway, I thank you for the official invitation."

They traveled down the mountain, skipping from boulder to boulder like mountain goats. As they neared the tree line, the boulders became smaller and farther apart. Soon they walked down through the thickets of spruce, birch, and willow.

A hummingbird *zzzz*ed past and they could smell wild roses somewhere close.

"I love this time of the year," Pelagian said. "It really pisses me off that we have to waste it on a war. By the way, thank you for everything you and the lieutenant did to help your mother when I was wounded."

"You're welcome. His name is Jerry; there are lots of lieutenants."

"But not many you are in love with."

"Good point."

"Halt!" a voice bellowed, seeming to come from everywhere at once.

Pelagian and Magda slid to a stop.

"Who are you?" the voice demanded.

"Pelagian and—"

"—his daughter, Magda!" she yelled.

"Oh, sorry we bothered you." A young man in Russian camouflage, but possessing long hair, stepped from behind a tree. The slap of straps on stocks and barrels attested to weapons being lowered.

"No, you were absolutely correct in challenging us," Pelagian said. "You all are doing a good job. Keep it up."

"Why do we have a skirmish line this far up the mountain?" Magda asked as they continued down the slope.

"They're part of our reserve, the last part before the Refuge. They're all volunteers and every one of them is willing to give their life to protect the Refuge."

"Papa, do you know of anyone who was drafted into the Dená army?"

He grinned at her. "Point taken."

The ground leveled slightly and they both stopped near a gun emplacement in the rocks.

"Any sign of the enemy?" Pelagian asked of the gun crew.

"Naw, I don't think we're gonna see that much action," the sergeant said.

"Within ten hours I will remind you of your words," Pelagian said with a ghastly smile. "Stay alert. When they discover how we have tricked them, they will be livid and out for blood."

"Our blood?" the sergeant said.

"You're Dená, aren't you? Watch out for our people in front of you."

Pelagian moved on down the mountainside and Magda followed.

★ 45 ★

"Major, we've made contact with the enemy."

Riordan looked up from the map spread across his lap, glanced at General Myslosovich, then opened the door of the command car. "Show me where they are on this map, Charly."

The two scouts looked at the map for a moment and Charly put his finger down next to the town. "They're right there, Major. Aren't they, Bondi?"

The other scout nodded his head. "That's where we find them, sir. Right on the other side of the town."

"They weren't in the redoubt?"

"The gates of the redoubt are gone; maybe they burned them, I dunno," Charly said, rubbing his neck. "The whole village seems to be deserted; we didn't see anyone. So we went on down the road and saw a scout car headed toward us."

"A Russian scout car?"

"Yes, Major, with a Zukhov tank right behind it."

"They're not supposed to have any tanks!" Myslosovich blurted.

"Sorry, sir, but I know a Zukhov when I see one," Charly said evenly.

"I don't doubt you, soldier," Myslosovich said quickly. "This is getting entirely out of hand."

Riordan unhooked the microphone from its clip on the dashboard. "This is Major Riordan, I want all three tanks to the front of the column—now."

Three clicks on the small speaker confirmed his orders.

The general frowned. "I thought your batteries were depleted."

Riordan glanced at him. "Our long-range radios are depleted. We can communicate only between our units."

The general held his gaze for a moment then turned to the scout.

"How many tanks did you see, soldier?" Myslosovich asked.

"At least three, General. But there was a lot of dust obstructing visibility and they were on a bend in the road. There could have been fifty behind it."

"You said there was a column moving up from Tetlin," Riordan said. "Could it be them?"

Myslosovich frowned and pondered. Riordan could almost see wheels turning and smell burning gear oil. Riordan stopped and coughed, knuckled one eye.

"They would have to be moving at top speed to be that far in such a short period of time. Based on the column I brought north, they couldn't have covered that much distance. This has to be the renegades from St. Anthony with their DSM allies."

"Good enough for me," Riordan said, picking up the microphone again. "All units, prepare to engage."

★ 46 ★

1,000 meters over Russian Amerika

First Lieutenant Jerry Yamato thought the rudder control seemed a little sluggish, but the Grigorovich fighter roared forward, as if eager to see what was over the next ridgeline. He had taken hits from both columns. Fire from the first target had only hit his left wing once, a mere nothing in the greater scope of things.

The second column put three rounds through the cockpit and God knew how many elsewhere in the aircraft. One of the rounds had blown a hole in the left side of the fuselage and shattered part of the windscreen. The second round had taken out the instrument panel with a great shower of sparks.

The third round had ripped along the side of his left thigh muscle, cutting him open. He had immediately tied it off with his belt. But Christ almighty, it hurt!

So far he had fought off the lightheadedness he recognized as a symptom of shock, and concentrated on just crossing the next ridge while ignoring the other ridgelines beyond his position. Not knowing the condition of his bird bothered him more than he thought possible. Perhaps it was because he had nothing else to think about?

"No, dammit, it's because I might be low on fuel or running hot!" he bellowed into the wind whipping past the open cockpit. One thing he knew for certain: an enclosed cockpit was infinitely superior to the alternative. All his life he had read stories about the early days of aviation—open cockpits, goggles and scarves catching the wind, seat-of-the-pants navigation.

He decided they had to be crazy or so bored with their lives they would do anything for excitement.

The next ridge passed beneath his wings and he peered through his goggles, trying to pierce the hazy air. A ribbon of reflection snaked from one side to the other and he realized he was looking at a river, a big river.

"Damn, that has to be the Yukon!" he shouted.

He ducked his head and studied the map Romanov had given him. According to the map, Fort Yukon was right on the river. He jerked his head up and searched for signs of civilization.

Too high, he decided, pushing the stick forward and arcing toward earth. Still nothing. The banks all looked wild and untouched to him.

He had to go right or left...which? How much fuel remained in the tank? Had one of the rounds holed his fuel tank?

The fact he didn't have a parachute throbbed in the back of his head like a whiskey hangover. He had to land safely or die. Flipping a mental coin, he angled to the left and flew directly over the river.

The river made a bend to the left and he put the Grigorovich over and followed the water. Something glinted in the distance on the right side of the river. He dropped to what he thought might be three thousand feet and stared hard at the spot.

And there was a village. Just behind it was a runway. Something big and fast roared over him and he snapped his head around to see a P-61 twist into a turn.

He pushed the lever to lower the landing gear and it stuck halfway. Fear ran through him like ice water. He had to lower his landing gear so they knew he didn't want to fight. So he could land!

He pulled the lever back and slammed it forward again. It stuck in the middle again. The Grigorovich rocked violently to the right as the P-61 buzzed him again.

He sat back and held both hands in the air, waiting. The wind beat on his gloves, tried to tear the sleeves off his flying suit. And a P-61 edged up beside him while the pilot closely inspected him.

Jerry pointed down and mimicked landing gear lowering. Then he slammed the lever forward as hard as he could.

The other pilot gave him a thumbs-up and peeled away. Jerry put his bird into a bank and lined up with the runway. He felt so happy he could almost cry.

★ 47 ★

Delta

"Lieutenant Colonel Janeki, our scouts report Russian armor ahead and in battle formation."

"Have you tried to contact them by radio, Vladimir?"

"Yes, Lieutenant Colonel. No response. We seem to get a lot of interference around here."

"I don't like this, gentlemen," he said to the officers gathered around him.

"We know that St. Anthony Redoubt has gone over to the enemy, Lieutenant Colonel," Major Brodski said. "They wouldn't answer us anyway."

"Have you been able to raise Third Armored?"

"No, Lieutenant Colonel, that interference again."

"Where the hell are they? They couldn't have been completely annihilated."

"Perhaps their communications have been knocked out?" Captain Vladimir said in a hopeful tone.

"Or perhaps they have been overrun by the damned Dená and their California allies." Janeki spat in contempt.

"If that's the case, Lieutenant Colonel, would there still be Russian crews in those tanks?" Major Brodski asked.

"Do you think Russian soldiers would join the Dená?"

The six officers grew quiet. Only two of the six would meet his gaze.

"I think they would, too," Lieutenant Colonel Janeki said. "Especially the lower ranks."

"If we capture any Russian renegades, I think they should be shot!" Major Pyotr Bulganin snapped.

"Absolutely," Samedi said. "For now, I want every weapon loaded and ready to fire. Put as many tanks abreast as the terrain allows, with the rest of our armor behind them. We're going to hit them with everything we've got."

The officers ran to carry out his orders.

★ 48 ★

Battle of Delta

Colonel Del Buhrman held the binoculars to his eyes and watched the Russian armor below the ridge where the 3rd PIR waited for events.

"I believe this thing is working, Sergeant Scally, both sides haven't wavered."

"They told us at the Weasel Works in Fresno that it would work better if you were closer to the target, but I think we're delivering hash to all concerned."

Buhrman lowered his binoculars and regarded the clear-eyed youth.

"Well, you just made first sergeant with your little magic box there."

"Thank you, sir! I can use the money." He bent back to the machine and gave one knob a slight nudge. "But it's really the scrambler doing all the work."

Buhrman stared down at the Third Armored and the unknown unit they had met. The Californians had watched the whole thing from their vantage point on the ridge. At first Colonel Buhrman thought there was going to be a fight, but the two units had parleyed instead.

The unknowns had Russian tanks but the Imperial double-headed eagle had been painted over with a stylized "IF" and the Russians hadn't paid it any mind.

"If they had Fremont tanks, I'd sure as hell want to know where they got them!"

"Colonel?" Scally looked up from his scrambler.

"Just talking to myself, Ryan. One of my bad habits."

"Gosh, Colonel, I didn't know you had any other kind."

"Sergeant Scally, mind your machine if you want to keep *all* of your stripes."

"Yes, *sir!*"

As they watched, the Russians began firing on each other.

★ 49 ★

Battle of Delta

"Incoming!" screamed Sergeant Yalushin of the Third Armored. A deadly rain of cannon shells impacted among the leading elements. One of their precious tanks took a direct hit and promptly exploded, raining debris across the column.

"Fire at will!" Major Riordan screamed. All seven remaining tanks of the Third Armored and the International Freekorps answered in unison, filling the road ahead with armor-piercing shells.

The Imperial Fifth Armored took massive damage, losing a fifth of their strength in moments. The entirety of the first wave of tanks and half of those in the second wave received direct hits, bursting their hulls and killing their crews.

Both columns rocked to a halt during the exchange but continued firing.

"Major Riordan!" General Myslosovich bellowed. "We are being annihilated." Explosions bracketed the column while tanks and APCs in the middle of the force took direct hits and exploded.

"We must surrender!" Riordan screamed back. "They're too much for us!"

"Agreed!"

A white flag surfaced almost immediately when the word of surrender passed back through the ranks. The terrible shelling ceased and five minutes later a scout car bearing a white flag emerged from the dust cloud hanging over the road.

General Myslosovich felt like taking his own life. He may as well: two defeats in six days meant his career had ended, no matter to whom he was related. The scout car stopped in front of them and an Imperial Russian Army major stepped out, straightened his tunic and marched toward their vehicle.

"That's a Russian column, isn't it?" Riordan said with defeat evident in his voice.

"Yes," said General Myslosovich, feeling an intense headache explode between his eyes. "We have been fighting our own people."

The major strode up to them and snapped to attention.

"In the name of Lieutenant Colonel Samedi Janeki of the Imperial Russian Army, I demand your immediate surrender."

"Christ, man!" General Myslosovich shrilled. "We *are* the Russian Army!"

★ 50 ★

Fort Yukon, Dená Republik

"Lieutenant Yamato, I don't think it's advisable for you to fly," Lieutenant Colonel James Burton said.

"You're the flight surgeon. You can order me not to go up, but if it's my decision, I'm on my way."

"Your wound is as good as it can be; the stitches make a big difference. I think you could use some more rest, but your responses are fine and I know you have more investment in this war than others."

"And I told them I'd be back with modern aircraft."

"That's a beautiful bird you brought in. The mechanics are treating it like royalty."

"They know quality when they see it, sir."

"Okay, you're back on the flight list. I'll call Major Shipley and tell him you're cleared."

"Thank you, Colonel Burton." With a salute Jerry was out the door and hurrying toward the flight line. He entered the Operations Building next to the hangar.

A sergeant in ROC uniform looked up from the front desk.

"May I help you, Lieutenant?"

"I need a plane."

"Your name, sir?"

"First Lieutenant Gerald Yamato, 117th Fighter Squadron, ROC."

"You were shot down out there in the wilderness, right, sir?"

"Yeah, I sure as hell was."

"Through that door, Lieutenant Yamato"—the sergeant pointed—"you'll find the Operations officer. He has all the planes. Glad you made it, sir."

"Thank you, Sergeant. I'm glad I made it, too."

He pushed through the door where a corporal glanced up from a typewriter. "Hi, Lieutenant Yamato, welcome back."

"Corporal Anderson, it's good to see you." Jerry immediately turned his attention to the Flight Status Board. "Wow, we have seven operational birds and all of them are on the ground?"

"We've been ordered to stand down, Jerry," Major Shipley said, coming out of his office. Captain Kirby and Lieutenant Currie trailed him.

Jerry snapped to attention and saluted his commanding officer. "Congratulations on your promotion, sir. Good to see you."

Shipley returned the salute. "Thanks, but I'd rather still be the XO and have Major Hurley back. You've done a hell of a fine job, Lieutenant, or should I say, Captain?"

"Major?"

"Actually that's wrong too. I received a message from Sacramento this morning promoting the entire squadron to the next rank. It seems we benefited from some good press over our battle with the Russian armored column."

"That's because there weren't any reporters there," Captain Kirby said.

When they finished laughing, Jerry asked, "So is the war over?"

"Not that I've heard. This morning we had orders from Dená Southern Command to stand down for the day, no reasons why, but then we're just a bunch of fighter jockeys, right?"

"Maj— Colonel Shipley, I have obligations which require the use of a P-61."

"You have military obligations beyond this squadron?"

"I told them at Delta that I'd be back with a modern aircraft and help them in the fight that's imminent."

"When you were debriefed upon your return last night, all the information was sent to DSC. Their orders as of this morning were quite explicit."

"May I have your permission to contact their intelligence people? Perhaps they didn't fully understand?"

"I have no objection," Lieutenant Colonel Shipley said. "We would all rather be flying."

They all followed Yamato into the radio room. Sergeant Reddy looked up from his lurid paperback and pulled his headset off.

"Traffic seems to be pretty quiet, Major Shipley. Lieutenant Yamato, welcome back!"

With a nod at Shipley, Jerry said, "Can you connect me to the Dená Southern Command?"

"Sure thing, Lieutenant Yamato." Sergeant Reddy repositioned his headset and turned a dial. "Chena One, Chena One, this is Cal Squadron one-one-seven, do you read?"

Jerry found himself holding his breath. There had to be a way around the ordered stand down: the woman he loved faced great danger and he had to do what he promised.

"Jimmy, that you?" the sergeant said. "Yeah, it's Bob Reddy, good to hear you again."

Jerry felt impatient. Hell, Magda was more military than this!

"Jimmy, listen, I have a lieutenant here who wants to contact your people. No, I don't know which ones, but I'm going to put him on, okay?"

Sergeant Reddy tore off the headset and motioned for Jerry to approach.

"C'mere, Lieutenant Yamato. Here put these on, yeah, that's right. Okay, this is Jimmy Sunnyboy you're talking to, he's with the Dená Southern Command."

Sergeant Reddy slid from behind his desk and motioned for him to sit. Jerry put the headset on and grabbed the microphone.

"Hello?"

"Yes, Lieutenant, what can I do for you?"

"Who is in charge there?"

"Here in the radio room or on the base?"

"The commander, over everybody."

"Oh, that would be General Grigorievich."

"I need to talk to him."

Jimmy Sunnyboy laughed. "That's not easy to arrange, Lieutenant. Would you care to tell me why you want to speak to the general?"

"I just flew in from St. Anthony Redoubt in an antique aircraft. The combined Dená and Russian defenders are facing three Russian armored columns. Our people, your people, are holed up in the rocks waiting for the attack."

"Yeah?"

"And I told them when I left that I'd be back with planes and fighters, to help them survive the Russian attack."

"Whattya want from us?"

"We got the word to stand down from you people! We need to be attacking, not sitting on our butts in the officers' mess!"

"What's your name, Lieutenant?"

"Actually it's Captain Gerald Yamato. I just got promoted."

"Congratulations, sir. I'll be right back."

The carrier wave collapsed into hash and Jerry glanced around at the other officers. They all stared at him. He concentrated on the heavy metallic-acrid odor of vacuum tubes and electricity that always registered in his mind as "radio."

"You there, Captain Yamato?" Jimmy sounded out of breath.

"Yes, I'm here."

"Okay, I'm putting on General Paul Eluska. He's in charge of the whole army while General Grigorievich is away."

"Thank you, Jimmy."

"What's the story, Captain?" the voice carried authority, interest, and empathy.

"General, this might take a few minutes." Jerry launched into the tale of his journey from the air base outside Sacramento, Republic of California, to Delta, Alaska. He left nothing out and ended with "... and the woman I love expects me to return with at least one modern aircraft to help turn the tide."

"You have a hell of a gift for story telling, Captain Yamato. Our governing council is negotiating with the

Czar through the British. All involved parties were supposed to stand down. From what you're telling me, the Russians are trying to pull another fast one on us."

Jerry glanced up at the other pilots; they were hanging on the general's words as much as he was.

"You have our leave and our blessings. Go get the bastards!"

"Thank you, General! I gotta go now."

Jerry ripped off the headset and tossed it to Sergeant Reddy.

"Make apologies for me, okay?" He raced out the door behind the other pilots.

The Ops sergeant had already hit the klaxon and a high-pitched warble pierced the air outside the building.

"Captain Yamato," the sergeant shouted, "you've got zero-three-four, okay?"

Jerry gave him a thumbs-up as he raced through the door.

★ 51 ★

Delta, Russian Amerika

"General Myslosovich, Colonel Janeki, this is Corporal Cliper," Major Riordan hesitated for a moment before continuing. "He is an Athabascan from this area. I have used his knowledge to good effect in the past."

"You're a turncoat," Colonel Janeki said.

"I am a realist, Colonel," Cliper said. "It does not take a genius to see which side is going to lose this conflict."

"I like this man," General Myslosovich said with a wide grin. "He knows of which he speaks!"

"Where are the people who live here?" Janeki asked.

Cliper's eyes took on a haunted cast.

"I don't know. I was here for three weeks about a month and a half ago. I come from far upriver and they would talk to me but there were times when I knew they were lying."

"So far he has no knowledge," Janeki said, staring at Riordan.

Riordan didn't respond. This young Russian lieutenant colonel wanted him as a trophy; he'd known it from the first moment they met. Riordan struggled to keep his face impassive: just when he'd had Myslosovich's command in his hands!

"I asked them what would happen if the Russians attacked them," Cliper continued.

Riordan tried not to show his contempt for the spare, balding Indian. He recognized him for a man who thought himself adept at manipulating others. Using him as a foil against Janeki might not work.

"They said they would take refuge in St. Anthony Redoubt."

"If they were attacked by Russians, they would go to Russians for protection?" Janeki asked, eyes wide in mock incredulity.

"That's what they said, Colonel."

"I hope you didn't pay him much," Janeki said to Riordan. "His information is as worthless as he is."

"He knew all about the magic woman, and her husband, the great warrior."

"And this helped you in what manner?"

"We knew who they were when we captured them," Riordan said sharply, instantly regretting enlarging the incident.

"So produce these people. I would speak with them."

"They escaped."

"I hope you had the guards summarily shot," Janeki said in a pompous tone.

Riordan glanced around the circle of men. Janeki had three armed men present. He suddenly realized the colonel was trying to provoke him, get him to do something stupid, and then kill him.

A male version of Bodecia, he thought wryly.

"We were all too busy fighting for our lives when it happened. The DSM ambush was cleverly laid and perfectly executed. I caution you to put nothing beyond their means."

"Well," Janeki said, his eyes wetly condescending while fastening fast on Riordan, "we're a bit more than a band of bandits, aren't we?"

Timothy Riordan had to reach deep down inside himself to his core of discipline to not tear this bastard's heart out with his teeth. He refused to give the son of a bitch the satisfaction of visible anger. Willing his eyes to be as bland as a monsignor at a baptism, he looked back at the Russian colonel.

"Well, sir, if your army of bandits can accomplish more, I'll applaud all of you."

"We fight for the Czar, for the flag of Imperial Russia," Janeki said with gravel in his voice. "If you insult this command again, I'll have you shot."

"No offense intended," Riordan let his eyes laugh at the man. "But if you try that, you'll need your entire army."

"Gentlemen!" Myslosovich said. "Please save your anger for the enemy. We need everyone we have to assure victory over the damned Dená."

"Anger, General?" Riordan said with a wide grin. "No such thing. The good colonel here and I are just establishing our bonafides, as my sainted father used to say."

Janeki visibly stifled a retort. Glancing around at the horizon, he called, "Sergeant Malute," then held General Myslosovich with his gaze. "I have an expert tracker from Kamchatka; he can follow your dreams. He will find our missing traitors and their DSM accomplices, and we will hang them all."

A small, bandy-legged man ran up, stopped at quivering attention, and saluted the colonel. "Sir?"

"I want to know where the villagers went."

"Yes, Colonel."

★ 52 ★

RCNS *Mako*
Village of Kilsnoo, Admiralty Island,
Russian Amerika

"Up periscope," Captain Vandenberg ordered.

He snapped down the control arms as the massive tube rose from its well and was peering through the lenses before the scope finished its ascent. He slowly went in a full circle before he relaxed and turned to the others on the small bridge deck.

"Well, no welcoming committee that I can see. Our security must be good." His grin couldn't disguise the tension in his eyes.

"Was someone to meet us in a boat?" Wing asked.

"No, Colonel, not at all. We're actually going to tie up to a pier for all of five minutes while you folks disembark. I was just worried that word had slipped out about our visit."

"Are all of your missions like this?" Grisha asked.

"Pretty much, General. This is one profession where paranoia is part of the job description."

"Yeah, I know what you mean."

"Excuse me, General, I've got to get you delivered."

He turned away and shouted, "Chief of the Boat, make ready to surface!"

The chief was no more than six feet away. He shouted back, "Aye, aye, Captain! All hands prepare to surface!"

Activity quickened all through the submarine and Grisha and Wing watched it all with wide eyes and total lack of understanding as the vessel made sounds different than anything they had heard before. The deck tilted upward slightly. Sergeant Major Tobias eased up next to them.

"Never in my life did I think I would find myself in one of these things," he muttered.

"Seems to work pretty good from what I've seen," Grisha replied.

"Give me the open air," Wing said. "I need to *see* my enemy."

"I concur, Colonel," Tobias said.

"Bridge watch to stations, line handling party to stations," Vandenberg ordered. The submarine began to slowly rock from side to side.

Men raced up the ladder to the conning tower, threw open the hatch and disappeared through a shower of seawater. A sailor carrying heavy jackets appeared next to them.

"Compliments of the California Navy. You folks will need these foul weather jackets; the weather out there is pretty nasty."

"Thank you!" Wing said with enthusiasm. "I was just wondering what to wear."

The pockets of each coat revealed an indigo knitted watch cap and a pair of warm gloves.

"These fellows think of everything," Tobias said.

They pulled on the gear and then followed Captain

Vandenberg up the ladder. Two sailors helped them step onto the wet steel deck. Wind-whipped rain blew past at a forty-five-degree angle.

Grisha laughed. "Damn, it smells good here!"

"How can you inhale without drowning?" Wing shouted.

The *Mako* was being pushed up against a dock by a small log tug borrowed from the local sawmill. Men on the dock threw lines to sailors along the hull of the submarine. The lines were quickly secured and tightened, pulling the sub up snug against the large rubber fenders hanging down from the dock.

On the dock, a hoist lifted a gangway across and placed it between the dock and deck of the submarine. The chief bosun gave the captain a thumbs-up.

"Good luck, General," Vandenberg shouted. "We'll be in the area if you need to leave quickly."

"Thank you, Captain. Our people owe you and your crew a party after this is all over."

"We'll look forward to it. Now, please let me get under way."

Both men smiled and shook hands. Then Grisha, moving carefully on his crutches, followed Wing and Tobias as they hurried across the gangway to the dock where a group of people in oilskins waited in the stormy afternoon.

"Grisha, how good to see you, my cousin." Paul Chernikoff extended his hand.

"Paul!" Grisha propped the crutches in his armpits and grabbed Paul's hand with both of his. "It's good to see you, too. Your brother sends his warm regards." He lowered his voice, "You and I need to speak privately very soon."

"I understand. Let's get in out of the weather."

He led them to an ancient Russian wood-burning omnibus. Once inside, the vehicle was pleasantly warm and cozy. Everyone pulled down hoods or removed rubberized mariners' hats.

For a few seconds each party looked over the other. Then Paul grinned again.

"You look healthy, cousin."

"Thanks. Except for an almost healed leg, I am. This is my wife, Colonel Wing Demoski Grigorievich, and Sergeant Major Nelson Tobias."

"Paul, I would know you anywhere. You look just like your brother," Wing said.

"Yeah, we get a lot of that. Welcome to Tlingit Country. Allow me to introduce our brand new diplomatic corps."

Grisha glanced out the window. The *Mako* had already disappeared. He turned his attention to the group. The bus moved through the storm and down a small road between stands of sixty-foot hemlock and spruce.

"General Sobolof is head of the Tlingit Nation Army and on the War Council. Colonel Augustus Paul is from New Archangel, Colonel Gregori George is from Angoon, and Lieutenant Colonel Titian Bean is from T'angass. I am from Akku, as is General Grigorievich."

"May I ask where we are being taken?" Grisha asked.

"To a safe place, Grisha," General Sobolof said. "May we dispense with formality and call one another by the names we all know?"

"Of course, Vincent," Grisha said smoothly. "If that's how you wish it to be."

"Good. How goes your war?"

"It isn't just *my* war, it's *our* war. The Imperial Russian government has ordered a cease of hostilities with the Dená Republik, the United States of America, and the Republic of California. However, I am told there is still a battle raging near Delta between a number of different armies, but I am sure we shall prevail."

"So *who* are *we* fighting?" General Sobolof asked.

"Vincent, we are all fighting your two-faced ally, the Empire of Japan."

"I know we are contemplating fighting Japan, but why are you?"

"We don't want to fight them *after* they have made military gains in Alaska. Do you not agree?"

"Yes, I do agree. But to be very candid, Grisha, we haven't much of an army to throw at them, and an even smaller navy."

"Actually, I believe we are here to discuss something different," Wing said. "Unification?"

"There are a number of viewpoints on that issue," General Sobolof said carefully. "We realize that things must change, that things *are* changing whether we wish it so or not. But we are an ancient people and have become set in our cultural ways."

As he hesitated for a moment, she plunged forward.

"You wish to change *some* things but not *everything*?" she asked with a smile.

"That's an excellent way to put it, Col—uh, Wing," Colonel George said with enthusiasm.

"So what do you want to change and what do you want to keep?" Grisha held his smile in his eyes.

The omnibus stopped.

"Please, let us discuss this over food," General Sobolof said. "You all must be hungry."

"I think we can all agree on that," Sergeant Major Tobias said, beaming all around.

The *Yéil naa*, or Raven clan house was large and comfortable. Many paintings and carvings depicting Raven decorated the walls. At the far end stood an eight-foot traditional carving of Raven done in highly polished black stone. The yellow cedar floor was nearly reflective enough to use as a mirror.

In the center of the building stood a blazing rock fireplace open on all four sides, and every rock was carved with hieroglyphics. Each red cedar plank wall featured a beautiful Chilkat blanket flanked by button blankets.

Wing turned to stare back at the entrance. The entire doorway was the open mouth of a huge totemic frog.

"That's the *Kiks.ádi* door," Colonel Paul said. "We are especially proud of that work."

"You have every right to be," Wing said in a hushed tone. "It's magnificent."

Four women stood close to the great fireplace, cooking on wide sheets of steel suspended over the flames. The aroma of exotic foods filled the clan house and a wave of *rightness* washed over him as Grisha suddenly realized how hungry he was and how familiar this all smelled.

★ 53 ★

Delta

"See?" Jimmy Deerkiller whispered. "Right through those rocks there, it's the guy who was asking all them questions a couple months ago."

Ben Teske stared hard, licked his lips and eased his .338 magnum up, balanced it on the rock in front of them and squinted through the telescopic sight. "Yep, it's him all right."

"There's someone with him," Jimmy hissed.

Ben moved the weapon slightly. "Looks like an Eskimo in a Russian uniform."

"They're trackin' us," Jimmy said as he lifted his weapon and laid it across the boulder beside Ben's.

"You take right and I'll take left," Ben said, peering through the scope.

"I'll do the count." Jimmy licked his lips again. "One. Two. Fire!"

The two trackers both fell backwards with destroyed heads.

Ben stared down the trail. Jimmy bent over, "Don't forget your brass."

"Yeah. Y'know, I think I killed a couple guys in

the fight that night, but I couldn't see 'em like this: up close and in the daytime."

"I think you better get used to it, brother."

Pelagian crept up behind them.

"Okay, guys, as soon as you see more troops coming toward you, fall back to the first line. Okay?"

"We'll do it, Pelagian." Jimmy turned and watched the big man fade into the brush. "Y'know, when I was a kid I used to be afraid of him."

"Why?"

"He's so damned big. I used to think he was some sorta monster."

"I always felt safe around him," Ben said, still watching the slope below them. "He never—hey, did you see that?"

"What?" Jimmy stared down into the hazy summer afternoon.

"I thought I saw someone, but they dropped before I could really be sure."

"Scan your side," Jimmy said and went silent.

They intently watched the 180 degrees of slope before them. Nothing moved; the ground lay bereft of life. Ben found himself staring at the boot propped up on a rock, where one of the trackers had fallen.

Motion flickered on the left in his peripheral vision and he snapped his gaze onto it without moving his head: two men in mottled green-to-black field dress. He grabbed Jimmy and pulled him down with him as he dropped behind the boulder.

"Wha—?" Jimmy blurted. The sound of his voice was abruptly obliterated by heavy machine gun fire chipping rock and blasting the top of their boulder. Ricochets whined off into space.

"Damn!" Jimmy said. "Thanks, man."

"We need to withdraw, right now."

"I'm right behind you."

★ 54 ★

Over the Dená Republik

Jerry felt totally at home for the first time in what seemed like forever. The P-61 responded under his hands like an eager lover who understands exactly what is wanted of her. Magda's presence suddenly suffused him and he forced the thought of her out of his mind.

This was deadly business and he needed to maintain vigilance if he wanted to kiss her again.

"Captain Yamato," Colonel Shipley's voice crackled in the headset. "You know where we're going, so you take point."

"Yes, sir!"

The Alaskan landscape rushed beneath them in full spring fecundity and bright morning brilliance. Numerous tree-shadowed lakes, large and small, reflected their swift passage. Yamato turned to the south and the flight crossed the wide, brown Yukon River and paralleled the famous Russia-Canada Highway. Jerry knew it led to Magda and St. Anthony Redoubt.

Shipley ordered the ten fighters to spread out. "Keep your eyes peeled; this is still Russian air space and until President Reagan says otherwise, we're still at war."

Jerry kept his eyes on the road below them, noticing the small outposts every few miles. What had Magda called them? He felt completely serene and ready to blow hell out of the Russian armor gathering at St. Anthony Redoubt.

"Colonel, Ellis here!"

"Go ahead, roger."

"We have bandits at two o'clock."

"Bandits?" someone said with evident disbelief.

"Cut the chatter!" Shipley ordered. "Okay, I see them. Ellis, Fowler, put your glasses on them and tell me I'm wrong."

"Wrong about what, Skipper?" Jerry asked.

"I count six Russian Yormolaev-2 bombers with eight Yak fighters and a Sturmovik flying cover," Fowler reported. "Looks like they're headed for Chena or Fort Yukon."

"I concur," Ellis said. "They must be out of St. Nicholas Airdrome."

"I don't think they've seen us yet," Shipley said. "Probably because they're an easy 5,000 feet higher than we are. Captain Currie, alert Dená Command, we're going to engage."

Jerry's heart fell, but he knew Colonel Shipley was making the only realistic decision.

"We're gonna hit them as hard as we can," Shipley said. "Major Ellis, you are now Sucker Punch Two. Take Currie, Donaldson, Cooper and Cassaro, cut right and stay on the deck until you're under the bombers, then blow them out of the air."

"Yes, sir." The five Eurekas banked and dropped almost to treetop level on a course to intercept the now-distinct Russian aircraft.

"Fowler, Yamato, Hafs, and Kirby—you're with me, Sucker Punch One. We're going to bore straight in and hit the fighters. If we're real lucky and they've all got hangovers, we might pull this off."

"This is a lot more interesting than hitting an armored column," First Lieutenant Hafs said. "And I love the odds."

"I always knew you were crazy, Mark," Yamato said with a grim laugh. "This just proves it."

"As soon as we know they've seen us," Lieutenant Colonel Shipley said, "drop your wing tanks. We're going to need all the agility we can muster."

Jerry felt the adrenaline singing in his veins while fear for Magda's situation ate at his guts. *We've gotta do this fast*, he thought. *I've still got to keep my word*.

The Yaks grew in his gunsights and he flipped off the safety cap over the trigger button on his stick. Suddenly the Yaks dropped away from the bombers and turned toward Shipley's flight. The ruse had worked.

As if on cue, the wing tanks dropped from beneath the wings of all five Eurekas. They roared up to meet the enemy.

★ 55 ★

Delta

"They're hiding up there in the rocks," Major Riordan reported to the general and lieutenant colonel. "It cost us two good men to get that intelligence. I've ordered a squad to engage the enemy and report their position. We'll envelope the area with cannon fire and eliminate the possibility of an attack. Then we can arrest the surviving traitors from Chena Redoubt and hang them."

General Myslosovich awarded him a wide smile.

Riordan wasn't watching the general; his eyes were on the lieutenant colonel.

"Not bad," Lieutenant Colonel Janeki said. "I would have done exactly the same thing. But how can you be sure they're all in the open?"

"No matter what, they'll be softened up after the barrage."

"I approve."

The radioman in Riordan's command car called out, "Major, the transmission is breaking up, but they're receiving fire."

"Coordinates?"

"Range four, vector three, sir."

Riordan snapped the numbers to the sergeant beside him and within thirty seconds every tank in the command fired at the ordered target. Explosions echoed back to them, one after another.

The shelling lasted five minutes, then abruptly ceased.

"Who's going to go look?" Lieutenant Colonel Janeki asked, staring at Riordan.

"My men are already up there. They'll report soon."

★ 56 ★

Battle of Delta

First Squad, Company B, of the International Freekorps, crept up the mountain. A week ago they had mustered thirty effectives; since the midnight attack of a few days ago they were down to nineteen. Lieutenant Alex Strom felt electrified with every sense wide open for input.

His record listed battles in Afghanistan, China, the Belgian Congo, Portuguese East Africa, and all the way back to his first as a Royal Austrian Fusilier private at the Siege of Berlin. Over the years and wars, he had worked his way up the muster list.

This was his second command as a lieutenant. His elevation to commissioned status came in the French Foreign Legion while serving in Africa. If this current arrangement failed, he could always return to France, which he now considered as home.

But the money was so much better in his present situation. Major Riordan had been less than forthright when he told the battalion they had a new war and they would draw standard pay. He hadn't mentioned the identity of the employer, nor when the next payday was scheduled.

He's never screwed us over, Strom thought. *Not yet.* He had yet to decide if he believed that Riordan would do that. As a naturalized Frenchman serving under an Irishman, he held a quiet skepticism as to the commander's grasp of reality.

He halted and waved his men down before thinking about it. There had been a noise, a very small thing, but yet something different than before. He waited, patience as much a part of him as his spleen, and just as hidden.

There! He heard the sound of a foot pushing at, or slipping on, gravel. Not with effort, he decided, but in eagerness. There were close to a firing line; someone waited for them.

He pointed to two troopers and motioned them forward. Both were well trained and veterans of at least three engagements. But in his heart of hearts, Strom didn't care for either of them.

They moved up the slope, keeping low and maintaining vigilance. They passed Strom's forward position. He watched them edge around boulders and slide down into what depressions the land offered.

They disappeared from sight. The lieutenant realized he was holding his breath and forced himself to continue breathing. He strained to hear anything, the least sound, or slightest suggestion of resistance, anything alive beyond their position.

The ground they traversed was torn and blasted, only splinters and pieces of leaves were left of the brush and trees which once grew here. Boulders held their positions but sat split and fractured; their shards had blasted through the area at high velocity. Strom took it all in silently.

Sergeant Verley, his immediate subordinate, motioned from the far side of their position.

Take cover? They were under cover! What did he mean by—?

He registered the rumble then and quickly screamed back at the men behind him, "Take cover. It's an avalanche!"

The universe filled with hurling rock.

★ 57 ★

Refuge, Dená Republik

Magda watched the succession of broken men and women being carried into the Refuge and wondered how this could have happened, not realizing she was speaking aloud.

"We didn't expect the artillery," Gregori Andrew said, making a sling for his bloody left arm. "Them rock pieces were flying all over the place. The one that did this"—he lifted his left arm with his right hand—"flew right through one of them Russian soldiers like he was a thin sack of blood."

"Go over to my mother, there; she'll help you." Magda felt angry, sick to her stomach, guilty, and relieved all at the same time. Her scout patrol was scheduled to begin five minutes after the attack started, therefore they were all still in the Refuge when the shells began falling.

Scout Two, returning from reconnoiter, had been wiped out.

"Magda," Uncle Frank said as he approached. "I'll bet I know what you're thinking." He put his hands on her shoulders and stared into her face. "It's called the 'fortunes of war' and nobody knows what will happen. It just wasn't your turn."

Her eyes felt hot and she didn't want to cry. "I hear your words but my heart still doesn't understand. Maybe next week or next month I'll finally get this all straight, but not yet. Right now I've got to get my squad moving. We don't have any eyes out there watching. Thanks for the support, Major." She saluted and he returned it.

Her squad consisted of a corporal and five privates. Even a week ago nobody had bothered with rank, but now everything needed to be exact and military.

Corporal Anna Demoski stood when Magda approached. "I've got the guys all ready to go, Sergeant." She handed Magda her pack and weapon.

"Thanks for minding my gear, Corporal. Let's move out."

The five privates—four men and one woman—rose to their feet and followed without saying a word. All prior levity had vanished with the artillery barrage. It finally hit home: they were in a shooting, and killing, war.

They passed through the wide cave mouth, which was being closed up as quickly as the work crew could manage. The passage to the outside twisted back and forth. Large boulders were being levered into a wall complete with firing slits backed by yet more rock so a satchel charge or a grenade would only harm the defenders in that location.

Only the turrets on the two Russian tanks could be seen under the ceiling of rock. Nothing was built higher than their lowest firing elevation. Machine guns poked through the wall like spines on a rock porcupine.

Magda stopped her people at the very end of the passage. Two sentries peered out at the summer morning.

"See anything?" she asked.

"Nothing yet, but we know they're out there somewhere."

"We'll get back to you on their location, okay?" She patted the radio strapped to her side, then waved her people forward and led them into the deadly open.

★ 58 ★

Battle of Delta

"I want you to go up that hill at speed," Lieutenant Colonel Janeki said to Infantry Captain Koseki. "Your wave will be followed by another, fifty meters behind you. Shoot everything that moves and any person who does not. Take no chances, understand?"

"Yes, Colonel! After the barrage there should be nothing alive on that mountain."

"That was our estimation also. But there were enough people left to trigger an avalanche. They can't engineer two of those on one mountain. But still—take no chances."

Captain Koseki saluted, clicked off the safety on his machine gun, and motioned his men forward. Sixty heavily armed troopers started up the slope as quickly as they could manage. The center of the wave had the easy task of following the tracks of many vehicles on the closest thing to a road the mountain offered.

The captain appreciated the honor of commanding the assault, but at the same time he fought to keep his fear at bay. *One had to ask,* he thought, *where was the destination of the vehicles they followed? Were*

*the Dená naive enough to leave their army exposed
on a mountainside?*

For two decades, Branif Koseki's father had served
as a counselor to the Czar. Baron Koseki went into
a total rage when Branif told him he had joined the
Imperial Army.

"Serving in the military is completely beneath you,
beneath this family! I will arrange for a commission
immediately. If you insist on playing the toy soldier,
at least you must be an officer."

Three years beyond the tirade, Captain Branif Koseki
had not again laid eyes on his father. *The old bastard
wouldn't understand anyway,* he thought. Watching
out for those who served under you was as alien to
the baron's mind as walking on the moon.

Sergeant Turgev's right fist shot into the air and
every man in line went to ground. Captain Koseki
felt grateful for the plentiful boulders, some newly
arrived, which offered shelter. He held his hand
open, palm up.

Turgev pointed to his right and left, held three
fingers stiff for a long moment and then grabbed his
wrist with his left hand. Machine gun nests, three
defenders each. Captain Koseki nodded understanding.

How the hell could they have lived through the
barrage? Fox dens? Trenches? Caves? He focused on
the tactical issue at hand.

He motioned for three men on both sides to go
wide around the enemy flank. Then he signaled for
two widely spaced men to move forward, along with
Lieutenant Taksis. The lieutenant gave him a withering
look and the three men moved slowly up the mountain.

Captain Koseki thought his lieutenant was a coward

who could still be turned into a fighting man, and he had just granted him the opportunity. The flankers faded from sight and Koseki felt sweat beading on his forehead beneath his helmet. Deep in his soul he cursed Colonel Janeki.

Heavy machine gun fire erupted on the right, frighteningly loud, far too close, and from a weapon larger than any of his men carried. A high-pitched shriek climbed to unbelievable decibels before choking off abruptly. A Russian grenade, distinctive with its flat popping sound—the men called them "Czar's farts"—exploded somewhere up in the rocks and brush.

Captain Koseki held his hand up and waved his men forward. He was the first to move slowly up the mountain, hunched over and frightened more of appearing cowardly in front of his men than of dying. He glanced back at his men.

Sergeant Turgev directed two squads toward the machine gun nests he had spied. The soldiers stayed as close to the ground as possible as they moved forward.

Machine gun fire abruptly tore through three of the soldiers, dropping them down into the rocks with the hammer blows of heavy rounds. Sergeant Turgev's men opened up, firing beyond Captain Koseki's field of vision.

Koseki and the men around him edged upward, eyes wide and casting about for targets and death. The captain eased around a large boulder and slid behind another. To his right the rocks abruptly decreased in size, creating an inviting path up the mountain that promised ease of movement.

Sergeant Turgev's men continued firing and the staccato roar of two heavy machine guns now bounced off the rocky slope. Captain Koseki knew that basic military logic ordained more than two guns would be guarding this slope. Corporal Kasilof edged up beside him.

"Do you want me to send somebody around that way?" He pointed toward the open slope.

"They would be killed instantly. That's a natural field of fire that even the poorest soldier couldn't help but notice. Our foes do not seem to be fools."

Corporal Kasilof's eyes widened as he stared at the slope. "My apologies, Captain. This is my first combat experience."

"Spread the word, when I blow my whistle, everyone goes over these rocks. We must do it together or the effect of surprise will be lost."

"Yes, Captain." The corporal hurried back and spoke to every man. One by one, they all turned and stared at Captain Koseki.

He climbed up as far as possible without show- ing himself above the covering boulder and braced himself. A glance back at his men determined they all followed his example. The first time he put the whistle in his mouth he trembled so violently that it fell from his lips and dangled on its cord.

He cursed and jammed the whistle into his mouth so hard he chipped a tooth. Subduing his fear for the moment, he blew a shrill blast and leapt up and over the boulder, firing his machine gun.

★ 59 ★

Over Russian Amerika

Captain Jerry Yamato knew his aircraft to be superior to the Yak growing in his gunsights. At 3,000 meters he fired short bursts from his wing cannons and watched the Yak run right into the tracers. The Russian craft shuddered and smoke poured from behind the propeller. The plane seemed to shrug and nosed toward the ground.

The fighter immediately behind it came through its predecessor's smoke like an avenging angel, cannon firing and no deviation in course as it headed straight for Jerry.

Jerry rolled to the left and dove at full speed before pulling the Eureka up at a steep angle to come up behind the Yak. At least that was the plan. He snapped *Satori*—every P-61 he flew induced *satori*—around and the Yak wasn't there.

Immediately he rolled to the right and tracers streamed past the cockpit. He felt at least two rounds hit the fuselage as he pulled up and fought for altitude. Glancing over his shoulder, he saw the sun flash off the Yak's wings as it pulled up to follow him.

He became aware of the radio chatter.

"Dave, you got one on your tail!"

"Good shooting, Currie, but watch out for the belly gun on the one behind it."

"Colonel Shipley, you got one coming straight down at you!"

Jerry looked back at the Yak. It had reached its performance ceiling and rolled back in a dive to lower altitude. Jerry grinned and nosed over, roaring down on the now vulnerable Yak with his wing guns blazing.

The Yak shook under the barrage as first smoke and then flame boiled out of it. It nosed over and hurtled toward the earth 6,000 feet below. Jerry didn't see a parachute.

Bullets smashed into his plane and two rounds came through the cockpit, barely missing his head. He felt the air movement of one as it passed his cheek. Suppressing panic, he twisted to the left and climbed as fast as the bird would go.

Abruptly the belly of another Yak filled his sights and he squeezed off a long burst and veered to the right as the Yak exploded, filling the sky with debris. A burning tire streaked through the air and glanced off *Satori's* nacelle. Jerry quickly thanked his ancestors that the thing had missed his prop.

"Colonel Shipley, Fowler here. I'm hit." The words poured out in a rush.

"How bad, Dave?"

Jerry could hear the man's rasping breath over the radio and twisted around trying to locate the others. His acrobatic flying had taken him over a mile away from the main fight. Unwittingly, he had moved close to the bombers, now fighting for their lives against Sucker Punch Two. One of the birds from Sucker

Punch One flew toward him, trailing heavy smoke. Jerry realized it was Fowler.

"Ain't gonna...make it. Chest wound. Losing lotsa blood, hard ta see."

"Where you going, Dave?" Jerry asked.

"Wanna take...a bomber"—he coughed and his plane dipped and bobbed up again—"...with me."

Jerry looked over at the four remaining bombers in time to see one of the Eurekas take a burst of fire from the leading bomber's belly gun. The Eureka tumbled and burst into flame.

"Bail out!" he shouted. "Bail out!"

"Major Ellis just bought the farm." Jerry thought it was Cassaro's voice.

"Tell 'im to wait," Fowler said. "I'll go with..."

Jerry saw Fowler's plane streak by. The cockpit was shot to pieces and part of the tail elevator ripped away as he watched. The plane arrowed directly into the leading bomber, colliding amidships.

A bright light filled the sky as the entire bomb load detonated, atomizing both aircraft. The shock wave knocked *Satori* out of level flight, rolling her violently to his left and into a spin. Jerry fought to pull her back into level flight. The second bomber took massive amounts of debris through the cockpit, nose gun, and top gun mount, killing those crew members. The bomber went into an earthward spiral.

"Jesus," someone breathed over the radio.

"Got him!" Hafs shouted. Another Yak torched out of the sky.

The two remaining Russian bombers turned left 180 degrees and dropped to a lower altitude as they abruptly reversed course.

"They're running away," Captain Currie said. "Want us to pursue, Skipper?"

"Negative that. Let the Yaks go, too. We've stopped their mission. I want a status report from everyone. Currie?"

"Quarter tank of gas, about a third of my ammo left, no damage that I know of."

"Cassaro?"

"Same on fuel, little bit less ammo, and I've got a piece shot out of my tail."

"Can you still maneuver safely?"

"I shot down the bastard that did it, so I guess so."

"Cooper?"

"Lead me to them!"

"Yamato?"

"Fuel at one quarter, ammo half gone, multiple hits including cockpit but no injuries and I'm still airworthy."

"Kirby?"

"Good to go, Skipper."

"Hafs?"

"I'm with everyone else on fuel and ammo, no hits and I scratched a Yak."

"Good work, men. Captain Yamato, you nailed two of them, didn't you?"

"Yes, sir. Can we go after the armored column now?"

"We have enough fuel to hit them once and then we haul ass back to Fort Yukon, got it?"

Seven comm clicks answered.

"Yamato, lead the way."

★ 60 ★

Battle of Delta

Magda and her scouts entered the front line of Refuge's defense. Anyone farther out was an enemy or terribly lost. No matter how you cut it, they would be targets.

The line consisted of four .30 caliber machine gun emplacements joined by a well-protected trench feeding into the second line of defense, 100 yards to the rear.

"They're on the other side of those boulders, Magda," Tom Richards whispered out of the side of his mouth. "You're better off here for the time being, okay?"

"Is that an order, Lieutenant?" She smiled when he glanced at her. She liked Tom. He had more Yup'ik blood than Athabascan, but he was a clever leader and the DSM could use a lot more just like him.

"For ten minutes, okay?"

Machine gun fire on the far right blotted out her response and everyone in the trench readied weapons.

"They're probing, Tom," one of his soldiers said.

"I know, Howard. Be ready for them."

Magda eased to the left to fill in the wide space between the machine gun emplacement and the rest of the people in the trench. Anna Demoski automatically moved equidistant between Magda and the soldier on the other side of her. Magda studied the terrain with the eye of a hunter.

The left flank Dená gun emplacements were within 30 meters of each other. Both had incredible fields of fire across rocky ground and could be brought to bear on the boulders in the center of the line. Putting herself on the other side, Magda winced when she realized what the enemy faced coming up that steep slope.

"They should just go home," she muttered, "and leave us alone."

Two heartbeats later, Russian soldiers poured over and around the boulders, screaming, firing light machine guns ineffectually into the air and at rocks. The Dená line answered with immediate precision.

The machine gun emplacements cut the attackers down with surgical skill. The attack foundered in less than a minute and ebbed back into the rocks leaving at least thirty causalities.

"I want volunteers," Lieutenant Richards snapped. "We need to pursue and harass."

"My squad is on it," Magda said, waving her people forward.

"Sergeant Laughlin," Richards yelled, "you and your squad go with them."

Athabascan warriors moved quickly and quietly among the boulders, intent on their mission.

★ 61 ★

Battle of Delta

"Majeur Riordan!"

Riordan turned to his executive officer. "René?"

The small man glanced around at the men working on machinery, cleaning weapons, laying about smoking and gabbing. He fixed his eyes on Riordan and harshly whispered, "The Russians are going to arrest you!"

"Say what? Why?" He put his hand on his holstered 9mm. "Or for that bloody matter, how?"

"They know about the mechanized scout incident."

Riordan scowled, glanced around, looked back at his comrade. "And how the hell did they tumble to that?"

"Someone sent them a message. I don't know who. The message said you shot a Russian officer in the head, at close quarters, from behind."

Riordan felt a chill slide down his spine and freeze his scrotum. He opened his mouth twice before he could actually say anything. "God's cod piece, René, *you* didn't even know that, only I did!"

"How could this be known by anyone?" René asked.

"Someone had to be there; someone I obviously didn't see. Jesus wept, we were out in the wilderness!"

"You must flee or they will have you on charges, *Majeur*."

Riordan felt sweat beading on his forehead. He was acutely aware of the smell of diesel exhaust and cordite, and of the fear that suddenly slid over his mind. The old anger welled up, the absolute source of his driving energy, breaking through bonds perfected over the years, refusing to be internalized one moment longer.

"They need me, damn them! Nothing I've done in the past can stop my greatness, my future."

"*Majeur*," René said softly, as if soothing a frightened child, "I have for you the motorcycle, just here, *non*?" He pointed to their BMW. "I will tell them you have gone on reconnaissance, to find a way around the enemy defenses, *non*?"

His hard-earned training kicked in and Riordan collected himself in an instant. "Yes, you're absolutely right, René. Thank you, my friend. I'll sneak in after nightfall and we'll take it from there."

"*Oui*. Now hurry; they will be here soonest."

Riordan mounted the motorcycle, noted that it carried water, rations, even a sleeping bag. He snapped the cover of his holster shut, grabbed the goggles hanging off the handlebars and pulled them on.

"René, I'll be back." The engine caught on the first kick and he accelerated off through the war machines and soldiers, heading for the rear. If he had glanced in the mirror, he would have seen René wave in farewell. But he only had eyes for the road ahead.

★ 62 ★

Lieutenant Colonel Janeki pondered the report from the only noncommissioned officer to survive the assault on the mountain. "How many rounds do we have for the cannon?"

"Approximately three hundred shells remaining, Colonel," Major Brodski said.

"This is the only enemy strongpoint before Chena, is it not?"

"Yes, Colonel."

"We cannot advance with this pocket of rebellion and potential assassination at our backs. Use half of the remaining ammunition; shell that damned mountainside until every boulder is reduced to sand."

Major Brodski saluted and turned to the waiting staff officers. In moments the first rounds whistled over and impacted the mountain. The barrage settled into a constant cacophony of high explosives.

"Colonel, there is the matter of the letter."

"What letter is that, Leonid?"

"The letter that accuses Major Riordan of murdering a Russian officer."

"Have you been able to find him?"

"I haven't heard back from the provost marshal, Colonel. I anticipate word at any moment."

A huge cloud rose from beneath the rain of destruction on the mountainside. Janeki peered up where the enemy had chosen to make their stand and tried to fathom their decision. A scout car stopped near him and two MPs stepped out with a mercenary captain between them.

Both MPs saluted and the sergeant reported. "Colonel Janeki, this is Captain Flérs of the—"

"I know who he's with," Janeki said crisply. "What about him?"

"He was observed aiding the escape of Major Riordan, sir."

Janeki turned cold eyes on the captain. "Captain Flérs, how did Riordan know he was being sought by our provost marshal?"

"I told him, Colonel."

"You are his second-in-command, Captain Flérs?"

"*Oui.* For the past three years I have had that honor."

"So there *is* honor among thieves and murderers?"

"We are neither of those things." Captain Flérs kept his tone conversational but Janeki detected a flash in the man's eyes that promised retribution. "We are professional soldiers for hire. We are very good at our profession and have enjoyed many successes."

"Do you consider mass murder a 'success'?"

"I do not know what you speak of, Colonel."

"Three, four days ago, did your brigands not kill every man in a Russian Army scout unit in order to rob them and steal their vehicles?"

Janeki saw the fleeting expression of the guilty

flash across the Frenchman's face. Flérs blinked and stared at Janeki.

"I don't know what you are talking about, Colonel. We did no such—"

"Take him out and shoot him!" Janeki bellowed, startling everyone in the area.

Two troopers had the presence of mind to grab the stunned Captain Flérs.

"Sir?" the MP sergeant said. "You want him shot, now?"

"Yes. He's a lying French weasel who abetted the murder of scores of Russian soldiers and—"

"Wait!" Captain René Flérs' practiced nonchalance fled from his face and fear crawled from every pore. "I had nothing to do with it, I swear." Tears leaked from the corners of his eyes and he blinked through them.

"The *majeur* listens to no one," he said with a catch in his voice. "He makes all *le réglement du jeu*—"

"Speak English or Russian," Janeki snapped.

"Sorry," Flérs said with a sniff. "He makes all the rule of the games. He thinks he is some sort of avenging Irish god."

"What does Irish have to do with it?"

"*Mon dieu*, where would one start?" Flérs threw his hands in the air, finally breaking the MPs' grips. His eyes widened even further.

"Only to suggest a question and he begins the lecture! The inhumanity of the British against the Irish is all he can speak of. And the Czar he is cousin to the King of England."

Janeki blanched. "Do you mean the man is an anarchist?"

A Gallic shrug from Flérs. "The case can be made, I'm afraid."

Janeki turned to the provost marshal, a senior lieutenant promoted from the ranks for heroism. "Place this man in solitary confinement; he is to speak to no one. Very carefully isolate the mercenary troops, disarm them, and place them under arrest."

"Colonel, we are in the middle of a battle. I have but ten men to police this regiment now, and there are over a hundred mercenaries."

"They will listen to me," Captain Flérs said in his executive officer voice. "They will fight for you."

"They murdered Russian soldiers! You didn't give them a chance to fight for their lives—"

"But you need us!" Flérs cried out, his face twisted in fear and supplication.

Janeki hesitated, thought for a moment. "All right; call your men together. Sergeant, you go with him."

"Thank you, *mon* Colonel. You will not regret this."

The men walked away toward the majority of the mercenaries waiting to go into battle.

Janeki stepped closer to his provost marshal and put his mouth within inches of the man's ear: "Lieutenant Kubitski, here's what I want you to do."

★ 63 ★

Battle of Delta

In a pocket between three boulders, Magda hugged the heaving earth as the salvos impacted around her. She and her squad had dropped Russians all the way down the slope. She stopped her people when they were within three hundred meters of the road and waved them back toward the Dená lines.

Halfway up, the mountain erupted in front of them. The first shells smashed four of her people into gory atoms and she screamed for the remaining troops to take cover. Armageddon rolled over them.

Each time a shell landed, the ground and rocks sprang into the air, hitting her, pummeling her, striking at her from directions she could not anticipate. It was a huge club of sounds, repeating over and over and over. The noise and concussion filled her soul with abject terror.

She looked around at her team, watching the flesh on their faces shake, their eyes going bright as if ready to cry, blood draining from faces leaving them pale as diluted tea. Her people looked older, flabby, and the only sounds she heard between the smashing shells were cries of prayer, pain, the rattle of teeth, and whimpering that reminded her of a badly injured dog.

As the barrage continued, the members of her team found shelter that, true or false, promised protection, and huddled where they could. The very earth proved to be their enemy as well as their salvation. Suddenly the world grew quiet and she suspected a trap.

After a full minute she raised her head and looked around.

"Sergeant Laughlin!" she yelled. Her voice sounded faint in her own ears.

The rocks and dust absorbed her shout. Nothing moved. No response answered her call.

"Anybody!" she shrieked at the mountainside.

"M-Magda?" a voice scarcely above a whisper registered on her consciousness.

She twisted from one side to the other trying to ascertain its source. A dusty, bloody hand reached over a rock and clawed at it, seeking leverage. Magda scurried over, grabbed the hand and hauled the person into view.

Corporal Anna Demoski bled from both nostrils and one ear.

"My God, Anna, are you all right?" Magda pulled the woman close to her and eased her down onto the rocky ground.

"Don't really know. I hurt like hell, y'know? Anybody else alive?"

"I'm not sure. Hell, I'm not sure we're alive!"

Anna laughed and a droplet of bloody sputum dropped from the corner of her mouth and hung, glistening, in the dust-filled air for a long moment before sagging to her uniform jacket and soaking into the sweat-darkened material. Anna visibly ebbed.

"I'm so sorry, my friend," Magda blurted.

"That bad, huh?"

"I really don't know. You don't look good to me, but I'm not a—" She threw her head back and screamed, "Medic!"

Two small men abruptly appeared. Magda thought they were a hallucination; they looked identical.

"Hi, I'm Tiberius Titus," one said, quickly examining Anna's wounds. The other winked and said, "I'm Titian Titus. We're twins."

"I'd have never guessed," Magda said, frowning. "Is she going to be okay?"

"She's concussed," Tiberius said.

"This isn't necessarily fatal," Titian said.

"But it could be," Tiberius added.

"I like how you each cover the other's ass," Magda spat.

"We'll do the best we can, Magda," Titian said.

"We promise," Tiberius said with a nod.

She backed away while they eased Anna onto a litter and then they disappeared through the rocks. Magda sat for a moment, waiting for others to make themselves known, then followed the Titus twins, wondering if she would see tomorrow's dawn.

★ 64 ★

Over the Battle of Delta

"There they are, Major!" Jerry Yamato yelled into his microphone. "Sitting ducks!"

"My gawd," Colonel Shipley said. "Look at all the targets! Hit 'em, guys, they're the last of the Russian forces threatening us!"

The flight dropped and strafed the column below them. Some antiaircraft fire answered, but nothing of any consequence. The squadron roared over, leaving death and wreckage in their wake. Then they turned and did it again.

Jerry noticed that most of the armor was in the front of the column and concentrated on hitting as much of it as he could. As he strafed the hulking machines he wished he had rockets or bombs to smash them. But he didn't.

As the squadron strafed the Russians for a third time, a click sounded in Jerry's headphones.

"That's it, guys," Lieutenant Colonel Shipley said. "Head back to the barn."

As replies clicked over the radio, Jerry turned and flew low over the huge cave, waggling his wings, before turning north with his squadron.

★ 65 ★

Battle of Delta

With Colonel Janeki's words bouncing about in his head, Senior Lieutenant Kubitski's knuckles whitened as he grasped the wheel of the scout car.

Get a trooper next to every one of the mercenaries and on your signal have them kill every one of those bastard bandits!

Leonid wasn't sure he could give that order. It was murder; therefore it had to be an unlawful order. But to defy Lieutenant Colonel Janeki was suicide. That the man was unstable had become manifestly evident even to the lowest private.

He didn't hear the aircraft or he would have immediately taken evasive measures. In one heart-stopping moment, the windscreen of the car vomited out onto the hood—Captain René Flérs blew to pieces before the man could even scream—and something punched Kubitski in the side of the head so hard that the impact flung him through the door and he was unconscious before he hit the ground.

Nails hammered into his head as adrenaline relentlessly shuddered him awake. He pressed his right hand to his head and pushed himself up with the left. Blood flowed from a perfectly straight gouge on the side of his head; a large caliber round had grazed his scalp.

If it had so much as nicked bone, his face would have been blown off. His massive headache suddenly seemed oddly reassuring.

A bullet whined by and he realized he was in the line of fire at about the same speed as his well-honed reflexes kicked in and he scrambled toward the back of the nearest large object.

Lieutenant Kubitski observed that he was taking cover behind a burning tank, a *Russian* burning tank. He willed his mind to function and surveyed the area with a soldier's eye. His scout car had rolled and now fed a petrol fire that engulfed the entire vehicle.

The battered red and blue kepi that Captain René Flérs had kept perfectly straight on his head lay in tatters in the middle of the road; blood and heavier material adhering to it pushed the felt and leather into the dirt. What was left of the captain was being cremated.

Half of the vehicles around him were in flames. Men screaming in fear and anger suddenly became incredibly louder as his ears popped and instantly added more pain to his head.

Something had gone incredibly wrong here.

★ 66 ★

Near Delta, Russian Amerika

The night before when the Russians began fighting the force in front of them, Colonel Buhrman had waved his men into cover. They went into cold bivouac and got what rest they could.

The morning's first Russian high velocity shell had dropped onto the mountain approximately an hour earlier. Every fifteen minutes after that, another shell had been fired. Buhrman was counting down the seconds until the next one when a man walked into the middle of their area with both hands in the air and an automatic rifle slung over his shoulder.

Buhrman shot to his feet. "Jackson, you sonuvabitch, you trying to get killed by friendly fire?"

Colonel Benny Jackson grinned and lowered his hands.

"C'mon, Del, you were the only one of your troops that saw me, and I know you wouldn't shoot me."

"How'd you do that? I have men out in every direction."

"Well, every fifteen minutes they couldn't hear much. On top of that, they weren't anticipating anyone coming through their lines from the rear. The only guy

I saw was tightening the laces on his leggings, and he only looked down at his hands for thirty seconds."

"Good thing you weren't on the other side," Buhrman said with a rueful grin. "Where are the rest of your people?"

"About a thousand yards beyond your perimeter. I wasn't about to chance the life of anyone else before making contact with you."

"What are you doing here?"

"What do you think? I'm joining up with you to fight the Russians."

"Good. I think the Dená are going to need all the help they can get. Once the—"

Another cannon shell screamed into the mountain.

"As I was saying, once the Russians figured out they'd been fighting their own people yesterday, I knew they were really going to be pissed."

Jackson chuckled. "Oh, that's precious, their own people! Let's just hope they were all good shots. But where are the Dená?"

Buhrman turned his head and quietly said, "Major Smolst."

"Heinrich!" Jackson shouted as the man materialized from the brush. "How good to see you!"

The men shook hands and grinned at each other. For the first time in a very long time, Colonel Buhrman was at a loss for words. Finally he cleared his throat and said, "So you two know each other?"

"Colonel Jackson was with Grisha when he and I reunited after a ten-year absence."

"Yeah, and in the middle of one of the coldest damn nights I've ever experienced," Jackson added. "My piss froze before it hit the ground, I shit you not."

"I believe you. Heinrich, have your sergeant tell him about Refuge," Buhrman said.

Sergeant Jerry Titus filled Jackson in on the story and location of Refuge.

"Okay, Del," Benny said. "What do *you* think we should do?"

"Link up with the Dená, and very carefully. Right now they've got itchy trigger fingers."

"Why don't we wait for the Dená to make a move and then we hit the Russians in the ass?" Jackson watched as Buhrman thought about it.

"That's good, Benny; that way we don't have to worry about anyone getting hit by friendly fire. But do you think the Dená will do something offensive or continue to maintain their defensive position?"

"They started this revolution because they were tired of taking shit from the Russians. I'll give you two-to-one odds they hit the Russians within the hour."

Buhrman's grin seemed wolfish. "No bet. I remember that poker party down in the Arizona no-man's-land. You only give odds when you have an ace in your hand."

"You're never going to forgive me for beating you in poker, are you?"

"I'm never going to forgive you for *cheating* me in poker!"

They both laughed at once.

"Bring your guys in; I'll let my people know. Glad you're here, Benny."

"Likewise, Del."

Colonel Buhrman quietly called his people together.

★ 67 ★

Battle of Delta

When Jerry's squadron attacked the Russians, everyone at Refuge had cheered, hugged one another and some even danced in circles. Then the planes were abruptly gone. Night fell and the firing slackened and died.

They slept fitfully, those who could sleep at all.

Magda felt bereft. Of all her squad only she and Anna had made it back. The artillery had blown seemingly safe rocks into blizzards of shards that sliced people to unidentifiable bits.

And the air raid by Jerry's squadron was still generating animosity.

"What the hell!" Sergeant Kasilof had screamed. "They call *that* an attack? Even the Russian Air Force could do better than that!"

"Well, you're damned lucky that you're *wrong*, Kenny," Magda snapped. "We haven't yet seen a Russian plane that wasn't ours. And that's because of the 117th!" Finally she also slept.

Chris Anderson woke all of them. "Hey, Pelagian wants to talk to us, right now."

Everyone had slept in their clothes. They groggily

followed him toward the center of Refuge. Smoke stung Magda's nostrils.

People were cooking breakfast over small fires and the aroma of hot food made her realize how incredibly hungry she was. She wondered if terror could suppress one's appetite since she hadn't been at all hungry yesterday.

The huge space contained so much life it seemed to breathe on its own, Magda thought. Two Russian tanks parked side by side, tread to tread, blocked the main entrance, their cannon pointing outward. Behind them the crowded vehicles and groups of people flowed to the sides and back into the dimness of the cavern's depths.

Nearly everyone had brought all their possessions and some of the "camps" looked quite comfortable. The cries of babies echoed back and forth. She noticed a long line at the only two latrines.

Sure glad they remembered that, she thought.

A long band of orange ribbon marked the area the military needed for operations. It wasn't crowded with people; it held brown-painted cases stenciled with a two-headed eagle and full of 7mm rounds. There were also olive-drab cases stamped with USA that held mortar rounds and new mortars still packed in protective Cosmoline. A pallet of ration cases each had ROC prominently displayed.

The civilians had been drafted to unpack and assemble the weapons and over two dozen worked at cleaning the preservative off the weapons. All traces had to be eliminated or the weapons, especially the mortars, would not operate properly. Magda felt gratitude for their help, otherwise there wouldn't have been enough time to do what they all had to accomplish. They finally reached Pelagian.

He stood in front of a split steel drum whose ends had been welded together and the whole thing turned into a grill. He turned moose steaks as the woman next to him fried eggs on a slab of thin steel.

"You folks hungry?" Pelagian asked.

"Jeez," Bernard Sunnyboy said in a tone of relief. "I thought we was going to have to eat Russians for breakfast!"

Stoneware plates, porcelain plates and everything in between found eager hands and the army ripped through breakfast. Pelagian put away his apron and shrugged into a flak jacket boasting a charging bear of the Republic of California. His gray steel helmet featured the imperial double eagle.

A question flitted through Magda's mind. She wondered if the Dená Republik would ever be its own master. She decided things would be fine as long as their official language wasn't Russian.

"We're going to hit the Russians," Pelagian said in a conversational tone. People stopped chatting and listened to him.

"They've been throwing an artillery round at us every fifteen minutes for the past two hours. I think they are preparing an all-out assault on our positions. I would like those positions to start a lot closer to them than they currently are to us. You have five minutes to finish your meal."

Conversation evaporated as everyone wolfed down food. Magda wondered for how many it would be their last meal. The five minutes went fast.

"Grab your gear; we got work to do."

Once through the sinuous entrance, Pelagian moved briskly down the mountain and the Dená with their Russian converts kept pace. The landscape had changed. Many boulders were now shattered and strewn over the formerly open areas. Shell craters pocked the ground.

They passed dead Athabascans as well as dead Russians. Magda saw an upright boot with the foot and shin still in it, nothing else of the person evident. Massive amounts of blood had sprayed rock walls, some thick enough to still be viscous.

Flies buzzed everywhere as the day quickly heated. The smell of dead flesh eddied about them like an incoming tide. Magda knew that would also get worse as the temperature rose.

The carnage lay evident on all sides, but still they maintained their rapid pace down the mountain, slipping around the larger rocks, hesitating brief seconds to ensure the way ahead was clear, then moving relentlessly onward. Magda felt the fierce collective determination as if it were a palpable part of them all.

They would not again cower before the Russian guns. They would bring the battle to the foe and they would either triumph or die. Tears slid down her face and she wondered if she would ever see Jerry again.

"Halt!" the order hissed over the rocks and all immediately crouched behind cover. Most of them could see the mass of Russian armor and troops beyond the last rocky ridge below them. They checked their weapons and waited for orders.

Suddenly Russian troopers moved up from behind the ridge and there was no more time for further reflection or fear. Three ranks of Russians abruptly filled the space between them and the ridge.

"Fire!" Pelagian bellowed in his best "voice of God."

Magda aimed and fired, aimed and fired, aimed and fired...

★ 68 ★

Battle of Delta

"Send everyone up that mountain!" Colonel Janeki screamed. "Kill everyone you find, spare nobody!"

He turned to find General Myslosovich staring at him, still chewing on a piece of bread from breakfast.

"Janeki, this has turned into a tragedy."

"Not at all, General. We will soon have this batch of rabble eliminated and then we can return to Chena and finish this once and for all."

"That's easy for *you* to say. *I've* been to Chena. This whole thing is coming undone. We do not have the Russian Army Air Force aiding us, nor do we have any allies willing to send troops. This has been political from the beginning and *we*, dear Janeki, are the damned pawns! The Czar has sacrificed us to move his bishops and knights elsewhere!"

"Are you finished with your histrionics, General?" Janeki snapped. "*We* are the avenging saber of the Czar! *We* will prevail here and in Chena! If you do not believe that, then you are a defeatist and you know what that will bring you!"

"Christ, Janeki, look about you. We have killed

enough of our own troops and destroyed enough of our own equipment to be suspected as traitors. The Dená still resist even though we have pounded their positions with heavy artillery. Why haven't we already *won*?"

Janeki turned to the old man, a man he loved, the man who had helped him through the Byzantine labyrinth of gaining rank in the Imperial Russian Army, the man he was now tired of placating and supporting. "Taras, you have to let *me* lead this army or—"

The left side of General Myslosovich's head abruptly exploded out in a grisly eruption. Bullets snapped and whined around them. Janeki whipped around and, in total disbelief, saw troops charging his position.

"Corporal of the Guard!" he shrieked. "Corporal of the Guard!"

Myslosovich's body thudded to the ground unnoticed.

A master sergeant and his squad of ten troopers surrounded Janeki and retuned fire. Janeki scurried away from the fighting, his heart in his mouth, wondering who these people were and how to deal with them.

★ 69 ★

Fort Yukon Aerodrome, Dená Republik

Upon landing the previous evening, Captain Jerry Yamato turned his P-61 toward the refueling station.

"Captain Yamato," Lieutenant Colonel Shipley snapped over the comm channel. "Where do you think you are going?"

"We've got to refuel and get back there, Colonel," he said in a plaintive voice. "They don't have a chance without us!"

"Stand down, Captain. That's an order. We have to reassess the situation and obtain further approval from high command."

"Colonel Shipley, you saw what those people are facing out there! We've got to get back there and help them."

"That's not our call, Captain. We're not running this war. Follow me to the line, sir."

With a sinking feeling in his guts and pain in his heart, Jerry complied. He wondered whom he could pay off to rearm and refuel his bird.

"All pilots proceed to debriefing," Shipley snapped over the radio.

Jerry turned the P-61 around and followed the rest of his squadron. His ground crew clustered around the plane and Master Sergeant Mike Marinig pushed the ladder close and climbed up to help Jerry.

"Did you kick their ass, Captain Yamato?" he said.

"Ran into a flight of Russian bombers and fighters headed north toward Chena. We lost Major Ellis and Captain Fowler, but we took out four bombers and a few Yaks."

Master Sergeant Marinig sobered and went still. "Major Ellis is dead? His kids and mine play together back at Fremont Field." The sergeant looked off into the distance for a long moment, his face working.

Jerry had almost forgotten what a close-knit family the ROC Air Force was. Everybody pretty much knew everybody else. The traditional military distance between commissioned and enlisted was for the most part minimal. Jerry thought that was one of the best things about the Air Force and exactly why he hadn't joined the Navy.

"Would you tell me *how* he died?"

"He died attacking a bomber. Through his efforts and those of Captain Fowler, two bombers went down and Chena was spared."

"Are you guys going to refuel and go back?"

"I don't know. Colonel Shipley says we have to wait for approval."

Master Sergeant Marinig frowned but didn't comment. "C'mon, let's get you out of there."

With everyone exhausted, the debriefing had been short and they all ate a good meal. Darkness, such as it was, fell and everyone turned in. Jerry slept hard but had nightmares featuring Magda being surrounded by laughing Russians trying to kill her.

At 0700, Jerry walked into the ready room; Colonel Shipley was waiting for him. "Captain Yamato, a word please?"

Jerry followed him to his office. Shipley didn't sit behind his desk; he sat on the front of it, facing Yamato. "Shut the door, Captain. What was that out there last night? You trying to be a general or something?"

"I told the Dená I'd be back with modern aircraft to help them fight the Russians. To my way of thinking three strafing runs didn't quite fill the bill."

"If we hadn't run into that Russian bombing mission—"

"Excuse me, Colonel. I know why we didn't stay over the battle, but I don't understand why we didn't immediately go back."

"Interrupt me one more time and I'll confine you to quarters, *Captain*. I understand that you have a very personal interest in the battle at Delta, but that does not preclude our mission nor does it give you military or moral authority to take over my command."

Jerry felt his face grow warm and he held his tongue, realizing that at this point he was far too angry to speak. He stared at his commanding officer and remained at attention.

"Before you say something damaging to your career, allow me to enlighten you that we have orders to renew the attack as soon as possible. The Dená at Refuge made radio contact with their people late last night and gave them the lowdown.

"It seems the Russian military in Alaska is fighting

their own private war. St. Petersburg ordered them to stand down three days ago. You are dismissed, Captain."

Jerry executed the best salute of his career, and when it was returned, performed a perfect about-face and left the office. Master Sergeant Marinig was waiting outside the door and fell into step with Jerry.

"Is it true? Are we going back?"

"Yeah. Right now."

"Your bird is warmed up and ready."

★ 70 ★

Village of Kilsnoo, Russian Amerika

Grisha sat in his chair and quietly ground his teeth. For two days they had circled like feral dogs, seeking advantage where none existed. The atmosphere in the beautifully appointed chamber lay heavy with animosity and distrust.

All of the kwan leaders had said the same thing in as many different ways as possible: *we want your help but we don't want to change our culture in order to get it.*

Colonel Gregory George finished his version and sat down in the ensuing silence. Grisha could feel them all staring at him.

"I apologize, gentlemen," Wing said, rising to her feet. "This has all been a colossal waste of time. We came here thinking you were ready to negotiate, even pulled an active duty submarine out of the war we all are fighting in order to get here safely, and for what?"

Grisha smiled in his mind. They were going to get it now!

"With all due respect to your military ranks and your stations in your culture, none of you are willing to compromise even an inch. You want it your way or the waterway. The underlying theme here is: if you don't agree with me, you are my enemy.

"I don't know your culture other than what my husband had shared with me. But I know people. All that the men in this room have shown me is disdain.

"You think we have an inferior culture because it is open to everyone, even women, to question, debate, confer, and to run. You are still caught up in your centuries of male superiority to the point you do not realize the world has changed around you.

"You are losing a war because you are afraid to lose status in your own villages. I am at my wits' end trying to show you the reality of your situation, and I am tired. I want to go home and let you explain to the Japanese how important you are in Angoon or Kake—I'm sure they will appreciate it much more than I do."

Wing took a deep breath and looked over at Grisha. "Can we go home now, General?"

Not smiling was the hardest thing he had ever done in his life. He glanced around the room at their angry faces, dark looks and total discomfiture. The only hope for this alliance was that Wing had cracked their common defense.

"Gentlemen, do we have anything further to discuss?"

General Sobolof rose to his feet and cleared his throat. Blood colored his wide cheekbones and he chewed at his lower lip, glowering at Wing and Grisha.

"I can appreciate the colonel's attitude. But as she has already stated, this is not her culture. However, to declare an impasse at such an early juncture in a political dialogue is—"

Wing stood up so quickly her chair fell over backward and slammed on the floor.

"This is more than an impasse, General! This is total disregard of a critical military situation in deference to a social norm. If that's what you want to spend your time discussing, that's fine with this delegate, but I refuse to *waste* my time here when I could be defending my people. General Grigorovich is absent when needed by his troops and his adopted country. He does not need *tradition* and *station* to prove his worth; he has already done so with his *courage* and *leadership*. And that is something I would highly recommend to every other *man* in this room."

She stomped out of the chamber and silence fell like a leaden shroud.

Despite surreptitious glances, Grisha held his tongue. Wing had done nothing more than to speak the truth and he was determined that if even one of them maligned her in any way, he would leave the conference and call for Commander Vandenberg and his submarine to take them away.

Colonel Sam Dundas rose to his feet, staring at the door through which Wing had disappeared. "I think I'm in love. Grisha, will you sell your wife?"

Every man in the room laughed long and hard.

Grisha kept his smile and waited for the laughter to subside. "Not for all the abalone in Angoon, Sam. I appreciate your sentiment but I know what a prize I have found."

General Sobolof stood and regarded Grisha gravely. "General Grigorovich, we all know you, have known you for your entire life. Your new station amazes us and gives us pause. Your wife gives us even more pause... because she is right."

Grisha tried not to hold his breath.

"We are frightened because we need help, yet we do not want to sacrifice what culture we have retained in order to maintain our freedom."

Grisha kept his silence and stared back at the general.

"If it hasn't been obvious, we don't know what to do."

He had thought it all out, but he knew he couldn't shove it down their throats. This was as close to a plea as he would get.

"I know you," Grisha said in measured tones. "I have known you all my life. But I need this to be very clear and succinct. Are you asking me for my advice?"

"In the name of Raven, yes!" Sam Dundas exclaimed.

Grisha nodded. "Very well. If it were me, I would go to the people and say..."

★ 71 ★

9 miles east of Delta

Yukon Cassidy drove slowly over the rock rubble known as the Russia-Canada Highway. RustyCan was closer to the truth and that is what everyone called it. His utility thumped and bumped over the uneven surface and he detected new squeaks from the vehicle chassis as well as the wood and metal lodge top swaying side to side over the road.

In the passenger seat, snoring softly as he rocked to and fro, sat Roland Delcambré. Cassidy glanced over at the small man and grinned. At first he had been skeptical about the man's advertised abilities, but his small frame was wiry and held impressive strength.

The thing Cassidy liked most about him was his quick mind and erudite tongue. Smart, well-spoken, dependable people were few and far between in these parts and the longer he knew Roland the more he appreciated him.

He did his unconscious left-to-right horizon sweep and movement caught his eye. Something small was coming toward him on the road. Motorcycle, he decided.

Courier? Scout? Deserter? The possibilities flashed

through his mind in a flash. The answer really didn't matter, but they needed to be prepared for anything.

"Roland, we have company."

Delcambré's eyes opened as if he had been awake all along.

"Looks like a motorcycle." He pulled a small pair of binoculars from the gear at his feet and focused. "Forsooth! It is a BMW motorcycle and not only am I very familiar with the machine, I am also very familiar with the rider."

Cassidy pulled his foot off the accelerator pedal and pushed in the clutch. The utility rolled to a stop and he put it in neutral and switched off the engine. No point in wasting petrol.

"Who is it?"

"Our mutual acquaintance, Timothy Riordan of the International Freekorps." Delcambré chuckled. "And the son of a bitch is *alone*! His bully boys have either been stomped flat in a fight or co-opted by a larger force."

Cassidy checked the clip in his .45 Colt automatic, then looked to his Sharps .45-.70. The buffalo gun was an antique, but still deadly and quite serviceable. His proficiency with both weapons was well known.

"Will he recognize you?"

"Absolutely," Delcambré said with a smile. "He loved to make me the butt of jokes because of my size. If we decide to shoot him, can I do it?"

Cassidy laughed. "He'll recognize me, too. I tried to stop him and his *soldiers* from taking everything they could carry out of a grocery store down in the Nation. They not only left a good man and wife destitute, they also left me unconscious with a broken jaw. If you want to shoot this bastard before I do, you'd best be fast."

"Wait a minute," Roland said, squinting at Cassidy. "Aren't you supposed to bring him back to Pa Sapa for trial? Isn't that what that Indian general, General Spotted Bird, wanted you to do?"

"*If* I can." Cassidy gave him a ghastly leer. "If I can't bring him back alive, Lawrence will understand. I just have to bring him back."

The motorcycle had neared to a hundred meters, and slowed to a crawl. The machine stopped and Riordan balanced the BMW between his legs and stared at them.

Cassidy waited.

★ 72 ★

Battle of Refuge

Janeki felt a shiver run up his spine from his ass to his skull. He had watched it all unravel. The easy win over a bunch of rebel deserters had turned into a battle of considerable proportion, with devastating losses.

Less than an hour ago he realized he no longer had the troop strength or equipment to strike at Chena. He couldn't obey his orders. But perhaps he could prevail here.

His troops were taking light weapons' fire from his left and rear flanks. So far the Indians and traitors on the mountain hadn't realized the distraction and acted upon it.

"Who is my adjutant?" he shrieked over his shoulder.

A thin, pale lieutenant hurried to his side and saluted. "Co-Colonel Janeki, I am your new adjutant."

"Who in God's name are *you*? I've never laid eyes on you before."

"Lieutenant Petrovski, I ... I was the assistant supply officer, Colonel. We did meet once, it was back in—"

"What is happening on that mountain? Are we facing new people or did the savages and deserters on that mountain flank us? That is all I want to know. I don't care who the hell you are or if I've ever seen your witless face before this moment!"

"I think we're losing more men than we can afford, Colonel." The lieutenant's voice was suddenly crisp and professional. "Please explain if and how I can help you change that situation."

Janeki felt another chill course through him. This would all be on his head if he failed. Taras Myslosovich had had the good sense to stop a bullet, but he would have been even more worthless now than he had already proven.

"Get me the provost marshal, quickly! I must rescind an order."

"Colonel, the provost marshal is at the aid station. He was wounded when the Republic of California Air Force strafed our column. The Freekorps executive officer was killed outright. They were in the same car."

"No! I didn't know that. Thank you, Lieutenant Petrovski . . ."

Good, he was going to need those mercenaries. They could die *for* Mother Russia here rather than at some worthless village on the Yukon.

"Colonel, we're losing our ass here. We need to pull back and regroup."

"They told me to stand down, you know," Janeki said in an absent manner, trying desperately to make sense of the situation without screaming.

"*Who* told you to stand down, Colonel?"

"St. Nicholas Redoubt, of course. Who else has that sort of authority?"

Petrovski stared at him for the longest time before bellowing, "Cease fire! Cease fire!"

"No!" Janeki screamed, feeling the wrath pour out of him. "Not yet!"

"We are no better than bandits without the full backing of St. Petersburg!" Petrovski looked around, seeking allies. Soldiers stared back at him curiously but none ventured closer than they already stood.

"He is ordering us to wage illegal warfare! Don't you see? We can quit, we can go hom—"

Janeki's bullet hit the lieutenant in the chest, a perfect heart shot at two paces. Petrovski fell backwards onto the rocks, already dead.

"Do we have any more traitors who wish to join him?" Janeki bellowed. The rage cleared from his mind and he assessed his situation clearly. "Sergeant, count off every other man here. Send half to the left and the other half to the right. We have a mission to accomplish."

The headache was back.

★ 73 ★

9 miles east of Delta

Riordan saw the twin flashes of light that told him the occupants of the truck had just surveyed him with binoculars and now knew more about him than he did about them. He hoped they were not enlightened, but if they were... He loosened his carbine in its scabbard and unsnapped the flap over his pistol as nonchalantly as possible.

He hadn't felt this alone since shipping out of Boston at the age of fifteen—a long time ago. He allowed himself to wonder if N'go had survived the fighting before concentrating on the threat at hand.

The battered truck with a homemade dwelling bolted to its back came to a complete stop. He would have to go to it in order to parley or pass, or both. If this were a real highway made of macadam and smooth as a baby's butt, he would simply accelerate past them without a nod.

But this was the RustyCan and consisted of a plethora of small boulders that would dump a motorcycle quicker than it would ever lend support.

I, Riordan decided, *am thoroughly screwed.*

He gently twisted the throttle and moved slowly up to the truck... and saw the pistol pointed at him.

"Good evening, Major Riordan," the man behind the gun said.

Riordan glanced up at the bright sky. "How can you tell it's evening?"

"The trees are dark and the bird calls are less strident. One can almost hear the Earth exhale as the Sun nods at it to pass on."

"Poetry has always eluded me," Riordan said, becoming nervous under the man's measured tones. "Perhaps we can discuss the situation?"

"Of the evening, or yours?"

"My situation, if I am to see other evenings."

The man laughed and the gun did not waver.

"You really don't remember me, do you?"

Damn, Riordan thought. *There is no way I could be this man's father and nothing else bears such gravity.*

"No, I'm afraid I don't. Should I?"

"Less than ninety days ago, you and your men roared into a small town in the First People's Nation, stole everything my friends had from animals to wheat, beat me senseless and left me for dead."

"You were the man in the grocery store who called us pirates, thieves and desperados, aren't you?"

"You *do* remember!"

"I remember your spirited defense, but not your face."

"Did you hear what I screamed when you rode off in your command car?"

"No. I wasn't aware you spoke."

"Because you didn't care what I, or any of your other peaceful victims, had to say."

"Trust me, I'm listening now."

"I'll *never* trust you, Riordan. I screamed 'I'll find you!' at the top of my voice."

Riordan glanced at the horizon where the road rose to a ridgetop. Beyond lay mountains dark with trees and snow-capped peaks. Then he stared down at the irregular pieces of rock constituting the Russia-Canada Highway, and sighed.

"Well, sir, it seems you have. What now?"

★ 74 ★

Battle of Refuge

"Del, we got 'em pinned down," Major Joe Coffey said, breathing hard. Gunpowder streaked his face and a slice had been taken from the sleeve of his combat blouse.

Both men crouched in a semicircle of rocks that offered excellent protection.

Colonel Buhrman nodded at his arm. "Did that hit flesh?"

"Nothing more than a nick, Del. Thanks for asking. They can't charge up the mountain for fear we'll flank their position. So we've got them cornered. Whattya want to do?"

"Where's Major Smolst?"

"Leading his men. They're trying to cut the Russians off on the east."

"Brilliant, then we have them boxed with nowhere to go."

"That's what Heinrich and I decided about twenty minutes ago."

Buhrman grinned. "The best part of this situation is that I get to make battlefield promotions and the army has to go along with it, *Lieutenant Colonel Coffey.*"

Coffey grinned. "You are the *biggest* asshole I have ever known. You will use every ploy at hand to realize your objective. Have I ever *not* gone above and beyond for you?"

Buhrman sobered. "Of course not. And you've never been able to say 'thank you' the first time around in your whole life. You've earned this, Joe. It isn't *just* manipulation."

"Thanks, Del. I really appreciate it. It would have taken another two years to get this through normal channels."

"Naw, we're in a war again. Keep your shit together and you'll be a bird colonel in three months."

"You still haven't said what you want us to do, *Colonel*."

"I want a runner, preferably one of Major Smolst's men, to go up that mountain, make contact, and have the Dená charge downhill in concert with our assault on the enemy flanks. Think that will work?"

"Hell yes! The Russians will have to surrender or die."

★ 75 ★

5,000 feet over Russian Amerika

"This is Delta Refuge, do you read me? Over."

Captain Gerald Yamato thought the transmission was a cruel prank at first.

"This is Delta Refuge, does anyone hear me?"

Jerry keyed his microphone. "This is Captain Yamato of the Republic of California Air Force. Who is in charge there?"

"Captain Yamato! This is Max Demientieff. We fought together when we hit them mercenaries, remember?"

"Max! I'm so happy to hear your voice and know you're okay. We're on our way to hit the Russians attacking you. Over."

"We got people out there, Jerry, be careful you don't get them too. Uh, over."

"Is there anyone in your front lines with a radio? Over."

"Yeah, hang on for a minute."

The radio burst with static and he turned down his volume. The 117th was no more than five minutes from the battle; he needed coordinates.

"This is Sergeant Haroldsson of Dená Recon. What do you need?"

317

Jerry couldn't believe his ears. "Magda? Is that you?"

"Jerry!" The catch in her voice tore at him. "Where are you?"

"Closing on the battle at five thousand feet! We're going to hit the Russians, but Max said there were Dená elements close to the Russians. What's the story?"

"The lines are all messed up and we're probably within fifty meters of the Russians right now."

His heart flew into his mouth. "You're *that* close to the Russians?"

"It's a war, my love. They damn near killed me yesterday with an artillery barrage. We do what we must."

"Magda, get away from the front lines, please!"

Despite the poor connection, the starch in her voice came through loud and clear.

"Don't *ever* ask me to let someone take risks in my name that I won't take myself! Don't you know me better than that, Jerry Yamato?"

"Of course I do. I don't know what I would do if anything happened to you. I fear for you."

"You would soldier on. But I promise to be careful."

"Thanks. We can see the dust and smoke from the barrage. Where do we hit them?"

"At the bottom of the mountain, where all their armor is concentrated. We'll take care of the rest."

"Consider it done. I love you."

"And I love you, over."

Colonel Shipley's voice sounded softer than it had at the beginning of the flight. "Captain Yamato, you have the lead on the first attack."

"Thank you, sir, I sincerely appreciate that. Permission to reconnoiter the area, sir?"

"Permission granted, Captain."

Jerry dove toward the base of the smoke cloud where it intersected with the RustyCan. He swept over the Russians so quickly they didn't have time to direct any fire at his plane. Their column looked pretty well shot up to him.

He banked left and right, following the highway while digesting what he had seen, and flew over a second, much larger, column. He stared incredulously at the long line of tanks and armored troop carriers. Just as his heart was sinking into the pit of his stomach, he realized they were not displaying Russian insignia.

"First People's Nation?" he blurted.

"What was that, Captain?" Shipley's voice sounded taut. "Where the hell are you? We've completely lost visual on your craft."

He pulled the P-61 up as sharply as he dared while machine gun fire erupted from dozens of locations in the column. Two rounds put holes in his left wing. Jerry took a deep breath.

That was too damn close!

"Colonel Shipley, there is a First People's Nation armored column less than five miles from the Russian position. It outnumbers the Russians by four to one."

"Who . . ." Shipley began and then faltered for a moment. "Whose side are they on?"

"Ours, I think. But they still put two holes in my left wing. They weren't expecting friendly aircraft."

"Friendly aircraft, hell," Shipley said with a snort. "They weren't expecting any aircraft at all! Tell me about the Russians."

"They're bunched up and hurting. But we have to make sure we don't hit the sides of the road; they're engaged in hand-to-hand combat there."

"Roger that. Good work, Captain."

"Thank you, sir." Jerry knew there would be a citation for this in his service jacket, but he didn't really care. His war had transcended nations; now it was completely personal.

"Gentlemen," Shipley said, "you all heard the captain. Hit everything in the middle of the Russian parking lot but don't shoot near the edges."

A bevy of comm clicks answered him and the 117th dove to the attack.

★ 76 ★

Battle of Delta

Provost Marshal Senior Lieutenant Kubitski screamed at his men to take cover when the Californian aircraft went over. Private Ilyivich stood watching as the plane buzzed into the distance.

"Get your dumb ass under cover!" Kubitski screamed. "Did I tell you it was permitted to move?"

His bandaged head throbbed where the cannon fire from the earlier strafing run had clipped his scalp.

"But the plane didn't fire, Lieutenant—"

"There will be more planes, you stupid bastard. Now get under cover!"

As his men went to ground he sprinted toward Colonel Janeki's position. Ten minutes after the colonel shot his new adjutant, everyone in the column knew about it. This had to be ended.

Bullets skitted past him and took cover. They were being flanked and Colonel Janeki was still obsessed with going to the top of this damn mountain. Fifth Armored had been Kubitski's life since he was sixteen and a sub-private.

The battlefield commission came as a surprise; he

just thought he had been doing what they trained him for. The promotion to provost marshal was an even bigger surprise; he hadn't thought he was hard-assed enough for the job.

He glanced about, seeking his men. Three feet behind him a bullet ricocheted off the fender of an armored car. He let his training take over and watched for the next shot.

Nothing happened. He wasn't facing an inexperienced recruit; this fellow knew what it was all about. He waited.

A volley of automatic fire erupted from a dozen places and Mother Kubitski's little boy Leonid dove for cover. His adversaries were just as professional as himself.

Perhaps more?

The fire drew attention from his troops and the enemy area received heavy machine gun and mortar fire. He utilized the lull in incoming fire by running toward Janeki's last known position. Just as he was about to go to ground again, a bullet clipped the side of his steel helmet and knocked him sprawling.

He lay stunned. His head throbbed worse than the most massive hangover he had ever experienced. Between the earlier graze and this near miss, he felt marked for death.

For a moment he saw two of everything and squeezed his eyes shut. The scent of flowers suffused him and he didn't know if he should enjoy the incongruity or worry about brain damage.

He had to get to Janeki before the colonel got all of his comrades killed. He wasn't going to argue with the man. He would just shoot him.

A roaring grew and for a moment he thought it was part of the concussion. It turned out to be aircraft, and this time they *were* firing. Provost Marshal Kubitski swiftly crawled under a truck and prayed it didn't take a direct bomb hit.

★ 77 ★

Village of Kilsnoo, Russian Amerika

"What do you think their answer will be?" Wing asked, staring at the closed conference room door and doing her best not to fidget.

"In my opinion, there can only be one answer: to agree with us or something very close to agreement." Grisha wished he had something to do with his hands. For a brief moment he envied cigarette smokers until he also remembered how they smelled.

"We don't have a lot of time left bef—"

The door opened, breaking her sentence along with her train of thought. Colonel Sam Dundas gave them a slight bow.

"General, Colonel, we would appreciate your presence."

Wing studied the man. She didn't know Sam Dundas like Grisha did, and therefore found his face unreadable. Grisha took her arm and they walked through the door.

She desperately didn't want this mission to fail. Not only did it signify the possibility of a unified Republik of Alaska, it also returned to her beloved

Grisha the status of which he had been robbed. She didn't think these people gave him much respect and that put her hackles up.

All five men stood when they entered. General Sobolof indicated the two chairs on either side of him at the head of the table. No one spoke as Grisha held Wing's chair and she sat. The others sat when Grisha did.

Wing tried not to hold her breath. From somewhere inside her she heard Blue say, "Don't ever show 'em that it matters." She forced herself to relax, give the men around the table her best "I'm on your side" smile, and wait.

"General Grigorievich, Colonel Grigorievich," General Sobolof said in his most ponderous, official tone, "we sincerely appreciate and salute your presence here, and we further understand what personal danger you endured in making this visit."

He's going to send us packing, Wing thought.

"To that end we wish to assure you that your efforts are not in vain. We have agreed to *most* of General Grigorievich's suggestions and are certainly open to further debate."

"You are?" Wing blurted.

All of the men except Grisha broke into laughter.

"What's so funny?" she snapped, trying not smile.

"You thought we were going to turn the whole thing down, didn't you?" Sam Dundas asked, wiping a tear from his eye.

She gave them her full grin. "General, I will *never* play poker with you, or any other game where I might lose money."

This time Grisha laughed too.

"Now that we've had our fun," General Sobolof said, "let's get down to business."

Two people, a woman and a man, came in through a side door.

"This is Captain Pletnikov and Lieutenant Davis. The captain will record our conversation on this machine, and Lieutenant Davis will transcribe everything said with her incredible command of shorthand."

Wing nodded in tandem with Grisha. The captain sat down and glanced at the lieutenant. She opened her tablet on the table and nodded back. He snapped a switch on the machine and it began to hum.

"This is General Vincent Sobolof of the Tlingit Nation Army. I am officiating at a meeting between members of our War Council and delegates from the Dená Republik. I will now have each of these people identify themselves, beginning with our guests."

Wing waited while Grisha spoke and then she identified herself and stated her rank. While the men around the table spoke, she allowed herself a glow of pride. They were making history here, and despite what happened later, this would be remembered, and matter.

★ 78 ★

Battle of Delta

Magda peered intently where she had seen the Russian troopers fall back. At least the artillery had ceased. The Russians were probably worried about hitting their people. Private Clarence Attla, hunkered down to her right, nudged her.

"Somebody is coming around that rock over there, Magda." He gestured with his chin and aimed at the spot.

"Could it be our people?" she whispered.

"Ain't we the right flank?"

"Supposed to be, but you never know who might have gotten off course. Don't shoot unless I say so."

"You're the sergeant," he whispered through a quick grin.

They both watched the slab of rock. The firing had died down to intermittent shots. They could both clearly hear someone moving slowly through the scree around the base of the rocks.

A head popped up and then down again. Magda glanced at Clarence. He shrugged. The head edged from behind the slab at a different spot.

327

She realized the person wasn't attacking; they were trying to make contact or surrender. She shared the thought with Clarence.

"And *how* do you know that?" he asked.

"If they were attacking, they'd just lob a grenade over here and charge in when the thing went off."

He stared at the slab and scratched his jaw. "That's good thinking, Magda. I agree."

"Be ready to shoot anyway." Her mouth went flat. "It could be a trick."

"Okay, you take it from here."

"This is the Dená Army," she said in a loud voice. "Stick your rifle straight up and ease around that rock if you want to live."

A rifle speared into the air. "Okay," a voice called. "Don't shoot, okay?"

"Okay," Clarence replied. "Get yer pokey butt over here."

Magda thought the rifle looked like a California carbine.

"Clarence? Is that *you*?" A man wearing ROC dungarees edged around the slab and moved toward them, keeping low behind the rocks.

"George? What the hell you doing out here? I thought you were still fishing down at Russian Mission. Get over here, man."

Clarence and George pounded each other's back and grinned.

"Magda, uh Sergeant—"

"Magda's just fine," she said through her smile.

"Uh, this is my cousin, George Hoyt from Russian Mission. I ain't seen him for years."

"Hoyt? What kind of a name is that?" she asked.

"My great-grandpa was one of them Moravian missionaries. Great-grandma sorta absorbed him into her way of life."

"What you doing out here, George?" Her voice went crisper than she intended.

"Yeah. I'm with Major Smolst from Chena and we got a bunch of California rangers and paratroopers with us. Them California guys want to hook up with the people at Refuge and coordinate an attack."

"That would be us," Magda said. "Anybody else with you, George?"

"No. Just me."

"Clarence, you stay here. I'm going to take George to Pelagian."

"Yes, Sergeant Magda."

George followed her along their line of soldiers. "You're a sergeant?"

"Is there something wrong with that?"

"Not at all. It's just that you're the prettiest sergeant I've ever seen."

"You're a flirt, George. It must run in the family."

Pelagian was suddenly in front of them. "Magda, who's this?"

"Father, this is George Hoyt from Russian Mission. He's Clarence's cousin. He's also a scout for Major Smolst and the Californians." She stepped aside.

"George." Pelagian shook hands with him. "Where are your people?"

George pulled a map from his blouse pocket and spread it on a flat-topped rock. "We're here, the California rangers are here, and the paratroopers are here." His finger stopped moving and he looked up at Pelagian. "And you know where you're at."

"This is great; we have them hemmed in on three sides. All they can do is retreat toward Tetlin."

Magda's radio beeped and she lifted it to her ear as she keyed a response.

"Magda, this is Jerry. I just flew over a column of armor less than five miles from Delta headed your way—"

"Oh Christ! How are we—"

"Let me finish! It's an FPN column."

"FPN?"

"You know, First People's Nation."

"I know what the letters mean, but what does it mean that they're *here*?"

"We are going with the assumption that they are on our side, even if they did put a few holes in my plane."

"Are you hurt?"

"Not this time. Don't worry. What is your tactical situation?"

"Here, talk to Dad." She handed the radio to Pelagian. "It's Jerry."

"Captain Yamato, how good to hear your voice!"

Magda watched her father as he listened. When he frowned she knew he had heard "FPN."

"What are they doing this far north? Have they declared war on Imperial Russia, too? This changes things drastically here, especially for the Russians. We have them enfiladed on three sides and I believe they are low on artillery shells."

He listened intently again and began shaking his head. "No, no more air strikes. We're cheek to jowl with them at this point and I would hate to lose our people to friendly fire. Your squadron has done an exemplary job so far and the Dená Republik will never forget your service and sacrifice."

He handed the radio back to Magda. She put it to her ear and turned away from her father and Private Hoyt.

"Jerry?"

"Yes, Magda?"

"We're so close to the end of this. Please be careful."

"I'm a hell of a lot safer than you are, my love. Please watch your step."

"I will. Dená Scout out."

"Yamato out."

She clicked off her radio and turned back to her father. "So what now?"

★ 79 ★

Battle of Delta

"Where is the colonel?" Kubitski demanded.

The corporal hunching behind a destroyed scout car jerked his head up when the lieutenant yelled. The tears running down the man's face only steeled Kubitski's resolve.

The corporal swiped his face with a sleeve and pulled himself together. "Over there, sir. No more than thirty meters. They have a bunker of sorts—rocks and machines in a circle."

"This is nearly over, soldier."

The lieutenant peered across the space separating him from the colonel. Very little cover to be seen or utilized. Not good.

The battle seemed to ebb, gunfire slackened to brief bursts here and there, but no mass movement. He allowed himself to think it all might be over. Perhaps Colonel Janeki had regained his senses.

"I want a full assault on that damned mountain! We have traitors to execute!" Janeki's voice rang across the space between them. Kubitski sprinted across the open area, moving his exhausted legs as fast as he could, feeling his heart bursting from his chest and nearly allowing himself to believe he had made it.

The shock of the bullet spun him in a complete circle and knocked him to the ground. Another bullet buzzed past his head as he rolled over and scrambled to his feet. If he stopped here, he was a dead man.

He knew he owed the absence of debilitating pain to shock, and that he couldn't function much longer. Another bullet clipped his left arm as he hurled himself at the small opening between two tanks. He stumbled and fell between the two machines. His body didn't want to move any farther; it demanded rest.

"What! My God, it's Lieutenant Kubitski!" Janeki shouted. "Help him! Get him a medic!"

Kubitski felt he was peering out of a deep well. Darkness had closed in on his vision and in the cone of remaining clarity stood Colonel Janeki. He forced himself to raise his wounded left arm and beckon his commander closer.

Janeki rushed to his side and bent over. "What is it, Lieutenant?"

"Deliverance!" Kubitski grated in a sand-filled voice and, lifting the pistol in his right hand, he shot the colonel through the brain. All went dark, but it was a good dark.

★ 80 ★

Battle of Delta

Major Smolst squirmed up beside Colonel Buhrman. "Just got word from Pelagian; blow a loud whistle twice and everybody charges the Russians."

"Thanks, Heinrich." He pulled a whistle from his blouse and blew two long blasts, put it back in his pocket and bellowed, "Charge!"

He was on his feet and running as fast as he could toward the Russians. Bullets whined past and he threw himself behind a medium-sized boulder. A quick glance around renewed his confidence; all of the California and Dená troops were advancing and firing like demons.

Colonel Buhrman pushed himself up and continued his headlong charge. He saw people moving down the mountain toward the other Russian flank. The roar of gunfire rose to a crescendo and began to ebb as some units engaged in hand-to-hand fighting. Russians were retreating to the mass of vehicles, some of which were burning brightly.

Smoke, cordite, feces, blood, sap, and diesel exhaust all assailed his nose. He couldn't remember being in a fight more fierce than this one. He glanced around at his people again.

He watched Lieutenant Colonel Coffey slam into an invisible wall, spin and drop.

Aw damn, not Joe, not now!

Russian fire picked up again: time for a reassessment. He blew the whistle again and bellowed, "Take cover!"

The Californians and Dená went to ground in one fluid movement.

Russian fire slackened and stopped for lack of targets.

He made his way back to where Joe lay writhing on the rocky soil.

"Medic!" Buhrman screamed. "Where you hit, Joe?"

"In the side. What's in the side right through here?" Lieutenant Colonel Coffey grimaced and let his head drop to the ground. "Shit, that hurts!"

A medic slid in, keeping himself behind the jumble of boulders shielding the two officers from enemy fire. "What's the situation, Colonel?" he asked Buhrman.

"Joe took a hit in the side, Doc."

"Let's have a look at you, Colonel Coffey..." He swiftly cut the uniform around the wound and gently tugged the ragged bits of uniform out of the wound.

"Augh!" Coffey all but shouted. "Why don't you just rip my whole gawddamned belly open?"

Doc pulled a hypodermic from his bag, carefully loaded it from a small bottle, and then injected Joe with the contents.

"You'll feel a lot better, right about now."

"Oh, hey," Joe said with discovery in his voice. "Where did the pain go?"

"Lay still, Major."

"Doc, I'm a light colonel now, didn't you get the word? I thought I told everybody."

Colonel Buhrman watched Doc explore the wound with his fingers, then feel around the torso to Joe's back. His eyes widened for a second; then he was pulling something greenish-brown out of his bag and stuffing it into the wound.

"Doc," Buhrman said softly. "What the hell are you doing?"

"Packing the wound with sphagnum moss, Colonel. The Dená taught me about this stuff. It's not only sterile, it's also slightly acidic, and it keeps the wound cleaner longer than anything else we've got."

"Where do you get it?"

"It, uh, grows on the ground. You're standing on some right now."

Joe had grown quiet.

"How is he, Doc?"

"Classic bullet wound, but I think only fat and muscle were hit. It went straight through him. Give him a month and he'll be good as new."

"How *are* we getting our wounded back to aid stations?"

"Carrying them. Our only aid station is about half a mile behind us. We have Major Nacht and a captured mercenary by the name of Revere working on our wounded. I don't know how they're keeping up."

"I've been busy. What are our casualty numbers?"

"Between our guys and the Dená, there's about forty to fifty wounded back there."

"Damn, we'd better wrap this up soon. We've hooked up with the Delta Dená and we're going to hit the Russians again as soon as everyone catches their breath."

"Colonel Coffey is going to make it, sir. You don't have to hang around. I'll take good care of him."

"Thanks, Doc. This guy means a lot to me."

Doc smiled. "Me, too, Colonel."

Colonel Del Buhrman, feeling strangely alone, hurried back to his men.

★ 81 ★

Battle of Delta

The firing died down and Magda signaled to her people. *Wait*. She wanted to see what the Russians would do next.

"Magda, they're waving a white flag!" Sergi Eluska shouted.

"Stay down, it might be a trick!" She peered around the boulder, knowing that if it were a trick, she would probably be dead within seconds. The Russians had proven to be excellent marksmen.

A group of Russian soldiers holding both hands in the air followed a sergeant who carried what looked like a bed sheet attached to a pole. If this was a trick, they were going to lose a lot of people in a very short time.

"They're surrendering?" she whispered.

"They're giving up!" she shouted to her people. "Let's take control before they change their minds!"

The Dená rose as one, aiming their weapons at the Russians who immediately stopped moving.

"We surrender. Please don't shoot."

Magda couldn't tell who yelled but she could see that all agreed with the statement.

"Sit down on the ground with your hands on your head, now!"

They complied. The white flag fell onto the dusty road.

"Who is in command of your force?"

A heavily bandaged man raised his hand.

"Two of you help him up and bring him over here."

She was not going to expose her people to possible subterfuge. From here forward the only people who would die in this place would be Russian.

The bandaged man proved to be a senior lieutenant.

"You are the senior officer?"

"Yes," he said crisply. "I am Lieutenant Leonid Kubitski. May I know your rank, please?"

"I am a sergeant of scouts, Dená Army."

His eyes shifted away from her, staring over her shoulder. She turned and saw men she didn't know completely surrounding her. She thought she had been deceived and felt a total dupe.

A man with a large moustache raised his hand.

"I don't know who is in charge here. I'm Colonel Buhrman, of the 3rd California Parachute Infantry Regiment." He nodded to the man at his side. "And this is Major Heinrich Smolst of the Dená Army. How can we help?"

Magda smiled. "You can wait for my father, Pelagian, who has been overseeing the evacuation of our wounded. He'll be here in—"

"I'm here, Magda."

He stood off to her side with a squad of six heavily armed Dená soldiers.

"Wow," Colonel Buhrman said. "I thought our guys were the only ones who could just pop up like that."

Pelagian smiled. "We live here, Colonel Buhrman, that helps a lot."

"You have more at stake here than we do. Please, sir, take the surrender of these people." Buhrman stood at attention and saluted.

★ 82 ★

Old Crow, Dená Republik

Gennady Ustinov watched the tall Athabascan slowly go around the crowded council meeting room and speak to every person, except Gennady.

He carefully scanned the group and decided that Hannah Weirmaker was the best person to approach; she owed him money.

"Hannah, what did that man ask you?"

"Gennady, every time I talk to you I owe you more money. Go away."

"We can be even if you wish."

"Even? Are you saying that if I answer your question I will owe you nothing; all my bills will vanish like my worthless husband?"

Gennady sighed. "Yes, that is my proposition."

"If you try to back out of this later, I will cut your balls off myself!"

"My word is my bond! Your debts will be dissolved."

She gave him a long, level look. "He wanted to know who I planned to vote for as delegate to that constitution thing. I don't even know who wants the job in the first place."

"You must vote for people you trust," Gennady exclaimed. "What they write and is agreed to will frame your life forever."

"How do I know what people really think? They just tell you whatever they think you want to hear and then go and do whatever they want."

"Did he ask you to vote for someone?"

"Of course he did!"

Gennady stared at her and raised his left eyebrow.

"He wanted me to vote for some guy called Nathan..."

"...Roubitaux," Gennady finished for her. "Does he think you are in his district?"

"I guess so, why else would he ask?"

"Has anyone else asked you to vote for them?"

"No. Everyone else is busy fighting somewheres, except you."

"He's not in your district."

"He thinks I am."

"What? Where is he from?"

"He says he's from Eagle, but nobody there remembers ever seeing him before."

"Thanks, Hannah. You have fifty rubles credit in my store as of now."

She grinned. "I won't forget that!"

He knew she wouldn't; neither would he. Gennady might drive a hard bargain but he never forgot his word. He moved purposefully up to the tall Athabascan, reached out and touched his arm.

"Excuse me. Might I have a few words with you?"

The man turned with a grin that faded as soon as he saw Gennady. "What do you want?"

"Who are you?"

"Alexi Popovich, who's asking?"

"You know who I am. You're campaigning against me."

"I am campaigning for Nathan Roubitaux. There's a difference."

"Not from where I stand. Since when is Nathan from Eagle? Nobody in the village knows him."

"He was born there. His parents moved to Tanana when he was a baby."

"And he hasn't lived there since. He doesn't live there now. How can he claim to live where he doesn't?"

"He was born there, Gennady!"

"Can he prove that? Was his birth recorded by the priest? Does Eagle even have a priest?"

"The church in Eagle burned a few years ago," Alexi said. "All records were destroyed."

"*That* was very convenient, wasn't it?"

"What are you insinuating, Gennady Ustinov?"

"*Insinuating!*" Gennady shouted. Every head in the room turned toward them: "I *insinuate* nothing! I *accuse* you of spreading false information about your *candidate*. And I accuse him of lying about where he was born. Nobody in Eagle or the rest of this district has ever heard of his family or any of their relatives."

Alexi's face darkened with blood and his composure slipped into a glare at the shorter man. "You accuse *me* of lying?"

"*Da*, unless you can come up with a better word!"

"I demand satisfaction! Either apologize at once or meet me outside."

Gennady grinned. "You are challenging me to a *duel*?"

Alexi maintained his glare and suppressed a smirk. "Yes. If you're man enough to face me."

Gennady's eyes seemed to glint. "I accept. Since you challenged me, I get to choose the weapon."

Alexi suddenly looked wary. "What do you choose?"

"Skinning knives at thirty paces."

"Skinning knives? What can you do with a skinning knife at that distance?"

"Do you accept my choice of weapons?"

Alexi smirked. "Of course." He straightened to his full height, a full head above Gennady, and shook his long arms as if to make them more limber. "But I think you'd better keep your distance."

Somebody shouted, "Duel! Clear the building!"

Everyone trooped out into the sunshine. Gennady thought it might be close to 70 degrees Fahrenheit, and no breeze to alleviate the oppressive heat. Temperatures in Interior Alaska during the summer could reach incredibly high numbers.

Waterman Stoddard stepped off thirty paces. He gave Alexi a skinning knife, and then approached Gennady, holding out a second blade.

"No thanks, Waterman. I have my own." He pulled his knife from its sheath and stared at his opponent, holding the knife in his right hand at his side.

"So what do we do now?" Alexi said with a grin, glancing at the crowd for approval. "Stare at each oth—"

Gennady snapped his arm up and his knife flew straight into Alexi's throat.

Alexi dropped his knife and grabbed his throat as he thudded to his knees. Staring at Gennady with wide, beseeching eyes, he pulled the blade out and dropped it, and grabbed his throat again. Blood gushed from the wound, soaking his hands, arms and the ground around him.

While his mouth opened and shut like that of a beached fish, Alexi Popovich fell over on his side and died.

The crowd stared in silence. Alexi looked around, staring into the eyes of every person there.

"I am an honest man. I pay my debts and I honor my contracts. I ask for your vote as delegate."

He walked over to the still-twitching body and picked his knife off the ground, wiped it on Alexi's trouser leg, and walked back into the meeting house.

★ 83 ★

Aboard the RCNS *Mako*, SS-45 Chatham Strait

The rumbling thunder of a Japanese destroyer rolled over them and Grisha felt his heart rise into his mouth. The submarine lay quiet on a shelf off Admiralty Island. Grisha had no idea how Captain Vandenberg knew the location of the shelf or how he could set his boat on it safely.

Clangs like hammers on steel suddenly rang through the boat.

"They've found us!" Captain Vandenberg bellowed. "All ahead full."

The rumble and hammer strikes vanished. Grisha looked at the men around him, slowly, carefully. He wanted to remember their faces for as long as he lived, and pay them honor.

As one, they sweated and strained, eyes upward. No, some stared at meters and dials as if watching the turn of a card or die that would render them rich or busted. Or dead.

"Sonar?" Vandenberg intoned.

"They're coming back around, Skipper. This would be a good time to jink."

"Thanks, Pete. Helm! Hard to port."

"Hard to port, aye!"

The submarine rolled to the right and Grisha was glad he had not released his hold on the framework. Something crashed to the deck behind him.

"Sorry, Skipper," Chief Fisher muttered. "I thought I had that secured. Give me a minute." He swished away and Grisha turned his attention back to Sonorman First Class Lawson.

"Skipper, they crossed our wake, fading to starboard."

"Anything else out there, Pete?"

"Not that I can hear, Skipper."

"Chief of the Boat, bring us up to periscope depth."

"Periscope depth, aye," Chief Busch said. "You heard the captain, guys, now get us there."

Grisha watched as wheels were turned and levers brought back a few notches in their arc. But he understood none of it. He couldn't remember ever being this frightened before in his life.

"Grisha!"

He turned and saw Wing's outstretched hand, grabbed it immediately. He hadn't thought of her for over five minutes and his cheeks flamed. He felt gratitude that the battle lanterns all had red lenses.

"What is happening?" she asked as he pulled her close.

"I have no idea. All I do know is that Captain Vandenberg had been through this before, so I don't think we have to worry."

Captain Vandenberg overheard him and flashed them a quick smile.

"Periscope level, Skipper," Chief Busch whispered.

"Up periscope," Captain Vandenberg said.

As soon as the eyepiece hit knee level, the captain was on it, snapping down the two little arms and walking them around the thick, still-rising shaft of the thing.

"Destroyer aft, six thousand yards and headed away from us." He continued to slowly walk the shaft in a circle and stopped abruptly.

"Second destroyer headed straight for us, balls to the wall! Open forward torpedo doors, now!"

Grisha saw the fear drop over their faces. This wasn't a sure thing. They all still might die.

"How can they do this day after day?" Wing whispered in his ear, echoing his own thoughts. He shrugged.

"Forward torpedo doors open, Skipper," Chief Busch said in a conversational tone.

"Fire one, fire two!" Vandenberg ordered.

"Torpedoes away, Skipper," Chief Busch said. "How long until you—"

The explosion slammed through the water and violently rocked the *Mako* to the left.

"Jesus Christ!" Busch shouted. "How fu—," he glanced at Wing and flashed her a grin. "How close were they, Skipper?"

"Too damn close. They just went to the bottom," Vandenberg said, eyes still glued to the periscope. "And here comes their cavalry." He snapped the arms against the periscope tube.

"Down scope, full speed ahead. Take her down to 300 feet, port full rudder, Chief."

"Port full rudder, 300 feet, aye, aye, Skipper."

The deck tilted down and Grisha maintained his grip on the stanchion with one hand and put his

other arm around Wing. Behind them he could hear
Sergeant Major Tobias muttering under his breath.

"What's that, Sergeant Major?"

"I was just telling myself that this is something
I needn't do again in my life. Once is more than
enough!"

Wing turned to him and forced a smile. "For once
I am in total agreement with you, Sergeant Major."

"Depth charges!" Sonarman First Lawson shouted,
jerking off his headset.

Thunder filled their steel universe.

★ 84 ★

**5 miles east of Delta on the
Russia-Canada Highway**

Yukon Cassidy aimed at the position from where Riordan last fired. His carbine weighed more than an ordinary weapon, of that he felt positive. The muzzle quivered no matter how hard he grasped the weapon.

"Where *is* that son of a bitch?" he muttered.

Time dragged and he decided that the quarry had different plans, but what? He knew Riordan wouldn't do anything to endanger himself in a real way.

What would I do?

Cassidy craned his neck and took in the whole physical area where they fought. To his right, a ridge lifted above the common denominator plain; the plain actually rose to meet the ridge, beyond which distant mountains could be glimpsed. He didn't have the luxury of speculating on what might lay immediately over the rise.

He just needed the high ground.

Cassidy crawled forward, wondering where Roland had disappeared. He had his doubts about Frenchmen and, as yet, this one was not changing his mind.

Riordan was fast. Cassidy had trained his .45 on the

man and talked while Delcambré had stepped out of the truck cab with a rifle. As soon as he saw the muzzle on Delcambré's weapon come up, Cassidy had pulled the .45 up and opened the truck door to get out. When Cassidy's left foot touched the road, Riordan kicked the door into him and accelerated his motorcycle down the road at such speed that Roland's shot missed.

Cassidy shoved the door away, dropped the pistol and grabbed his .45-.70, took careful aim at the motor-cycle and blew a hole in the back tire. The BMW skidded wildly on the rocky road and Riordan leapt off the machine as the wheels caught and it began to flip sideways. Riordan had the presence of mind to grab his rifle from its scabbard then rolled when he hit the ground.

"The son of a bitch disappeared!" Cassidy exclaimed.

"He is very good at that," Roland agreed. "I suggest you take cover."

"He has to be dazed. Let's get up there and grab him."

"After you," Roland said with a wide smile.

Cassidy grabbed his pistol off the truck seat and holstered it. Holding the rifle close to his chest he went down the road at a dead run.

Riordan's first shot went through the crown of his hat and snapped it off his head like magic. Cassidy threw himself behind the biggest rock within a meter. It wasn't a very big rock since he couldn't fit all of himself behind it.

A quick glance behind showed no sign of Roland Delcambré. Cassidy aimed toward where he last saw Riordan, and waited.

A bullet, so close to his head it sounded like a

hummingbird in full flight, buzzed past. Another bullet whined above him.

Where the hell is he?

Cassidy carefully surveyed the ground immediately around him. The terrain was flat on both sides and gained elevation up to the rise. With Riordan ahead of, and above, him, he didn't have a chance of flanking the bastard.

Where the hell is Delcambré?

Cassidy had the largest rock within five meters. Engine noise behind him suddenly registered.

This is either a very good thing or a very bad thing.

Without really thinking about it, he rolled over and over toward a larger rock five meters distant. After the fourth roll he felt disoriented and stopped, completely in the open. The engine sounds were louder and he scrambled over to the rock.

Blood pounded in his head but he felt relieved to have some decent cover.

Rifle fire behind him added to his decision to just stay put for a moment. He watched the area from where Riordan had last fired, and waited.

He heard Roland shout, *"Que est vous?"* and heard the answer: the damned Freekorps. Then Riordan shouted from somewhere in front of him. The damn terrain made it sound like his voice was everywhere.

The voices behind him suddenly ceased. The quiet stretched too far into his nerves to be comfortable.

"Are you soldiers with me?" Riordan shouted.

A voice Cassidy didn't recognize answered, "Sorry, Major, this is your fight. But we'll watch."

"Bastards!" Riordan shrilled. "After all I've done for you!"

Cassidy realized he knew where Riordan was, off to his left side, and started inching toward him.

"Riordan, you have dropped our balls in the dirt for the last time. I hope they hang your ass!"

Cassidy grinned and quickened his pace. In moments he was out of the roadside dirt and rocks and on softer, quieter sphagnum moss and lichens. He stopped to rest in a shallow depression, wishing he could take a quick nap on this delicious bed.

He heard a scuffing sound and raised his head to look Riordan in the face less than a meter away. Immediately Cassidy threw himself forward and used the .45-.70 to block the rifle Riordan quickly tried to aim. They parried, both swinging their weapons at the other, both still on their knees.

A furious battle of rifles as quarterstaffs ensued. In an effort to gain height, Cassidy shuffled to his right and his knee came down on a sharp stone. For the briefest moment his attention diverted to the piercing pain in his knee and in that moment Riordan clipped the side of his head.

Cassidy, stunned, rolled away and Riordan, still in the fierce heat of the fight, swung his rifle back and with all his force brought it down where Cassidy's face lay blinking at the sky.

Cassidy jerked to his right. Riordan's rifle stock hit a rock the size of two doubled fists and shattered.

"Damn!" Riordan shouted.

Cassidy reared up and swung the .45-.70 at the Irishman's head and missed when Riordan fell onto his back, scrambling for his pistol.

Cassidy pulled back the hammer on the .45-.70 and aimed at Riordan's head. "I know you're not from the Great Plains, but I'm sure you've heard of a buffalo gun."

Riordan pulled his hand away from the pistol and held it in the air. His other hand lay on the ground, shaking with desire and exhaustion.

"Yeah, I've heard of 'em."

★ 85 ★

**9 miles east of Delta on the
Russia-Canada Highway**

Lieutenant Alex Strom of the International Freekorps
wondered how to end this once and for all. Riordan
and the other guy could fight all night at this rate.
Yet Roland Delcambré sat behind him with a weapon.

The three truckloads of mercenaries behind Delcambré had no idea what was going on. They merely
waited for Strom to give them direction. He finally
decided to call Roland's bluff when suddenly a tank
reared up over the ridge and slammed down on the
road surface. The dusty, faded paint depicting a Kiowa
war shield adorned the front of the machine.

"Shit!" Strom said, dropping off his elbows onto
the ground. "I know when I'm licked."

Three more tanks followed. All stopped and their
cannon and machine guns pointed at the vehicles
carrying the remnants of the International Freekorps.
Riordan and the other man stared at the machines.
Roland's friend lowered his weapon and stepped back
from Riordan. Both gasped in exhaustion.

"I'm getting out of here," Gagne said. "Don't wait
up. You have a good life, Alex. Roland, can I leave?"

Delcambré nodded and Strom watched Gagne slip away from under the car and disappear off to the right. One of the FPN gunners fired a quick burst in that direction but made no indication he had hit anything. Strom wondered if they'd hang him.

A man about his father's age climbed down off the lead tank. He had the air of command about him and wore two small silver devices on his shoulders. He stopped in front of the man Riordan had fought with and extended his hand to pull him up.

"Once again Yukon Cassidy gets his man."

Riordan, still lying on the ground, quipped, "But he didn't beat me!"

Cassidy glanced down at him. "That can be arranged."

Soldiers poured over the ridge and surrounded Strom's scout car and the three trucks. Strom nodded when one of the soldiers deftly plucked the pistol off his belt and the two carbines out of the car. The officer walked over to the scout car.

"Name and rank?"

Strom decided the devices were representations of the sun that meant the man was a brigadier general. He stood at attention.

"Lieutenant Alex Strom, International Freekorps, General."

"You're a prisoner of war, Lieutenant Strom. It will be determined later if you are guilty of war crimes or merely bad judgment in following that worthless bastard." He nodded at Riordan.

"I've already convicted myself of the latter, General."

"You're smart; that's why you're a lieutenant."

"Maybe I'm not smart enough?"

★ 86 ★

Port Lemhi, Republic of California

The RCNS *Mako* slid into her berth and sailors on the dock tied her fast while a gangway was expertly lowered to her deck.

Wing felt completely drained of emotion. It seemed a miracle to see sunlight, solid ground, and the last of this horrible, smelly submarine. Still, she had to be polite.

"Colonel Grigorievich," Captain Vandenberg said, holding both of her hands in his, "your unflinching bravery gave all around you added determination."

"Captain Vandenberg," she said earnestly, staring into his eyes, "it's a true wonder I didn't soil myself. I have never been that frightened before in my life. You and your men have to be the bravest people I know to go down and do that day after day."

"Thank you, ma'am. I'll make sure my crew hears your words. We're proud to have helped make your quest more successful."

She didn't hear what Grisha said behind her. She didn't care. She just wanted off this terrifying boat once and for all.

Lieutenant Commander Hills waited at the bottom of the gangplank.

"Welcome back, Colonel. How was your trip?" His wide smile gave him a boyish look.

"Hell, Commander Hills. Total hell. I really need a drink of something stronger than tea."

"Perhaps I can interest you in a shot of twenty-year-old brandy?"

"I have never drunk liquor before, so..."

"Maybe a nice glass of California wine would be a better choice then."

Grisha and Sergeant Major Tobias walked down the gangway, deep in conversation. Wing wondered what subject they discussed. Once on land Grisha turned and saluted the *Mako*, then bent down and kissed the ground.

The watch standers on the submarine all laughed and applauded.

"Commander Hills, it is a true joy to see you again," Grisha said.

"The trip was that bad, huh?"

"Have you ever been in a depth charge attack?"

"No, General, I haven't. You don't see any dolphins on my chest. I'm in awe of those guys, but I'm not crazy."

"Commander Hills has offered us a glass of wine."

Grisha regarded her with an odd expression. "But you don't drink."

"Today I do, perhaps for the only time in my life, but getting back here alive deserves a celebration."

"As long as you don't overdo it." Grisha smiled and offered his arm. As they walked to the black sedan, Grisha whispered in her ear, "We have to return to Tanana as soon as possible. The election is getting ugly."

Wing felt her spirits slump. "I was afraid that would happen."

★ 87 ★

4000 feet over the Dená Republik

"Give me a damage assessment," Colonel Shipley ordered.

"This is Cassaro. I'm out of ammo but they didn't lay a finger on me."

"Hafs here. I'm getting frostbite from a hole on each side of my canopy; other than that I'm just fine."

"I'm fine as frog hair, Skipper," Currie reported. "As far as I'm concerned, we could hit them again."

"Yamato?" Shipley's voice had gentled and his concern was obvious to all who heard it.

Jerry cleared his throat. "No injuries, no aircraft damage, Colonel Shipley."

"Well, gentlemen," Shipley said in a more fulsome voice. "This is our last mission. We've been ordered back to Fort Yukon. We're being relieved."

"Excellent!"

"Man, that's the best news I've heard since we came north."

"Who's replacing us, Colonel?" Yamato asked.

"I'm not at liberty to say over an unsecure frequency. But suffice it to say they will add a lot of speed to the war."

Jerry frowned. *What the hell was he talking about?*

As they angled down toward the runway at Fort Yukon, an aircraft whipped past them at an incredible rate of speed.

"What the hell was that?" Cassaro yelled.

"It's a plane. I can see that much," Hafs said.

"That, gentlemen, is the future of aviation," Shipley said in a reverential tone. "That was an RCAF F-82 Swordmaster, the most modern jet fighter aircraft in the world today."

"What the hell is a *jet*?" Currie asked.

★ 88 ★

Tanana, Dená Republik

"I want Gennady Ustinov arrested and tried for murder!" Nathan Roubitaux bellowed.

"Who did he murder?" Grisha asked, keeping his tone neutral.

"One of my oper—one of my campaign workers! A man named Alexi—"

"Popovich," Grisha finished for him.

"Then you already know about it. Why hasn't this man been arrested?"

"For one thing, there's still a war being fought. And from what I heard, your *campaign worker* challenged Mr. Ustinov to a duel and lost. There is the issue of personal responsibility here. Mr. Popovich shouldn't have been so free with his challenge."

"You're siding with them against us?"

"Who are *them* and who is *us*, Nathan? I thought we were all on the same side here; the Athabascan People, the Dená Republik."

A murmur eddied around the Council Chamber.

Grisha and Wing had been summoned to the chamber ostensibly to give a report on their meeting with the Tlingit Nation Army. But they knew much more needed to be dealt with than the stated subject; they had been warned.

Grisha, Wing, and Sergeant Major Tobias had arrived in Tanana the previous day to a welcoming committee of four: General Eluska, Lieutenant Colonel Blue Bostonman, Major Lauesen, USA, and a man named Waterman Stoddard.

Introductions had been quick and General Eluska summed up with, "We represent four situations: I'm military, Blue is politics, Major Lauesen is intelligence, and Mr. Stoddard is trouble."

Grisha's grin died quickly when he realized Paul wasn't kidding. "So tell me."

"There is a battle under way at Delta; we heard it might be finished, but nothing official has come through. The Republic of California has sent a—"

A quickly growing roar filled the air and a formation of four aircraft shot through the sky over them and dwindled into the distance.

"What the bloody hell!" Sergeant Major Tobias blurted.

"Couldn't have timed that better if I tried," General Eluska said with a grin. "That was part of the squadron of fighter jets the Republic of California has sent north."

"Jets?" Wing asked, glancing at the sky again.

"I'll handle that part, Colonel," Major Lauesen said in a low voice.

"We still have about fifteen hundred people stationed at Bridge," General Eluska continued, "and the Dená Army is pretty damn thin everywhere else.

But we still have the ROC and the USA bolstering our pitiful numbers." He nodded at Major Lauesen. "I think you should go next, Elstun."

"Thank you, General Eluska. General and Colonel Grigorievich, a great deal has transpired since you left on your mission. And please allow me to congratulate you both on the results; I wish I could have been there."

"How could you know what happened?" Wing said. "We just got here."

"You came by submarine, Colonel. I received a report by radio."

"The Tlingits said they would let us break the news," Wing snapped.

"It wasn't the Tlingits who told me," Major Lauesen slightly blushed, "our intelligence did."

"The US has a spy in the Tlingit Nation Army?" Grisha asked, sand in his tone.

"No more than I am, here, General. Military advisors arrived in Tlingit country about the same time you embarked on the *Mako*."

"What else?" Grisha felt he had been ambushed by words, and he realized the battle hadn't really started yet.

"The current situation in the Dená Republik is quite good. Colonel Buhrman's 3rd PIR reports that the two Russian columns and the International Freekorps have surrendered; they were all decimated to the point of annihilation. An armored column fielded by the First People's Nation cut off the retreat of elements of the IF, and are maintaining station."

"Exactly where?" Grisha fought a sense of bewilderment.

Why did the First People's Nation send an armored column into Dená territory?

"They're about six miles outside of Delta." Major Lauesen waited for a beat and then continued, "Conflict outside Alaska has been intense and devastating to the units involved. The Republic of California declared war on Japan, as did the Kingdom of Hawai'i."

"I thought the Japanese attacked Kodiak," Wing said in a puzzled tone.

"And Sitka," Lauesen said with a nod. "They destroyed the Kodiak Naval Station but lost a destroyer at Sitka and have withdrawn all naval elements from Alaska, except for an Imperial Marine battalion they abandoned on Kodiak."

"Why did they do that?" Grisha asked.

"The Republic of California Marine Corps parachuted elements of the First Brigade into interior Kodiak and ambushed the Japanese marines advancing on the town of Kodiak from the rear. The battle has yet to end, but the Japanese have no hope of winning that one."

"What else, Major Lauesen?" Wing bit off each word.

"Yes, let's get back to the rest of the world," he said blithely. "The reason Russia has largely ignored us here in Alaska is—"

"Ignored!" Wing snapped. "We've fought with everything and everyone we had!"

"No argument, Colonel. But my government anticipated a much larger war here. The Imperial Russian government sent token forces compared to what she had at her disposal."

"That's exactly what I've thought all along," Grisha said. "I kept waiting for the real attack to begin."

"It won't. That charade they perpetuated on you down in California paid huge dividends."

"My *trial*?" Grisha said through a grin.

"Yeah. The Russians didn't think the Dená would actually pull you out of a field command to answer criminal charges. They planned to use your non-appearance as propaganda against both the ROC and the USA for supporting a criminal rebellion."

"How would that really help them?" Grisha suspected there had been more to the situation than he had been told.

"Alliances in Europe were changing on a daily basis. The situation in the rest of North America hinged on European alliances. Russia lost political face when she had to withdraw her charge, not to mention your performance garnered high praise from most of the members present."

"I'll bet I can name the unimpressed ones," Grisha said, relishing the moment.

"I suspect you're correct. The CSA halted hostilities with the USA; they were losing anyway. Texas and New Spain are negotiating yet another border, which has been a typical Texan thing to fight about ever since they left the CSA over New Mexico back in 1852."

"Stay on subject, Major," General Eluska said with a hint of a smile.

"Right!" He flipped a page in his small notepad. "All saber rattling in Europe has ceased with the understanding that no more European troops would be sent to North America, forestalling an arms race that would bankrupt all involved."

"We're like one of those little soldier pieces in that game you like, aren't we?" Wing asked, staring into Grisha's face.

"Yes, my love, we were nothing more than a pawn to most of the world. But we are a very fortunate pawn."

"Couldn't have said it better myself," Major Lauesen said.

"Those airplanes?" Wing prompted.

"They are called jets. They don't have a propeller. Don't ask me how they work because I don't know, probably magic. The Japanese are openly using them, as is the Republic of California."

"What about the USA?" Grisha asked.

"Ours are still a military secret," Lauesen said with a laugh.

"Which brings us to politics," Blue said. "Dená politics."

"Just when I was starting to relax," Grisha said. He noticed that Major Lauesen had pulled Sergeant Major Tobias off to one side and was speaking earnestly into his cocked ear.

"And I'm part of that, too, General," Waterman Stoddard said. He glanced at Blue and added, "President Roubitaux is trying to steal the constitutional convention."

"It was my understanding we were here to report on our meeting with the Tlingit Nation Army, Mr. President," Grisha said, staring into Nathan's eyes, "not to dispense justice or right civilian wrongs."

"We will get to your report in good time, General Grigorievich, but I feel it is imperative to inform you that a schism has developed in our cause and threatens all of the Dená Republik."

"Politically, but not militarily, Mr. President?"

"It could lead to military action, General."

"May I have a word in private, Mr. President?"

Nathan, caught flatfooted, opened his mouth but

said nothing for a quarter minute. Grisha could almost see wheels spinning in the man's head.

"Of course, General." Nathan stood and indicated a door in the corner of the room.

Grisha opened the door and interrupted an intense embrace between a female staff sergeant and a male corporal. "You're both dismissed. Go somewhere else for that."

They fled and Nathan came through the door, his face like thunder. As soon as the door shut, he rounded on Grisha.

"You're siding with the Village Faction, aren't you?"

"I'm not siding with anyone, Mr. President. Why are you?"

"There seems to be a lot of people out there who do not fully understand the situation. They could endanger the constitutional process, make us look like fools in the eyes of the world."

"The world already thinks we're fools for fighting Mother Russia. Why worry now?"

"Don't be clever with me, Grisha! This is serious business."

"Getting shot at *isn't* serious business, Nathan? I think you've forgotten that a lot of people have died to keep you in the position to which you seem to have become accustomed."

Nathan had the good sense to back off, let the pomposity fall from his features and continue in a more contrite voice.

"Of course. Getting shot at is about as serious as it gets. I apologize if you feel I was denigrating anyone's service or sacrifice."

He is really smooth! Grisha thought. *I almost believed that.*

"Not to worry," Grisha said. "But I must tell you that a great many people are of the opinion that you are out to steal the election."

"To what purpose?"

"To load it with people you have picked. This has to be a democratic process, Nathan, or everything we have done is wasted."

"Have you *met* Gennady Ustinov?" The sneer in his tone was unmistakable. "He's a storekeeper in Old Crow who thinks he understands the whole political landscape of the Dená Republik."

"Maybe he understands that you believe you invented it?"

"And thou, Brutus!"

"Don't throw your university education at me, Nathan. I'm too damned tired to give a shit. And don't give me that old 'you're either with me or against me' stuff, because it isn't true.

"But I do want you to remember that I took an oath, one that *you* administered, to serve the Dená Republik to the best of my abilities. And I plan to do just that—serve the Republik, not you personally."

"Thank you for being so candid, General Grigorievich. I appreciate it."

Before Grisha could respond, Nathan hurried back into the Council Chamber.

"Lunchtime, folks!" he called out as he went through the front door without slowing or looking at anybody else.

★ 89 ★

6 miles east of Delta

Magda and Pelagian sat in the back of the scout car as Major Smolst drove them and Colonel Buhrman toward the three tanks blocking the road. She held a machine gun with the barrel pointed forward and up. They could easily see the Kiowa war shield displayed on the tank hulls, even though the paint was pitted and dusty.

They had already passed at least three squads of soldiers. Many of them wore feathers and other bird and animal parts in their hair. Considering that all of them also wore camouflage battle dress it made for an interesting ride.

From between the tanks three men walked toward the scout car.

"That's Yukon Cassidy!" Pelagian said as he hopped over the side of the car and hurried toward them. He grabbed the shortest of the three and they hugged, slapped each other on the back and danced in a circle all at the same time. Pelagian towered over his friend by more than a foot.

"I take it they've met before," Colonel Buhrman said with a grin.

"They've been friends for over twenty years," Magda said. "Cassidy is one of those people you either hate or love. Our family loves him."

Pelagian and Cassidy stopped and spoke with the other two men. Pelagian turned and motioned for the others to join them.

In moments they all stood face to face.

"This is Colonel Buhrman of the Republic of California Army 3rd Parachute Infantry Regiment, Major Smolst of the Dená Army, late of the Troika Guard, and my incredible daughter, Magda, who is also a sergeant of scouts in the Dená Army."

Magda didn't wait any longer; she rushed forward and hugged Cassidy. "It's so good to see you again! You just disappeared after the first part of the battle."

She pulled back while her father introduced the other two men.

"Gentlemen, this is General Lawrence Spotted Bird and Colonel Franklin Fires-Twice of the First People's Nation Army, and my old, dear friend Yukon Cassidy."

After hand-clasping all around, Colonel Buhrman immediately went to the crux of the matter.

"What are you people doing this far north, General Spotted Bird?"

"May I ask you the same question, Colonel Buhrman?" General Spotted Bird asked.

Buhrman didn't lose his grin. "*Touché!* We were invited by the Dená Separatist Army to provide aid and assistance. We've been providing both for over six months."

"Commendable," General Spotted Bird said. "We followed a bandit and his cohorts north."

"With an entire armored column?" Major Smolst blurted. "You must have really been pissed."

"Well put, Major. The International Freekorps went through our country like a plague of locusts, killing, looting, burning and fleeing when met with equal force. Then the British Canadians had the temerity to attack us with the fiction that they were merely passing through to get to the United States.

"We defeated the British and chased them back into their own country and, just for the hell of it, took a big part of their territory and kept it. However, we didn't find *Major* Riordan since he had gone north where he thought we wouldn't follow. He was wrong."

"We have a lot of IF prisoners of war, but I don't know if he's one of them," Colonel Buhrman said.

"He isn't. Cassidy brought him in yesterday. He's back there in our jail lorry." General Spotted Bird nodded toward the tanks behind him.

"What are your plans now, General?" Pelagian asked.

"First, to offer any help we can give. Second, to get home as soon as we can. My men are tired and they've fought well."

"We offer you the hospitality of Delta, Dená Republik." Pelagian grinned. "I think there's going to be a celebration very soon now."

★ 90 ★

Tanana, Dená Republik

While two of the new F-82 Swordmasters flew a
combat air patrol overhead, the side of the Tanana
Aerodrome was lined with aircraft. The remaining
ten P-61 Eurekas, patched and tired, were flanked
by thirteen of the new, gleaming jets.

Captain Jerry Yamato stood at parade rest in the
front rank of the 117th Attack Squadron personnel.
Both officers and enlisted men wore their dress uniforms, sent north specifically for this occasion. To their
right were mustered the officers and enlisted of the
24th Attack Squadron.

Jerry noticed the 24th had three times as many
officers as did the 117th. Over the next two hours that
would change forever: the 117th was being disbanded
as an active unit. He tried not to think about it.

The command sergeant major snapped tall.

·"A-tenn-SHUN!"

Every man on the field went as ramrod straight
as he could.

Five officers moved out of the shadowed hangar
and into the bright Alaskan sunshine. Jerry couldn't

believe how damned *hot* it was. He was no stranger to heat and he calculated it had to be right at 90 degrees Fahrenheit.

One of the officers was Brigadier General George "Jud" Caldwell of the Republic of California Air Force. Every man in the RCAF revered him. Jud had gone from an enlisted sergeant-pilot to a battlefield commission of lieutenant. He then opted for four years at the Presidio where he graduated fifth in a class of 187.

Every airman in the RCAF knew that "General Jud" would never ask anything of them that he wouldn't do himself. He was the best and they would follow him anywhere. He had come north on the same plane that carried their dress uniforms.

The general's adjutant, Colonel Ust, carried a small stack of boxes: decorations to be presented. The other three officers with General Jud were unknown to Jerry. All were in the Dená Republik Army and wore a combination of ROC and USA army uniforms. The two men wore the rosettes depicting dentalium shells in a star pattern and executed in beads, gold on a field of blue: generals.

The woman wore the depiction of the sun resting in a moose rack. She was a colonel. Jerry gave her a closer look than he did the men. She was strikingly beautiful despite the scar on her cheek; he decided she had to be Athabascan.

The party halted in front of the 117th.

"Airmen of the 117th Attack Squadron," General Jud said in a conversational voice, "you have brought honor and glory to your service, your country, and your flag. A grateful nation salutes you."

All five of the officers saluted at the same time.

For a moment the 117th froze, and then returned the salute, officers and enlisted alike. None of them had ever seen that done before.

"It is my great honor and pleasure to award the following decorations," General Jud said.

"To Lieutenant Colonel Benjamin Hurley, late commander of the 117th Attack Squadron, for actions above and beyond the call of duty. In an action against an armored Russian column, he led by example and gave his life to bring about the destruction of most of the enemy column. A grateful nation awards Lieutenant Colonel Hurley the Republic of California Congressional Medal of Honor, posthumously. The award was presented to his widow three days ago in Sacramento."

Every man in the 117th applauded long and hard. Jerry felt tears on his cheeks and didn't give a damn. They'd even promoted Major Hurley to Lieutenant Colonel; that would help his widow in terms of a pension.

The applause died down and General Jud gave them a moment to collect themselves. He cleared his throat.

"Major David Fowler. In an action over Russian Amerika, he shot down two enemy fighters and, although mortally wounded, piloted his aircraft into an enemy bomber, resulting in the destruction of that craft and a second bomber, which resulted in an enemy retreat. A grateful nation has awarded him the Distinguished Flying Cross."

In his mind's eye Jerry again saw Dave's plane arrow into the Russian bomber and explode. As far as he was concerned, that deserved a Medal of Honor also.

"Lieutenant Colonel Roger Shipley, front and center."

Lieutenant Colonel Shipley moved out smartly, stopped in front of the general, and came to attention.

"Lieutenant Colonel Shipley consistently and professionally led his squadron against the enemy, never wavering in his duty to his squadron or his country. He is hereby promoted to full colonel and a grateful nation awards him the Air Medal."

Colonel Ust handed General Caldwell the medal and the general pinned it on Colonel Shipley's chest and then shook his hand. Jerry couldn't hear what the general said to Colonel Shipley, but the colonel was visibly moved. In moments the colonel was back in ranks.

"Captain Gerald Yamato, front and center."

As Jerry stepped out and came to attention in front of the general, he wondered why they would award him a decoration. All he'd done was try to stay alive and keep his word. Only dead men should receive honors.

"Captain Yamato turned adversity into opportunity when he was shot down over Rainbow Ridge in the same action that claimed four of his comrades. He persevered through an attack by a Russian survivor of the armored column the 117th destroyed. He was instrumental in saving the life of the Russian and making him his friend.

"Captain Yamato, still a lieutenant at the time, joined forces with elements of the Dená Separatist Movement and led a group of infantry volunteers against a well-entrenched column of professional mercenaries and successfully destroyed enough enemy armor to reduce their military threat significantly."

General Caldwell looked up from his paper and grinned at Jerry.

"This is like reading a novel, Captain!" he said in his San Fernando Valley drawl.

Quickly suppressed laughter eddied through the ranks.

"Being deprived of his P-61, Captain Yamato flew an antique 1940 Grigorovich in first a reconnaissance flight over three hostile armored columns and then later returned to attack all three. Captain Yamato was wounded in this last action yet piloted his damaged antique aircraft to an airfield two hundred miles distant where he had never been before.

"In addition," General Caldwell theatrically wiped his brow causing more laughter in the ranks, "then-Lieutenant Yamato led a strike force back to the Battle of Delta where the 117th surprised a Russian bombing mission on its way north. Captain Yamato shot down two enemy fighters in the action where Major Fowler gave his life, and proceeded to lead his squadron back to the Battle of Delta where they depleted their armament on the forces attacking the Dená Army."

General Caldwell stopped and looked at Jerry. "I am proud to know you, sir. A grateful nation bestows upon you the Distinguished Flying Cross, the Purple Heart, and the Air Medal, Major Yamato."

Jerry stood, stunned, as General Jud Caldwell pinned medals on his chest. They had blown everything out of proportion: he didn't deserve this.

The general stepped back, shook Jerry's hand. Then he saluted him.

Jerry returned the salute automatically, feeling oddly detached from himself, as if he were watching this happen to someone else.

"Our hosts have something to add," General Caldwell said and stepped back.

One of the Dená generals stood in front of him, held out his hand. Jerry shook it.

"I am honored to meet you, Major Yamato, I have heard much about your actions. I am General Gregori Grigorievich of the Dená Army. We are a new army, part of a new nation, one that you have helped birth.

"As yet we have no military history, no tradition. All is new. General Eluska and Colonel Grigorievich here, and I, have conferred and created the first decoration for valor in the defense of the Dená Republik."

General Grigorievich paused and swallowed. Jerry realized the general was more nervous than he was. The colonel passed something to the general and he held it up with both hands for all to see.

"Allow me to explain what you are seeing," General Grigorievich said.

"The four-inch-wide band of dark blue cloth is backed with moosehide and set off with bead rosettes signifying the North Star on each side. Twin ranks of dentalium shells cascade down to a piece of very old copper taken in trade over a century ago. Both the copper and dentalium shells denote rank in the Athabascan culture.

"This is a unique piece of art, created specifically for this occasion and for Lieutenant Colonel Yamato, his rank in the Dená Army from this day forward. Since only a citizen of the Dená Republik can be commissioned in the Dená Army, Gerald Yamato has been adopted into our people and culture: he is now one of the People."

General Grigorievich put the necklacelike decoration around Jerry's neck, stepped back and shook his hand.

"Welcome, Colonel Yamato. We would be honored if you would have dinner with us tonight."

"Thank you, General Grigorievich. I thank you for the great honor and would be proud to dine with you."

General Grigorievich grinned, making him look years younger. "That's settled, then. I'll have someone come by and pick you up."

Jerry saluted the officers and returned to ranks. The ceremony wasn't over. Hafs, Currie and Cassaro were all awarded the Air Medal, as was Major Ellis, posthumously.

Once everyone was back in ranks, General Caldwell spoke again.

"President Reagan has awarded the 117th the Presidential Unit Citation. The squadron will go into history with a legacy of duty, honor, and glory. Thank you for your service. You are dismissed."

★ 91 ★

Delta, Dená Republik

Toe-tapping fiddle music resonated through the town of Delta. The townspeople had gratefully and quickly descended the mountain to return to their homes. The square in front of the former St. Anthony Redoubt was filled with tables, chairs, benches, and piles of blankets where babies and small children watched the commotion. The aroma of cooking food permeated the area as moose haunches and entire caribou carcasses turned on spits over mounds of glowing coals.

Magda knew she should be as happy as everyone else but she felt very alone. She wanted Jerry here. He deserved to be here as much as anyone else—more than some, in her estimation.

She sensed someone beside her and looked over to see her mother.

"You miss him, don't you?"

"Of course I do, Mother." The tear that escaped her left eye surprised her. "How can I celebrate without the man I have come to love?"

"He'll be back. I know that for a certainty," Bodecia said with a nod. "He's as smitten with you as you are with him, maybe more."

Magda sighed. "I'm not sure that's possible."

Bodecia laughed. "You're wallowing in self-pity. At a time like this, that is a waste of your intelligence. Besides, your father wants your opinion on the latest situation."

"What situation? Didn't we win?"

"We won *this* war. Now we're faced with not losing the victory."

Magda jumped to her feet. "I don't understand, but explain on the way."

The late afternoon increased in tempo. People danced to fiddle, guitar, and balalaika music. Someone had even brought out an antique harpsichord and was playing it with exquisite expertise.

"Suddenly we are faced with factions within the Dená people," Bodecia said as they moved briskly through the happy crowd.

"Factions? What kind of factions?"

"Basically, many have different opinions on where do we go from here."

"Anywhere we want to! I don't understand this."

"Well, I do and I don't. Oh good, there's your father; he will make us both understand. He's good at this nuance stuff."

Two FPN drummers, one Pawnee and one Sioux, added their harmony to the music. Laughter and loud talk echoed around the square. Dená girls walked with FPN warriors close to their own age, chatting and flirting.

Magda knew there would be many babies made this night. Was that why she was so morose? Is that why she wanted Jerry to be here with her? She realized their war was over and now she could examine the emotions she felt for him. She wanted to do that with him—not alone.

Pelagian sat on a folding campstool conversing with General Spotted Bird, Colonel Fires-Twice, Colonel Romanov, Yukon Cassidy, and a small man she didn't recognize. On the perimeter of the group others sat or stood.

"Ah, here's my clear-thinking daughter. This is Magda, a sergeant of scouts and the pride of my life."

She stopped and came to attention. "Gentlemen," she said with a nod.

All the men stood. Pelagian introduced everyone, ending with the small, dark man. "And this is Roland Delcambré, who is traveling with Yukon."

"Sir." She nodded again. Magda glanced at her father. "Mother says there are factions. Please explain what that means."

"First it means that the war is over and we won. I'm not sure how we did that as quickly as we did, but the fact remains that we've run out of Russians to fight. So now we're free to fight each other."

"Why? What is there to fight about?"

"Please give me your opinion on this: where does the Dená Republik go from here?"

"We form a government, of course."

"I agree. How?"

"We've already started. We pick delegates to a constitutional convention and they write a constitution and we do whatever the constitution says to make a government."

"So who do you pick to write your part?"

"I don't even know who's running. Delta is our whole district, yes?"

"Yes."

"So who is running?"

"Konstantin Mitkov for one."

"Viktor's father?"

"Yes."

"Who else, Father?"

"Me."

"What?" Bodecia jumped like a bee-stung pup. "Shooting Russians is one thing, but if you go into politics, you'll have Indians shooting at you!"

"Why, Father?" Magda asked.

"I'm sorry to spring this on you both, but there is no time to spare. The election is a week away and I haven't had a chance to tell people how I see the situation."

"How *do* you see the situation?" Magda didn't know why, but she felt very apprehensive about his decision.

"We are a brand-new country filled with people who were born here and others who have helped us fight for our liberty. Who are the citizens of this new country? Just those born here, or also those who were willing to die for it?

"And what about land ownership? Does our new country recognize the deeds of those who owned land under the Czar, or is everything up for grabs again? Who decides if Dená who didn't fight against the Czar have the same rights as those who did?"

Magda blinked. "You're right. I hadn't thought about any of that, and I know you would be essential in a constitutional convention if it were to be fair for all. How can I help you?"

"How can we all help?" Yukon Cassidy asked.

"Are you even a resident?" Pelagian asked Cassidy.

"If six years of running a trap line on the Charley River doesn't make me a resident, then nothing will."

"He's a resident as far as I'm concerned," Doyon Isaac said from the edge of the circle. "As is every person who fought for the Dená Republik. Who could argue against that?"

"Konstantin Mitkov, for one," Pelagian said. "He believes that if you're not at least half Athabascan, then you're not a citizen."

"Remind me, old friend," Yukon Cassidy said. "Where was it that this Konstantin fellow fought?"

"He didn't. He was one of the first to reach Refuge and he grabbed as much space as he could. When the evacuation began, he was told he couldn't have that much area and he argued about it."

"Yet nobody shot him?" Cassidy's grin made everyone else laugh.

"You've made my point," Pelagian conceded. "This is why I must run, and why I must win."

"May we be of help?" General Spotted Bird asked.

"I guess you could talk to people."

An FPN Army sergeant suddenly ran up to the group and saluted General Spotted Bird.

"What is it, Sergeant Fox Dreams?"

"Sorry to bother you, General. Major Riordan has escaped."

★ 92 ★

5 miles northwest of Delta

The motorcycle backfired for the third time and the engine died. Riordan coasted to a stop and stepped off one side of the machine and let it topple the other direction into a deep ravine, causing a small landslide of rock and gravel that covered the motorcycle. His water and food were strapped to him, part of his constant vigilance attitude.

They had probably found the dead guard by now, wrapped in his blanket and on the cot in the half-assed jail built on the back of a lorry. It took him all of a half hour to unhinge the door. It took another ten hours for the right circumstances to make his escape.

He jogged north with glances over his shoulder every thirty paces. They might wait for dawn, and they might not: it wasn't that far away. He couldn't take anything for granted. Where the hell was Klahotsa?

If he could reach that village he would be safe, perhaps. But there was nowhere else in the new Dená Republik where he could find sanctuary. Kurt Bachmann was the man who had hired him; that's who he had to find.

Riordan glanced over his shoulder again and when he looked forward again he saw the glow. He slowed to a fast walk and peered ahead. Finally he realized he was seeing the reflection of a campfire off the edge of a vehicle on the side of the road.

He stopped and let his breathing subside into something normal. This had to be done carefully and a panting, wild-eyed apparition out of the night would be problematical to say the least.

Ten meters from the truck he yelled, "Hello the camp, one man coming in."

Two young Indians stoically watched him emerge into the firelight.

One waved him forward and nodded to a rock on the other side of the snapping, flame-engulfed wood. "You hungry?" he asked.

"I'm starving. Haven't had food since breakfast."

The other one peered into the darkness. "You on foot? I didn't hear any motors."

"Had a motorcycle. It died about five miles back that way." Riordan nodded his head, never taking his eyes off the men.

"Where you going?" the first man said as he handed Riordan a steaming plate of stew.

"Thank you!" He grabbed the food and shoveled a spoonful into his mouth and yelped as it burned his tongue. After a moment he chewed and swallowed. "I'm going to Klahotsa. You folks going that far?"

"Naw, we're only headed to Nowitna. But that's a lot closer than you are now."

"I'd love a ride."

★ 93 ★

Tanana, Dená Republik

Precisely at 6:45 P.M. a dented, but spotlessly clean, scout car pulled up in front of the old hotel where the RCAF billeted their pilots. Jerry felt ostentatious in his dress uniform with all the decorations but returned the snappy salute the sergeant major gave him.

"Is there a problem if I ride in front, Sergeant Major Tobias?"

Tobias grinned. "I won't tell if you won't, Colonel."

Jerry settled in the front passenger seat. "I'm not used to all this yet, so don't worry about being formal."

"It's not just 'formal,' sir, it's also respect for rank and honors." The sergeant turned around in the dusty street and they bounced along at ten miles per hour.

"That's the other part of it," Jerry said, bracing against the dashboard, "I don't feel like I did anything that the next guy wouldn't do in the same situation. And being one rank in the RCAF and a different rank in the Dená Army is just nuts."

"I'll give you that, sir. I've never seen the like in all my thirty-odd years of soldiering. But as for deserving it, well, that's not for us to decide, is it now?"

"Where exactly are you from, Sergeant Major?"

"Originally?" He lapsed into silence for a moment. "Boston, down in the United States of America."

"The state of Massachusetts, right?" Jerry said.

"Very good, sir. Most folks don't know their geography nowadays, or much else found in books for that matter."

"You sound like one of my school teachers back home." Jerry laughed.

"I was a school teacher once, a long time ago."

"Then you're a college graduate?"

"That I am, although I would appreciate it if you didn't tell anyone else."

"Hell, Tobias, you could be an officer."

"Nothing personal, Colonel Yamato, but why would I want to do that? Here I am at the top of my game, being involved in all the big things, and yet have no responsibility if it all goes to hell in a hand basket."

"So you're happy where you are?"

"Let's just say I'm satisfied with my lot in life. I've had it much worse. Ah, here we are: Dená Army Headquarters."

Jerry took in the three-story building. "When did they build this?"

"This is an old Russian Army hospital. The USA and your Republic of California have modernized it and it is now the most up-to-date hospital in the country. The left wing on the bottom floor has been turned into quarters for officers. General and Colonel Grigorievich have the nicest apartment in the place."

"Tell me about them, please."

"Ah, no time, Colonel Yamato," he said with a wolfish grin, "you'll just have to fend for yourself."

Jerry followed the sergeant major up the walk and

through the doors. A sentry snapped to attention and Jerry returned his salute. The tile floors were polished to the point that one could use them as mirrors with which to shave.

Sergeant Major Tobias stopped and knocked on a door. It immediately opened and Colonel Wing Grigorievich waved them in. She looked incredibly feminine and Jerry realized she was wearing a dress that more than accentuated her excellent figure. Magda rested in his thoughts for a long moment.

"Colonel Yamato, Sergeant Major Tobias, please come in."

"Thank you, Colonel," Jerry said, clutching his hat in both hands.

As he stepped through the door, she neatly pulled the hat from his hands. "I'll take care of that. Please join the general in the parlor, or whatever that room is." She flashed him a quick grin and he realized he wasn't the only nervous person here.

"Yes, Colonel." Tobias had disappeared and Jerry's steps on the wooden floors seemed unnaturally loud. General Grigorievich sat on the far side of the room holding a telephone to his ear. He waved at Jerry, smiled, and pointed to the sideboard where various bottles of liquor and wine stood.

Jerry wandered over to the bottles and read the labels. He found a California wine and poured himself two fingers in a glass, then sat in a chair and waited.

"Of course that's important, but you can't expect me to come out on either side. What? Because I'm a professional soldier, that's why."

General Grigorievich glanced up at Jerry and rotated a finger near his head and smiled.

"For the last time, I cannot help you with this. This is a political situation and I am military; we cannot take sides."

He put the phone down on its cradle and stared out the window at the subdued twilight.

"They just don't get it, Colonel Yamato. Every Athabascan with a problem thinks they have the right to call in the army to get them what they want. That's not our mission and I'll be damned if the army will get pulled into this political faction thing."

"Colonel Yamato, relax," Colonel Grigorievich said, coming into the room. "You've chosen a wine. Please tell me which it is and why you chose it."

Jerry realized he had been sitting at attention. He forced himself to relax and swallowed the contents of his glass. He went over to the sideboard where she stood.

"I chose a California wine because I know the label and actually know the vintner. This merlot has a complex body as well as a nice nutty and fruity finish. I don't know how you got this bottle up here but I am impressed and gratified."

Throughout his critique she had watched his face and he watched hers. She went from amused to impressed and nodded as he finished.

"Well done, sir! I'm glad the general chose you. Neither he nor I know a thing about wine."

"Chose me?"

A bell rang and Sergeant Major Tobias stepped into the room. "Dinner is served on the veranda."

He motioned to double French doors both of which stood open and inviting. Colonel Grigorievich poured herself a glass of wine and Jerry poured himself another and followed her. A table set for three and illuminated by candlelight dominated the space.

Jerry glanced up and saw mosquito netting draped over the entire area. The faint buzz of the insects could be heard if one listened for them. The colonel stopped at a chair and Jerry held it for her while she sat.

General Grigorievich ambled out onto the veranda holding a bottle of beer and pulled back the remaining chair.

"Do be seated, Colonel."

Both men sat and a waiter instantly appeared with a tray holding three steaming plates.

The general smiled and said, "I hope you aren't tired of moose yet."

"Actually I have developed quite a taste for it, sir."

Grigorievich held up his hand. "While you are my guest, I am Grisha and my wife is Wing, is that okay with you, Jerry?"

"Of course, si—Grisha. Thank you for the honor."

"The honor is all ours, Jerry," Wing said. "I think you could run for political office in the Dená Republik and win right about now."

"Please let me say something here and now." Jerry looked at both of them and didn't proceed until both nodded. "I am not a 'hero,' I am still alive and all I ever did was what anyone else would do under the same circumstances: keep my word and try to stay alive."

They both broke into hard laughter. Jerry wasn't sure what he should do, but he damn well didn't feel like joining them.

Grisha held up his hand. "Please," he coughed and chuckled again, "please don't be offended. I said damn near the same exact same thing when they told me

I was a 'hero' after the Second Battle of Chena. I know exactly what you're feeling and I can tell you how to deal with it."

"I would be forever in your debt, sir!"

"Get used to it."

"Damn!" Jerry blurted before he could catch himself. Grisha and Wing both laughed again.

"Please," Grisha said, "let's eat before the food gets cold."

Jerry cut a piece of moose steak and chewed for a moment before realizing it was the absolute best moose steak he had ever encountered.

"This is incredible!" he said as he finished the first bite.

"It's my mother's recipe," Wing said, "using only native herbs and the best cuts."

"I would love to thank her!" Jerry exclaimed, taking another bite.

"You may get the chance some day. She lives in Nulato, but I give you welcome in her stead."

Grisha dug into his meal and Jerry tried to do the same, but he felt bothered.

"Wing, earlier you said 'I'm glad the general chose you.' What did you mean by that statement?"

She smiled and nodded at Grisha.

Grisha frowned at Wing theatrically and suddenly Jerry realized the intense bond between them. They both completely understood the other and accepted what they found. He wished that Magda could be here to witness this with him.

"My wife speaks out of turn, which happens a lot," Grisha said with a laugh. "But she passes judgment on you, which is not to be ignored."

"Judgment about what?" Jerry pressed.

"I want you to be my attaché from the Republic of California. I need someone who knows the ROC military, politics, and government intimately. Someone I can trust."

"Grisha, you just met me tonight. How do you know you can trust me?"

"By that decoration hanging around your neck. You have proven yourself to be a friend of the Athabascan People to the point you risked your life more than once. We don't do that sort of thing for just anyone.

"Whether you like it or not, we think you're special, Jerry. And from what I've heard, we're not the only ones. You have an incredible amount of political clout in this new nation and you don't seem to know it. I want to use you, in the best possible meaning of the term, to help keep this fledgling republik alive."

"How do I do that?"

"Accept my offer. It might mean resigning your commission in the RCAF. But I guarantee you that you will receive a higher rank in the Dená Army and equal if not better benefits."

"I admit to feeling somewhat dizzy at this point, Grisha."

Grisha laughed. "Hell, man, so do I! I was a slave when I first got into this outfit and Wing helped save my life. Top that one!"

"You're kidding me, right? You were an actual slave?"

"You want to hear the story? Wing, please grab me another beer. Well, it all started down in Akku..."

★ 94 ★

Delta, Dená Republik

"Pelagian, you need to wake up."

He rolled over and looked up at Yukon Cassidy. "Why? I was up late last night campaigning."

"You were drinking and campaigning. I know because I was there."

"So why are you up already?"

"Because I have been in elections before—you haven't."

"And I must rise from my comfortable bed because?"

"Konstantin Mitkov and a number of his friends have surrounded the two polling places and are stopping everyone."

"What?" Pelagian sat up and for the first time noticed Bodecia wasn't beside him. "That's not allowed."

"Perhaps you need to tell him that. I'll go with."

"Where is Bodecia?" he asked, pulling on his clothes.

"I think she's out giving Konstantin a lot of grief."

"Shit!" Pelagian pulled on his boots and stood. "Show me!"

Bodecia stood in front of two young, burly men. As he closed on them he heard Bodecia say, "You do not have the right to stop anyone from voting."

"I have the right," one of the thugs said in a condescending manner, "because no one can stop me."

Pelagian walked up behind the two men, putting his hands on their shoulders and leaning between them briefly.

"You should have listened to her," he said and jerked his head back, "it would have saved you pain!" He slammed their heads together, dropping them in a heap.

"It's about time you got your butt out of bed," Bodecia said.

"You might have woken me, my love."

"Don't start with me, you'll lose! You have two more coming up behind you."

Pelagian turned as two young men stopped in their tracks and glared at him and Cassidy.

"Why you beating up our friends?" one demanded.

"Because they are assholes," Pelagian said. "Do you have a problem with that?"

"It's pretty easy to take two guys from behind," the other one said. "Might be harder if you were facing them."

"They were impeding voters. That's against the rules."

"*What* rules?" the first said with a snort.

"*My* rules."

They both glanced at each other and in that instant Pelagian stepped forward and cracked their heads together, and stepped back as they fell to the ground. He looked around at Bodecia and Cassidy.

"This election work is tiring. I'm hungry. Is there breakfast to be had?"

"Perhaps. Follow me."

"Haven't I always?"

"Don't be impertinent. Have you voted yet?"

"No, I've been busy."

"Go back and vote. Then come over to the house; we're feeding everyone."

Pelagian and Cassidy walked back to the school where he'd encountered the young men. As he walked through the door someone grabbed him. It was Konstantin Mitkov.

"Who you gonna— Oh, it's you." His face went pale and he stepped back.

"Are you grabbing everyone who walks in here?" Pelagian demanded.

"I can ask, can't I?"

"What do you do if they tell you it's none of your damn business who they're voting for?"

Konstantin's face clouded. "I ask 'em why!"

"You are breaking the law. No one is supposed to try and tell people who to vote for."

Konstantin grinned. "Ain't no law like that here, yet."

"Well, maybe this will work." Pelagian hit Konstantin in the side of the head and the man collapsed. "Okay, someone show me how to vote for myself."

"Can I vote here?" Cassidy asked with a grin.

"Everyone knows you're a resident of this area; of course you can vote here," Pelagian said.

Two old women sat at a table containing a ledger. Pelagian stopped in front of them and asked, "What do I do now, Aunties?"

"Sign your name here," one said crisply.

"And then mark your ballot," the other one said, holding out a small ticket of paper.

"When you've voted you put your ballot in there," the first said, pointing to a keg with a slot cut into the top.

"How many people have voted so far?"

"Not too many. That jerk Mitkov keeps stopping them."

"We'll fix that," Cassidy said with a bow. "May I sign the ledger?"

★ 95 ★

Tanana, Dená Republik

Magda watched the ground rise up to meet the RCAF transport carrying her and her parents. It had been a long time since she last flew, and the novelty was enough to keep her glued to the window.

No wonder Jerry loves this so much!

The aircraft touched down on the newly laid tarmac, courtesy of the Republic of California as an aid to their Air Force, and quickly decreased speed as the engines cut back and the flaps on the wings dropped. She couldn't see much of Tanana from the plane window. This was her very first visit to the new capital.

So much had happened and so quickly. Her father had won the election for delegate by a landslide: 898 to 27 votes. Pelagian immediately hired Yukon Cassidy as an aide; then he hired Magda also—he could have two. He told her the hiring order was because he saw Cassidy before he saw her after the election.

She worked hard at not being miffed as far as others were concerned. Actually, she didn't really care. Jerry was here somewhere and she would see him soon. She wondered if he knew she was flying in today since communications had been haphazard.

The aircraft stopped moving and rocked to a full stop. They all unhooked their seat belts and moved toward the door. She wondered what had to be done first: the convention began in just two days.

The door swung out and a figure stepped into the aircraft and out of sight across the aisle into the galley. She followed her parents and when she came to the point where she would turn and exit the aircraft, a voice to her right said, "Magda!"

She saw Jerry just before he grabbed her in a tight embrace and kissed her.

They held the kiss until applause broke out and they pulled apart. Magda felt she was in a surreal dream: her parents on one side of her and Jerry holding her tight on the other.

"Magda," Jerry said, dropping to his right knee, "would you do me the honor of becoming my wife?"

She nearly fell. But her father grabbed her arm and whispered in her ear, "I think this one is a keeper. What do you think?"

So much at once! She felt overwhelmed and suddenly hesitant.

She smiled down at Jerry. "Yes. Yes, he is. But, Jerry, can we take this a little more slowly? The war is over and we have the time for the luxury of a normal romance."

He frowned and got off his knee. "So you're willing to marry me, or what?"

"I'm at ninety percent, Jerry. This is the first thing involving me in what seems like forever that hasn't been rushed. Can we just slow down?"

His eyes searched hers and she knew when he made his decision.

"Sure, we can slow down, just as long as we keep moving forward."

"Oh, thank you!" She grabbed him and kissed him with as much feeling as she possessed.

"Can we get on with this day?" Bodecia asked in a mocking tone.

★ 96 ★

Tanana, Capital of the Dená Republik

Two loud raps of wood against wood cut through the multiple conversations in the hall. The constitutional convention delegates grew silent.

"I am Nathan Roubitaux, the provisional president of the War Council of the Dená Separatist Movement, the precursor to the Dená Army. Some of you know me well, and the rest have laid eyes on me for the first time.

"I would have you all know that this cause has been the most essential element in my life over the previous four years. After the First Battle of Chena, I thought we were doomed due to the loss of so many of our finest warriors and strategists. But others came forth and filled the gaps in our armor.

"This has been the most remarkable time of my life and I would not have missed it for sainthood. The people in this room carry a great obligation to the Dená People; you are going to pattern the path they will travel from this point forward. I had hoped to be a part of this assembly of quick wit and deep thoughts, but I was not elected.

"Therefore, my last act will be to lead the election of the presiding officer of your constitutional convention. Do I hear any nominations?"

A woman stood. "I am delegate Blue Bostonman from Aniak. I nominate General Grisha Grigorievich."

Another woman stood, "I am Eleanor Wright from Nulato, I second the motion."

Nathan frowned. "General Grigorievich is not an elected delegate."

Blue stood again. "Nathan, we're making the rules here. We can elect anyone we wish. I think Grisha would be a good choice because he has proven his loyalty to the Dená People and yet has no ties to any village."

"He's married to a woman from Beaver," Nathan pointed out.

"Wing hasn't lived in Beaver for almost fifteen years and she's smart enough and honest enough to not favor one village over another. Are you miffed that I didn't nominate you?"

"I am only trying to follow what little protocol we have established thus far. Are there any other nominations?" Spots of color darkened Nathan's cheeks.

A tall man stood and glanced around the room before addressing the chair. "I am known as Pelagian and I am from Delta. I see many faces here that are new to me. Could we adjourn for an hour or two so we all might meet one another?"

"There is a motion and a second on the floor," Nathan said. "We have to deal with them before anything else can be entertained."

"Fine," Pelagian said. "I move that the motion and second be tabled for two hours. Somebody want to second that?"

Gennady Ustinov stood, identified himself, and seconded the motion.

"All in favor of the motion to table signify by saying aye."

Everyone in the room loudly intoned, "Aye!"

"Are there any nays?" Nathan looked over the room and rapped his gavel. "The motion carries, the vote is tabled and we are in recess for two hours."

Conversational buzz immediately filled the room and people moved around, shook hands, introduced delegates they knew to people who were still strangers, and formed small discussion groups. Nathan left the room but nobody seemed to notice.

Pelagian went around the room, from person to person, until he had shaken every hand and heard every name. Just before the two hours had elapsed, General Grigorievich arrived; a cane in his hand aided his limp. Applause broke out.

He raised his free hand in the air and the delegates quieted.

"I have been told that my name is in nomination to be the presiding officer at this convention. You honor me beyond my abilities. I am not sure I could correctly herd this argumentative bunch." He grinned and most of the delegates laughed.

"Seriously, I don't think I am the right person to do what you ask. There are others with more education and experience who could handle this much better than I can."

"Grisha, would you hear me out?"

"Of course, Blue."

"You don't have relatives anywhere in Dená country. You don't care if someone is upriver or downriver or even from the Yukon. No one has any doubt about your loyalty or abilities. You're the only person in Tanana who fits that description. You're perfect for this job and we need you to do it."

She sat down and the room grew quiet.

"Who agrees with her?" Grisha asked.

Everyone stood. A few stood more slowly than the others, but in the end all the delegates were on their feet.

"In that case I guess I'll do it. Let me know when you want to start." Grisha turned and left the building. Applause broke out behind him.

★ 97 ★

Tanana, Dená Republik

Jerry knocked on Colonel Shipley's door.

"Come in," sounded through the wood.

Jerry entered and stood at attention. "Request to speak to the commanding officer, sir."

"At ease, Major Yamato. Of course you can speak to me. Have a seat. What's up, Jerry?"

Jerry sat and looked across the desk at his commanding officer.

"I didn't think I would ever hear myself say these words, but I'd like to resign my commission in the Air Force."

"I wondered how long it would take you to decide."

"Sir?"

"General Grigorievich spoke with me about putting you on his staff, said he didn't want to go behind my back but wanted you to make your own decision. I agreed with him."

"It's not that I don't love my country or honor my commitments, Colonel—"

"Nobody would believe that of you, Major, least of all me. You have been immersed in a culture that fascinates you, you have met the person you want to spend the rest of your life with, and her culture has made you part of it in a very special way. I would do the same thing you are, hands down.

"But I want you to be aware that you can be seconded to the Dená and still maintain your rank and service in the RCAF."

"I did know that, Colonel. After a great deal of thought I decided that this might lead to more duties in the Dená Army and, to be honest about the situation, I should join them from the start. How do I start this process, sir?"

"You can end it by signing these three sheets of paper. When General Grigorievich told me of his intentions, I had the paperwork drawn up and ready for you. This *is* an efficient branch of the service, you know."

"Yes, sir, I know."

Jerry quickly scanned the papers and then signed all three. He laid the pen on the desk and smiled up at his former commander.

"If you'll still be here on August first, I would appreciate it if you would attend my wedding."

"I'll make a point of being here, Colonel. I wouldn't miss it for the world. Just think how many California cocktail parties I can dominate with this story."

Shipley stood and offered his hand. "All the best, Jerry, you deserve it."

"Thank you, Colonel," Jerry shook his hand. "It has been an honor serving with you."

Jerry turned and left the office before the lump in his throat could progress into something potentially embarrassing.

Tanana, Dená Republik

The Tlingit delegation flew in on a rainy day, which pleased Grisha no end.

They'll feel right at home.

The twin-engine propeller aircraft stopped in front of the new terminal and the whining engines slowly faded to silence. Grisha glanced over the honor guard with pride. The eight men and women all wore the new Dená Republik Army uniform, designed by two Athabascan women and manufactured by a company in the Republic of California.

The aircraft door opened just as the portable stairway rolled into place. General Sobolof stepped out and glanced at the sky which threatened heavier rain and soon. He moved down the steps followed by four more Tlingit Army officers and four civilians, three of which were women.

The Dená honor guard formed up on each side of the walkway and saluted as the group passed through. Grisha waited at the end with Wing and General Eluska flanking him. Off to the side stood Lieutenant Colonel Yamato, Captain Pietr Chernikoff, and Sergeant Major Tobias.

"Grisha, it has been too long since I last saw you."

Grisha smiled. It had only been a matter of weeks since their last conversation. "You're a sight for sore eyes, Vincent. Welcome to Tanana, Dená Republik."

"We have much to discuss, Grisha. But first allow me some pleasure." General Sobolof stopped in front of Captain Chernikoff, who stood even straighter if that were possible.

"Captain Pietr Chernikoff, it my great pleasure to promote you to Lieutenant Colonel in the Tlingit Nation Army. Your effectiveness here in the Dená Republik has been exemplary. Besides, we had to keep you and Paul looking the same, didn't we?"

At that moment Paul Chernikoff emerged from the aircraft and in quick strides covered the distance between him and his brother. The two men embraced.

Grisha heard Wing mutter to Yamato and Tobias, "My God, how will we tell them apart?"

"Would you all please join us for lunch?" Grisha said.

"With thanks, General Grigorievich," Colonel Sam Dundas said. "I'm starving!"

Everyone boarded a dilapidated Russian omnibus for the ride to the hospital. Abruptly the sky opened and heavy rain sheeted down. Thunder reverberated through the bus, smothering conversation and causing a few apprehensive glances out the windows.

"I refuse to view this as an omen," General Sobolof all but shouted.

Grisha nodded.

The bus halted as close to the front of the hospital as possible. Sergeant Major Tobias was first out the door and ran the few meters to the hospital doors and flung them open. Then he ran back and assisted as people exited the omnibus.

By the time Grisha got to the door, Tobias was soaked.

"Sergeant Major, don't you catch cold. I'm going to need your energy in the next few days."

"Not to worry, General. I have a dry uniform inside."

Thunder rumbled again but the storm had moved west and the worst seemed to be over. Wing led everyone into the largest room in the building where tables had been arranged in a large circle with openings on two sides. Everyone would be facing the center.

Each place setting was marked with a small placard bearing a person's name written in beautiful calligraphy. Off to the side stood the constitutional convention delegates. A pair of tables held pitchers of water and a large samovar of tea.

The groups melded and conversations bloomed and flourished. Sergeant Major Tobias, in a crisp uniform complete with all of his decorations and badges, edged up to Grisha who chatted with Paul and Pietr Chernikoff about family and friends back in Akku.

"Excuse me, sirs." Tobias nodded to the two colonels. "General, whenever you think everyone is ready to eat just nod and we'll ring the dinner bell."

Grisha looked from one cousin to the other. "You two ready to eat?"

"I know our bunch is ready to start gnawing table legs."

"Sergeant Major, ring your bell."

"Very good, General Grigorievich."

Moments later the ring of a small, crystalline bell cut through all talk. In the sudden silence, Sergeant Major Tobias inclined his head to the group and said,

"Ladies and gentlemen, if you will take your places we will now begin lunch."

Grisha smiled as everyone quickly found their assigned places. It seemed there had been surreptitious recons taking place. Four servers entered through the kitchen door and set platters of food on the tables.

Grisha snagged a strip of squaw candy and began chewing.

★ 99 ★

Klahotsa on the Yukon, Dená Republik

"I thought you were bringing a small army of mercenaries with you, Major Riordan," Kurt Bachmann said in a snide tone to the obviously weary man standing in his doorway.

"The situation changed many times since we spoke with your agent. I have traveled a long way; may I come in?"

Bachmann nodded to the two heavily armed men flanking the major. "It's okay. You men did a good job. Come on in, Riordan."

As the door shut behind him, Riordan said, "Those two would make good mercenaries. I had no idea they were around until they told me to halt."

"One used to be in the Russian Army, the other has served under arms but I have no idea where. What happened to your International Freekorps? They all following you at a distance?"

"I wish!" Riordan dropped into a chair and looked around. "You got anything to drink? Water for a start?"

Bachmann went behind his bar and poured a cup of water and carried it to the table. "On the house."

Riordan drank it all and handed it back. "I'd be forever grateful if you could fill it with whiskey now, just this once."

Bachmann glanced down into the cup and back at Riordan. "How grateful? You going to repair my truck?"

Riordan winced. "Please don't say truck. Brings back recent bad memories."

Bachmann retreated behind his bar again and filled the cup with British Canadian whiskey. "Do share the memory," he said, putting the cup in front of the Irishman.

After an appreciative sip, Riordan twisted his lips into a wry smile. "Met two Indians way the hell down by Delta; they had a truck and I needed a ride. They asked me where I was headed and I said Klahotsa. They were headed for Nowitna but said I could ride that far."

Bachmann suddenly grinned. "You should have never told them you were coming here."

"Got that straight! I thought I'd be able to get the drop on them at some point and arrive here in style with my own truck. Those bastards never stopped watching me; they even took turns sleeping."

"But they *did* give you a ride?"

"Yeah, right to the junction where you turn to go to Nowitna. Then they pointed down that desolate mess of rocks you people call a highway and said I only had another hundred or so miles to go. Since one of them was holding a rifle in his hands, I thanked them for the ride and started walking."

"Didn't even bother to try and steal a vehicle?"

"I knew they distrusted me and would warn everyone in Nowitna. Since I've no wish to get shot to death over some crappy lorry, I decided to walk. Took me three days. If I hadn't met a trapper who fed me all the muskrat I could eat, I would have probably starved."

"Takes longer than three days to starve," Bachmann said. "So why did you come here?"

"Because you hired me. Timothy Riordan keeps his word."

"What possible good can you do me by yourself? I hired an army, not a damned advisor."

"I'm temporarily without an army, true. But you do need an advisor, Bachmann. More to the point: you need me."

"What the hell for?"

"How many more fellows like those two I met you got around here?"

"A few, so what?"

"Every one of them is a loose cannon if it comes to a fight. Right now they're all a bunch of individuals. You need someone who knows how to turn them into an army."

"An army loyal to me, of course?"

"As long as you meet payday," Riordan said with a smile.

Bachmann walked back and picked up the whiskey and a second cup, sat down at the table and poured both cups full.

"So how much of a wage do you require, Major Riordan? And what *exactly* do I get in return for paying it?"

★ 100 ★

Tanana, Dená Republik

Grisha set his empty cup on the table and grimaced at General Vincent Sobolof. "Now I have to make a speech. This is the part of the job I hate."

Vincent grinned. "I promise to applaud."

"I just hope the Dená do too."

He stood in one of the two openings breaking the ring of tables. He wanted to be able to see everyone's face without constantly turning in circles. All conversation ceased and all eyes were on him.

"Delegates, this is a special day in an historic time in our country. I have agreed to preside over the constitutional convention for the Dená Republik. However, the scope of this assemblage has changed even before the task begins."

He nodded at Vincent before continuing.

"Some weeks ago, Colonel Wing Grigorievich, my lovely wife, and I were dispatched to the Tlingit Nation as ambassadors. We were to sound them out on possible unification of our two fledgling nations."

Some of the Dená were exchanging puzzled glances complete with raised eyebrows. A few were frowning.

413

"After much talk, and a lot of argument," some of the Tlingits laughed at that point, "we came to a consensus. Just as they have here in Dená country, the old order had to willingly change if this concept had any hope of success.

"So they sent word to all the villages: elect a representative and send them to us. They had even less time than we did here. But it was done, and they are with us today."

Agitation among the Dená became noticeable and Grisha nodded at Wing who had suggested place names so there could be no whispering at this point.

"I promise you all the opportunity for questions and debate when I have finished my opening remarks. Every person in this room was elected by their people to represent them and create a new nation where freedom, equality, and peace can be realized by every citizen. It is not going to be easy.

"But we are not talking about the Dená Republik any longer. We are creating the Alaska Republik, a nation that will stretch from the Arctic Ocean to Dixon's Entrance—"

"Do the Eskimos know about this?" Gennady Ustinov blurted, rising to his feet. "Are they gonna walk through the door next?"

"Mr. Ustinov, I promised you an opportunity to speak when I was finished." Grisha let ice coat his words. "I am not yet finished."

Gennady sat down in silence.

"I was about to address the point that the Eskimos have not been contacted yet. Mainly that's due to the fact they are not in the midst of creating a nation—yet. They certainly know about the war being newly finished but beyond that we have no idea what they know.

"First we need to create the promise and then offer it to them. They can take it or leave it. The most recent intelligence we have received is that the Russians have completely pulled out of northern Alaska and are preparing to do the same in central and southeast Alaska. The only area in Alaska they have not left is Kodiak, where they are still fighting a Japanese invasion."

This was news to most in the room and Grisha let the silence linger as they digested the meaning of his words. Before anyone in his audience could comment, he continued.

"We have prevailed in this contest with the Czar for two reasons: we had help from very powerful North American nations and, the Czar had other problems much closer to St. Petersburg that threatened his empire. To put it bluntly, he wrote us off like a bad debt."

Grisha hurriedly drank half a glass of water.

"Which doesn't mean we're out of the woods yet! We have received help from the United States, the Republic of California, and the First People's Nation. That help comes with a price we have yet to learn or are in any position to repay and still maintain the sovereignty for which we have fought.

"Think about that! You people have to create something here that will deal with and transcend all obligations. I further charge you Dená, and you Kolosh, to come together and create an Alaska Republik. I will now take questions."

Gennady Ustinov was on his feet instantly.

"General, there is much happening here that was totally—oh, what's the word?—uh, *unanticipated!* We were supposed to create the Dená Republik, nothing more, nothing less. We're not ready for this!"

Blue Bostonman shot to her feet and stared at Gennady. "What, you think your people elected you to do something easy, something that just benefited you and to hell with them? All of us here carry something sacred: the belief of our friends and neighbors that we can give them hope, equality, and the promise that no one else can do it better. You people got a lot to live up to!"

Four more people stood up.

Grisha pointed to a Tlingit woman. "Ganaxxa."

The other three people sat down.

"I am Ganaxxa of the Hutsnuwu People. I live in the village of Angoon. This is a frightening thing for us, this constitutional convention.

"We don't know you people, the Dená, very well. For centuries our two peoples have traded but nothing more. Until the Russians came we were a warrior nation and all other peoples were frightened of us.

"We still have that heritage; we will fight anyone who tries to conquer us." She shrugged. "We might not *win*, but we *will* fight!"

Many delegates laughed but all paid close attention.

"We are here to see if we want to join you in this republik thing. Our peoples have more in common with each other than we do with the Russians, or Californians, or the Japanese. We must build a nation of strength and this will not be an easy thing to do.

"So let us begin as equals. You have impressed us by choosing General Grigorievich to be first speaker of this thing. I have great hope for all of us."

She sat down and all the other delegates stood and applauded.

Grisha waited for the delegates to quiet before he spoke.

"Next question?"

Slowly the delegates came to know one another.

★ 101 ★

Klahotsa on the Yukon

"We thought we'd find you here, Major," Private N'go flashed his sharp smile.

Riordan grinned widely at the six men. The guards had brought them in minutes before. All six were armed and seemed to be in good condition.

"You remembered where we were going before getting messed up in the Russian thing. Very good, I'm proud of all of you. Your timing is excellent. Mr. Bachmann and I have come to an agreement and the thing I needed most was trained cadre. And here you are!"

Private Dierks nodded at N'go.

"N'go got us here in one piece, even caught food so we could eat."

"Thank you, Rudy, I appreciate your input." Riordan looked at N'go fondly. "Why did I bust you to private the last time?"

N'go scratched his bald head. "Damn if I remember, Riordan. Why?"

"I couldn't remember either. Well, you're a lieutenant again. The rest of you are sergeants. We have people to train."

N'go grinned. "First lieutenant or second lieutenant?"

"First lieutenant, you've earned it."

"How many people do we have to train?" Sergeant Dierks asked.

"So far we only have sixteen. But I want to train them first to be assassins and snipers, so this is going to be intense."

"And brutal," First Lieutenant N'go said with a wide smile.

"The lieutenant is correct." Riordan nodded toward the door. "Let's go meet the trainees, shall we?"

★ 102 ★

Yukon River between Tanana and Klahotsa

Dená Army Sergeant Sergi Titus used the shaft of the "kicker" motor to steer the twenty-foot aluminum riverboat as it drifted downstream with the current. Four fishing poles angled off the boat, two to a side, and their lines cut tiny wakes on the rolling Yukon River. The main motor, a 40-horsepower Swedish Evenrude, was tilted forward and locked down so the shaft and propeller didn't touch the surface of the brown river.

Not a single cloud marred the bright sky. A constant warm breeze wafted over them, carrying the scent of fir trees and blossoming flowers as well as pushing away any mosquitoes that might be in the area. Bird song sounded on both sides, barely audible out here in the middle of the nearly mile-wide river.

"This is the life," Sergeant Bob Frieze, RCAF, said. "We really appreciate you bringing us out here, Sergi."

"For sure," Corporal Ken Tilgen said. "Right, Carpenter?"

The other RCAF corporal tilted his bottle of beer toward Sergi and grinned. "I could do this all day, man."

"I just wanted to show you guys that there's more to Alaska than you've seen at the airfield. Besides, I really feel that the Dená People owe you more than you'll ever see in your pay packets."

"This has been an adventure for most of us," Corporal Tilgen said. "Who would have thought we'd see a constitutional convention in action? That's something you don't see down in the Republic. I heard they've almost got the thing finished."

"They had some pretty good models to work from," Frieze said. "The US, the CSA, the Texans and us all have pretty much the same wording."

"Preambles are different," Tilgen said with a shrug, "but essentially, you're correct."

"They been at it ten weeks, right?" Carpenter said. "How long would it take to copy the best parts of the others and just sign the thing?"

Sergi Titus laughed. "It ain't that easy. We're trying to get *all* the Dená *and* the Tlingits to agree on one document that they're gonna have to live by."

"So?" Carpenter said.

"There's a lot of old animosities and distrust to get past. That kind of thing takes time. Indian time."

"What's 'Indian time'?" Tilgen asked.

"Pretty much the idea if you don't get it done today, there's always tomorrow."

"Oh, sounds a lot like Spanish Mexico time," Carpenter said with a laugh. "*Mañana!*"

The other two Californians laughed.

"That means the same thing, huh?" Sergi said with a grin.

"Precisely!" Carpenter said.

Abruptly one of the poles jerked down and the

reel sang out as something on the other end of the line grabbed the bait and ran with it.

"Holy shit, I got something!" Frieze shouted, bounding to his feet. "You guys get your lines out of the way!"

Titus and Tilgen both jumped up to grab their poles. Carpenter decided there was too much going on at the moment for him to get in the middle of it, so he stayed put and took another swig of beer.

Suddenly Frieze's head exploded, then Tilgen's, and Titus screamed as something went through his chest. All three men were knocked into the water. Before Carpenter could sit up, he heard the rifle reports carry across the water.

"What the *hell*?" he shouted.

The boat rocked and a bright hole appeared in the gunwale. Another rifle report echoed across the Yukon.

He lifted his head to look at the east bank from where the shots originated. Something buzzed past his head close enough that he felt the breeze it created.

Another hole punched through the side of the boat. He rolled over to the main motor, grabbed the control arm, pulled it down and let it go. The engine slammed down into operating position.

Carpenter pushed the control arm with his foot so it turned the boat toward the west bank. As soon as the boat turned, he sat up and grabbed the arm, pushed the ignition button and, like a lunatic, laughed aloud as the engine roared into life.

Another hole appeared beside the motor and something hit his left boot, tearing the heel off and throwing it over the front of the boat.

Carpenter gave the control arm a hard twist and the motor bellowed as the front of the boat rose and tore west across the Yukon. A round splanged off the top of the motor and Carpenter turned the boat to the left and back again to the right.

Until the sob burst from his throat, he didn't realize he was crying. He kept the boat moving upriver toward Tanana, but not in a straight line. He thought the war was over.

★ 103 ★

Tanana, Dená Republik

"You were in the *middle* of the river when this happened?" Colonel Smolst asked again.

"Dammit, Colonel, I've told you that twice already!"

"Calm down, Carpenter!" Colonel Buhrman snapped.

"It's okay, Del," Smolst said. "He's had a damn lousy day."

"Why would anyone want to kill us?" Carpenter said in a pleading tone, looking from one officer to the other. "The frigging war is *over*, isn't it?"

"We thought it was," Smolst said. "Okay, just one more question and you're dismissed. How long do you think it took you to get back to Tanana?"

"It seemed like forever, but..." Carpenter stared at the ground and frowned in thought. "Between forty-five minutes and an hour, Colonel. I think we were about twenty-five miles downriver when it happened."

Tears leaked from the corners of his eyes. "Those guys were the best buddies I ever had."

"Go see the doc, Carpenter," Colonel Buhrman said gently and patted the man's heaving shoulders. "Tell him I said to give you the good stuff."

Head down, Carpenter limped away, not bothering to compensate for the damaged left boot.

Smolst looked at Colonel Buhrman. "This isn't good. We must have a band of rogue Russians out there."

"But there aren't any Russian outposts unaccounted for, are there?"

"No. But there had to be more than two people shooting to get that many shots off in such a short amount of time."

"Colonel!" The shout came from the bank where the shot-up riverboat had grounded at high speed.

Both officers hurried down.

An RCAF first lieutenant was examining a bullet hole with a magnifying glass. He looked up. "Gentlemen, this is a very peculiar situation."

Buhrman glanced at Smolst. "Lieutenant McVey was a police crime scene investigator in civilian life."

"Excellent!" Smolst said. "Why peculiar, Lieutenant?"

"We have entry holes, but no exit holes. These holes are larger than a regulation rifle round would make, which could be attributed to a lead-point round, perhaps even a dumdum—both of which are illegal by treaty throughout North America.

"But what makes this event even more puzzling is little or no evidence of what had to be a high-power round. There were no other boats on the river, so the shots had to be fired from the bank, approximately a half mile away. If the rounds had been standard military, there would be holes in the other side of this boat, and they would be lower than the entry holes."

"Which would have sunk the boat, right?" Buhrman said. "So what are we dealing with here?"

"I would say mercury. To prove that, I am going to swab this area with cotton and send it to a real lab to be examined under a microscope to search for trace amounts. But that's the only thing I can think of that would create a pattern like this."

"Mercury-tipped bullets?" Smolst said. "Why would anyone do that?"

"For an assassination," Buhrman said. "But whose?"

"Can we go back to the mercury tips for a moment, Colonel?" Smolst asked. "Why mercury?"

"It was probably between a .30 caliber and a .300 magnum round that made this hole," the lieutenant said. "But the entry area is twice what it should be and the lack of exit holes is pretty much a giveaway. When a mercury tipped round hits a human head, the head explodes—it just ain't there anymore."

"Why?"

"Because mercury is a heavy metal, a liquid heavy metal. When the brass tip of the round fragments, the mercury keeps moving at the same velocity and it spreads. You don't just get wounded with one of these rounds, you get killed."

"Oh. That's why all three of the men who were hit were knocked completely out of the boat."

"Yup, you got it, Heinrich," Buhrman said. "And keep in mind all three men were hit from half a mile. These people might be monsters, but they're damn good shots."

"What are we going to do about them?"

"Find them and kill them, the sooner the better."

"We don't even know how many we're up against."

"You bring your five best and I'll do the same. I think the odds will be on our side."

"I hope you're right, Del."

"Go get your people. We'll meet up here in one hour, ready to travel cross-country."

Colonel Heinrich Smolst hurried up the riverbank.

★ 104 ★

Tanana, Dená Republik

"Has every delegate signed the document?" Grisha asked from his desk in front of the ten tables where the delegates had hammered together a constitution.

Eleanor Wright stood. "Mr. Chairman, every delegate has signed our new constitution. It is ready to be presented to the people of Alaska."

In less than a heartbeat, all of the delegates were standing and applauding, as was Grisha. Emotion filled him and he hoped this effort would bring the benefits every person in the room thought it would. Only time, and history, would tell.

He let them stop of their own accord before speaking. "Each one of you has my heartfelt gratitude for the time you have given to create a framework for our new nation. I'm sure that August 16, 1988 will come to be known as Constitution Day for the rest of the Alaska Republik's history.

"Now we have to give each of our states about five months to form their governments and ratify what we have done here. This is going to be an interesting winter. I declare this constitutional convention to be adjourned."

He rapped his gavel for the last time.

★ 105 ★

Village of Klahotsa

Major Timothy Riordan stopped in front of Trooper Smythe and examined the man intently for some reason to gig him. He snatched the rifle out of Smythe's hands, opened the bolt and spun the weapon so he could peer down the barrel. The bore glistened with a light coat of oil and the rifling looked pristine.

He threw the weapon back and Smythe caught it and returned to "present arms" in a blink. Riordan inspected the worn, but immaculate, uniform. Not even a loose thread.

"What country does that uniform come from?"

"Rhodesia, Major."

"You're a long way from home, Trooper Smythe."

"As the major well knows, home is where the paycheck is, sir."

Riordan allowed himself to smile and moved to the next trooper. He wished all of his new people were as military as Smythe. His most slovenly soldier was First Lieutenant N'go.

Now he remembered why he had busted the man to private months ago. But N'go had done something none of the others had ever done: he had saved Riordan's life.

That was worth a silver bar, Riordan thought.

Although twelve years in the past, the memory of lying on the steel deck of the freighter, bleeding from a severe beating only two days outbound from Boston, sprang unbidden into his mind. On the run from the Boston Police Department, which included his father, he'd taken a berth as apprentice seaman. Immediately he'd made the mistake of thinking that his status in the Feral Cherubs would mean something outside of the slums of Boston.

Bosun Collette had tried to kill him for his insolence. N'go stepped in at the last moment and told the bosun he had done enough. N'go stood nearly two meters in height and his solid, muscular body filled out his frame.

The huge African kept the crew at bay until they made landfall in Banjul, Gambia, where they both jumped ship. N'go wanted to flee before the authorities could be notified. But Riordan had correctly surmised that the bosun would be one of the first granted shore liberty.

Before Bosun Paul Collette could even have a beer, he was ambushed and beaten to death with an iron bar by Timothy Riordan, who never forgot a slight or a debt. Even at a twelve-year remove, Riordan still appreciated the irony of the whole thing. Before he left Boston he was an avowed darky hater. At this point he would die for N'go, the closest friend he had or was ever likely to have.

He forced his mind to the present. He stopped inspecting his small band and took a stance in front of them. "You've all done well. It's a pity one of your targets was able to escape last week, but I doubt it will matter in the greater scheme of things. Your marksmanship is excellent and I congratulate you all."

The twenty-four troopers, five sergeants and one first lieutenant all grinned at him.

Maybe this is the size of force I should have led all along.

"Todd and Foster have perimeter guard, the rest of you are dismissed."

The men scattered to their duties and the few distractions of Klahotsa, Bachman's store being first and foremost. N'go walked over to Riordan.

"Are you sure that there will be no retribution for the shootings, Tim?"

Away from others, rank disappeared between them.

"What can they do, send a cop? The Dená are all wrapped up in their little civics class. Everyone is too busy to investigate three shootings."

"I have my doubts of that, Tim," N'go said carefully. "*Everyone* has friends."

"You're proof of that!" Riordan said and laughed.

★ 106 ★

Near Klahotsa on the Yukon

Colonel Del Buhrman didn't like all this snow. It put a damper on their efforts. Not to mention it was getting damn cold for guys from the Republic of California. But they knew who their quarry was and where they could be found.

They had stopped in Nowitna to ask questions and replenish their supplies. At the Titus Brothers Mercantile they asked if anyone had seen any strangers.

"Why you askin'?" Sergi Titus gave Major Smolst a hard stare.

"Because someone murdered three innocent men on the river eight days ago. We want to find them before they kill someone else. That all right with you?"

Sergi pulled back, glanced around the busy room, and then nodded toward the back of the room. "Follow me, please."

Smolst followed but grabbed one of his men to come too. Sergi Titus didn't argue about the extra man when he saw who it was. He led them through a door and spoke only after the door shut.

"My cousins, Prospero and Iago Titus, were driving

back from Delta and met this man who came in by himself, no vehicle or anything. He was hungry and tired and said he was going to Klahotsa, could they give him a ride."

Smolst squinted at the man. "Prospero and Iago?"

Sergi grinned and shrugged. "My Auntie Ruth likes to read. When the twins were born she was reading a lot of Shakespeare. What can I say?"

Smolst laughed. "So did they give this fellow a lift?"

"Sure. This is the bush. Everybody helps everybody."

Smolst frowned and said, "So why—"

"Allow me to finish. My cousins were immediately suspicious of the man because of his destination. The man who runs Klahotsa is a tyrant, a cheat, and not to be trusted."

"Who is that?" Smolst asked.

"Bachmann. He showed up in Klahotsa one day about ten years ago with a signed deed for the store. Everybody who looked at the paper said it was the signature of the old owner, Konstantin Demientieff. But no one ever saw Konstantin after that: he had vanished."

"So you pulled us back here to tell us that?" Smolst said.

"No. There are two men out there in our store that we don't know. They could be Bachmann's men."

"Did your cousins give you a description of the man to whom they gave a ride?"

"Yeah, they did." Sergi described Riordan perfectly and succinctly.

"We won't forget your help, Sergi. You have our thanks."

"Just be careful, Major Smolst. Bachmann has

gathered a number of men around him, all strangers to us, and they are all killers. Let us know if we can be of more help."

"Is there a back way out of this room?"

"Through that door, Major Smolst."

Smolst walked out and found Colonel Buhrman. After telling him the situation, they decided to find the two spies. It didn't take long.

"So who are you people?" Buhrman asked the two men tied to adjoining trees about half a kilometer from the village of Nowitna.

"We're—" said the first.

"Tellin' you nuthin'!" said the second.

Buhrman pointed at the second one. "Peterson, Kyle, take this guy over there about a hundred meters, make sure you're out of hearing from us, and question him further."

While the man was moved, Buhrman stared at the first man as if he could see through him. After five minutes of silence, growing increasingly nervous throughout, the first man blurted, "Listen, we haven't done anything wrong!"

"So what *have* you done?" Colonel Buhrman asked in a disinterested tone.

"Some training, that's all."

"Training?"

"Yeah. Basic tracking, some fieldcraft, a bit of marksmanship . . ."

"Using what kind of weapons?"

The man licked his lips. Light snow started falling which gave the space around them more visual intimacy.

"Uh, .30-06 mostly. Just run-of-the-mill weapons."

"What kind of rounds did you use?"

Fear suddenly radiated from the man's eyes and Buhrman knew he was close to long-sought answers.

"B-bullets. Just regular bullets."

"There's this thing I have, not sure what to call it, but I absolutely know when someone is bullshitting me. As soon as this thing goes off in my gut, I start losing control of my better nature. And then I tend to hurt people who bring this thing on me.

"You have just slipped into that category." He lost his good-natured mien and sharpened his voice. "And if you want to live through the next hour, you need to be truthful with me, otherwise at the end of the hour you will be begging us to kill you!"

"Th-this is crazy! I don't know any—"

"Is Bachmann paying you enough to die under torture?" Buhrman demanded.

The man's face blanched and he nearly fainted.

"Answer me!"

"No. No, he isn't."

"How many men does he have?"

"Th-thirty. Two dozen troopers like me, five sergeants, a first lieutenant and that g-gawddamn major."

"That would be Major Riordan?"

"Yeah. If you know everything, why you asking me questions?"

"To see if you'll lie to me and then I can hurt you."

"L-look, this thing with Bachmann has gone all wr-wrong from the beginning. I haven't hurt anyone and I want out of this mess."

"What's your name?"

"C-Clarence Needham."

"Where were you born?"

"Ohio. What does this have to do with anything?"

"Because if I let you go and I find out you lied to me, I will hunt you down and kill you."

"I haven't lied to you, dammit!"

"I haven't finished asking questions yet."

Needham chewed his lower lip and, despite the growing cold, sweat ran down his forehead.

"Who shot those guys in the riverboat three weeks ago?"

"Smythe, Lockhart, Innoko Mike, and Murphy over there." He nodded toward the man Smolst and two soldiers were interrogating.

"What kind of rounds did they use?"

"Mercury tips."

"Why?"

"Bachmann wants us to kill some people and he thinks we'll only have time to get off a couple of shots."

"What people?"

"Some Indians who he says are pushing him around."

"How many of these pushy Indians does he want to kill?"

"We're training to hit six people at once."

Murphy screamed something at Smolst, drawing their attention. Smolst knocked the man flat.

"He's got a boot knife," Needham blurted, "and he's fast with it!"

Murphy came off the ground and lunged at Smolst. Colonel Buhrman snapped up his rifle and shot Murphy through the head. He lowered the weapon and stared at Needham.

"You just redeemed yourself somewhat, Mr. Needham."

Smolst walked over, glanced at Needham and then

gave Buhrman a sidelong look. "I knew you were fast, Del, but that was amazingly quick."

He gave Smolst a big grin. "I wish I could claim full credit, but Mr. Needham here told me that Murphy had a boot knife. We would have hung him anyway; he was one of the killers."

"Well, you've certainly done better with Mr. Needham than I did with Murphy. I couldn't even get him to tell us his name."

Needham cleared his throat. "When you people came into the mercantile, Murphy knew you were looking for the shooters. He thought we could bluff it out and get away later."

"You've stopped stuttering!"

"I knew I could talk my way out of your threat, but I also knew Murphy would kill me if I did."

"You're not out of the woods yet," Buhrman said.

Needham's mouth twisted into a small smile. "But I'm willing to tell you everything I know."

Colonel Buhrman smiled in return. "Heinrich, let's find some transport back to Tanana. We have a trap to set."

"What about Murphy?"

"Pay someone to bury him and forget where they did it. Mr. Needham, you are my prisoner for now. Sergeant Papke and Corporal Badberg here will see to your accommodations."

The two had come up behind Needham and he didn't know they were there until they nudged him and pointed toward the mercantile.

"So what kind of trap do you have in mind?" Smolst asked.

"The best kind, of course!"

★ 107 ★

Tanana, Provisional State of Doyon,
Alaska Republik

Sergeant Major Tobias answered his knock on the door.

"Colonel Yamato, please come in. The general is expecting you."

Jerry stamped as much snow off his feet as possible and then entered the warm apartment, pulling off his large, fur-lined mittens. "I have never been this cold in my entire life!"

"Jerry, how good to see you!" Wing said, entering the room. "I see you have learned how to dress for the Alaskan winter."

Jerry hung his parka on a hook near the door, draped his wool scarf over that and pulled off his knit cap and jammed it into the parka hood. He sat down on a chair and untied his mukluks.

"It's a good thing I agreed to work for you folks when the weather was warm. I'm not sure I would have agreed so readily if I had already spent a winter here. The thermometer outside my cabin only goes to minus forty and the mercury has been down there for a week!"

"It's about sixty below zero right now," Wing said, "but you seem to be doing fine."

He pulled off the mukluks and fished out the felt booties and put them on over his heavy socks. "I had no idea when I was given these things that they would save my life."

"Your wolf parka is one of the most beautiful I've ever seen, and I've seen a lot of them."

"Won't it smell like wet dog if it rains?"

"You don't wear a parka like that in the rain," she said. "You wear your old RCAF raincoat."

"I just hope it warms up enough to rain someday."

Tobias and Wing both laughed.

Grisha walked into the room. "What's all the noise? Oh, hi, Jerry, glad you made it."

"General," he nodded. "Good to see you, sir."

"Jerry, you're in my home."

"Sorry, Grisha, this takes some getting used to."

Wing laughed. "It's January! You're more set in your ways than my grandfather was."

"Not fair, Wing," Jerry said. "Military titles have a reason. I've been bending my head into the military mold for five years now. Some of this stuff is habit forming."

"What do you hear from Magda?" she asked.

He sighed before he could stop himself. "She misses me. Hell, I miss her! She doesn't understand why I have to be here and she has to be there."

"Why does she have to be in Delta?" Grisha asked.

"Grisha, if my future father-in-law was more intimidating than he already is, he would be illegal."

"What does *he* have to do with it?" Wing asked. "It's Magda's decision."

"Well, this isn't exactly San Francisco. I can't just ask my fiancée to move in with me."

"You don't think that people who love each other don't live together before marriage up here in the frozen north, not to mention people who just *like* each other?"

"Wing, I couldn't ask her to do that!"

"You mean you *haven't*? Jerry, you're in your twenties, but you're acting like a man in his fifties!"

"And there's a lot of attention on me from every direction. I wear a uniform that has no tradition or history. We are all making that history and we have to be somewhat circumspect to be responsible to the People."

"Bravo!" Grisha shouted and applauded.

"Jesus, you *are* my grandfather!" Wing said, feigning shock.

Jerry tried to smile but his heart wasn't in it. "I think she has a point, you guys. Why do I need to be up here in Tanana. Couldn't we talk by radio?"

"Sure," Grisha said, abruptly losing his grin. "And everybody north of the 55th Parallel would be in on the conversation."

"We don't have secure communications of any kind?"

"A courier that you trust is about it. We use the old Russian telephone system for most of our traffic. Although we don't need operators any more, anyone could tap into a phone line that goes for hundreds of miles through the wilderness."

"I could act as your liaison from there if we had regular meetings. I could fly back and forth in one of the P-61s the RCAF gave us."

Grisha's grin flashed back. "Ah, now I understand! You get to see your girl *and* you get to fly!"

"I think it sounds like a good idea," Wing said. "We need to spread our people around more."

"But Tanana is the capital of the republic, or will be." Grisha waved one hand in the air.

"Are you sure of that? It will be up to the first legislature to sort out—if we ever sort out the legislature."

"Wing has a point, Grisha." Jerry suddenly reflected that he used to think the RCAF was informal, but he had never before called his commanding officer by his first name. "Once each state gets set up and sends a delegate to the AR Council, there's going to be a fight over the location of the capital."

"Well, they won't be putting it farther north, that's for damn sure," muttered Grisha. "I'm just afraid that if they put it in Sealaska, the Tlingits will dominate the government."

"Which is what the Tlingits, Aleuts, and Eskimos think the Dená are doing now," Jerry said quietly. "Major Lauesen said his people are getting that message from all directions."

Grisha rubbed his jaw, and stared at something only he could see. "Well, I'll be amazed if they all send a delegate. I'm afraid they'll all declare themselves republiks and do it all their own way."

"They can't afford to do that since Doyon State already has the majority of US and ROC military bases. They'll send delegates, but the price will be a capital that isn't on the Yukon or Tanana Rivers. I'll put money on that," Jerry said.

"We'll find out next May," Wing said. "Are you both ready for dinner? Sergeant Major Tobias and I have worked up something we think will please you both."

★ 108 ★

Delta, Provisional State of Doyon, Alaska Republik

Pelagian came through the door, kicked it shut behind him, and dropped the load of firewood in the dented and scarred box next to the stove.

"I think it's warmed up to about twenty below."

Magda diced carrots furiously. "This is the longest winter I can ever remember. These carrots are about gone."

Bodecia looked from the roast she was preparing and smiled at her daughter. "That's because you've never had a reason to look forward to the arrival of spring before this."

"I've *always* welcomed spring, Mother! It's almost magical how the ground thaws and plants appear. Leaves suddenly pop out on the trees, the air warms and the world becomes a different place."

She looked up from the carrots to see her parents regarding her with smiles.

"This is also the first spring you've been in love," Bodecia said. "That always puts a different spin on things."

Magda grinned. "Yes, I freely admit—"

A roar thundered through the house and Magda felt elation flash through her entire being.

"That's Jerry!" She dropped her knife and ran outside.

She watched the P-61 circle around in the distance and come tearing back toward her. She jumped up and down and waved madly as the aircraft again zoomed over the house, waggling its wings.

Bodecia came out and touched her daughter's shoulder. "Get your coat and some warm footwear. Rudi is already warming up the truck."

With a laugh Magda raced back into the house. She felt like she could have run to the aerodrome dressed the way she was, but knew that would be foolish, let alone dangerous.

As she slipped into her mukluks, she remembered stories of people who, after a long spell of severely cold weather, would rush outside with little protection when the temperature rose to minus twenty degrees Fahrenheit, and suffer frostbite.

She pulled on her parka and zipped it shut. As she went out the back door while pulling on her mittens, Bodecia called to her.

"Why don't you invite Jerry to dinner?"

She chuckled as she slammed the door on her parents' laughter. The drab utility sat wreathed in a cloud of its own exhaust, running smoothly. Rudi and Pelagian had rebuilt the engine and the little VAZ, as Rudi called it, purred like a contented cat. She slid into the passenger seat and smiled at Rudi.

"A soon as I hear plane in distance I crank up utility, knowing you will wish ride as soon as possible, yes?"

"You're such a smart man, Rudi. I'm very happy you decided to stay with us."

"I am honored your parents allow me to intrude into your lives. Otherwise would have had to join Dená Army for rations and place to sleep. Now am proud resident and proprietor of finest garage in Russ—ah, Alaska Republik."

Magda laughed with him. At this point she would have laughed with anyone. But she was pleased that the former Russian sergeant had accepted Pelagian's offer of the room over the garage.

The garage was nearly as big as the house with space for two vehicles as well as a spacious workshop in the rear. A large woodstove in the corner of the workshop kept the entire building comfortable as its stack went through the ceiling of the shop into the second-story room before going through the roof. They had all been surprised at Rudi's deft touch with engines and other things mechanical.

Pelagian immediately helped Rudi start an engine repair business and rented half the garage and all of the shop and upstairs room to Rudi for a percentage of his revenue. It also didn't hurt that Rudi was almost pathologically protective of the whole family and that the dogs loved him.

"Cermanivich Services" already had a backlog of work that would take him through spring to finish. Magda noticed he wore clean clothes instead of his customary greasy mechanic's coveralls.

"How did you get cleaned up so quickly?"

He smiled and kept his eyes on the icy road. "Was apprised of impending arrival of the lieutenant colonel so as to be prepared."

She stared out at the snow-laden trees lining the road for a moment.

"How long have you known he was coming?"

Their headlights bounced off the six-foot snowbanks on each side of the road. Except for them, the road lay empty.

"Two days, I think."

"And you didn't tell *me*?"

"And ruin happy pilot arrival? Not in script, sorry."

"Why, you plotter, you!"

"Please, both Pelagian and Bodecia also know of this, not just poor, lowly mechanic."

"I'm surrounded by plotters!" Magda couldn't be happier. She realized if she had known Jerry was coming, she would have been a total mess at this point. But, still!

By the time they traveled the four miles to the aerodrome next to St. Anthony Redoubt, the short day had descended into total darkness and the lights of the aerodrome looked particularly inviting in the frigid afternoon. A quick glance at the sky promised no deeper cold this night as the clouds that hid the stars also kept the air temperature constant.

Rudi pulled up in front of the office where pilots checked in and filed flight plans. Magda was out of the utility cab before it had stopped moving and raced through the office door.

Dominick Demientieff looked up from a book. "Can I help you? Oh, hi, Magda. What's up?"

She frowned. "Didn't a plane just land here? One buzzed our house..."

Jerry's voice came from behind her, "Yeah, a plane just landed. What's so important about it?"

She turned and jumped into his arms, kissed him deeply and tried not to cry. They broke the embrace only when Dominick cleared his throat.

"Why don't you two go find someplace a little more appropriate?"

"Oh, Dominick, you're such a stick in the mud!" she said with a giggle. She turned back to Jerry. "But I think he has a good idea there. Whattya say, soldier?"

He hadn't stopped staring at her since their embrace. "I have missed you so much!" His voice went husky. "I'm not sure I can wait until August to marry you."

"Me too," she said. "You're invited to dinner by the way."

"Let's go. Hey, thanks for everything, Dominick." He grabbed a duffel bag near the door.

"Good seeing you, Jerry. Have a great time you two."

Jerry held the truck door open and Magda scooted over next to Rudi; he threw the duffel into the back and slid in beside her.

Once the door closed, Jerry leaned forward and shook hands with Rudi.

"I hear you've become the proprietor of your own business, Sergeant Cermanivich."

"Please, no longer sergeant. Am now happy civilian and *part* owner of good business. Is good to see you, Jerry."

"Magda mentioned something about dinner. I'm starved." He put his left arm around her and pulled her tight against him.

Rudi turned and drove back toward the house.

"I talked him into it, folks."

"Who is *him*?" Rudi asked.

"General Grigorievich."

"And what is '*it*'?" Magda asked.

"To be stationed in Delta."

"When?" She all but shrieked.

He looked down at her and the dash lights reflected off his smile. "As of now."

By the time Rudi pulled up in front of the house, Magda had regained control of herself. She thought her heart would burst when Jerry told them the news.

I hope I always feel this way about him.

As she and Jerry exited, Rudi said, "Will be in directly to share happy meal with all."

"Thanks for the ride, Rudi," Jerry said.

"I owe you many more, my friend."

Magda rushed into the house and shouted, "He's being stationed here! Isn't that wonderful?"

Once Jerry removed his cold weather clothing, he hugged Bodecia and Pelagian in turn.

"Magda, please help me finish preparing dinner," Bodecia said.

She frowned and started to protest before remembering he was going to be here from now on. They had time, a lot of time.

"Of course, Mother."

"Do you have something for me?" Pelagian asked Jerry.

"Yes, sir, I do." He pulled an envelope out of his jacket and handed it to the large man.

Pelagian ripped it open and eagerly read the message. Both Magda and Bodecia watched him as he walked across the room, opened the firebox on the wood stove and threw in the letter and envelope.

"Well, that was certainly dramatic!" Bodecia said in a tone that demanded enlightenment.

"Well, the main gist of it all is that I am running for First Speaker of the Alaska Republik."

The way the words rolled off his tongue told Magda that he was taken with the idea.

"We don't even know if we have a republik yet!" Bodecia snapped.

"Why are you upset?" Pelagian said.

"Because you haven't talked to me about this at all, and here you are, putting yourself and us in the crosshairs of every mentally deficient, politically frustrated, would-be messiah out there. Did it occur to you that we might want some input into this momentous decision?"

"Bodecia, my love, nobody outside this room knows anything about it. I'll happily listen to anything you and Magda have to say about it."

"And then go right ahead and do what you want anyway!"

"Mother, you're being unfair. Let's have a meal and a quiet discussion about this crazy idea Father has come up with."

Bodecia laughed but Pelagian didn't. Jerry looked uncomfortable. At that point Rudi hurried in and firmly shut the door behind him. His quick smile faded as he looked around at the others.

"Am I too early for meal? Will be happy to return at later time."

"Dinner is ready, Rudi," Bodecia said in a listless voice. "We're all absorbing the idea of Pelagian running for Czar."

"First Speaker," Pelagian said in the most neutral tone he could manage. "We call it First Speaker."

"Is possible to discuss *and* eat?" Rudi asked.

★ 109 ★

Klahotsa on the Yukon

"You ever see anything like it before?" Trooper Bates asked.

"What? I can't hear you through your scarf," Corporal Smythe said in a low voice.

"The lights, ever see anything like them before?" He pointed up to the aurora borealis filling the dark sky with light and dimming the distant stars.

The aurora curtained across the void with sheets of cold flame that seemed to be hundreds of miles wide, knife-blade thin, and stretching upward into outer space. The lights wavered, shifted; the color changed from opalescence to a mild emerald and bent into a scroll.

"You're supposed to be on perimeter patrol, not watching pretty lights in the sky, you dumb bastard!"

"How can you *not* watch them, Smythe. Is there no poetry in your soul?"

"It's *Corporal* Smythe to you, *Trooper* Bates, and if you don't attend to your duty, I'll put you on company punishment!"

"Yes, Corporal."

"I wish to hell it would cloud up," Smythe said. "When it's clear like this the temperature plummets."

"What are we doing out here, anyway? Nobody in their right mind would be poking around here in the middle of a night this cold."

"What Major Riordan *wants*, Major Riordan *gets*," Smythe said. "We get paid to follow orders, not question them."

"What's that?"

"I said—"

"No! Over there!" Bates said in a whisper, pointing into the dark forest.

Corporal Smythe stopped and peered into the trees, trying to pierce the heavy darkness. Above them the aurora twisted and writhed, color shifting to a rose blush that reflected off metal for just an instant.

Smythe quickly raised his rifle and fired into the darkness next to where the glint had vanished.

The gunshot shattered the still night and four shots, fired nearly simultaneously, erupted from the trees.

Two rounds hit Bates in the chest, knocking him back against a tree, dead before he hit the ground. Two rounds found Smythe, one grazing his skull and the other shattering his left scapula. He fell unconscious in the snowy forest, his blood melting snow crystals before freezing into a red pool that reflected the dancing aurora borealis.

★ 110 ★

Nowitna, Provisional State of Doyon,
Alaska Republik

"That's the slowest damn retreat I've ever made,"
Colonel Del Buhrman said, holding the cup of tea
in both hands.

"If you break a sweat in weather like that," Lieutenant Colonel Heinrich Smolst said, "you die."

"Why?"

"Because you breathe deeper, strain for more air,
and the air is cold enough to frost your lungs—and
kill you."

"Extreme place, this Alaska of yours."

"And full of extreme people," Smolst said with a
nod. "Like you."

Buhrman grinned and looked up from his cup of
tea when Iago Titus came through the cabin door.

"How's our patient?"

"My auntie has stabilized the wound, but we need
to get him over to Tanana as soon as possible. She
says his arm needs surgery."

"Damn, I was afraid of that. I'll see if I can get a
plane in here to pick him up."

Smolst shook his head. "It's somewhere between fifty and sixty below out there, Del. The air is too thin for small planes and we can't get a big one into Nowitna—the strip is too small."

"What do you mean, 'the air is too thin'?"

"All of the moisture is frozen out of it and a small plane has trouble getting any lift without a bit of moisture in the air."

"You're pulling my leg, right?"

"I had the same response when they told me that one back in Siberia in '79. So I asked a pilot about it and he verified the story."

"I'll be damned. You learn something new every day."

"If you pay attention," Smolst said.

"So we can't get out by air unless it warms up. I sure as hell hope it doesn't get any colder."

"Which begs the question, Colonel Buhrman: why are you still here?"

Colonel Buhrman gave him the squint-eyed, half-smile look that told Smolst the man had an ace in the hole. They had played innumerable games of poker to pass the hours waiting for things to happen and Smolst lost a lot before he began recognizing the colonel's "tells." This time the ace in the hole wasn't a card.

Smolst pressed on. "After all, the war with Russia is over. The war with Japan is all but over. And except for a few bands of rogues like Riordan's, things have gotten pretty quiet. Yet you're still here and in the field despite the fact that most of your people returned to California."

Buhrman's grin grew under the heavy moustache.

"That's what I like about you, Heinrich, you're smart."

The door flew open and a bundled figure hurriedly slammed the door behind him. After he pushed back the parka hood and pulled the scarf from around his face, Buhrman recognized First Sergeant Scally.

"My God, but it's cold out there! I think my balls have shrunk up to my esophagus."

"Now there's an image I really don't want to dwell on," Buhrman said. "Do you have anything further to report?"

First Sergeant Scally hung up his parka, turned to the colonel, and saluted.

"Our pickets report nothing other than an incredible display of the northern lights, sir."

"At ease, Sergeant. You performed well out there tonight."

"Thank you, Colonel. I found the mission to be exhilarating as well as incredibly frightening."

"Well put. I have to agree with you."

"So what do you want the men to do now, Colonel?"

"Stand down, take it easy. I don't anticipate the enemy doing anything crazy for at least three days. They have no idea where their opposition originated or where it went."

"Are they really that dumb?"

"No, Sergeant, they are really that paranoid. We'll happily use that against them."

"Works for us, Colonel. We'll be in the main lodge."

"Tell the bartender to give everyone a drink on my tab. Once."

"Everyone? No matter who's in the bar?"

"Everyone, friend or foe."

"Class act, Colonel. Thank you." First Sergeant Scally saluted.

Buhrman retuned the salute. "Dismissed, First Sergeant."

The sergeant grabbed his gear and bolted through the door. The general store was no more than fifty meters from where they sat.

"You're a real pushover, Del," Heinrich said with a wide smile.

"Not at all, Colonel Smolst. I reward achievement and am quick to acknowledge it."

"So why are you still here?"

"My government gave me the task of seeing the first elected government in the Alaska Republik to fruition. Until there's a First Speaker elected and sworn in, my mission is not complete."

"Sweet Baby Jesus, you could be here for years!"

"You say that like it's a bad thing, Heinrich."

Smolst laughed. "Is it? Do you like it here, Del?"

"I admit to having developed a taste for moose meat. I've never tasted anything better."

"Seriously."

"I am serious! I like moose meat. I also like the idea of helping a new republik get its shit together. This is the first mission I've ever had that really makes an historic difference and I want to do it right."

"My God, you're a visionary!"

"Screw you, Smolst. You're much more hardened than you think I am."

"Not really. I applaud your stance. I think you actually mean it."

"Well, I do. I've been through a lot in my career and until now I really didn't give a damn about the outcome. I just followed orders and endured. This time I actually care about what happens. I care about the people I'm working with and I care about their future. I attribute it all to my advanced age—I'm just getting soft."

Smolst laughed from the bottom of his belly. "You're a fraud, Del, why don't you just admit it?"

"I will when you do."

"I'm glad you're on our side, Colonel Buhrman, and I'm glad you're here."

★ 111 ★

Klahotsa

"What do you mean, 'you found nothing'?"

"One of our guys hit someone, but there was just frozen blood and no body."

"Those sons of bitches!" Riordan shrieked. "Why don't they fight fair?"

Everyone in Bachmann's store remained silent.

"We've got a dead man and a seriously wounded man with no medical support."

"We do have a village health aide," Bachmann said as if mentioning an exotic flower.

"Has he treated a gunshot wound before?"

"*She* has treated many gunshot wounds. People hereabouts tend to hunt for their own meat and accidents happen."

"Why the hell isn't she here already?"

"Nobody asked her," Bachmann said in a flat voice. "You seem to think that everyone anticipates your needs. You need to lose that illusion."

"Get her here! Now!"

"James, would you please ask Auntie Andi if she would please come over and look at our patient?"

The man disappeared into the night.

Riordan turned his attention back to his men.

"Sergeant Dierks, how did these people escape?"

"The best guess we have is that they walked away, Major. Probably had a vehicle a few miles down the road."

"Walked?"

"If you move faster than that you tend to frost your lungs, sir. And that will kill you within minutes."

"So our pursuit was at a walk also?"

"We didn't even mount a pursuit, Major. There was no point in doing so."

"You arrived at this conclusion all by yourself?"

"No, but I take responsibility."

"Do you know the penalty for failure in the Free— in my company?"

"Yes, sir. But I also recognize futility when I encounter same."

"Major Riordan," Bachmann said, "I would like to talk to you in my office."

"I'm busy right now, sorting out a sergeant."

"And I pay *both* your wages. Keep that in mind on the way to my office!"

Riordan fought the wave of rage that welled up from deep inside his soul. He wanted nothing more than to kill the arrogant bastard.

But I don't know where he hides his money.

The rage subsided but his anger didn't.

Riordan slammed the office door behind him. "What are you trying to do, make me look bad in front of my men?"

"Shut up, Riordan!" Bachmann snapped. "I want you to understand that I'm running this operation, not you. You obviously don't know shit about arctic survival; your sergeant did exactly the right thing."

"He didn't do *anything*!"

"Precisely! Keep in mind we're training killers, not soldiers; expert assassins, not mercenaries. I want these men to hit their targets and get out of the area."

"What's the point of killing a bunch of people if you're not going to gain any territory?" Riordan felt baffled.

"Are there snakes where you come from?"

"Snakes? There are no snakes up here."

"That's where you're wrong, Major Riordan. We have an ample supply and your men are going to render them headless."

"Kindly tell me what the hell you are talking about, Bachmann."

"The Dená, the Tlingits, or Kolosh, and the Eskimos are planning to create an Alaska Republik. The Russians are gone for good. Political and civic venues are in upheaval and I mean to take advantage of that to secure my future."

"And I thought *I* was an optimist! Do you really believe that you and me and thirty, uh, twenty-eight guys good with weapons are going to take over an entire sub-continent?"

"If you take out the top thirty people in a small nation, that doesn't leave much above a colonel. We can handle colonels with our second shot."

"Do you think they're all going to line up for you in one place?"

"Actually, I do. But first we have to figure out who is harassing us and take care of them. Probably something to do with those men your guys used for target practice. Send two of your men to track them, but each one alone and a half hour apart."

"So we know when and where the first one dies." Riordan allowed himself a slight smile. "You're good at this stuff, Bachmann. You could go places."

"I fully plan to. And if you play your cards right, you can go with me."

★ 112 ★

St. Anthony Redoubt, Provisional State of Doyon, Alaska Republik

"Lieutenant Colonel Yamato, how good to see you again," Colonel Stephan Romanov said. "Please, sit down."

The only thing that had changed in the colonel's office was the absence of the Russian flag and he now wore a different uniform.

"Thank you, Colonel," Jerry said as he eased into the chair. "I am pleased to see you here, as well as Sergeant Severin. The Alaska Republik Army needs all the good people it can get. Not to mention, you know the area well."

"You honor me and my men."

"Having served so long in the California Air Force and now in the Republic's army, my discipline has slid somewhat. Do you mind if I call you Stephan when we are not in proximity of others?"

Romanov grinned. "My pleasure, Jerry. How is your fiancée and prospective in-laws?"

Jerry mirrored Stephan's grin. "Magda is fine. I feel so incredibly lucky to have found her."

"The way I heard it, *she* found *you*."

"Well, yeah, that's probably closer to the truth. Pelagian and Bodecia are both well. And we're all happy that the war is over."

"A most remarkable war, I must admit. Frankly, I thought I would end up in front of a firing squad at some point. I had no idea that events outside Alaska would make such a difference here."

"Nor did I. General Grigorievich asked me to take stock of what personnel and material we have here. I figured you would already have that information."

"Rightly so. We lost a third of our troops, and three officers, in the Battle of Delta. Two officers and nine troopers elected not to stay when I, and the majority of the garrison, went over to the Dená. So currently we have five officers and sixty-two soldiers."

"Compared to the rest of the army that's not bad. The Dená lost a lot of people in the war and, since the cessation of hostilities, a good number have quit the uniform and gone home. I think there are more US and ROC troops in Alaska than Republic troops."

"Is that something we need to worry about? Foreign troops on our soil?"

Jerry laughed. "Said the Russian to the Californian!"

Stephan chuckled. "But we have found a new country, even helped create it. I haven't seen that many US Army or ROC personnel changing uniforms."

"First of all, I don't think we have to worry as long as both allies have a presence here. If one pulls out, then we might have to take measures. Second, I think that in the end, a lot of the 'foreign' troops just might elect to stay, despite this insane cold weather."

"I am amazed that you stayed, Jerry. I understand that California doesn't have winter as such."

"Northern California has winter, but nothing like this. Besides, I fell in love and I think I can better adapt to Alaska than Magda can to California."

"I envy you. You have found happiness and a lovely, accomplished mate."

"I've noticed that there are a lot of lovely, accomplished Athabascan women out there, Stephan. And a lot of them are single and looking for a good man."

"Perhaps I don't get out enough."

"Back to the inventory," Jerry said, pulling a notebook from his pocket. "What do we have in the way of equipment?"

"We *had* a Grigorovich fighter until a certain lieutenant flew away in it." Stephan grinned.

"You still have the fighter. That lieutenant managed to get it, and him, shot up a bit. Both are good as new and the Grigorovich will be returned to Delta Aerodrome so I can face Sergeant Suslov again."

Stephan's face lost its animation. "He would be proud that you remembered his name, and happy that you kept your promise. But we lost Yuri Suslov to Russian artillery in the Battle of Delta."

Jerry winced. The sergeant's good-humored face shining with gap-toothed pride flashed through his mind. So many good people, promising people, had been lost.

"I am bereft to hear this. I wanted him to work on our P-61s. He was a superb maintenance sergeant."

"Yes. We also have a Sikorsky helicopter and most of a Yak 3."

"Helicopter? Do you still have a pilot for it?"

"We have two, much to my surprise."

"I don't understand."

"Our pilot officers are sons of a nobleman in St.

Petersburg who is very close to the Czar. Without the influence of the Czar, neither of these men would have made it through officers' training let alone flight training. Until we made contact with the Freekorps, both men were abject alcoholics.

"One was wounded while they were on a reconnaissance flight over the Freekorps and nearly bled to death. This event sobered them in more ways than one. They both ceased drinking, became very good officers, and elected to stay here rather than go back to Russia."

"And they both made it through the war?"

"Indeed, and brilliantly led troops in combat. I was astounded to say the least."

"Is the helicopter airworthy?"

"Oh yes. We didn't lose all of our mechanics, just the best one."

"With your permission, Stephan, I would like to have the airfield named after Sergeant Suslov."

Stephan's eyes brightened. "I can think of no better name, nor a better way to show your Russian-born citizens that they made a difference and are fully accepted in this new republik. Thank you for that gesture."

"No thanks needed, sir. It's the very least we can do. I hadn't thought of it as a unifying gesture, but you're right. If we both sign the request, I think Tanana will agree."

"It probably helps that you will soon be related to the First Speaker."

"Pelagian hasn't been elected yet. He has a lot of campaigning to do before the May elections. People up north don't know him as well as folks around here. Gri—General Grigorievich is going to take him down to the Tlingit country, uh, Sealaska State, and introduce him around. The general was very impressed with Pelagian during the constitutional convention."

"I am amazed at the speed with which all of this is happening," Stephen said, shaking his head. "After all my years dealing with the tortoiselike bureaucracy of the Imperial Russian Army, this is like falling off a cliff!"

"We're a small nation in population, but with vast distances. I'm amazed at how many people know each other yet live hundreds of miles apart. They sent Yukon Cassidy up north to talk to the Eskimos because they knew him. Yet he was born down in the First People's Nation."

"Cassidy is a good man; I'm proud to call him friend," Stephan said.

"I can't call him friend just yet, but I'm working on it."

"We keep straying from the official purpose of your visit. We also have a number of field artillery pieces, I'm not sure how many at this point, as well as three old Zukhov-1 tanks. Beyond that we have a few dozen tripod-mounted machine guns and cases and cases of rifles."

"Scout cars, trucks?"

"Oh, yes. We have one command car that is nearly an antique, three scout cars, four or five armored personnel carriers and twelve lorries; one is rigged with a dump mechanism."

Jerry wrote furiously for a moment and then looked up. "Great. Some of the machines might get sent elsewhere but you'll be consulted first."

Stephan Romanov smiled. "It is just past the noon hour. Would you please join me for lunch?"

"Thank you, I would be honored."

★ 113 ★

On the RustyCan between Nowitna and Klahotsa

"Just like the colonel said, there's another one trailing behind." Corporal Bennett sounded like a kid on Christmas morning.

Private Hendrix kept the binoculars to his eyes. "Isn't the colonel always right? That man gives me the creeps! He ain't natural."

Corporal Bennett wasn't listening; he had pulled his radio from inside his coat, extended the aerial and flipped the switch.

"Field Fox One, this is Field Fox Two, come in."

Hendrix lowered the binoculars and joined Bennett in staring at the radio. New equipment was always suspect until it operated correctly under field conditions.

A tiny voice clearly said, "This is Field Fox One, go ahead Field Fox Two, over."

"Oh, shit, I forgot that 'over' part," Bennett muttered. "Field Fox One, the second target is in range, moving slowly. You want us to take him out? Over."

"Take him alive if you can. If he threatens either of you, kill him, but bring in the body. Over."

"Understood. Field Fox Two out." Corporal Bennett

gave Hendrix a level stare. "Did you make marksman back home?"

"You know damn well I did."

"Then you stay here. Keep your sights on him at all times. If he looks like he's even thinking of shooting me, blow him away."

"Is this gonna get me a PFC stripe?"

"It will if I have any say in the matter."

"Go get him, tiger!"

Their vantage point was on a hillside where the road turned to the left behind them. The target point was straight downhill at the apex of the curve. Bennett hurried down the back of the hill, out of sight of the lone scout, and across the road to a fall of boulders.

They had already set the site and he squirmed into position, rested his scoped rifle on the rock in front of him, and waited. He could see Hendrix out of the corner of his right eye, sitting up there like an archangel in winter camouflage.

Bennett watched the road, letting his mind wander a little. He was grateful that it had warmed to ten below zero and then marveled at the concept that that temperature could be considered warm. Still nothing moved on the road.

That son of a bitch should be here by now.

He glanced up at Hendrix. Hendrix wasn't there. Bennett didn't move.

If there were people uphill from them, there might be people down here, too. Very slowly, without moving his body, he turned his head to look behind him.

Two men stood two meters away with weapons pointing straight at him. He dropped his rifle and raised his hands.

"Turn around," one of them said in an accent Bennett couldn't place. He did as he was told. He still reclined on the rocks.

"Anybody else with you other than the Kaffir up the hill there?"

South Africa, Rhodesian probably. "No, just the two of us."

"Good."

Bennett didn't hear the shot.

★ 114 ★

Nowitna, Provisional State of Doyon, Alaska Republik

"Any word from Field Fox Two?" Colonel Buhrman asked.

"No, sir," First Sergeant Scally said. "And it's been more than a half hour since they broke contact."

"Silent alert, now. Get your weapon ASAP."

"Sir!" Scally flipped a switch that turned on a red light in every house in Nowitna. The electricians had enjoyed the exercise and the residents thought it a novel way to communicate. None of them had ever believed it would be used.

Soldiers and armed villagers moved into prearranged positions. Radios were switched to the combat channel and locations were whispered into the microphones. Then they all waited for orders or action.

The village of Nowitna sits on a relatively high bank opposite the side where the Nowitna River enters the Yukon River between three islands. The Nowitna River bends and turns through a massive floodplain dotted with hundreds of lakes and ponds that entice millions of waterfowl every year as well as the ubiquitous muskrats valued for their fur. Moose populate the area in large numbers and the first Athabascans to come through the area thousands of years before probably thought they had found the most perfect place on Earth.

Now it lay swathed in a meter of snow, much of it deposited by the constant wind blowing across the frozen river and myriad lakes. Dark spruce and tamarack trees mingled with the denuded branches of willow, birch, and alder. A moving object of any size in the open could be seen over a mile away.

Colonel Buhrman and Lieutenant Colonel Smolst had their men watching the tree line, the clumps of Labrador tea, rosebushes, and various berry bushes. With the wind blowing small clouds of snow, it was difficult to tell whether or not humans worked their way forward through the growth.

Nowitna lay buttoned up; the houses on the north and west side of the village were all secure forts, with six to eight riflemen waiting at darkened windows or chinks in the log walls. The Titus Brothers Mercantile was one of the three two-story buildings in the village. Centrally located, one could see the entire swath of the region from northeast to southwest.

Buhrman, Smolst and two radiomen hunkered on the second floor, glassing their perimeter. Buhrman had the north and northwest; Smolst had the west and southwest.

"Do you really think they'll attack us, Del?"

"I'd bet the family farm on it. They think we don't know they're coming. They're pissed and want us out of the way for whatever they have planned down the line."

"The guy we caught could give us a lot of that information."

"Maybe there'll be time for that later."

"Colonel," Easthouse, the radioman said, "is it okay if I smoke?"

"You make any kind of light and I'll shoot you myself."

"That would be a 'no,' then," Easthouse said. "And I thought the biggest thing I had to worry about was lung cancer."

"The last thing we want to do is make a light in here that can be seen from outside." Colonel Buhrman glassed over his area.

"Don't those lenses reflect light?" Easthouse asked.

Colonel Buhrman froze and dropped below the window area. "Jesus, he's right—"

The glass in the window above his head suddenly blew in with a rush of cold wind and snow sprinkles. The rifle report echoed across the icebound flats.

"Did anyone see where that shot came from?" Colonel Buhrman snapped. He hadn't been this pissed at himself since the fight in the Arizona no-man's-land years before.

"Nobody saw a thing, Colonel," Easthouse reported.

"Can you reach Tanana or Fort Yukon with that lash-up?"

"Sure, who do you want to talk to?"

"General Grigorievich, the sooner the better."

"Give me a few..." Easthouse fiddled with the radio for a moment. "Tanana this is Field Fox One, do you read me, over?"

"Loud and clear, Field Fox One. Over."

"The O in C wishes to speak to General Grigorievich soonest. Over."

"Give me five, Field Fox One. Over."

"Aren't they in the same building?" Smolst said from his window.

"Yeah," Buhrman said. "But remember, it's a big building. Stay back from that glass, Heinrich. You're the only poker player I have who is any good."

"Why are they waiting?"

"They think we're going to make a mistake, get excited or impatient, and go after them."

"They're the ones in the cold and snow," Smolst said. "We can outlast them."

"Until it's dark. Then they'll attack."

"So what are our choices?"

"We're going to go after them," Buhrman said, "but not in the way they anticipated."

★ 115 ★

St. Anthony Redoubt, Provisional State of Doyon, Alaska Republik

Lieutenant Colonel Yamato sipped the last of his wine and considered if he wished a second one or not. Colonel Romanov was drinking up the last of his glass also. Jerry decided he would follow the colonel's lead.

Sergeant Severin stepped into the room. "My apologies, gentlemen. Colonel Yamato is needed in the radio room. There's a call from Tanana."

Yamato stood and nodded to the colonel. "By your leave, sir." He stayed on Sergeant Severin's heels until they reached the radio room.

"This is Corporal Desonivich, Colonel Yamato."

"What do we have, Corporal?" Jerry asked.

"Do you wish a private headset, Colonel?"

"Did they say this was classified?"

"Not yet."

"Then put it on speaker and give me the microphone." The corporal complied.

"Tanana, this is Yamato at Delta, over."

"Jerry, this is General Grigorievich. Is your plane operable?"

"Of course, General."

"Have it loaded with machine gun rounds and antipersonnel rockets."

Jerry nodded at Sergeant Severin who immediately picked up a phone and started talking.

"What's going on, General?"

"Colonel Buhrman and Lieutenant Colonel Smolst are in a tight spot. They need a fighter over Nowitna as soon as we can get one there."

"Once I'm in the air, I can be there in under an hour."

"I wish I could send someone else, Jerry. Since the 24th Attack Squadron returned to California, you're our only fighter pilot at the moment. We need to address that lack as soon as possible."

"Yes, sir, I agree wholeheartedly."

"Once you're in the air, we'll give you coordinates and updates."

"Yes, General. Delta out."

"Thanks, Corporal," he shouted over his shoulder as he dashed out of the room. "Sergeant Severin, get me a car!"

★ 116 ★

Nowitna, Provisional State of Doyon, Alaska Republik

"They're sending who?" Lieutenant Colonel Smolst asked.

"Yamato, that kid from the 117th who got shot down over Rainbow Valley while my guys were jumping on the Battle of Chena, where you guys were getting your asses kicked."

"I was wounded in that battle, Colonel Buhrman, otherwise you would have a much nicer reception." Smolst glanced out the window. "We're losing our light. If he doesn't get here damn soon, he'll be fighting in the dark."

"Not much I can do about that, Heinrich."

"Colonel, we've got an incoming message." Easthouse switched on the speaker.

"This is Yamato calling Field Fox One, do you read me? Over."

Buhrman grabbed the radio microphone. "Colonel Yamato, this is Colonel Buhrman. Nice to hear your voice."

"Happy to help, Colonel. Where do you want the delivery?"

Colonel Buhrman quickly described the area. "They're in the brush and tree line from the north to the west. You flush 'em and we'll pick off what you don't get."

"Roger that, be there in five minutes. Yamato out."

★ 117 ★

On the edge of Nowitna

"I'm just about frozen solid, Major."

"Quit whining, N'go. It's going to be dark in less than an hour; then we get to take 'em out."

"At l-least we'll be moving. Do you hear an engine?"

"No, I—oh damn, it's a plane!"

"In this weather?"

"It's a fighter, you dumb bastard!" Riordan shouted. "We've got to get out of here right now!"

Stiffened with cold they scrambled to their feet and stumbled deeper into the tree line. The engine noise rose to a roar and six lines of bullets raced past them, blowing trees and frozen tundra apart. Explosions burst behind them as the aircraft streaked over them.

Tears of rage ran down Riordan's face. He stopped beside an icy birch whose trunk was the size of his thigh and looked back at the carnage. The aircraft spat rockets and machine gun fire at the northern sector where most of his men lay waiting.

He saw three men leap to their feet to evacuate but they pitched forward after a few steps. The people in Nowitna were picking them off.

"That damned plane!" Riordan pulled one of his

mercury tips out, chambered it, and leaned against a tree for support. The plane was coming back for another run over his old position and it was coming fast.

Riordan took aim through his scope and as soon as the crosshairs centered on the cockpit, he fired.

★ 118 ★

Over Nowitna

Jerry had enough ammo to make one more strafing run and then he would have to leave. The arctic afternoon was fading fast and he didn't want to fly back in the dark. He bore down toward the first area he had hit, turned to the right a few degrees, and squeezed the trigger button.

Something hit the front of the plane and oil streamed out the side of the fuselage. The engine stuttered, roared full blast and then died.

I've been shot down again?

He turned away from the forest and aimed for the frozen Yukon. Air shrieked past and he held his microphone button with one hand and the stick with the other.

"Mayday! This is Yamato; I'm hit and going down over the Yukon near Nowitna. Mayday! Mayday!"

The P-61 lost speed and he had to hold the stick with both hands, willing it to stay in the air. He cleared the trees along the river by a few meters and felt a wave of relief wash over him. He stared at the frozen surface of the river and fear walked up his spine with cat claws.

The river wasn't smooth like a frozen pond. It had

ridges, bumps, hummocks, and chunks of ice that looked like boulders. And he was out of time.

"This is going to get ugly," he muttered.

He suddenly remembered he had two wing tanks nearly full of fuel that would hit first. And explode. He hit the switch and they impacted the river within seconds.

The explosions gave the plane a few feet of lift and he saw the trail running through the smoothest portion of that part of the river. He edged toward it, not wanting the bird to catch a wing and cartwheel—he couldn't survive that. He was moving *so* fast and there just wasn't any more time.

The icy river reached up and grabbed the plane; the frozen propeller immediately bent back under the nose and the plane bellied in, straight down the narrow trail. For an insane moment he worried about hitting a dog sled. The trail went through a cut in what looked like a hill of ice and he knew that's where it would all stop.

Both wings hit at the same time and ripped off the aircraft with shrieks of tearing metal. The fuselage shot through the cut, peeling aluminum off the sides of the bird and chunks of ice out of the abrupt wall on either side. The wreck slid to a stop and a gust of wind howled over it, throwing snow crystals like frozen sand.

"I'm still alive!" Jerry shouted. He keyed his radio. "Can anyone hear me? This is Yamato, can anyone hear me?"

The wind moaned again as it assaulted the plane. The radio was dead. He was the only thing out here that wasn't.

He had to figure out if staying inside the aluminum fuselage would be suicide. The aircraft had no insulation worthy of the conditions Jerry now faced and the inside would actually become colder than the outside. In a matter of hours the shredded fuselage would become an icy tomb, but it might offer protection from the incessant arctic wind.

"Sure glad I brought my cold weather gear!" he said loudly. He realized that he was afraid and needed to get himself steadied before doing anything at all.

"I wasn't afraid the last time," he said to the wind buffeting the wreck. "Why am I this time?"

Because last time you didn't have anything other than your life to lose—now you've got Magda, maybe.

He nodded. That was it. Now he really had the promise of a life, and he wanted to enjoy a lot more of it. He unfastened the parachute harness, reflecting that he was glad he hadn't had enough time to use it—God knows where he would be by now.

What to do? Every survival manual he had ever read said to stay with the aircraft if possible. But would that be wise here?

He pulled on his parka over his flight jacket and the mukluks on over his flying boots. He felt warm. Would his body heat keep the cockpit warm enough to live through the night? He decided his chances were as good here as out on the frozen surface of the wide Yukon River.

He wished he had a candle. The heat from a single candle could keep an enclosed space such as an ice cave, or a sealed cockpit, warm enough to survive extreme temperatures. He made a vow he would never venture into a subarctic mission without one ever again.

Pulling the wolf pelt parka tight, Jerry relaxed and tried to sleep despite the howling icy wind and his fear of freezing to death.

★ 119 ★

Nowitna, Provisional State of Doyon, Alaska Republik

"What the hell hit him?" Colonel Buhrman bellowed. "He was knocking the shit out of them and suddenly he goes down."

"Could they have shot him down with one of those mercury bullets?" Lieutenant Colonel Smolst asked.

"I keep forgetting how good those people are with a rifle. That has to be it."

"Which means there is still at least one man out there."

"He's probably headed for Klahotsa as fast as he can safely go. We have to go get Yamato's body, or what we can find of it."

Both men had seen the explosion far upriver and out in the middle of the frozen expanse between two of the icy islands. Nobody could have lived through that.

"I hope he didn't blow a hole in the ice and the wreck sinks," Buhrman said.

Smolst grunted. "No chance of that, Del. The Yukon ice is about twenty-five feet thick right now, and hard as concrete."

Buhrman turned to Corporal Easthouse. "Get me General Grigorievich. I want to tell him myself."

★ 120 ★

Delta, Provisional State of Doyon, Alaska Republik

Magda answered the knock on the door with a wide smile, expecting Jerry. Colonel Romanov stood there, blinking in the sudden light, looking grave.

"May I come in?"

"Oh," Magda said releasing a breath, unaware she had been holding it. "Of course, Colonel." She shut the door behind him.

As soon as she had seen him, a dread descended upon her like a shroud of hooks. She didn't want to know why he was here and not Jerry, yet she had to know instantly or go mad.

"What happened?" she asked.

Pelagian and Bodecia stood silently on the far side of the room.

"There was a band of killers attacking Nowitna. Colonel Buhrman called for air support. Jerry is the only pilot we have, so he went."

"I thought I heard a plane," Pelagian said, "but decided I was wrong."

"Let the colonel finish, Father," Magda said in a brittle tone.

"Yes, well, he was making his third strafing run over the outlaws and suddenly radioed that he was hit and going down. His engine ceased operating and he glided out over the Yukon."

"Which is frozen solid this time of year," Pelagian interjected.

"True," Colonel Romanov said. "But Colonels Buhrman and Smolst both reported an explosion when the plane hit the ice."

"D-did he have a parachute?" Magda asked, trying not to cry, seeking possibilities.

"Yes, but he wasn't high enough to bail out, it wouldn't have had time to open before..."

"He's not dead. I would know if he was dead. And he's not!"

Her mother came up behind her and put her arms around her, holding her tight. "Magda—"

She broke out of the embrace. "He's *not dead*, dammit! I won't believe he is until I see his body!"

Colonel Romanov threw out his hands. "We have no way of finding out, Magda. It's hundreds of miles to Nowitna. It would take days to drive it in this weather."

"Don't you have a helicopter?" she demanded.

He blinked. "Yes, yes we do. I have dismissed it so often in the past—I will dispatch it at first light and we will investigate for ourselves."

"I'm going with you, Colonel. Don't you dare try to leave without me."

Colonel Romanov looked at her parents.

"If it were Pelagian out there, I'd say the same thing," Bodecia said. "Come on, Magda, let's get you outfitted. It's not only cold up there, the wind also blows like a banshee's scream."

★ 121 ★

On the Yukon River

Jerry roused from a light doze and looked around the cockpit. Frost covered everything and he wondered at his ability to see anything in the middle of the night. He looked straight up through the amazingly undamaged canopy and saw the full moon between gusting clouds of blowing snow.

Despite the circumstances, he felt warm and toasty. The thought of trudging across the lumpy, uneven surface of the Yukon held no appeal and he was happy he made the choice to stay with the plane. But how long could he stay here with no food and no water other than the canteen he always carried?

There were other natural processes to consider also. When his bladder signaled need of release, what would he do?

Cross that bridge when I come to it.

He closed his eyes and retreated into sleep.

The wind shrilled over the fuselage.

★ 122 ★

Klahotsa

The door of the general store crashed open and Bachmann started in alarm. Two snow-covered figures staggered in and kicked the door shut behind them.

"What's going on?" Bachmann tried to make his voice hard with authority, but the words came out in a squeak.

"Don't crap yourself, Bachmann," Riordan growled. "It's just me and N'go." Both men went to the large pot-bellied stove in the middle of the room and all but embraced it.

"Where are the others? Why are you here? Did you find the people who attacked us?" He wanted to stop and make each question deliberate, something that must be answered immediately. But their arrival had brought fear into his soul and he wanted it evicted as soon as possible.

"Shut up," Riordan said. "I'll tell you everything, but just shut up.

"We surprised them with our tactic of shadowing our own scouts. Got two of the bastards, but they got our first man. They didn't shoot him; they captured him.

"So we moved in to pick them off but nobody

showed themselves. Not even a kid went outdoors. They were buttoned up tighter than a virgin's blouse.

"It was close to dark so I decided to wait and we'd move in and take them all out, cabin by cabin. Somebody in there was smart enough to call in a fighter plane. It blew the hell out of us.

"When our men tried to run into the tree line, the people in the cabins picked them off. I put one of the mercury tips in my rifle and when the plane came at us again, I shot the pilot. The plane crashed and burned out on the Yukon.

"Never shot down a plane before..."

Bachmann realized that both men were exhausted. "All the others are dead?"

"Far as I know. Didn't see anyone following us when we retreated."

"Then these hunters at Nowitna know you all came from here." Bachmann immediately wished he hadn't said that out loud.

Riordan gave him a look of pure hatred. "You're such a chickenshit. You worried that all your little schemes are going to come back to bite you in the ass? Afraid that you're going to have to take responsibility for your own actions?"

"Riordan, you're forgetting who's in charge here!"

"Then act like it! We can still pull this thing off if you'll stop pissing yourself."

"How do you see it working now?" Hope hammered in Bachmann's chest.

"Well, first we lay low for a while..."

★ 123 ★

Over the Alaska Republik

Magda tapped her foot on the aluminum deck as the helicopter racketed along below the clouds. Straps over her chest and lap kept her pinned firmly in the observer's seat. At least she could watch the land beneath them.

The Captains Fedorov, as she called them in her mind, had maintained a running argument from the moment they took off over an hour ago.

"Georgi, we have ample fuel to reach Nowitna!"

"And if we spend too much time over target and run out of fuel, Ivan, who comes to search for *us*? Are we not in the only helicopter in this country?"

"Where is the wild beast brother I once had? The one who loved to tweak the nose of chance?"

"He nearly bled to death last year. Don't you remember? You were there, right where you're sitting."

"Give me heading for Tanana Aerodrome; we will refuel there."

Magda smiled grimly. Colonel Romanov had told her these men were the best helicopter pilots in the Alaska Republik. However he had neglected to mention they were the *only* helicopter pilots in the Republik.

"There, Georgi, must be Tanana; aerodrome is immediately behind village according to map."

"*Da,* I see beacon. Oh look, they light up runway lights for us!"

"They have runway lights," Ivan said in an awed whisper.

The radio crackled. "Delta helicopter, this is Tanana control. Follow the instructions of the landing officer with the wands."

"Acknowledge, Tanana control. We see him."

"Can you hear me, too?" a different voice said.

"*Da,* loud and clearly."

"Set down between me and the hangar, there."

Through the blowing snow Magda could see the man with glowing orange wands in each hand. The wands went from far apart to close together and pointed toward a series of buildings with snow-packed roofs.

"Affirmative!" Georgi said and landed the machine without a bump.

Magda considered that they just might be good pilots after all, as long as they weren't talking to each other. The rotors swooshed to a stop. The door next to Magda suddenly opened and a cold blast of air sent snow through the aircraft. Colonel Wing Grigorievich looked up at her.

"How about some tea and a sandwich?"

"That sounds wonderful," Magda said, looking down at the harness and belt assembly. She picked at it with gloved hands. "If I can just get this damn thing off!"

"Allow me." Wing reached in and snapped a catch and the whole thing came apart in the front.

"Oh, I guess I should have paid more attention when they strapped me in."

Wing offered a hand as Magda exited. "You were probably thinking about other things. This way, please."

Magda followed her through the numbing wind into one of the buildings. The room temperature radiated about 75 degrees Fahrenheit. The walls boasted dark, polished wainscoting and photos of men and aircraft from the beginning of aviation history.

In the center of the room sat a large table with a steaming samovar and a tray holding a dozen or more sandwiches. General Grigorievich stood next to it. He stepped toward her, holding out his hand.

"Magda," he took her hand in both of his, "I wish I could say I was happy to see you. I just wanted to tell you that if anyone can come through this, it is Jerry."

She tried to swallow the sudden lump in her throat. "Yeah, but I'm not out there to help him this time."

"He saved a lot of lives yesterday. And, as always, he didn't hesitate to take the mission."

"Jerry and I are going to talk about that quirk of his," Magda said. "I want a husband, not a memory of a hero."

"Grisha," Wing said in a gentle voice. "Let her eat, she has a long day ahead of her."

"Of course. May I get you some tea, ladies?"

"Thank you, yes," Magda said. "With a bit of milk if you have it?"

"Black for me," Wing said. "But you knew that."

When they smiled at each other, Magda nearly burst into tears. Instead she looked down at the sandwiches.

"Is that real ham?"

"Yes," Wing said. "One of the California pilots brought us two cases. Please help yourself. Take some for later; we have a lot."

The Captains Fedorov came in, poured themselves huge mugs of tea and grabbed sandwiches. Georgi put two in his pockets before eating a third in four bites.

Magda wrapped four sandwiches in a cloth napkin and put them in the pocket of her parka. After eating two, she was still surprisingly hungry. She walked over to Wing.

"Tell me about Nowitna. I've never been there."

"It's a small village, up a large bank on the north side of the Yukon. There are two or three islands in the river, very close to the village, and the river is about three miles wide. Farther upriver the Yukon narrows to about a mile but there are islands all along there.

"From the reports we've received, Jerry went down in one of the open stretches of river between islands. The weather there is worse than it is here, so visibility is at a minimum."

Wing chewed her lower lip for a moment. "Magda, if he crashed and burned, which is the current conjecture, it's going to be hard to take."

"Wing, his plane may have crashed, but he is still alive. I *know* it!"

"I hope you're right, cousin. My prayers are with you both."

An RCAF officer came through the door. "The Delta helicopter is ready to go."

Magda followed the Captains Fedorov out into the wind and cold.

★ 124 ★

On the Yukon near Nowitna

Colonel Del Buhrman pulled himself out of the dogsled and looked back at the musher. "That was fun, Mr. Anderson. I wish we were out here under different circumstances."

Lieutenant Colonel Smolst poked at metal shards and regarded Buhrman. "There isn't enough here for a whole plane. Where are the wing parts and fuselage?"

Wind whistled down the ice-locked river and blowing snow whirled and capered around them in the bright day. Blue sky could be intermittently seen straight up, but at ground level, visibility was less than fifty meters.

Colonel Buhrman peered at his compass. "He was headed that way." He pointed upriver and the wind suddenly stopped for a long moment and visibility stretched to a half mile. Metal reflected in the distance before the wind again ripped snow off the ice and swirled it over the searchers.

Buhrman climbed back on the sled, Smolst onto another. The dogs responded happily and tore across the frozen river. Less than five minutes later they all stopped at an ice ridge.

"This is just the wings," Smolst shouted over the wind. "Did he actually fly *through* this cut?"

"If he did, he didn't get far!" Buhrman responded through a grin. He realized that the explosion they had seen the night before was either armament or something else. The plane had landed on the icebound river in one piece.

"Let's go through the cut and see what we find," Buhrman shouted.

In moments they found the fuselage. They studied the ice-rimmed aluminum for a moment. The canopy was translucent with frost on the inside.

"It occurs to me," Smolst said in a tone of conjecture, "that if there wasn't something warm in there, there wouldn't be any frost."

"Excellent deduction, Doctor Watson!" Buhrman said in a bad parody of an English accent.

Both men laughed, feeling their tension evaporate with the almost certainty of a happy ending to their quest.

Buhrman stepped up and pounded on the side of the fuselage.

They waited. He pounded again. No response.

"How do you open these damn things?" Buhrman asked with a sidelong glance at Smolst.

"Do I look like I know anything about aircraft, Colonel?"

"No. Sadly enough you look as ignorant as I feel. Let's try and figure this out."

★ 125 ★

Over the Yukon River

"There are people down there!" Ivan shouted over the roar of the engine.

Georgi banked and brought the Sikorsky back around for another look.

Magda shouted, "He's right! They're waving at us!"

Georgi landed on the river and cut the engine.

Magda stared through the window at the fuselage of the P-61. From this angle she could see the closed, frosted cockpit and the lack of a body out on the ice. She burst into tears.

Georgi opened his door and shouted at the people on the ice.

"Who are you?"

"Colonel Buhrman, RCA, and Lieutenant Colonel Smolst, ARA."

"What is 'ARA'?" Georgi shouted back.

The helicopter blades ceased revolving and reduced the background noise.

"Alaska Republik Army!" shouted Colonel Buhrman.

"Is good, is good, no need to shout," Georgi said.

"We're trying to see if there's a downed pilot inside this bird. Can you help us?"

"We are here to search for Lieutenant Colonel Yamato," Georgi said.

"That's who we're looking for! Who are you people?"

Magda unhooked her harness and stepped up between the two pilots. "I'm Magda Haroldsson. Jerry Yamato is my fiancé. We flew in from Delta to help look for him. Is he still alive?"

"We don't know, Miss Haroldsson. We think he's still in there but we haven't been able to rouse him."

"Please, it's Magda, Colonel Buhrman. Isn't there a latch or something?"

"That's what we were looking for when you folks showed up."

Captain Georgi Fedorov emerged from the helicopter. "What kind of a plane was this?"

"P-61 Eureka," Magda shouted over the sudden gust of wind. The snow striking her face felt like tiny slivers of glass and she pulled her parka hood up.

"I don't know that kind of aircraft." Georgi stared for a moment. "But it is much like a Yak. Therefore..." He moved close to the fuselage and ran his hand along the base of the canopy.

"Aha!" He pulled a handle and the canopy popped back a few inches.

Colonel Buhrman tried to climb up on the wing stump and the fuselage rolled toward him, pushed by the wind. He scrambled to keep on his feet.

"Well, damn!"

"Pull the canopy back," Smolst yelled over the cutting wind.

Buhrman grabbed the canopy and jerked it aft. The wind caught it and ripped it free of the fuselage and whirled into the air over their heads. It disappeared in the blowing snow.

Jerry sat hunched over in the cockpit, completely covered by the wolf pelt parka.

Magda scrambled up to him and pulled the hood back.

"Jerry! Jerry, are you all right?"

He stirred as if deep in sleep. One eye cracked open.

"M-Magda? Is that really you?" He sounded weak and disoriented.

She felt tears well up. "Of course it is, you silly man!"

A long gust of wind blew a shower of snow crystals over them and Magda tried to cover his face.

Buhrman, Smolst, Georgi, and the two dog mushers all helped pull him free of the wrecked plane and carried him to the helicopter. Without stopping, they slid him into an insulated sleeping bag brought for that purpose.

"Can we go now?" Magda asked. "I want to marry this guy before he gets away from me again."

"I feel warmer already," Jerry mumbled deep in the sleeping bag.

★ 126 ★

Klahotsa on the Yukon

"So the whole idea is to shoot as many elected officials as possible when they are presented to the public?" Riordan asked.

"Exactly. Think about it. It would devastate everyone there. Chaos would reign. All it would take is a voice of authority to bring them into line."

"And that would be you, right?"

"Who else, Mr. Riordan?"

"That's *Major* Riordan, thank you."

"Of course."

"Even if they have no idea in hell as to who you are?"

"Won't matter. Pass me the bottle, please."

Riordan regarded the whisky bottle as if it were a relic.

"I think it may be empty," he announced, and threw the bottle over his shoulder with force.

It smashed against something.

"Hell, I can fix that," Bachmann said. He pulled himself out of his chair and staggered behind the bar. "Let's have the good stuff. Nobody ever buys it anyway."

"When do I get paid?" Riordan asked.

"For what?"

"For being the officer in charge of your troopers. Whattya think?"

Silence reigned and Riordan twisted around to peer at Bachmann on the other side of the store.

"But you got them all killed. Why should I pay you anything?"

Riordan suppressed the instant flash of rage. He willed it to evaporate like dew on a sunny morning. This was important.

"*Who* was in charge of this entire plan?" Riordan asked as nonchalantly as possible.

"Well, I was."

"So *whose* orders did I follow to the letter, like it or not?"

"Mine?"

"Exactly. It was *your* plan that got them all killed, not mine."

"But you led them—"

"Following *your* orders, doing exactly what *you* ordered and exactly when *you* ordered it!"

Silence drifted through the store.

"What did we agree on?"

"Two hundred fifty in gold," Riordan said.

"Stay where you are. I'll be right back."

"Sure."

As soon as he heard the office door close, Riordan leapt to his feet and hurried to the back of the store. He eased the door open and through the crack saw Bachmann opening a door built into the wall of the building.

I would have never found that.

He pulled out his pistol, opened the door, and stepped into the office.

Bachmann whirled about and yelled, "I told you to wait!"

"Too late," Riordan said, and shot him through the head.

★ 127 ★

Over the Yukon River

"Colonel Buhrman," Ivan said from the pilot's seat, "there is a radio message for you." He handed him the headset.

"Buhrman here, go ahead."

They all could hear the crackle of the voice in the earphones but none of the words were intelligible.

"Does that tally with our body count? Okay. I'm sure Captain Fedorov told you we found Jerry. He's cold but he's alive. Thanks, Buhrman out."

He handed the headset back and turned to the others.

"Our people have accounted for every one of the attackers except for Riordan and his buddy, N'go. The store at Klahotsa was empty except for the body of Bachmann. Someone shot him in the head at close range."

"When thieves fall out . . ." Smolst muttered.

"But where the hell are they going to find shelter in this weather?" Buhrman asked.

★ 128 ★

Klahotsa

"I have heard nothing for hours, Tim," N'go said.

"Me neither. But it could be a trap."

"Let me go look. This tiny room is crushing my soul."

Riordan pushed the safety off his weapon and slowly turned the latch on the door. He eased it open and only darkness greeted them. The door made no sound; Bachmann had kept the hinges of his secret vault well oiled.

Riordan pulled out the tiny torch he always carried and aimed it at the floor before he switched it on. They had moved Bachmann's body, but his blood lay frozen in a small pond where he had died.

"Don't slip," he murmured to N'go.

The large man flashed a smile and nodded before he moved out into the office. He inched the office door open and waited. Silence reigned.

Abruptly N'go slipped through the door and into the general store. Riordan hurried to the door and waited a long moment before sliding through the narrow opening. His heart thudded in his chest while he waited for a shot or a command to surrender.

"There is nobody here, Tim." N'go's voice was as soft as a lover's whisper.

"We need to check outside."

Riordan went out the side door and nearly fell over something in the path. After a full minute of frantically searching the area without moving anything other than his head, he knelt and moved the blanket away from Bachmann's frozen face. The man still looked angry.

N'go eased around the front corner of the building.

"They all left in the lorry that brought them." He nodded at the covered form. "That be Bachmann?"

"Yeah. Probably put him out here to keep him cold."

"I would wager they will not return until warmer weather."

"Good," Riordan said through his sudden grin. "That gives us somewhere to live for a couple of months."

★ 129 ★

Tanana, Provisional Capital of the
Alaska Republik

"Where did you get flowers in the middle of winter?"
Bodecia asked.

"Colonel Shipley brought them from California on
the transport," Magda said as she peered into the mirror and edged the garland of woven flowers slightly
to the right. "Is that straight now?"

"It's fine, now leave it alone. That transport was
jammed with boxes and people. It was nice of the
RCAF to stop and pick us up; don't know how we
would have made it otherwise."

Bodecia admired their similar dresses in the mirror.
Both were made of split moosehide so thin it could have
passed for silk. The hide had been worked until attaining
a pearl sheen. The beadwork on both enhanced their
individual forms. A band of beads began at the neck,
ran down the slope of the shoulders and dropped to
the end of the short sleeves and then continued from
the armpit to the hem on both of them.

Bodecia's dress featured intricate florets across her
bosom that seemed to twist and drop to the midriff.

Magda's dress featured a jagged, lightninglike design that shot out from the band beneath the armpits and curved down and across her midriff as if to hold up her bosom. Both dresses were stunning in their simplicity and rich from the beadwork.

Nobody can bead better than an Athabascan woman! Bodecia thought.

"General Grigorievich asked Colonel Shipley to stop for you. I'm glad he agreed. But I was surprised to see Rudi."

"He said he wouldn't miss this wedding for all the gold in St. Petersburg, even if he did have to take his life in his hands and fly here."

"Is everything ready? How much time do we have left? Are the—"

"Magda! Calm down. Everything will be fine. You have to trust that all is going according to plan."

Wing hurried through the door; her flushed cheeks set off the sparkle in her eyes. "Are you ready, Magda? There are a lot of people out there waiting for you."

Magda turned from the mirror and stared at Wing. "Did they do a good job with the hangar? I always thought I would get married in a church!"

"Oh, my dear, just wait until you see it. What they have done out there couldn't be attempted in any church I've ever seen. And you look so beautiful!" Wing's facial muscles twitched and Bodecia realized she barely maintained her composure.

Bodecia felt so full of emotion she couldn't speak. Her only child, her wonderfully close friend for so many years, was going to leave her house now. This was a natural thing, even a needed thing, she knew that, but it still didn't dampen the ache in her heart.

How can something be so right and yet so painful at the same time?

Through the wall came the strains of fiddles, accompanied by at least two flutes, a balalaika, and William Williams' accordion. Bodecia had to concentrate for a moment before she recognized "Blue Skies of California," the RCAF anthem. How on Earth had William got his accordion clear up here?

"That's our cue, ladies," Wing said brightly, stifling a slight sniff.

"Mother?" Magda said, holding out her hand.

Bodecia moved next to her daughter, carefully held her face in both hands, and drew her face down so she could kiss her cheek.

"I am so proud of you, Lieutenant Magda Anton Haroldsson, and I love you with all my heart. Now let's go begin your future."

She took Magda's arm and they walked through the door held open by Wing and into the largest hangar at Tanana Aerodrome. Immediately the organ segued into "Lower Yukon Waltz."

Bodecia and Magda gasped at the same time. The hangar had been transformed into a military fairy tale.

Two gleaming P-61s had been parked at an angle to each other and festooned with ribbons and long ropes of braided flowers that crisscrossed in a net pattern. The ribbons and braided flowers from each aircraft met over a small dais that was flanked by the flag of the Republic of California on one side and the new Alaska Republik flag on the other. Behind the aircraft were deployed white silk parachutes lending the suggestion of clouds.

Vivid floral bouquets lined the carpeted aisle that

stretched from where they entered to the dais behind which stood Pelagian in a formal suit so ancient he looked like an illustration in a fashion history book.

"Where did he get that suit, Mother?" Magda whispered out of the side of her mouth.

"He's had it for years. Where I don't know, else I would have destroyed it and found him a new one," Bodecia whispered back. She could feel Magda laughing but nobody else seemed to notice.

Pelagian seemed to be a mélange of emotions. Bodecia could see his pride in a wonderful daughter, his happiness for her happiness, the fear that her safety was now out of his control (as if it *ever* was under his control!), the honor he felt for being the master of ceremony on this memorable occasion; and yet there was something else.

It took her a moment to recognize his use of theater in this ceremony. Bodecia felt her throat tighten and willed it to relax. Pelagian knew if he made a hash of this for any political reason, he would never live it down in his own home.

That gave her a sense of peace and she walked the carpet with her daughter between rows of folding chairs mostly occupied by military from a number of nations on one side and a wonderful assemblage of Aleuts, Athabascans, Kolosh, Haidas, Yup'iks, Sioux, Cheyenne, Pawnee, Tsimpshean, Malemiut, and other Peoples she did not recognize, all in their best regalia.

During the Russian surrender at Delta, one of Colonel Buhrman's men had taken a photo of Magda, surrounded by her exhausted troops, looking behind her at the sudden appearance of the Republic of California Army and the men under Lieutenant Colonel

Smolst. Not yet aware they were allies, her expression is one of combined disbelief, despair, and anguish. Once the photo was printed in the *Sacramento Bee* with the caption "Beauty among the beasts," it went all over the world.

Magda immediately became the face of the Alaskan War of Independence. She felt embarrassed by all the undeserved attention, but Pelagian said there was no harm in being lauded, especially when it kept their struggling nation in the eyes of the world. Her promotion to first lieutenant for her actions in the Battle of Delta gave her pride.

Bodecia thought her daughter deserved every ounce of praise that came her way. Ahead of them, Jerry stood in full uniform to the left of the dais. Rudi stood beside him wearing an impeccably tailored Russian Army uniform displaying his old Russian Command Sergeant Major rank complete with five rows of impressive decorations. She thought both men looked very handsome and striking.

They arrived at the dais and Bodecia released her daughter's arm. Magda gave Jerry a dazzling smile. Pelagian cleared his throat.

"Family and friends, we have come together today to hear these two people pledge their troth to each other. As witnesses we sanctify and give their union recognition so they may face the future together with honor. Both Jerry and Magda have prepared their own vows.

"Jerry, tell your bride what you vow."

Jerry turned to Rudi and took a ring that he slid onto Magda's finger as he spoke. He stared into Magda's face and Bodecia saw he was close to busting with emotion.

"I pledge you my love, my fidelity, my trust, my

fortune, and my unending companionship from this moment forward. You are my dream come true, my future ennobled and blessed. I vow to always stay with you in heart, mind, and body through all trials, tribulations, and blessings. I love you without reservation."

Pelagian had to clear his throat. "Magda, tell your groom what you vow."

Bodecia carefully put the ring into her hand. Magda took Jerry's hand and slid the ring firmly on before she spoke.

"I will always love you for the man you are, for the warrior you have become, and the protector you promise. I vow you my faithfulness, my support, my strength, and all my love. You have given my heart limitless horizons and a new world to explore by your side. I thank you for your honesty, your fidelity, and the hope that rages within me for our life together."

"What these two people have pledged today, let no one doubt or deny." Pelagian sounded hoarse. "Jerry, you may kiss your bride."

Bodecia noticed that the ensuing cheer made the parachutes ripple. Then she had to wipe her tears.

General Grigorievich stood and seven other officers, some RCAF and some ARA, all in full dress uniform, also shot to their feet. The eight men had been strategically seated so that they were all an equal distance from each other. In a flash there were two rows of four standing at attention facing the newlyweds.

"Center face," Grisha ordered. The two rows now faced each other.

"Arch sabers." With a fluid motion all eight of them pulled sabers from their scabbards, and as they lifted turned their blades in a clockwise motion so the sharp edge presented skyward and created an arch of brilliant steel.

Jerry and Magda walked back down the aisle, their smiles nearly as bright as the honor through which they walked. As soon as they passed the last two men, Grisha said, "Carry sabers."

All blades returned to their scabbards.

"Rear face."

The eight men pivoted and followed the happy couple.

"They had to have practiced that a lot," Bodecia said to Pelagian who had come up beside her.

All of the other witnesses in the hangar broke into applause.

Abruptly the parachutes rose like so many curtains to reveal long tables filled with food and drink. In the center was a three-tier wedding cake.

Jerry and Magda leisurely ambled over to the cake and waited as their guests left their chairs and surrounded them.

Bodecia took hold of Pelagian's arm and pulled him over to where a somewhat bewildered couple stood slightly away from the others.

"Mr. and Mrs. Yamato, would you please come with us?"

Both nodded and smiled.

"I've never seen a wedding quite like this one," Mrs. Yamato said.

"Me either," Bodecia said with a chuckle. "Magda and her friends planned part of it and Jerry and his friends planned the other part."

"Let me guess," Mr. Yamato said. "Jerry and his pals came up with the sword part."

Pelagian chuckled. "Actually, General Grigorievich and Colonel Buhrman planned that part. Jerry and the other pilots of the 117th designed the aircraft displays and the parachute curtains."

"We have very talented children," Mrs. Yamato observed.

"Yes," Bodecia said. "We are truly blessed."

They all watched as Jerry and Magda cut the cake with Jerry's saber. Then the party began.

★ 130 ★

Four Months Later
Tanana, Provisional Capital of the
Alaska Republik

"This is a test." The sound of the microphone rose to a shrill squeal and everyone held their hands over their ears. Warm breezes wafted through the summer afternoon beneath a flawless blue sky.

"Sorry about that," General Grigorievich said. "We're all new at this stuff."

The huge crowd chuckled. Tanana was jammed with people from all over the Alaska subcontinent. Official requests for space were more than triple what was actually available. One local man had made his fortune selling tents at three times what he paid for them originally and renting space on his property in which to pitch them.

"Never in the history of this planet has an event like this taken place. Much will transpire this day that will affect our lives and the lives of our children and their children. It is my incredible honor to preside over this assembly."

Applause rose from all quarters.

General Grigorievich stood at attention until the applause died down.

"I present the elected delegates to the first Alaska Republik Congress." He called their names as they stepped up on the stage in front of the podium.

After all twelve were called and identified, he added, "These are the first generation of lawmakers selected by the People. Honor them, and watch them carefully!"

Laughter mixed with the applause.

"Among these twelve, we must elect a First Speaker, which falls to those present."

Grisha called out the names of all twelve legislators, but only two elicited more than moderate applause: Pelagian and Nathan Roubitaux.

Once the noise died down to conversational level, Grisha announced, "By universal acclaim, the two candidates for First Speaker are Nathan Roubitaux and Pelagian Haroldsson."

The applause built and transcended what had gone before. Grisha wondered who was the true recipient. He saw Jerry and Magda in the crowd; they both looked radiant.

The applause finally died down.

"Who votes for Nathan Roubitaux?"

Hands shot into the air and Grisha waited while official counters made a tally. Finally one waved him on.

"Who votes for Pelagian Haroldsson?"

It seemed to him that more hands shot up than previously, but he also realized he may have seen that which he wished to see. He rubbed his face with his left hand and waited along with the crowd for the verdict.

He had known Nathan for a longer time but he

had taken to Pelagian immediately upon meeting the man. Nathan always seemed to have an ulterior motive for everything that he did, whereas Pelagian seemed to do what was needed at the moment.

Up on the stage the two candidates stood next to each other, smiling and staring at the crowd.

The chief counter came over to Grisha. "General, as far as we can tell, they are within ten or twelve votes of each other. We're going to have to do a paper ballot to make sure."

"I thought that would happen." He walked back to the middle of the stage. "We can't get an accurate count by a show of hands."

Somebody booed and others shushed him.

"We have four ballot boxes ready to go and a booth at each corner of the area." He pointed. "Look for the white flags. Each person is given a piece of paper and if you want Nathan as First Speaker write an 'N' on it. If you want Pelagian as First Speaker, write a 'P' on the paper.

"When you put the ballot in the box, you will have the back of your right hand stamped with ink that takes a few days to wear off. You must show the back of your hand before you will receive a ballot. All right, citizens, let's vote."

Pelagian turned to Nathan and held out his hand. "Good luck!"

Nathan shook his hand and smiled. "Good luck to you, Pelagian."

Grisha got into the shortest line and chatted with the woman in front of him who happened to be from Sealaska.

"This won't sit well with people from other states,

General. The crowd here is almost all Dená. I would wager there aren't even any Aleuts at all, and damn few Tlingits other than you, me, and my husband."

"No argument. I doubt that our two candidates would get the same acclaim in Akku or Kodiak. But this is a beginning for us on which to build. By the next election we will have a capital city and no doubt a variety of political parties."

"Yes," she said. "A lot must happen in the next four years. I think Sitka would be a good capital. It's worked for three centuries."

"For the Russians," Grisha said with a small laugh. "But all of their administrative offices were in St. Nicholas on Cook's Inlet."

She smiled. "Perhaps we need regional capitals."

"You may have something there. You're next to vote."

★ 131 ★

150 meters from the platform, Tanana

Timothy Riordan decided that Bachmann had been barking mad if he thought thirty men could stop this government thing with the Indians. Yet here he was, twenty feet off the ground in a tree, rifle with telescopic sights and all. He had seen his old guest, Pelagian, through the scope.

If it had been Bodecia, I probably would have fired!

The thought made him grin. He actually admired her even though she had been nothing but a pain in the ass for him. He suspected the attack on his camp had been a direct result of his capture of the three of them.

He winced at the memory of how little he had regarded the military prowess of the Dená. The Russians were what he feared then.

Good old 20-20 hindsight.

He glanced down at N'go, stationed at the bottom of the tree in a clump of bushes. The huge black man was staring at something in the opposite direction of the village.

Riordan twisted around to see if he could spot the

distraction. His sphincter clenched when he saw the line of armed men moving slowly downslope toward him approximately five hundred meters away. They kept a six- or seven-meter distance between them, and if he could see six men there were probably more.

How did they know he was out here? *Did* they know he was out here? Perhaps this was just a security patrol?

No, that's too organized for this lot. Even the Freekorps wasn't this military.

He knew he had to move; they would be here in less than ten minutes. He untied the rope holding him in place. It went over the limb above him and was firmly tied to the harness he wore.

With a flick of his wrist the coiled rope dropped and the end landed next to N'go, who looked up and nodded. Carefully, Riordan slowly slid his butt off the branch and eased himself down the tree, inch by laboriously slow inch. Quicker movement would catch the wrong eyes.

Applause erupted in the village. The Alaska Republik had its first president, or whatever they called it. He wondered which of the men won the vote.

A quote by Ben Franklin surfaced from somewhere in his memory: "We have built a republic, gentlemen, we must endeavor to keep it if we can."

Riordan shook his head. *I don't have time for this kind of crap; I must be losing my mind!*

N'go grabbed his ankle and steadied him as he lowered the last couple of feet. He pulled the rope over the limb and caught it when it dropped from the tree.

"We gotta get out of here, my friend," he whispered.

"They have us hemmed in," N'go whispered back. "All we can do is hide in this bush and hope they don't see us."

More applause sounded from the village. An amplified voice said something and more applause drowned it out.

One of the men coming through the trees yelled, "Okay, guys, let's wrap this up and join the party!"

The men dropped discipline and all hurried toward the village.

Riordan and N'go both huddled on top of their weapons, hoping their camouflaged clothing would blend with the shadows in the clump of bushes.

Out of the corner of his eye Riordan saw the boots of the man closest to them as he hurried past. The men had not found them; he and N'go were safe.

"Let's get out of here," Riordan whispered. "We have a long way to travel before we can stop looking over our shoulders."

"Agreed!" N'go mumbled.

They crawled out of the bushes and, watching the men hurry toward the village, stood up to stretch.

"Drop the rifles or you're dead!" a voice ordered.

N'go released his weapon and raised his hands.

"Shit," Riordan said as he let his rifle fall into the decomposing leaves from last year. He looked around. "Oh hell, not *you*!"

Yukon Cassidy, Roland Delcambré, and Colonel Del Buhrman all smiled, but their weapons did not waver.

"Roland," Cassidy said. "Would you do the honors? They're in my pack."

"My most distinct pleasure!" The diminutive man handed his weapon to Colonel Buhrman and reached into the pack on Cassidy's back. He pulled out chains.

"You don't have to do that," Riordan said. "We'll go quietly."

"Yeah, you would," Cassidy said. "But how long would you stay? We're not going to give you the opportunity to kill another gullible, young guard."

Riordan seethed inside. They might chain his arms but he could still run like the wind given the opportunity. Delcambré seemed to have an awful lot of chain for just two men.

"Turn around and face the village," Cassidy ordered.

"Damn," N'go said softly as he complied. Riordan did as ordered.

"Riordan, put your hands behind your back."

Cassidy was beginning to get on his nerves.

Metal clicked around one wrist, then the other. Both manacles were tightened to the point of pain, but he was damned if he would give them the pleasure of hearing him whine.

"Now put your feet together!"

Riordan's heart sank as Delcambré snapped leg irons on his ankles just above his boots.

So much for running. He wondered if they would hang him.

Delcambré went to work on N'go. As a final insult, the little bastard chained him and N'go together.

"There we are. They can shuffle but they can't hide!"

All three of the captors laughed.

"Start for the village. You first, Riordan."

He almost fell with the first step. His feet could only move a foot from each other. Now he was very sure that he hated Yukon Cassidy and, if the tables ever turned, would kill him in an instant.

It took forever to reach the edge of the village. A

utility waited and four armed soldiers watched him hobble up to them.

"So this is the bad-ass Riordan?"

"That's him, Heinrich. Do not give him a chance of any sort. He has killed two men in cold blood to escape and been the cause of the deaths of many others."

Heinrich looked around at his men. "You all heard the man. Now put these two where they can't get into any more trouble."

The men grabbed them and threw them into the back of the utility. Two crawled into the bed with them and, once the others got into the cab, rapped on the roof. The vehicle lurched off over uneven ground throwing Cassidy and N'go about like unsecured crates.

After an eternity of painful buffeting and slamming against the metal sides, the vehicle stopped. Riordan and N'go were slid out and pulled upright. The heavy log building boasted welded steel bars at the three windows Riordan could see.

"Move out," Heinrich ordered.

"How long will we be here?" Riordan asked, biting off each word.

"Until your trial. And after that until they hang you."

He felt like weeping.

★ 132 ★

Tanana, Provisional Capital of Alaska Republik

"Mr. First Speaker, we captured Riordan and N'go. They are the first prisoners in the new jail." Cassidy grinned. "So how do you feel, Pelagian?"

"Euphoric and hopeful. I know this is going to be a tumultuous four years. But since we're all brand new at it, I think we can pull it off."

★ About the Author ★

Stoney Compton has had novelettes and short stories published in *Universe 1, Tomorrow, Speculative Fiction, Writers of the Future Vol. IX* and *Jim Baen's Universe*. His novel, *Russian Amerika* (Baen Books), was published in 2007, and *Alaska Republik* is the sequel.

He is a native of Grand Island, Nebraska. He served an enlistment in the U.S. Navy where he had the honor of being a crew member on USS *Yorktown*, CVS-10, as well as in VR-24 Det in Naples, Italy.

During his thirty-one years in Alaska he worked as a produce apprentice; shipping & receiving clerk; gandy dancer for the USAF/Alaska Railroad; emergency firefighter for BLM; school bus driver; cameraman and film editor for KTVF-TV in Fairbanks; media specialist for Tanana Chiefs Health Authority; art director for *Tundra Times*, an Alaska Native weekly newspaper; freelance artist in Fairbanks and Juneau; and art director for KTOO-FM&TV public broadcasting for Juneau. He operated Ptarmigan Ptransport & Ptours in Juneau, was a Motorcoach Commander for Princess Tours, and worked for the Alaska Departments of Fish & Game, and Health & Social Services. For a year and a half he worked for the National Oceanic & Atmospheric Administration at the Alaska Fisheries Science Center in Seattle. His fine art has been in juried shows from New York to Hawai'i, and Alaska to California.

He now lives in the Las Vegas, Nevada, metro area with his wife Colette, their ever-changing number of cats, and Pullo, their energetic Australian Blue Heeler. He is an avid hiker and velocipede enthusiast. He is a Visual Information Specialist at the 6th Combat Training Squadron, Nellis AFB, Nevada.